THIRST OF THE VAMPIRE

She was ready. The sweet pain of yet another penetration would only enhance her rising bliss. I kissed her throat again, slowly, lovingly, as she moaned, nearly in tears from the extreme sensations.

I went in behind her ear, hard and quick, my fangs coming forward to pierce skin. To get a good grip, I relied on smaller fangs positioned back farther and curved in the opposite way. My venin went in, just enough to enhance her swoon, and then the blood flowed out thick and hot, and I had to restrain myself from ripping through and causing a mad gush.

It was madness, this gripping need to merge into her and take more and more of her. I was pushing her out of her skin to take over her soul. We couldn't both be in this same space; she had to yield, and she did. Her breath came fast and her skin was aflame. I sank in deeper and bit to get more flow. . . .

<u>BOOK YOUR PLACE ON OUR WEBSITE</u>
<u>AND MAKE THE</u>
<u>READING CONNECTION!</u>

We've created a customized website just for our very special readers, where you can get the inside scoop on everything that's going on with Zebra, Pinnacle and Kensington books.

When you come online, you'll have the exciting opportunity to:

- View covers of upcoming books
- Read sample chapters
- Learn about our future publishing schedule (listed by publication month *and author*)
- Find out when your favorite authors will be visiting a city near you
- Search for and order backlist books from our online catalog
- Check out author bios and background information
- Send e-mail to your favorite authors
- Meet the Kensington staff online
- Join us in weekly chats with authors, readers and other guests
- Get writing guidelines
- AND MUCH MORE!

Visit our website at
http://www.kensingtonbooks.com

THE
HEAT
SEEKERS

Katherine Ramsland

PINNACLE BOOKS
Kensington Publishing Corp.
http://www.kensingtonbooks.com

Prologue

Ana looked over the balcony for some sign of the vampire among the writhing dancers below. There had to be more than four hundred costumed people squeezed wall to wall into that midsize Goth club, all of them fiercely holding their ground in the sweaty crush and none of them aware of what was going on in a world just beyond their reach. Most would give their fake vampire teeth—and more—to possess her secret, yet she wished it had come into anyone's hands but hers. She'd never forgive herself for her hasty theft, let alone for the diablerie it had wrought.

She hadn't believed the document would affect her. She'd thought she'd just read it and put it back, but it hadn't been so easy. The thing had worked on her, enticing and confusing her, until it was possibly too late to undo the damage. She'd been careless and now she prayed for time—even just an hour—to rectify her mistake.

She had to find the vampire. Once he realized what she had, she'd be rid of the burden. He'd know what to do.

With rising desperation, she surveyed the room below. Ana knew from experience that many of these dancers were unaware of the others around them. They might not even realize that the deafening *thump, thump* of industrial music was coming from *Götterdämmerung*, a four-man band on the stage four feet above them. Most had taken something that sent them out of this room toward the deities, oblivious to anything but their own bodies.

The whole thing was grimly amusing. These kids, dressed up like bloodsuckers, role-played them, and even claimed to be secretly connected to the "Real Ones." They believed they shared the vampires' energy. They wanted so badly to get close, yet they never realized how close they actually were. When they ingested this psychoactive substance, which they believed was some synthetic drug, E or K or Godsend, they didn't even guess that a vampire's venin flowed transiently through their veins. In that entire room, perhaps only Ana understood.

But none of that mattered now. What mattered was the one she had to find. She thought his name was Cacilian, although in this secretive underworld names were chameleonic. Everyone adopted one to meet his or her ephemeral needs, whether to hide, impress, or engorge a fantasy. She'd seen this one several times before, long-haired and standing head and shoulders above everyone else. He generally dressed well but not flashily in something Victorian, had hair as dark as everyone else, and usually had numerous female followers attracted to his aura. Yet he'd never been this hard to spot. She feared he might not be there, though it was difficult to tell. The scene down below was an undulating ocean of black from which gesticulating hands rose up here and there as if in need of rescue. Ana herself had dyed her blond hair raven for that night. The last thing she needed was to stand out and be noticed.

She shifted her weight from one booted foot to the other. Her skin tingled and she needed something to calm her, but had no time to make a deal. If she didn't find Cacilian soon, she might as well kiss her hard work good-bye—along with the doorway she'd finally found into her own Dionysian fantasies. She had no one else to turn to, and she had to get the manuscript she'd taken back to its author now, tonight.

The image of her friend Tonia slipped unbidden into her thoughts. Only last week they'd been laughing over Ana's Jack-and-the-beanstalk filching, and now Tonia was dead. An "accident," the police had said, but Ana knew better. Three nights ago, Tonia had been found near the E train tracks. From the burns all over her body, the police had assumed she'd fallen onto the electrified middle rail. Yet no one had come forward to say they'd seen her, and Ana knew why. That was not where Tonia had died. She'd just been tossed there after she'd proved useless to the invisible power. There was no telling what she'd suffered, but Ana was sure it had been bad.

And it—this thing—was at her heels now, as if her very awareness made her a magnet. Just *knowing* set her apart.

But it was more than that. She had the one thing that some very desperate people were after. She couldn't let them have it, and anyway, it belonged to the vampires—in particular to the *kumu,* the elder. She'd betrayed him, though she hadn't meant to. She'd only wanted to know him better. She hadn't understood the document's frightening life force.

Touching the small metal key that Tonia had sewn under her skin beneath her left breast only hours before the "accident," she scanned the people below. The spot still stung and the incision was raw, but it was the only way to keep this key out of the wrong hands. She couldn't put it into her purse nor wear it around her neck. Sewing it inside had seemed the only option, much as it had hurt. She remembered Tonia bent over her work, her pixie-cut brown hair falling into her face as she drew the needle nine times through Ana's flesh. Ana wished now that she had told her friend before she'd died about the creature with the green eyes. Now she could share that with no one, not even her twin sister—especially not her twin.

She peered through the hazy darkness for the color red. The vampire always wore something crimson, whether it was a rose, a handkerchief, or an embroidered vest. She knew that he came here on a regular basis and was to some extent protected. Obviously a handful of other humans knew about him. The trick was to get past his guards. If she just managed to touch him, he'd "read" her. He could do that, and then he'd do whatever was needed to alert the others of his kind about the thing that was coming for them.

Red and blue strobe rays swung out from the stage, shooting the room full of alternating blasts of darkness and colored light. Squinting, Ana thought she saw him, and then she wasn't sure. Gripping the railing, she tried to appear calm. At all cost, she had to avoid unwanted attention.

Down on the stage, an emaciated young singer with bright red hair twisted into braids that fell over his chest was screaming garbled threats into a mike pressed hard against his raw lips. He'd cut himself with a razor just over his eyebrow and the blood flowed down the right side of his face, over his neck, and into his black shirt. He pushed the kids hard against their limits, urging them to reach for more than they'd been promised. "This is our secret abode!" he cried out. "And here you can find your magic."

Then Ana felt a nauseating jolt. In the back of her throat, she tasted crackers and onion soup—her dinner that night. She made herself stand still. She knew the feeling. She was being watched. She closed her eyes.

There was menace in it and it was male. Knowing not to react, she kept her grip on the balcony rail and breathed deeply. She could not let him—whoever he was—know she was aware. If he was one of *them,* she was dead.

A young man to her left jostled her and Ana opened her eyes. Glancing at him, she saw that he was just a kid. Long blond hair cascading over a royal blue velvet vest and white colonial shirt told her he was here to see the band, nothing more. She glanced down at his hand and saw the familiar work of a craftsman she knew well—a silver-covered hand shaped to resemble predatory claws. It was all just part of the vampire scene. The young man caught her eye and winked.

"You here alone?" he asked.

One of those drippy lines. How trite that all seemed now. No man could compare to the immortal she'd found. She envisioned his eyes, green with dark horizontal slits that proved that a human could indeed transform utterly. He'd let her touch his skin, knowing she'd be repulsed but enticed. Like a man aware of his leverage, he'd palpated her most vulnerable spot—her love for all things different. He knew her in a way that no one else ever had. She suspected that no mere woman had ever known him so well, either.

Ana shook her head at the boy. She felt so detached from this world of vampire clubs now, once her home away from home, but she wasn't yet part of the other one, either. She was treading water, floating in limbo. How simple it would be just to merge back among these kids and pretend she'd never witnessed the magic, but she was enlightened now. She had to go forward.

She glanced beyond him toward a black leather couch on which three people were sitting, two of them

apparently engaged in clandestine activities. That was
what it meant to be up here in the Black Lounge: you
could get away with certain things. Not everyone had
access, but those who did had privileges and expectations. A skinny girl with white hair cropped so close she
looked like a boy was helping her bare-chested date sort
through some pills. They both looked desperate, and
the girl's long maroon nails kept knocking the tiny tab-
lets from his hand. To Ana, they appeared to be moving
in slow motion.

Next to them an older man slouched. Ana could not
tell from his half-closed eyes if he was watching her or
just stoned out. He didn't acknowledge her looking at
him, so either he wasn't interested or he had a job to
do—regarding her.

She turned away. If they were already that close, she
figured she'd be stopped any moment now.

Once again scanning the surging crowd below, Ana
searched for Cacilian. He had to be there tonight; he
just had to.

She pushed away from the balcony's edge and slipped
toward the head of the stairs. If someone was following
her, she couldn't tell, because there were just too many
people crowding together up here. They lined the steps
all the way to the bottom, their eyes on the band. In
the event a fire broke out in this building tonight, a lot
of them would die.

Ana pushed and shoved against the crowd, annoying
everyone in her path. A hand slid between her and another woman, seeking a cheap caress, and someone
grabbed her arm, but she kept forging ahead. Suddenly
her silk dress tightened as if she'd caught it on something, and cold liquid ran down her right leg into her
velvet boots. She heard a piece of ice crush under her
foot and tried not to slip. Finally she got to the stairs
and freed herself from the claustrophobic throng.

She noticed that one of her boots was stained and one of her black stockings torn at the knee. Ignoring it, she practically leaped down the steps, not daring to look behind her.

The last thing she wanted was to alert the watchers to her attempt to elude them. That would just make things more difficult. Better to look like a girl about to step out onto the overcrowded dance floor.

Then just as she reached the bottom step, Ana spotted him. The vampire was well beyond her, moving down a hallway, passing easily among people who remained oblivious. That was under his control, she knew. If he wanted their awareness to permeate his, it would happen. If he wanted a boundary, it was instantaneous. Just the fact that he still walked told her that she was not too late. She felt the key again.

But indecision froze her. If she went after him, she'd alert whoever was tracking her, yet if she merged into the crowd and pretended to listen to the band, she'd waste precious time.

Then she got a break. *Götterdämmerung* ended the song they were shrieking and the singer announced that they were taking a few minutes. He looked weary as he removed his sweaty guitar strap from around his neck and shoulder.

Ana glided quickly toward the spot where she'd seen Cacilian. He'd gone down the long hallway where the merchant tables were located. She passed a jeweler, a tattoo artist, a table full of used CDs and plastic-coated comic books, and a woman offering pottery made with her own blood as an ingredient. There were several tarot readers and a psychic, all dressed as some Hollywoodized version of an Eastern European vampire, and all attempting to assert their aura of secret knowledge. Little did they know what clandestine lore really was, and it didn't come from Eastern Europe.

She came to an open doorway that led to a steep,
ill-lit stairway under a black arch that went down. Two
women chatting about their Egyptian-style makeup were
on their way up. Ana squeezed past them and continued
down into a murky, smoke-filled corridor. It smelled
both sweet and stale. Squinting through the haze, she
saw three young men standing around with cigarettes,
and then she spotted the one she was seeking.

Now she ran. It didn't matter who might be watching;
she was nearly to her goal. If she could only touch him,
he'd glean from her what he needed to know and then
in seconds shield himself and be gone.

Coming up behind the tall figure, Ana tapped his
back. "I need to tell you something," she said, "but not
here."

He turned and she saw at once that this was not Cacilian. She noted the red rose, but this was someone
else. In fact, the man looking at her with a question in
his eyes was clearly human, an imitator. She guessed
that he wore his hair long and his clothes in the Victorian style to mimic the vampire as a way to convince
girls of his powers. He was known for turning naive
young women into his slaves—though he used some
medieval term to romanticize it. He made them sleep
on the bare floor next to his bed, perform sex acts with
each other, and allow him to bite them on the back
with his specially sharpened fake fangs. Ana, who despised this man, backed away.

"Who are you looking for?" he asked. There was
something guarded, even menacing, in his expression.

God, she hoped she hadn't stumbled right into one
of *them*.

Then she spotted two men seated outside a door.
They looked like guards. That must be where Cacilian
was.

Ana pushed past the demon gigolo, but he gripped her arm and asked again, "Who are you looking for?"

"Never mind," she said.

"I know who," he told her. "What do you want?"

She struggled out of his grip and went straight to the closed door. The two men watched her but made no move to stop her.

"I want to go in," she said. "Now."

One of them shrugged. He was so loaded with silver prongs, rings, and black beads pierced through his skin that he looked like a human necklace. The other one sat without a word. He had painted his skin entirely white, even his head, which he'd shaved. Only his lips stood out, lined with bright red lipstick. He looked like a bloodsucking leech that had just pulled away from its host.

Ana reached for the doorknob and turned it. To her surprise it wasn't locked. She looked again at the leech, expecting him to stop her, but he just sat there blinking as if doped out of his mind.

The tall man in black with the red rose watched her as well. They seemed to know something. She suddenly felt that entering this room was a bad idea.

Yet she was already inside.

The place was dark, illuminated in one area by a free-standing silver candelabra on which three black candles had burned out. She closed the door to shut out the noise and let her eyes adjust. She was alone. No one else was in here, although she could smell the recent odor of pot. She realized that this was one of those after-hours rooms reserved for the inner circle's clandestine activities. By two A.M. it would be filled with people.

Then she noticed someone there. A large man was sitting in an overstuffed chair off to the right, hidden in the corner. He was obviously watching her. They'd let her in here to give her to this man. She'd been lured into a trap.

Yet he said nothing, though she could feel his eyes on her. Was he waiting for the others to come in and grab her? Or maybe he was wasted, too.

Ana breathed slowly to steady herself. She wanted to say something but couldn't find her voice. The key under her breast itched and burned, but she dared not touch it.

Whoever this guy was, he seemed to have no special power. She felt nothing from him, not menace, not control. He just sat there.

She took a hesitant step toward him. He still didn't move, so she took another. Something about the way he sat began to bother her. She wondered if he was dead.

Reaching into the velvet satchel she kept tied around her wrist, she found her carved silver cigarette lighter and brought it out. She flicked it into a small flame and held it toward him. The light shone on his face.

Ana was horrified.

It was he, Cacilian. He was sitting right here in front of her, but he wasn't looking at her. He wasn't looking at anything.

She rushed to him and knelt before him, touching the motionless hand that rested on the arm of the chair. He couldn't be dead; he was a vampire. She pushed at him and even pinched him a little, but he didn't respond. He seemed vaguely aware but trapped in some kind of torpid trance.

Then she realized: *it* had already come and had taken this one's spirit. Cacilian could no longer function. He was deadweight. He might as well be a corpse—in fact, he would be better off if he were.

Stepping closer, she tried to see if his eyes indicated anything at all, but the room was too dark. Whatever he felt, whether terror, boredom or nothing, she couldn't tell.

Fingering the key, now useless, Ana felt tears well up. This was her fault. If she hadn't delayed, this would never have happened. More to the point, if she hadn't stolen the document in the first place, this would certainly never have happened. Then she wondered if it had gotten the others. Were they, too, sitting upright in chairs or lying in the sand in their secret abode, unable to move or cry out? She couldn't imagine it.

Then she was grabbed from behind. She dropped the lighter. A hand went over her mouth as an arm slung her back against a large male body and long fingers stuffed something down her throat. She choked, but despite herself she swallowed. More hands gripped her arms to hold her still. She was bound tight with nylon rope, and then lifted and carried through another door and deeper into the darkness. Her last conscious thought was of the green-eyed vampire who awaited her.

One

Christian

We'd first sensed the danger coming just days before Jamie Farrelly arrived to look for her missing sister. Something had probed our memory fields. It was in the air, in the ground, even in our bodies, and we were no more prepared than a cornered rattler that can't see where to strike. This nemesis used our own vampire ways to target us, and we had only one immediate defense.

Of all things, it rested on the genetic map of this woman, Jamie. She was a temp, an ordinary mortal who had no idea what we planned for her. But she also had no choice. We were desperate. So we went looking for her to bring her to our home. Bel and I were sent as the scouts, since it was our habit to ride the nightly transit trains from Trenton to Manhattan. We knew the streets as well as any night creature could, and I believed I could win this woman's trust. I hoped to gently entrance her with the certainty that we had something she wanted. That ploy had never failed me.

As we mapped the places she would likely go, we narrowed down her sojourn to the Village/SoHo area and climbed to the tops of the lower buildings for a better view. It seemed the most logical place for her to search, and it didn't take long for us to find her. Over the course of several hours, we'd surveyed three other women who slightly resembled her picture, but when we actually saw her there was no mistaking who she was.

"Ana," Bel whispered. "They look so much alike."

Bel had been a lithe and slender adolescent when she seduced a vampire, but she'd seen the turn of at least one century. Her nickname, Bel, was short for cascabel, one of the most venomous rattlesnakes in existence. They're known as the Whispering Death, and the bite of these reptiles is most effective when closest to the heart. Bel's appearance was profoundly deceiving. She seemed just a young blond out for fun, but she was lethal. Sometimes she even scared me. She and I had been constant companions ever since I'd first been summoned into our *kamera*. The only time she went off without me anymore was for her private hunt.

I watched without a word as Jamie walked down a dark street just outside the Meat Packing District. Her energy signature was potent, repressed but spicy. There was clearly more to her than even she knew. I was three stories up but I found her heart. She was the kind of victim that drew me: passionate and complex but vulnerable.

The sensory pits inside my cheeks swelled up to suck in the nuances of her warmest body parts. I tasted the warm air to learn her fragrance. No matter what I could see of her, my scenting cells were far more discriminating. My skin is a mass of infrared receptors that eroticize my every move and tell me the source of greatest heat, and the closer I get the stronger my response. In fact, when a warm-blooded person is near, the venin I use to seduce them floods first through my body like a potent drug. Once it works on me, it's hard to restrain myself. It fills me from my brain to my groin and demands release.

No one else was with her, which made me breathe in some relief. She'd be ours before the night was over, which meant we might survive. Whatever was closing in had started in Europe several weeks before, and we'd thought that was where it would stay. But then it had hit home before we'd had much time to prepare. Its withering hand had tapped Cacilian, one of our New York intimates, and he had gone like a balloon losing air. He hadn't lived in our *kamera*, but he was associated with us, and that suggested that the thing was close and bearing down fast. It had hooked into our *mana*, our energy field.

As we padded in pursuit along the tops of the uneven buildings, I suddenly stopped. Something had pierced my aura. Looking down, I saw a brownish red smudge that appeared to be dried blood. I focused more sharply to ween it, which means to make an assessment quicker and more exacting than mortal perception can ever be. It takes energy to achieve this focus, but it pays off. I feared that others might also know about Jamie—others who might thwart us. They would gladly see our entire *kamera* perish, and if they knew what we wanted with her, they'd squash her like a bug.

I glanced down at Bel and saw her watching me. The top of her platinum head came only to my chest.

"It's a vampire," she said.

She had weened the bloodstain, too, and looked around. As a rule, she said little but I generally knew what she was thinking. Over the years we'd developed a tacit clarity of each other's minds from our shared anamnesis. In dreams we intertwined to absorb each other's skills, and that intimacy is more profound than any other. Bel was alert but unafraid, yet she failed to pinpoint the source of this disturbance. I passed to her the task of sentinel while I turned back to watch the woman below. Now that we'd spotted this Jamie, we had to keep her in sight. Whatever dangers might lie around us, she was our ultimate priority.

I liked the look of her. She was tall and artistically thin, and her flowing wheat-colored hair matched my own. I admired the way she glanced around at the streets as she *click-click*ed along in her spike-heeled boots, scoping out every detail of her surroundings from the garbage-strewn sidewalk to the ominous star-spangled sky. She was a distiller; that much I could tell. She took in the array of singularities in her path—a plastic cup rolling near her feet, the smack of a car door—and imbued them with anxious significance. She had a rare intelligence. I wanted to guzzle her aura.

Had she looked over her right shoulder and slightly up, she might have spotted us, though we can hide as fast as any viper in the wild. A quick shift toward a shadow, an instant black stillness, and she'd never have known. The art of a swift exit through the smallest holes and the ability to blend with anything were my own special gifts.

But she didn't look. Instead, she continued on her way.

With barely a glance, she passed one grimy shop after another. Tiny black teardrop pearls wobbled at her pierced earlobes. I could almost feel their slight erotic pull. A silken lace scarf of crimson embraced her neck and draped over her shoulders, flowing down across a tight black leotard and black cotton skirt. I smelled new leather against her skin, padded by a fresh layer of per-spiration, and wondered for what intriguing purpose she had bought that binding corset. It seemed dissonant with her energy. Her sister would have worn that easily, but not her.

I smiled. Some interesting game was astir. I loved the way these mortal girls run to their "vampyre" clubs with waists cinched tight, breasts plumped up, and legs encased in netting, as if that exotic attire transformed them into creatures of night. It set them apart from fashion, I guessed, which they interpreted as power. At any rate, at least now I had a better idea of where Jamie was going. It was almost too obvious. I didn't yet know precisely which club, but there was no doubt of the general area.

Winking at Bel, I said, "This will be fun."

She just shook her head and kept her eye on our girl. She didn't like those loud, frenzied places, preferring jazz clubs if she had to mingle with temps. Bel was weary of pretense of any kind, even the role-player's affectation that was entirely self-aware.

I rolled my tongue through my lips so that the tip caught the evening air and along with it the pungent scent and bitter taste of Jamie's nervous musk. It raised the hair on the back of my neck. I hungered to get closer. She seemed to me more substantial than her twin, which said a lot. Perhaps that was the energy from her desperate mission, perhaps something else. In any event, it was bound to remain with her as long as she was searching for Ana. She was here now, we had her, and she belonged to us.

And it was only by mere serendipity that we even knew.

A week ago, Gail Hawkins, whom we called Ana, had disappeared without a trace, and no one had a clue, although we felt certain it was connected to Cacilian's demise. The herd—that bustling throng of media reporters and their mindless audience—had buzzed about it for days. They quickly learned that Gail had been investigating vampire cults in Manhattan for a magazine story that never saw print. One night after leaving her home, she had simply vanished, and now everyone seemed suddenly quite curious about these so-called aficionados of the "Dark Realm." Interviews with cult members had sprung up in all the major papers, drawing out those who throve on drama and perverse attention. Some wanted to tell all, while others preferred a coy and seductive game.

Each evening before members of our *kamera* went out, Eryx—who looked more like an Ivy League lawyer than a collector of the bizarre—read these accounts to us. His passion for tabloids, long a joke among us, had quickly become an advantage. He picked up bits of information we wouldn't otherwise have known, and he loved his sudden importance. Most significantly, we were able to learn a few things about Ana's movements.

Savvy comments from youngsters on what it meant to be a bloodsucker were amusingly absurd. One of them showed the reporter his implanted false fangs, sharpened to such a point that his lower lips were callused. There was even a photo of him doing this. He giggled, according to the account, and said that he'd been born in the dark and now could not go out into the light. "I'm a vampire," he said. "My skin is hypersensitive."

I smiled at that one. In fact, our skin thickens and grows colder even as it becomes more sensitive. Its function is to help us better feel the nearness of prey, not to alert us to skitter out of the sun. In fact, our skin actually hungers for the prey. It inspires us to go out rather than remain indoors. Yet this wasn't the first time we'd heard such diverting comments from vampire cults.

Now when I say vampire cults, don't confuse them with us. Some of us do thrive in a group—a special kind of family—but vampire cults are human. Mortals. Temps, i.e., temporary beings on this planet, compared to us. Vampire groupies, some call them. We have our own appellation for these people who dress exotically in black and file their teeth into points or insert dental acrylic shaped into fangs. Sometimes we call them shadows because they crave so deeply to become us that they adopt what they think are our ways. In other words, they shadow us. Otherwise we just refer to them as temps. They actually poke each other full of holes to sip their bloody cocktails. Of course it hurts. It's nothing like our sweet, sensual penetration that disorients, feeds, traps, and swallows the soul. In one erotic step, we exploit our victims' memory fields to promise the fulfillment of some personal lack, which addicts them to us in an instant.

I admit that we do feel some affinity with them. They're romanced by their dark sides, as were some of us at one time. Phelan, our beloved artiste, calls them reenactors, like some obsessed Civil War buff who runs to Gettysburg every July to "be" a Confederate soldier. They get lost in their borrowed identity, and that's okay with them.

They guess that we come among them—they call us the Real Ones—but they're not sure what to look for, so they dress flamboyantly in vampire drag to signal who they are—in case we wouldn't otherwise know. Those shadows who "recognize" me press themselves against me, yielding their heat—exhaling their very breath into me, begging me to take them. It's a slow dance, a subtle tease, the most delicious agony. Male or female, I absorb them all. I love the feel of their piquant bodies, arched toward ecstasy with a driving need they can't articulate.

But I'd never beguile them there at the clubs. Mine is the gradual embrace, isolated and alone. I wrap the energy field around them like the body of a boa, so surreptitiously they don't even know they're held fast. They look into my eyes, which are slightly enlarged for hunting at night, and my swollen black pupils subliminally entice them. Only at the last do they gasp and struggle against the inner suffocation, and then . . . too late.

But we don't just suck their life juices from them. We first envenom them in such a way as to deprive the brain's left temporal lobe of oxygen, because that heightens the transcendent sensation that they're now among the gods. Our vampire elixir is an entactogen, which means "touching within." It works on the nerve endings to mimic a psychoactive drug, and our prey becomes immersed in the liquid sensations. We call it venin, rather than venom, because it's more refined than a viper's poison. It's a far more captivating annihilation.

Yet not all vampires function this way. Most are loners, but a few with special qualities get invited into groups. In our *kamera* our kinship lies with the snake. It's stealthy, clever, inscrutable, agile, and deceptive. The snake is the most feared creature on earth, but it actually spends less time killing than does the lynx or piranha. In fact, snakes can be healing. Aesculapius appeared as a snake to cure a Roman plague, and his emblem of health was a staff with two winged snakes. To the Incas, snakes symbolized knowledge, while poets like Rimbaud "rode the snake" as a way to court their muse. More potently, snake venom from some pit vipers heals the heart, and cobra juice is like morphine. In Egypt, snakes are gods.

But back to the vampyre clubs, where Jamie was now going.

There's a small group whose members consider themselves the dark gatekeepers. They claim that other mortals must go through the proper "screening" and say the right words in order to get close to the Real Ones. That means they must join some chosen inner circle. It doesn't matter which: Bloodists, Sanguinaries, Lazarati. They all have their rituals, but all are equally limited by the unyielding walls of mortal experience. These temps remind me of the tragic boy whose senseless death had propelled me into this state. He, too, had loved the idea of ripping the immortal seam.

"Christian," Bel whispered. She laid cold fingers on my arm. "She's nearly there."

Bel always sensed things before me. That came from the clarion pitch of her mental focus, sharpened by decades of practiced stillness and mental stretching. She was truly a receptor, and her specialty was the spirit world.

I glanced below.

Jamie turned down an alley and we watched to be sure she came to no harm. It was unwise, walking these streets at night, but at least she had immortal guardians.

Then I sensed another. Close. Very close. I was astonished that I hadn't weened it long before, but even more so that he or she had gotten past Bel. Alarmed, I glanced toward the shadowed depths of a building across the street. I saw movement. Next to me, Bel tensed. Whoever this was, the creature's abilities were clearly superior—and that made it dangerous.

Manhattan was not our territory, but we were generally allowed to roam there without interference. I sent out a signal to learn what we were dealing with. Possibilities raced through my head: that this was the thing that was after us or that it was another predator with an evolved means of trapping us. I moved protectively in front of Bel. She hated when I did that, and in fact in such confrontations she was probably more powerful than me, but had anything happened to her I'd have been utterly bereft.

In the meantime, I was losing my awareness of Jamie below. I believed I knew where she was heading, but this unexpected encounter thwarted my ability to track her.

Then out of the shadows came a shapely leg covered in stretchy black velvet. A scuffed boot of sooty leather decades old. I sniffed the air and extended my tongue. I tasted something familiar.

One of ours. I knew the flavor of those memories. I was relieved but then alarmed again. Why had she guarded herself and why was she there?

In an instant she was fully revealed.

It was Lachesis. She'd taken her name from one of the three Fates—the one who measured the length of the strands of each life—and thereby fated herself to become part of our *kamera*. The lachesis is also the bushmaster, the world's largest viper.

I sensed urgency within her. Something had happened. I weened it through mental waves passed from her to me. An image slowly formed of a boy in a house not far away, and then of someone dead. A chill snaked down my back.

No! That wasn't supposed to happen. Bel and I were to bring Jamie back ourselves, not force her with fear and violence. How could we possibly expect her to cooperate if she hated us? I silently communicated my annoyance.

But the deed was done. Lachesis ignored my feelings. She was tall and strong, and through her feminine facade radiated a powerful sense of clarity and self-assurance. Anyone meeting her would have come away believing that she'd been born when the world began, so impressive was her knowledge and confidence. Despite the effort she put into making a striking female presentation, with her curled mahogany hair, arched eyebrows, and flawless makeup, she could hold her own in a battle of wits with any of us.

Thus what I thought didn't matter, and Jamie would come now without a doubt, driven by grief and desperation. Clearly, the *dominie* was taking no chances. It didn't surprise me that he could be cruel; I'd seen that before, but what could he be thinking? He hadn't told us this plan, and I felt off balance, even a little betrayed.

Then I realized that something larger was at stake. Lachesis was not there alone.

Just above her, atop a taller building, I was shocked to spot Dantalyon. He stood like the Apache warrior he once had been, framed by moonlight, hips thrust forward, knees slightly bent, the wind gathering his black hair to whip it like a banner. I felt the fierce stare of his dark eyes and gestured that I understood. He withdrew, a black racer sliding into deep waters. Yet he was still there.

The obvious message was that this night's task had passed to him. Otherwise there was no way he'd be here. He never left Naje unless sent away.

Or that was what I'd always believed. What happened from that moment forward was to surprise and change us all.

Oblivious to us, Jamie continued to walk fast down the street. I looked past her and then I knew for sure. She was two blocks from the Slaughterhouse. My club. I hung out there because the shadows who frequent it live on the edge. I like the fervor. When I'm really hungry, I leave my little white-haired familiar and cruise to the Slaughterhouse to become the demon lover.

I wondered if I might have that opportunity tonight. Jamie would come to us now, anyway. She had no choice, so why not have some fun on my own? We still had several hours before sunrise.

"Don't go," Bel said. "He'll know." She generally deferred to those more powerful than us, but if there were no orders to the contrary, I followed my own course. I saw no harm in doing that.

"I'll meet you back at the train," I said. "I have time." She shook her head and left me. Though she was wiser than me, she rarely argued. I think she assumed that eventually I'd learn to curb what the others scornfully dubbed my "dissocial disorder." Taking my own path held me back from all that can be achieved in the *kameric* center, but I still had that need. Lachesis would just call it immaturity.

I continued along the rooftops until I reached the Slaughterhouse just ahead of Jamie. It was at this very place where I had first met her sister. She'd been easily lured through her hungers to our country dwelling and had jumped at the chance to be part of our experiments. We'd promised her an amaranthine transformation if she'd submit to a risky procedure that yielded to us her unique genetic configuration. Without hesitation—without even understanding what we meant to do—she had said yes. Risking her life was of no consequence to her, not when measured against more transcendant possibilities. There were no attachments to the world for her; she'd left family and friends behind, and her drive to pierce into our world was nearly an addiction for her.

Ana had known instinctively that what we said about the different ascending levels of the soul was true, and she had wanted to expand. That attitude alone put her on the first level—submissive trust in the reality of the moment. I thought she'd been ideal for the work, but something had happened. Something had gone wrong, and it wasn't long afterward that we'd been struck. We'd thought of shifting the procedure, and Ana was game for that, too, but then she was gone.

That meant we needed Jamie. Immediately. Our doom was closing in.

This was no vampire plague, no devil's karma. It was infiltrating our memory cells in the same way we did to mortals, and injecting us with a paralyzing ennui. Yet it didn't kill us and it didn't wear off, which meant an eternity of conscious inertia. Only those within our *kamera* had met the invisible slayer, and we had no clue where or how it would strike next, but it was most deliberately bearing down on *us*. For all any of us knew, this could be our last night. It could be *my* last night. If so, I wanted to enjoy it.

I watched the lanky blond take determined strides toward me as I waited by that mortal hellhole. I was curious. She seemed to have a plan and she had obviously dressed in a way that agitated her soul. She disliked what she was doing, but she was not deterred. I weened that she knew something that we didn't, something about Ana, but I couldn't get any detailed information. That meant I'd have to follow her and see what she was up to.

More secretly, I wanted her to see me before Naje had his way. Once she saw him, he'd have her, body and soul. He was the most dangerous among us, the most physically impressive, and the most skilled. For that, he had the most allure. He wasn't our leader so much as our focal point—the philosopher king—and with good reason. I didn't hold a candle to him, and I had no doubt he'd use all of his skills to persuade Jamie to do what we needed—including seducing her.

Silently I dropped down to street level, where Jamie was, and came close behind her. I was curious as to why she'd come and why, in particular, she was here in this place.

Initially she had dismissed her sister's disappearance. When the tabloids had interviewed her, she'd been uninterested, even cold, and her brusque attitude had been exploited to add "family conflicts" to the sympathetic portrait of the missing victim. That had made the event even more newsworthy.

Fortunately for us. That was how we had discovered her. Eryx had brought Naje's attention to the fact that

Ana had a twin. That was significant. It meant that what we had planned for Ana could be transferred. The genotype was the same. We could keep the calibrations and continue to refine them, rather than begin all over with someone else. There was still hope.

Yet Jamie was a wild card. No one knew how she would react. She might be as willing as Ana had been to help, but even for a temp who worshiped vampires, Ana had been an exception. She'd been authentically daring and untroubled by the possibility that she could get hurt. I'd met few of her mind-set, and it was unlikely this Jamie, who knew nothing of our breed, would be quite so eager. In fact, it seemed more likely that she'd fight us tooth and nail.

But there are those among us who could get her co-operation. They're the most adept at manipulating the memory field. In other words, they know how the mind invades the body's cellular structure and influences its emotional patterns. They ween what triggers any particular individual, either to fear or to crave a specific type of experience. That was why they're the executives among us and that's why we stay close. Their skills could not be taught, only absorbed, and it took years—even decades—to go from one layer of achievement to another. Obviously Naje had considered the potential problem of Jamie's resistance. After he'd sent Bel and me off to find her, he'd told his exquisite consort, the dark-eyed Dantalyon, what must be done, asap, to make this mortal "cooperate."

I followed close but silently as Jamie made her way to the Slaughterhouse's arched double doors, which were painted bloodred. It was an ordinary brick building, just an old warehouse, but inside would be a modern rendition of the Inferno—a crowded one. I weened that she was unprepared for what she'd find and I wondered if I should catch her outside the door rather than wait.

I moved quickly to catch up to her. I was only three steps away, about to touch her shoulder and use my serpentine wiles to draw her to me, when I stopped and shot back against the shadowed wall. A dark-haired man dressed in black jeans and a T-shirt stepped forward to greet her.

I was astonished. I knew him.

It couldn't be that she had joined with this man. How had he found her first?

Withdrawing into darkness, I watched him show her inside. He glanced around, but I was already impossible to spot. Like a snake, I pushed into a slim space between two walls and let my flexible bones collapse sufficiently to fit. His eyes narrowed as if he faintly sensed my presence. He muttered something that I didn't comprehend, so I assumed it was another language. He took one more step in my direction and I pressed further into the wall. I sent a quick pulse to scramble his memory, but he seemed already to have given it up. Touching Jamie's arm, he ushered her inside.

I came out to the sidewalk, but stayed in the shadows, breathing deeply to restore my shape. This process was painful, but as long as it wasn't prolonged, getting back into shape lasted only a minute. When I felt solid again, I went immediately toward Penn Station. I had to report this unexpected turn of events. The fact that Jamie had made such a contact was very bad news for us.

Two

Jamie

Jamie had arrived the night before in the historic university town of Princeton, New Jersey, with her eight-year-old son, Devon. She was vaguely aware that the American Revolution had turned its tide here, that presidents had picked it for their residences, and that the town was now a prominent academic and information systems center. With some relief, she'd left an unemployed, alcoholic husband, Greg, who passed out most nights and often slept through to the next afternoon. Sometimes he even soiled the couch. She'd begged him to get help, but since she was supporting them all, he saw no reason to do anything about the situation. To him, things were just fine the way they were. Jamie's only recourse had been to just pick up and go, but where her actions would lead she had no idea.

Although she'd long been interested in biochemistry, she never had the money, thanks to her dissipated mate, to go to school. Her education had come in bits and pieces when she could save enough herself to pay for it. Once she'd interned with a forensic serologist, but that had been the extent of excitement in her education. She'd found the reading of blood spatter patterns to solve crimes fascinating but was unable to take it any further. She wanted so much more, but she had been trapped by a singularly bad decision to marry and have a child with a man who had so little to offer. Now she had the opportunity, even if on the tail of tragedy, to see what else was out there in the world. Whether or not she found Gail, she intended to look into possibilities for herself.

When she'd first heard about her sister's disappearance, she'd been struggling to keep a part-time job clerking at an on-again, off-again racetrack for horses in Arizona. Her husband's problems had forced so many absences that she'd finally lost the position, so she'd decided to use the dead space between jobs to look into this matter with her sister. Gail had always lived on the edge, and Jamie did not believe that she was in serious trouble. Still, it had been almost a month with no word from her. That wasn't altogether unusual, but given her disappearance, it was disturbing. And the media had made such a big deal of it, as if Gail's absence, coupled with her involvement with some sort of satanic cult, meant that she'd come to some violent end.

"Does your sister often go out with people like this?" one reporter had asked her.

"Yes, as far as I know," Jamie had said.

"As far as you know? Doesn't she talk to you? Is there some trouble between you?"

Jamie had pushed away from the man, a sandy blond who'd looked so polished in his suit and tie that she could have used him as a dining room table. He'd persisted and she'd found out the next day in the paper that dear sweet Gail had no family ties. If she were missing, no one would even go looking for her.

So now Jamie was looking. It was true that Gail did not often call, but that didn't mean there was trouble between them. They just didn't see the world in the same way, and conversations that were anything but superficial inevitably became frustrating. Gail was so intense, and she wanted Jamie to take her ideas seriously. She was always looking for the ultimate experience, the doorway to something greater, and she seemed to feel sure that one experience or another would get her there. That meant drugs, men with serious character disorders, extreme fasting, extreme exercise, meditation—anything and everything that kissed possibility, even if it were dangerous. Her brushes with various subcultures had gotten her into some trouble, but her determination made Jamie's warnings moot. Gail would do whatever she set her mind to do, which Jamie thought was just too careless. Their differing philosophies set them in conflict, and Jamie ultimately had given up trying to warn her sister. The only way to keep from worrying was just not to know anything.

Nevertheless, she had a key to Gail's town house near Princeton. "If you ever need it," Gail had said many times, "just come." She had never liked Greg and had expected that Jamie would eventually get some sense into her and leave him. But that was just one of the many ways in which they were different. Jamie had made a commitment. She didn't let go easily.

Flying from Phoenix to Newark with Devon, she got them onto a shuttle into Princeton's town center at the Nassau Inn, and then transferred to a cab. As the driver loaded their luggage into the trunk, he smiled at Devon.

"Hello, young man," he said. "Welcome to Princeton."

Devon stuttered a response and then shied away behind Jamie.

She looked at the man apologetically. He was a young Hispanic, dressed in jeans and a dark green T-shirt imprinted with a quote from Einstein: *The most beautiful thing we can experience is the mysterious.* For the first time in a long time, she smiled. She knew that her son turned heads, but with all the stress in her life she'd lost sight of that. Devon's large, brown eyes were barely visible under a mop of light brown hair. She pushed his hair back and leaned over to give him a kiss. He was the one bright spot in her life, and she felt so grateful to have him. Still, she knew that his life with an alcoholic father had been rough. Greg had wanted another child, and Jamie had resisted, but only halfheartedly. She, too, wanted another child, but just not under these circumstances.

She gave the driver directions and was soon in front of her sister's place.

Entering Gail's home was the first clue for Jamie that something might be seriously wrong. She seated Devon on a flower-patterned couch and gave him his computer game to keep him busy while she had a look around. As she walked through the apartment, she sensed that things were missing, but she didn't know Gail well enough to know what those things might be or who had taken them. What made her nervous was seeing certain items that she knew Gail would not leave without, like her driver's license. That meant she had not just decided to take a trip. Wherever she went, she'd either left in haste or against her will. Or she'd known she was in danger and had left her license as a message.

In Gail's bedroom, Jamie found a framed photo of herself and Devon, smiling happily together. She'd hand-decorated the frame for Gail herself, carefully painting the carved wooden edges with colorful miniatures of Gail's favorite flowers, red posies. The one thing they shared was a deep love for things made by hand, believing that part of the crafter's soul resided with the object. If received as a gift, it was to be cherished. That Gail had kept this photo and frame close to her bed filled Jamie with a sense of remorse. She really ought to have made more effort to keep in touch.

She found nothing else of significance, which increased her concern. There was no evidence that Gail had packed up and left, but it did not appear that she spent much time here, either. Jamie thought that Gail had had a lover who lived elsewhere, but she'd never been sure. Gail was tight-lipped about her intimacies, mostly—as she once pointed out—because she had learned that Jamie usually disapproved.

Opening one closet, Jamie stepped back in surprise. It seemed like every dress or jacket or silk blouse hanging there was black or red, and on several hangers were black leather harnesses and lace-up corsets. On the floor were more pairs of boots than anyone should ever need, and caught on a crooked nail inside the door were several paddles and whips. Jamie closed the closet, feeling as if she were closing off her sister. She wasn't quite prepared for what this might mean, but she certainly did not want Devon to step in here and discover it for himself.

It was her intent to stay in the town house with Devon for a week or so. School was out for the summer for him, so the only thing he was missing was his gang of friends. Since he liked to read and could get immersed for hours in video games, Jamie knew he would quickly adjust to being alone with a sitter. Fortunately, she had found Jorja, a sophomore history major on short notice through the university's employment system. In the event that her search took longer than expected on any given day, Jorja had said she could stay. Jamie would have to go into Manhattan, and while trains ran regularly, she had little idea yet where to begin. She might even have to put in some night hours, since that had been the framework of Gail's life. Given how little time she had, she would have to start right away.

The following morning Jorja was prompt, and Jamie had intended to spend some time allowing Devon to get used to her. However, when he took to the sitter right away, she decided to get on an earlier train. The more she'd searched through Gail's clothing and papers, the more she felt certain that her twin had been into some very disturbing things. She'd even found a small loaded handgun in a sock drawer.

"Don't be gone too long, Mom," Devon said. "Please."

"I'll be back as soon as I can," Jamie promised, "but Jorja will be right here. She can take you for ice cream and read to you."

"I don't like it here," he said. "I want to go home."

"We won't be here long," Jamie promised him. She caressed his hair, but she was unable to look into his desperate eyes. "I may have to stay out late one or two nights, but I'll be back as soon as I can."

"Okay, Mom."

Devon watched from the window, his eyes red and his cheeks wet, as she got into a cab. On her ride to the train, she tried to put his distress out of her mind. It was just that the place was unfamiliar, that was all. He'd adjust. She needed to make this effort to find her sister, and she couldn't take Devon along—not with what she'd already seen of Gail's risqué lifestyle. Family called to family, and Gail now seemed the one most in need. Emotionally torn, Jamie forced herself to go forth.

On the train, she reviewed what she knew and studied a map of the city that she'd found next to Gail's computer. There were several Xs marked in red pen. The last place Gail had been seen, Jamie read in a newspaper article, was in a club in lower Manhattan. Something called the Slaughterhouse. It sounded awful, but that was the gist of Gail's lifestyle. Since the place did not open until evening, Jamie had to find other sources of information, so her first stop would be the New York Public Library. She wanted to read all of the newspaper accounts of Gail's disappearance, just in case someone had stumbled upon a clue or had talked with an acquaintance of Gail's. She thought she might see a lead where the reporters had not.

The library wasn't far from Penn Station, and she was impressed with the noble statuary outside, of magnificent lions. Walking up the wide steps and through one set of double doors, she came into a vast, rather intimidating hall. The ceilings were high and the double staircases imposing, but she made herself ask at the information desk for the reference rooms. Then she climbed the steps to find where she needed to go.

Once settled into the routine of looking through microfilm, Jamie prepared to spend several hours pulling up all the articles that had been written by or about Gail in the past month. These were numerous, but mostly repetitive, and she eventually narrowed it down to the few that indicated that the author had made some real effort to solve the mystery. She slid the microfilm through a machine and prepared to take notes.

Only half an hour into her project, she sensed someone watching her. Looking around, she noticed other people at nearby desks, busily working on their own projects. One was a dark-haired woman in a short yellow dress who kept pulling at it as she read. Another looked like a homeless man in ragged clothing; a third was apparently a coed at one of the many city-based colleges, and the only other person there was a man in casual clothing who appeared to be keenly interested in a newspaper article. No one looked up. Jamie pulled her chair closer to the machine and then made another quick glance to both sides. No one seemed to care what she was doing.

The feeling was gone, too, so perhaps someone had come to the door, looked in, and then left. Gail was her twin, it was true, but they had long cut their hair in different styles, and Gail wore much more makeup. No one would take her for Gail, not at a glance. She shrugged off the feeling and focused on the articles lying in a pile in front of her.

The first thing she noticed was that several people who'd been questioned referred to Gail as "Ana." She wasn't sure why Gail would adopt a false name, especially one so apparently tame and mundane. Then a young woman who called herself Black Asp explained it.

" 'Ana' is short for Anaconda," Black Asp said to one reporter. "We know they have some affinity with snakes."

"They?" he had asked.

The woman had only smiled enigmatically—or so he had written.

That was the only mention of snakes that Jamie could find, which was a relief. She avoided snakes with a passion. While hiking as a child, she'd been bitten by some kind of venomous black snake and had received medical help in time to save her life, but she'd never forgotten how painful it had been, how her ankle had swelled up, and how much it had frightened her mother. Jamie was thankful her mother had died several years ago, spared this recent concern with Gail.

The rest of the articles were about vampire cults. Apparently Gail—Ana—had become involved with these Goth types, and the Slaughterhouse was one of the places where they came together for parties.

Jamie knew nothing about vampire cults, but she understood perfectly the lure of transgressive symbols. She herself yearned for the feeling of expansion that such images inspired—who didn't?—but she'd always turned away. Now that she was far from her life with Greg, she felt the tug of freedom. It seemed these vampire enthusiasts did as well. The things that were said about them alarmed her, but she pushed on.

The *Times* actually featured a photograph and a full interview with one of these people, a man who called himself Judas. He had an exotic name for his "lair," the Bloodroom. The whole place, according to the reporter, had been decorated in dark red velvet against black walls that were textured to look "as if dried globs of blood were covered with a thin veneer of demonic ink."

Jamie blanched at that and read on. Judas actually had long canines, but whether they were real or the result of some dentist's artistry was never clarified. He was only twenty years old. He disliked sunlight, he claimed. He always had. He had become a vampire by drinking "the blood of the Other," and now he quenched his dark thirst by sipping blood from cuts inflicted over strategic places on the bodies of friends—safe sex, vampire-style.

"It's a liquid voltage," he said, but the reporter to whom he spoke seemed to think he was a little wacko. The tone with which the writer described his encounter was condescending and snooty. He clearly wanted to keep Judas at arm's length.

Then it got interesting. Judas claimed to be part of a vampire subculture, a netherworld that met in an abandoned Presbyterian church. They relished the perversion implied in that paradoxical clash of spiritual cultures. As disciples of dark alchemy, he explained, they fully understood the rituals of transformation from within. They had their own special music, secret names, sensual wardrobe, and ceremonial rites. They also had a whole set of clandestine mythologies akin to those of any church or religious organization. The difference, he said, was that they really believed in what they were doing. They did not just go through the motions or mouth creeds that crumbled like stale bread. Their practices were fresh, spontaneous, and sincere. And they welcomed all who were willing to endure the initiation. Judas did not offer any details on this particular practice, and Jamie wondered if Gail had gone through something like that.

Judas claimed that he did not know Ana personally, but he certainly knew of her. She had a reputation for having made contact with the "Real Ones." It was whispered around that she was being inducted into their coterie, and that they were a unique group with highly evolved abilities.

It sounded to Jamie like some sort of alien abduction jargon. Who were "the Real Ones"? What "evolved abilities" could they possibly have? And how did Gail have access to them? Did it have something to do with her disappearance?

As Jamie read the rest of the article, she concluded that these "vampires" were just a new breed of thrill-seeker, wandering around without a set of trusted values and looking for some form of power-based identity. The vampire was for them a new hero . . . even a new God. She certainly understood what it meant to be powerless, but these people were trying it on like some spectacular coat of many colors. At first she thought them a bit pathetic, but the more she read, the more it seemed that they felt they had found something that satisfied an inner longing that she herself had never dared express. As she read, her heart pounded.

She went through more articles that delved into the world of after-hours vampire types, but none shed light on what might have happened to her sister. Each of the "vampires" interviewed denied having encountered such a journalist, and they certainly did not coerce "victims" without consent. They didn't need to. There were more than enough people coming into the clubs who begged to be taken, overpowered, subdued, and made to surrender. Not everyone attracted to these groups chose the dominant role. In fact, claimed a "psychic" vampire named Eboni, there were far more willing "donors" than vampires, and that was something of a problem.

Jamie sat back and thought about this. She could barely imagine what it would be like to fully surrender to some demonic creature who gazed with full focus on her. Would it have blazing red eyes, as Hollywood always insisted, or something more alluring? More human. She almost felt the sweet touch of cold fingers on her skin, the hungry mouth moving close to her throat. The liquid release of all responsibility.

The image scared her. It also reminded her of Devon and how much he needed her.

To break the spell, she stopped reading and sat back. Just as she did, she caught a glimpse of the tallish man who sat several carrels away—the one who'd been wearing casual clothes. He did not meet her eyes, but she was sure he'd been watching her. He was lean, with brown hair that curled to just below his ears, and he wore faded jeans, black tennis shoes, and a light blue denim shirt—ordinary. Nothing about him seemed threatening, except that she was sure she had attracted his interest.

Still, it was daylight hours, almost noon. He could not be one of these so-called vampires. He certainly didn't dress as though he were. Maybe he was just a nerd who couldn't get up the courage to ask girls out, so he hoped he might encounter someone in a library.

Just to be sure, Jamie leaned toward the leather purse at her feet, flipped through it as if looking for something, and then grabbed it, got up, and walked away. Slipping around the corner, she waited a few minutes. Then she looked back at the microfilm booth where the light on her machine still lingered with a slight buzz on the last article she had read.

The man had not moved. In fact, he seemed quite intent on his own work. He wrote something on a small pad of paper, rubbed two fingers against his close-shaven cheek, and then returned to what appeared to be full concentration on a book that lay in front of him.

Jamie felt foolish. No doubt this guy had simply glanced up at her, exercising his eyes or just looking her over as a woman, and she had caught him. Just coincidence. He had no real interest, it seemed. He was busy with his own concerns.

Walking along the wide, arched hallway, she searched for a phone. One article she'd read had provided a phone number for access to "everything vampire." *Great idea,* she thought sarcastically. *Give these kids easy access, like reporting how to hot-wire a car to a bunch of hot-blooded teenage boys who needed to get somewhere fast.*

Still, the number might be useful to her. She wanted to find out where such cults met. She needed to know that these people really existed and that someone in this city might have encountered Gail in the course of her research. Someone the reporters had not questioned or had not questioned well.

Jamie had already talked with the police by phone. One detective, Sean Monty, had tried to dissuade her from going off on her own. She had appreciated his concern, but had not been impressed with his attention to her sister's case. He had provided her with a vague rundown of what little information they had and then had warned her that she was getting into dangerous territory. She had listened, not quite believing. She had felt that the police were not doing enough. The case had seemed low-priority for their overworked personnel, especially when they had discovered that Gail had

frequented these clubs on a regular basis. It seemed at
that point that they had written her off as a kook.

"You play with fire," Monty had said, "you get
burned. She knew these people. Knew them pretty well.
Some of those cult members who said they'd never
heard of her were lying. Maybe there were drugs involved. Maybe she offended someone or witnessed
something she shouldn't have. Or maybe she just shed
her identity like so many of them want to do and slipped
into someone else. It's possible that she doesn't want
to be found."

That had been enough to motivate Jamie to go
through with her plan. These people had obviously dismissed her sister as a hot piece, a girl who liked to get
a little wild and who had probably gone too far. No
crime in that. And no corpse had been found to prove
that anything had happened to concern them.

Jamie found a phone and dialed the vampire intelligence number. After four rings, a tape recording informed her that should she want a pair of vampire
contact lenses of any type or color—all black, all white,
all red, *"Lost Boys," "Interview with the Vampire,"* or "special effect" lenses—she could pick them up immediately. If she wanted fangs—regular or deluxe—they had
to be fitted, but they would be available in two hours,
with a one-year guarantee.

For more specific and personal information, there
was yet another number to call. "If you're a Bloodist,
a Genetic, a Goth, a Nightliner, or any other kind of
vampire or vampire supporter, we have information on
meetings. Ask for Lady Almedia or Loki. We'd love to
have you as a member. Or if you just want to talk about
your desires, give us a call. We understand. We really
do."

Jamie copied the other number but did not feel ready
to call. Knowing now that there were numerous cults

around the city, she wanted to look though more articles that could shed some light on which one her sister might have preferred. The last thing she wanted to do was visit them, one by one—especially if it meant that to get in, she'd have to fake the desire to want to drink blood. Returning to the microfilm room, she rounded the corner and stopped short.

The man from the other carrel was standing there at her desk, reading.

She had caught him!

Unsure what to do, she hesitated. What could he possibly want with those articles? But she couldn't just let him keep reading. Whatever he wanted, he could ask. Feeling bolder, she stepped forward to confront him. "Excuse me," she said. "Did you need something?"

He turned to her, startled, but regained his composure at once. She found his hazel eyes disconcertingly direct. There was no doubt in Jamie's mind that, as he scanned her, he was thinking of her sister. He knew Gail—or had known her, whichever the case might be. She could see it in his expression.

He was at least six inches taller than Jamie, who at five foot seven, was no slouch. And he seemed not the least bit chagrined at being caught.

"I'm sorry," the man said. "I just noticed . . . I figured you were . . ." He stopped and cleared his throat. Then he looked at her, his eyes bright with mystery. "I knew your sister," he said. "My name is Allan Coyne. I'm a reporter. I noticed your resemblance to Ana and thought maybe you were here trying to find her."

"Ana?"

"Sorry, I meant Gail."

Jamie crossed her arms over her chest and said, "And what is that to you? How did you know her?"

"I gave her some connections. She did some research for me once."

"You gave her some connections? For these vampire kooks?"

Allan Coyne shifted uneasily from one foot to another. "I'd be careful what you call them if I were you," he said. "But, yes, for the vampire cults. That was what she wanted. She was researching them."

"And I suppose she did something for you in return?"

Jamie noticed his eyes narrow slightly before he said, "We were friends. But she got a little crazy at times and I wasn't always willing to go along. Maybe if I had, she'd be here now."

"What's that supposed to mean? Do you think she's dead?"

Jamie's heart began to beat faster. As little as she had in common with her twin, she could not bear the thought of losing her. That meant losing part of her own self—the enticing, sinister part that acted on what it wanted, no matter how dark or frightening.

"I don't really know," Allan said. "But I do know that she liked to do some pretty dangerous things, and that the stories she pursued took her to strange places. Listen, would you like to have coffee somewhere? I mean, we got off on the wrong foot here. I didn't mean to snoop. I just wanted to be sure I was right about who you are. Maybe we can put our heads together and sort it out. It's possible that Gail said something that makes no sense to you but might give me some clues."

Jamie stiffened. She knew nothing of this man. If he was in fact a friend of Gail's, then what he suggested made sense, but if he wanted to block her from finding out what he or others might know, his friendly manner could be a cover. For all she knew, he'd kidnapped, harmed, or even killed her twin. He might do the same to her, and she had Devon to think about. Or maybe he was after some angle on a story and was willing to exploit her in any way he could.

"I don't know . . ." she said. She wished she were more decisive, that she could just judge people on the spot. There were so many different reasons why this man might want to get her away from the library.

Still, she had nothing else. She knew no one in this city who had known Gail. She had found nothing in Gail's home yesterday to shed any light, no phone numbers, photographs, nothing. That in itself was alarming, as if someone had cleaned out her place to erase any leads. Much as Jamie tended toward caution, this was no time to lose a potential connection.

Allan reached into his back pocket and withdrew a wallet from which he took a business card. He presented the card to Jamie. She read it and acknowledged his affiliation with the *Post*. It looked legitimate.

On the other hand, anyone could make up a business card.

"The coffee shop is quite close," he said. "If you're worried . . ."

"Okay," she said. "Let's have coffee."

Allan guided her to a place down the street that smelled of coffee, cinnamon, and fresh croissants. Somehow that was comforting. All the while, he kept up a stream of friendly talk that seemed calculated to put her at ease. She kept up her guard. In the café, he found a seat for them by a large window that provided a view of the people scooting by, then went to the counter to give their order to a black-uniformed waitress with kinky brown hair.

It was then, as he turned away, that Jamie noticed a red mark stretching across his neck, as if he had been freshly hung and had managed to slip from the noose.

Her mind moved toward images of autoeroticism with rubber cords. She started to rethink her decision to come with him. He apparently wasn't quite what he seemed.

Allan sat down with the same disarming smile. After a few more minutes of small talk, Jamie stopped him and asked, "What were you doing in the library this morning? Did you follow me there?"

He shook his head. "I was already there, but I'll admit to following you into the reading room. I was on my way out when I spotted you and saw your resemblance to Gail. I knew she had a sister—she told me. I thought perhaps we could assist each other."

"Then why didn't you just approach me? Why spy on me?"

He shrugged. "Chalk it up to a reporter's snoopy ways. I wanted to be sure about you first."

"I'm not telling you anything for print," Jamie warned him. "I don't want to see any of this in your newspaper."

He held up a hand. "This isn't about a story. Gail was my friend. I'm concerned. I knew her about as well as anyone did, I think, and I really have no idea what happened to her. I want to find her as much as you do."

"Why did you call her Ana?"

Allan considered this and then got right to the point. "Your sister wasn't just investigating vampire cults," he said in a voice so low it was almost a whisper. "She had a real affinity with some of the people there. She wanted to be with them, quite desperately at times. That was the name she took in order to be among them, and she insisted that I call her that."

"Affinity?" Jamie asked. "What sort of affinity?"

The waitress came with a mocha latte for Jamie and

black coffee for Allan. He waited until she was gone to respond.

"She talked about them all the time," he said. "At first, she read books and spent hours on-line, dragging in confessions of creepy practices from all over the world. She was like a vacuum cleaner sweeping through hell. She just couldn't get enough. She wanted to know everything that was possible to do, everything that people practiced in their satanic or witchy groups, how they felt, what they dreamed about, what they dared themselves to do. Anything unusual. Risk was an addiction to her."

"Why?"

"I think she felt that something was missing in her life. She thought she might find an answer among people who claimed to push the envelope, to explore every possibility for expanding their awareness and enriching their perceptions. She never judged them. She just wanted to know. I have to confess that some of the things she told me turned my stomach. Sometimes it even scared me."

"Scared you?" Jamie watched him, trying to sense whether he was telling her the truth. She poured a spoonful of sugar through the cinnamon-flecked foam of her latte.

"You have to understand that people with a vampire fetish tend to take one of two directions. They're either in it for the romance—the sort of highly sensual mythology that a vampire image suggests. Gothic stuff. Or else they want the gore. They want the bloodiness of it, the power, the violence, the dangerous sex. They love the predatory angle, with its control over others and its indulgence in total, unbridled blood lust. Those are the kind who hurt others, like those kids from Kentucky who killed an elderly couple just to experience their deaths. That's not romantic. That's just sick. But there are cults out there that cater to either taste and everything in between. It's become quite a fashionable thing to be among people who identify with vampires and ghouls. It's attracted tens of thousands of people."

"And what did you say to all of this? Did you discourage Gail from pursuing it?"

Allan shrugged and looked away for a moment. Jamie sensed he was uncomfortable. "Not at first," he admitted. "I'm afraid that I was curious, myself. I even got a few stories out of it. And I have to admit, as disgusting as some of it was, I thought maybe she was on to something. It was fun to watch Gail talk about it. Her eyes would light up and she'd confess secret desires of her own that made me pretty hot. But after a while she really did start to change, like she'd discovered something."

Jamie leaned forward. "Did you sleep with her?"

He hesitated, then reluctantly admitted, "Yes, I did, but I wouldn't say we were lovers. I don't think she thought that way of me. She just wanted sex, but no accountability. No relationships. I wasn't about to turn down an opportunity. She was beautiful. She was fun. And she asked me for nothing."

"Was fun?" Jamie raised an eyebrow. This was the first indication that Allan Coyne might actually know something that he wasn't revealing, and that her sister might be dead.

"Just an expression," he said with a shrug. "She's not around now. I haven't seen her since a week before she vanished."

"In what way did she change?"

Allan considered this for a moment before he said, "It's hard to describe. It was like she'd discovered something extraordinary. Something real, that she believed was some sort of answer to all her searching."

"Did she tell you what it was?"

"She didn't. She suddenly got secretive and disappeared for days without communicating with anyone."

"Anyone?" Jamie perked up. "You know her friends?"

"I knew one . . . Tonia. But she . . . she had an accident. She's dead."

Jamie raised an eyebrow. "Dead? You think it was an accident? What happened?"

"I don't know. People get pushed on subways sometimes. She fell onto the tracks. That's what investigators decided. Who knows? Anyway, that was my source if I wanted to find Gail, and now they're both gone."

Jamie sipped her coffee. This was a piece of disturbing news, and she felt more convinced that something bad had happened to her sister. She took a deep breath and asked, "So what do you think I might know? It sounds like she told you a lot more than she told me. In fact, I didn't know anything about this vampire stuff, other than some of her crazy Halloween forays."

He shrugged again. "It was just a thought. She spoke about you, so I figured you two were close. Women sometimes tell other women things they would never reveal to a man."

"Sorry," said Jamie. "We really weren't that close. She didn't appreciate my concern for safety."

Allan sipped his coffee. "Well, maybe there's another way." He looked down as if pondering whether he ought to say anything further and then took a deep breath before meeting her eyes again. "You may think this is crazy, but I'll just say it. I thought of this when I first saw you. It's tricky, but it might work. Because you look like her, and with a different hairstyle you'd resemble her pretty closely, you might be able to pose as her and get information that I can't seem to get. Maybe you could dress like her and go into one of these cults. Maybe you could get some answers."

Jamie stared at him. In truth, she'd already considered this plan herself. As much as the idea frightened her, it seemed the only alternative to the official avenues that had turned up nothing. "I think that's a possibility," she told Allan, "but I don't know where to begin. She left no journals or addresses or anything that I can find that gives me a clue."

"Well, I know some of the places she's gone. I know a few of the people she's talked with. We could start with them."

"Did you tell any of that to the police?"

When he hesitated, Jamie sensed again that he knew something that he was unwilling to say. It annoyed her, considering what he was asking of her.

"I'll go with you," he assured her. "I won't leave you stranded. I'd rather not bring the cops into this. I'm afraid I'll lose my connections with these people if I do. The police have done what they can, and the people whom I know have nothing to say to the cops, anyway. They'll talk to me more openly than they will to the law, and so far, they've told me nothing."

Jamie did not believe that. She took a sip of her latte and let the heat of the steamed milk spread over her tongue as she considered her options.

"There's something you're not telling me," she finally said.

He was ready for her, as if he'd anticipated this statement. "There's a lot I'm not telling you," he conceded, "but that's because this is all much more complicated than you can imagine. If you'll trust me, I can explain it further tonight, but there are things I have to show you first."

Jamie considered this. Allan's secrecy disturbed her, but she also felt that now was not the time to recede into her usual reserve. A plan of action had been presented—a viable one. She could not think of a single good reason not to at least give it a try, and she'd certainly feel better going into one of these clubs accompanied by a man than going in by herself. He did not seem to be a threat, only a man with information that he had not yet revealed.

She nodded and said, "Okay, then. Tell me how I need to dress and where I need to go. Let's do it tonight."

Something passed across Allan's face that she could not identify. He seemed satisfied. Almost too satisfied. As if this had been too easy. Whatever he wanted from her, she was sure there was far more to it than merely finding her lost sister. Something else was clearly at stake.

"I'll make some arrangements," he said.

Three

Christian

I sat with Bel on a coppery brown vinyl three-seater on the train back to Trenton. I was on the aisle. We stayed toward the back of the car so people looking for seats or getting off could brush up against me. This was just one way we'd discovered of pilfering their body heat unnoticed. We could have entranced them, but this game was more fun. I didn't actually have to touch them to get it, but I liked to. As they brushed past, I sucked it up.

For me, the pleasure was oral. I felt deep inside my mouth the approach of some eroticized torso, and the sensation intensified into glowing embers as that person came closer. My fangs would begin to twitch forward from the grooves in which they otherwise lay dormant, overwhelming me with a surging desire to pounce and inject my venin. I'd feel them swelling in my mouth, so ready for action I was nearly in a swoon, but then as the person passed by, they'd retract back, unfulfilled. Each time I told myself I might make my move, might entwine my prey with the seductive glide of an asp, and quickly bite. Once fastened, I'd never let go. All part of the fantasy. I never knew if I would strike or be still.

Despite the bright fluorescent tubes that ran the length of the car to heighten visibility, there were so

many oddly dressed kids returning from their diverse
late-night outings that we blended right in. We didn't
look that different, anyway, but our tastes tended to
buck fashion—like these kids. I even saw the flash of a
well-crafted fang in the mouth of a girl with long black
hair and a gaudy purple-and-red gypsy skirt. She turned
to me, her gold earrings catching a glint of the overhead
light, and boldly winked, as if she were the predator
and I the prey. She wanted me to think that she was
quite audacious and could have me or not, as she
pleased. I weened that she hoped this would entice me.

I smiled in response. I enjoyed this little joke. How
I loved these temps who wanted to be anything but
themselves. They were so close to my former mortal
soul that I could taste it.

If only they knew what it really meant to become what
they so often fantasized. It wasn't just an enhancement
of the physical experiences and mortal powers they already had. It was a total transformation into a predatory
perspective that tightened our body cells into hyper-
alertness. They would have to thrive as their blood commanded, the shifting moods distributed randomly by
some force none of us understood. It wasn't even a
physical need so much as the compulsion to absorb that
which was of most value to the prey—the stuff that made
them hot.

Bel and I had spent a lot of time over the years calculating which night trains carried home the largest
load of people, because that meant human warmth
from bodies high on night energy all pressed close together, particularly bodies that were permeated with the
flames of alcohol. Although we couldn't ingest as we
desired, we absorbed, so to speak, the secondhand
smoke.

I watched a young college student in the seat ahead
of me. His reddish brown hair was short, clipped neatly

enough for me to see the slight pulse behind his ear. I stared for a moment, mesmerized. This was my favorite place to drink. So secret. So seductive and throbbingly hot. Just looking at it aroused me.

Bel's elbow shook me loose from my erotic reverie. She was always nervous that if I indulged too much, I'd lose control.

Next to us, a white-haired man with facial skin falling into his neck pulled a cell phone from the pocket of his suit jacket. He punched in a long string of numbers, and in a moment began to shout to another party, who apparently lived in Hamburg, Germany. It seemed it was his first experience using such a device, because he repeatedly exclaimed his wonderment at how he could speak to his friend from a train car in New Jersey. And he kept losing the connection. He'd mumble as he punched in the numbers again and then start to yell to his long-distance friend. I smelled stale breath, which revealed his age as tellingly as the dried scales of skin on the back of his hands. He didn't interest me.

I felt Bel on my other side as she glanced over at him. She was annoyed. I knew she might go for him, even if there was little payoff. Just because. Had she lived as a mortal, she'd have been one of those psychopathic adolescents who terrorize people to fulfill some interior demon. Despite some of her more refined traits, Bel could really have been evil.

The man looked like an ordinary businessman making the final dash in his long race. He seemed tired and a bit perplexed by the wonders of technology. Using this phone had been a small victory in a world that sought to edge out his type. His hand trembled slightly as he held the portable phone to his ear. I saw the blood pulsing in his neck, smelled his anxiety. I began to feel the slightest stirring.

There's nothing we crave more than passion in some

form, whether it is fear, love, excitement, or enthusiasm. It's fiery; it's alive. In someone like him, fear was probably all he had left. But its nuances fascinated me.

When the train stopped in Metuchen, the man stood to get off. He grabbed a brown leather briefcase from overhead and walked toward the nearest door. Swift and silent, Bel followed him. There was nothing threatening about her, looking as innocent as she had on the day she had cleverly seduced a vampire at the age of thirteen to turn her. I knew what she was up to. I wanted to go with her, but she disliked it when I watched. She preferred taking her prey in private. If she guessed I was there, she would give up the pursuit and be annoyed with me for days. Yet I had ways to scramble the psychic bond so she couldn't be sure.

Just before the doors closed, I got up and moved into the passage between the cars. I was just about to step out when I spotted Dantalyon in the next car back. I stopped. I hadn't expected him here. I thought he'd long ago caught a train back. His brown eyes met mine and that moment of hesitation decided my next move. The closing doors clipped my chances of catching Bel, but I sensed it was better to remain on the train. I moved into that car and sat in the two-seater next to the dark-skinned renegade.

The immediate intimacy of his presence nearly overwhelmed me. We'd been on hunts together, and he'd even been the one to invite me into the *kamera*, but rarely did I get this physically close to him—rarely would he have let me. The seats were small, which pushed us against each other. He was warm, which meant he'd taken a victim. I guessed that he'd been part of the abduction of Jamie's son. I tried to allow myself only the merest contact of shoulder against shoulder, but his knee quickly brushed against mine. He wanted from me whatever I had taken from the shadows that evening.

I gladly yielded and felt the transfer of heat. I wished he would take more. I would give him anything, everything.

Then I realized that something disturbed Dantalyon. Never forthcoming, he wouldn't tell me what it was, but he was also blocking my read of the memory fields that enveloped us. That didn't surprise me, since Dantalyon reserved familiarity for Naje, his *kupua*. Only a random whim ever inspired him to give us a taste, so sitting with him now was a real treat.

"You got the boy?" I asked. I didn't have to say who I meant. We all knew that Jamie had a son.

He nodded. He didn't reveal what they had done, so I searched for a way to engage him further. I didn't care what we talked about because I didn't know how long we had together. From this point on, the train would stop about every ten minutes, and he might depart at any moment.

"How will you get her to come?" I pressed.

Dantalyon raised an eyebrow, as if to let me know this was a silly question. Of course Naje would have a plan.

I nodded and sat back to absorb what I could of his presence. In our *kamera*, there are several levels of refinement and ability, because the development of a *kamera* is the process of joining disparate souls into a unity. Few vampires enjoy this heightened existence, and most don't even know about it. It's not just a frat house gang of immortals; it's the blending of special talents to create a greater force for all of us to imbibe and exploit. When we work together and honor our center, we're much more powerful. The trick was to submerge ourselves.

We're often enamored of those who are a step or two more advanced, as if falling in love with our own potential powers. Dantalyon was the most exquisite among us, especially when sated, with his burnished skin and radiant hair. He spent his best moments with Naje, whom we variously called our elder, *kumu*, or *dominie*. They were like lovers who could not drink enough of each other, though their union throve on something beyond my comprehension. For me, this was a most privileged moment.

Within a *kamera*, the second most elite position is that of consort, the *kumu*'s companion. Typically, one vampire might make another to stave off loneliness. They might stay together or, eventually uninterested, drift apart, as I did rather quickly from my progenitor. They may suffer a brief infatuation or a long-term ache, but being made a vampire is as a spark to a blazing inferno compared to the vested position of the elder's consort, which, due to its innate power and precariousness, is quite rare in our world. Few can bear the tension, even with the privileges it entails. It happens only within a *kamera*, and even then it's unique, in part because it's so dangerous.

First, by way of explanation, it's important to know that a vampire's actual age has little relevance among us. What matters is our resonance, and this happens on two levels. First, there's a cultural resonance, because we're attuned to the culture's emotional tones and we become what the collective spirit desires but represses. We can shift and change with the times, and we do. Just look at how Dracula, one of the most dreaded creatures in the 1930s and 1940s, now appears on candy wrappers and cartoons. He's a joke. Yet the vampire still has a threatening shape in an entirely different persona. It's much more confusing and paradoxical these days, which means it's more easily embraced by the postmodern mind.

But the other resonance is the more important one to us and most relevant to understanding the consort:

once transformed and invited into a *kamera*, we resonate to a certain predatory species. Whether it's a lynx, wolf, or lion, it pervades how we dress, wear our hair, adorn our bodies, and affect a pattern of manners. As I said before, our own *kamera* resonates to the snake. Other *kameric* resonances, like bears or panthers, can coexist with us, though we'd rather go our separate ways. Those that become like the hawk or eagle make us as anxious as we make scorpions or rats. They wouldn't necessarily hunt us, but in a confrontation we each go for our own advantages. And they will take prey from us.

We draw into ourselves the spirit of our resonant species and become quite literally possessed by the mind of a creature that thrives on the hunt. Some of us even choose species-specific names, like Cascabel, Eryx, and Naje, although I had not yet done so. We're chosen for the *kamera* because of some unique ability.

As the expression goes, we can "morph" into that to which our mental facilities attach. We're psychological shape-shifters. Mind and body act as a unit, but the power of mind is preeminent. Our thoughts can change our entire cellular structure. It takes some practice to make dramatic leaps, but the most skilled among us can do it. Or so the legends tell us.

In fact, Naje, whose original name none of us knows, drew his appellation from the humanized cobras that surround the Buddha in many depictions. The Nagas guard treasures, especially pearls. Naje is as close to the snake's mystical abilities as anyone can get without being one. It was he who chose the resonance after roaming the world in search of shamanic magic. Then he formed the *kamera*, one member at a time, over the course of at least two centuries.

During our vampire sleep, we're made to dream repetitively of that to which we resonate, and gradually the imagination works on our bodily substance to bring about the Quickening. The predatory mind takes over, not as an animal but as a higher order being with shared crossover characteristics. Our own small group—those who live in our country mansion—have kinship with the pit viper, refined and steady in our pursuit. The full transformation, which entails the ability to use a full and diverse range of animallike powers, can take time, but that makes no real difference to us. The more gradual the transformation, the more sensual, and like snakes, we can digest a single meal for days, even weeks, before having to go out again. And we have shedding cycles. It's not the skin we shed, however, but an inner identity. As we evolve, we move from one transient stability to the next.

And the resonance can change at some later point. I might experience for an entire decade the identity of a cobra, for example, and then find myself taken over by the diamondback. My dreams will tell me when it's time. Churning throughout my vampire sleep, these dreams lead me from one destiny to another. They inhabit me and possess my soul. Vampire identity is that fluid.

Should I evolve from the snake to something else, say, a grizzly or even a snake that devours its own kind, my *kamera* would rip me to pieces in self-defense. Even a consciousness transformed will have some links to its former *kamera,* and that state of mind presents a threat to the survival of the group toward which he is moving. We can only hope that our dreams will remain intraspecies, else we're finished.

And there's no hiding it. The snake knows when the hawk is near; the hawk knows the snake. Where there's no resonance, there's only the posture of preservation.

Those vampires who resonate specifically to similar temperaments or occupations then share a peculiar affinity for one another. That was how the various *kamera*s form, and how within *kamera*s smaller groups like ours develop. Within each *kamera* a focal member emerges, defined by how well he or she crystallizes whatever is sacred to the group. That vampire becomes the center. We in Solebury honor the artful mind, so the one who leads us is determined by his or her comparative degree of aesthetic intelligence and the spiritual level to which his soul has ascended. Strength among us comes not from age, but from wit and the deepening of perception. Naje holds our highest respect. None would challenge him. Some of us won't even approach him.

Then there's the consort, which brings us to Dantalyon. A supreme vampire such as Naje may decide to draw someone—mortal or vampire—more fully into his sphere. His decision is based on the person's capacity for absorbing the resonance and for holding his attention. That one becomes the consort. The chosen one then inherits the *kumu*'s soul and the two develop as one, fully entwined. While that has its advantages, it's also quite vulnerable. Any given vampire, powerful as he or she may be, can have only one such liaison at a time; to chose another is termination for the first. And conversely, if the *kumu* has chosen badly, he or she may be drained of all power by the consort. Trust and integrity on both sides is paramount. They must honor the eternity of a devoted love or suffer a destiny of betrayal.

Many of those in the center chose not to bond with a consort due to its obvious danger, but our Naje simply could not resist. He'd been celibate in that way for centuries, which meant that the one who could provoke his attention had to be spectacular. Dantalyon was as near perfect in beauty and form as a man can be, and he bore his status well, if enigmatically. He was also gifted in many ways that Naje valued.

He'd chosen Dantalyon over a century ago. That

meant Dantalyon had absorbed a lot of Naje's mind. He felt what Naje felt, saw things as Naje saw them, knew his powers to some degree, and wore the hushed aura of the chosen. He was special. He possessed more intensity than the rest of us in aesthetic sensation, intellectual cunning, and emotional sophistication. Yet he was also exposed. He could be snapped out of existence like a flame blown out. That was the price.

In fact, the legend among us was that he'd resisted at first. He'd understood the cost and had declined. That had made Naje even more determined. Whatever powers he had used to persuade Dantalyon were unknown to the rest of us, but the manifestations were vibrantly visible. He'd not have taken a consort against his will; that was too dangerous, so something irresistible had been done to entice the reluctant Apache. Over a century later, they were still entwined. Those two had only to enter the same room and you could feel the power surging from within their awareness of each other and the abilities they cocreated.

We loved to just look at Dantalyon, whose name derived from demons that turn men's thoughts to evil, and he enjoyed the attention. Still, he held us at arm's length. He'd been a prince among his people and he was the prince among us as well. Yet tonight something seemed different.

"You don't like this plan?" I asked him.

He shrugged. "He knows what he's doing."

"Then what's bothering you?"

He looked out the window. Lights flashed by as we came into the New Brunswick station near Rutgers University. I felt myself slide into his brooding soul and sought some foothold. The perilous thing about being a vampire is how easily our identities can shift, especially in close proximity to those who are stronger. We're always on guard over our boundaries.

"Shall we get off here?" I asked. There were places in New Brunswick to have a good time. College kids who would swoon over us. We were both tall and well built, though he was much more imposing. We could certainly find some clandestine role-playing parties. Maybe that was all he needed.

Dantalyon shook his head. Then he reached over and stroked my hand as it rested on my thigh. I knew he felt me inwardly recoil, though it was not from revulsion or lack of desire. Had I made this gesture with him, I'd have performed a forbidden act. No one touched the consort except Naje.

But tonight, it seemed, Dantalyon sought a small rebellion, a little game. His forefinger rubbed the sensitive web near my thumb. I didn't move. I didn't breathe. I allow the pleasure to flow into my loins. I liked what he was doing and wanted more. His contact with me traveled from the surface of my skin to the nerve endings of my aesthetic imagination. This exquisite tension was probably what he felt whenever Naje touched him— the infusion of vitality and warmth, like cocaine or ecstasy flooding a mortal soul. I held still and let it take me.

He smiled at my response. He opened his legs slightly to brush the side of his left leg more fully against my right. I started to tremble a little. He enjoyed that. It must feel good to have power over others in this way, I thought, when one was generally the receiver.

If I were to describe this moment to Phelan, who was in love with Dantalyon from afar, he'd never believe me. He might even be upset by its potential for imbalance in the group. He'd definitely be jealous.

"Let's go to New Hope," Dantalyon whispered close to my ear. "I'm in the mood. Who knows how long we have? I'm restless. I want to burn. Let's find someone who can give us that."

I nodded. I was in that mood, too. Maybe it was the effect of imminent annihilation; I didn't know. But I was jittery, too, and to have the most beautiful vampire in our *kamera* as a companion was more than I could have hoped. He was everything I wanted to be, with his sleek black hair and large, dark eyes in a face of the most ethereal contours. He was over six feet tall, with a full chest, small hips, and long-boned, muscular thighs. Naje had chosen well, although I was sure his reasons had been influenced by Dantalyon's more occult qualities—those that had become nearly mythical among the rest of us as we exercised our imaginations outside their closed door. When vampires blend their energies during our daytime trance in a spiritual embrace, it creates a vision that augments their mental dexterity. I've done it with others in our group to surprising effect, and we knew it was a regular exercise for these two. I'd once been invited to share it, and when I emerged from it the following night, I knew I'd been altered in ways I still don't comprehend.

I couldn't wait to go. I would get to see Dantalyon's hunger rise, watch him play, observe his burning seductions. I thought there might be a special treat in it for me, if only to be a witness.

And that was what he seemed to want from me.

I had heard that Dantalyon enjoyed being watched, and nothing fed my own passion more than getting close to the act as a master performed it. I grew more solid at the thought, my whole body swelling, which had a contagious effect. I sensed Dantalyon's excitement and wished the force of my own will could speed the train as effectively as it moved mortals from this place to that. I wanted to get to New Hope. It wouldn't be long.

Four

Jamie

The Slaughterhouse was far noisier than Jamie had expected. She could hear nothing above the din of electric guitars, thumping drums, shrieking singers, and kids yelling to one another. The smoke from cigarettes and pot was so thick she began to cough against the sickly-sweet aroma. The deeper into the throng she went, the more like the inside of a pottery kiln the place felt: hot, sticky, enclosed. She adjusted the leather corset to keep it from pinching her skin. She was sure, if she removed it, she would find it soaked with sweat.

Allan had hold of her arm, but Jamie feared losing him in the crush of leather and lace-clad members of this outlandish club. He had made arrangements to meet someone here and had warned her what to expect, but none of his descriptions had quite prepared her for the degree of overt hunger she saw on the quick glimpses of young, garishly made-up faces she managed to catch as she passed by. Some of these kids seemed so desperate for attention.

She saw women with buzz cuts and pierced, black-tinted lips, boys with long, scuzzy hair and spidery tattoos. Eye shadow of every conceivable shade lay heavy on the lids of both genders, with thick black liner framing eyes that spoke from within of equally thick layers of alienation. Everyone was dressed in something tight or something black or red. Fleshy bosoms burst out everywhere. Some kids looked ready to perform any S&M act requested. One dark-haired, overweight woman wore high-heeled boots laced up the back in red, a tight microskirt, and black garters showing from beneath held a sinuous bullwhip. She smiled at Jamie in invitation and raised an eyebrow. Jamie turned away.

They were not staying here, she knew. They were merely meeting someone who would give them the address of a much more clandestine group meeting. She supposed this was some kind of gauntlet to be run to prove their mettle before getting the prize of a secret location. Kids yelled to one another over blasts of music.

"Dahlia, let's try the darkroom—"

"Come on, baby, give me one—"

"I need some eyeliner!"

Allan claimed to know the people who were sending them, but now that she was in the midst of all this sizzling cacophony, Jamie was not so sure she was doing the right thing. She thought of Devon and prayed that this night would not end badly. She thought about just canning it and heading back to the train.

Against her instincts, she had decided to go ahead and meet these people who supposedly "knew things." Now she feared that this might very well have been the way that Gail had disappeared. And who would know if the same thing happened to her? No one here had any idea who she was, save Allan, and she had said nothing to him about her son back in Princeton. He wouldn't even know who to contact. At least Jorja had her home number in Arizona.

Keep calm, she said to herself. *You'll soon be out of here. This is no time to turn back.*

They went down a long staircase strewn with the bodies of people high on something or undulating for someone in a moody mating dance. Jamie was sure that one couple was actually having sex right there in the open—a girl with hair the color of a pumpkin's insides, sitting on the lap of a boy, rocking in erotic rhythm—but she tried not to look. Their self-absorbed moans were drowned by three young men chattering loudly to her right who were passing something to one another. They barely noticed as Jamie squeezed past them and followed Allan to the lower level.

They pushed their way down a long stairway lighted only by a dim lamp at every fourth step. Jamie wondered if they'd be able to see anything at the bottom.

They made their way through a crowded, smoke-filled hallway, getting a quick glimpse inside some of the rooms where doors stood ajar—just enough to see that each room had its own hellish theme. Jamie noted what she thought was a game in progress in which one could change clothes right there in the room and join the action. People inside in various states of undress were getting prepared. She glimpsed a muscular set of buttocks separated by a crimson thong as a man bent over to slide on a pair of leather pants.

The room across the hall seemed to be reserved for quieter fare. Jamie wished she could enter it and not come out, just to get away and breathe, until she saw a short blond man with green eyes slash open his arm at the crook of his elbow and offer it to a slim girl with jet black hair who gripped him and drank eagerly. A stream of red ran down her chin. Jamie turned away, only to be caught in the arms of a shirtless male with long, sandy locks who looked no older than fifteen, although his manner was bold and aggressive. He smiled and she saw his pointed canine teeth.

"Interested?" he asked. Jamie shook her head and pulled away just as Allan caught her arm and dragged her farther down the hall.

They were halted by a small procession. Five shirtless young men in black boxer shorts carried a redheaded girl on their shoulders. She lay prone, dressed in a long, white robe of silken material. Jamie noticed red smears on it. The girl opened her eyes just as the procession passed Jamie, and reached toward her. There were dark smudges on her fingers. Jamie backed away.

She and Allan were beckoned into a dark room where people lined the walls, talking animatedly with one another as if making the deal of a lifetime. Now Allan and she were doing the same.

Jamie watched as Allan slipped money to a sweaty young man in a full leather bodysuit, with a beard dyed scarlet, as if he'd just had his sloppy fill of a vampire's meal. The man next to him—a twin to the "vampire" named Judas from the *Times* interview—looked her over. His eyes narrowed. She sensed that possibly he had met or known Gail, so she affected a cockier pose. She put her hands on her hips and raised her breasts provocatively. The leather encasing her ribs slipped a little from the sweat, but she stopped herself from pulling at it and revealing her naivete about this scene. His nostrils flared as if he were learning her scent, and she felt certain that at any moment he would point at her and denounce her.

"Thought you dyed your hair," he commented.

She gave a quick and noncommittal shrug. Not knowing whether it was true, she wanted him to believe she dyed it back and forth at whim. Jamie tried to appear nonchalant, even bored. He continued to stare and she wondered if he was looking for some signal from her that only Gail would offer, but finally the "vampire" seemed satisfied. He leaned over to Allan and said something that Jamie could not hear.

Allan signaled a thumbs-up and they made their way back through the sweaty press of partiers. They were jostled from both sides, and Allan lost his grip on Jamie's arm again. She nearly panicked as people came at her from all sides. Someone whispered something in her ear and she felt a sharp prick on the back of her neck, as if that person had decided to sample the goods. Allan found her and got her outside. She rubbed the spot where she'd been hurt and breathed the fresh air in relief. Balmy as it was, it seemed cool in contrast to the inferno of bodies inside.

"I know," he said, laughing. "It's quite a scene. But I couldn't have gotten this address without you. They had to see you to believe that you were Ana."

"And did they?"

"I think so. They were a little surprised, but they never really ask questions. Live and let live, that's how they exist."

"Gail dyed her hair?"

Allan shrugged. "She did a lot of things. I hadn't seen her right before she disappeared, so she might have."

"Don't these people worry about AIDS?"

"Not really. They feel immune, or else they think, 'What difference does it make?' "

"And this next place?" Jamie said. "Will it be as bad as this?"

He shook his head. "Much more mellow. We're off now to see the real practitioners. They come here only to pick their kills—"

"Kills?"

"A metaphor. Not to worry. Role-playing requires total authenticity. You never leave the role. So when they talk about a one-night stand or a pickup, they call it a kill. But before we go to the next place, you've got to make yourself think more like your sister. They haven't met her, so that's an advantage, but they know about her. They certainly know that she was used to this. Nothing fazed her. She wouldn't have gawked the way you were doing. She relished it all, and even flirted with it. They'll expect that from you."

Jamie nodded. She was thinking of the temporary tattooing process on her arm that Allan had urged her to endure that afternoon, and the damp leather corset that pinched against her ribs. She adjusted it and said, "I'll be ready. But why are they willing to meet with me? That doesn't make much sense."

"I told them you were doing a sympathetic story and that a rival clan tried to rough you up, so you went into hiding for a while. Now you're ready to take it up again. They're eager to speak with you. This particular group seeks positive publicity. One of them even went on *Ricki Lake* for one of her Halloween shows some time back. They're trying to get society at large to recognize their rights—that consenting adults should be able to do whatever they want—so they may divulge enough to give us some leads. It's worth a shot, anyway."

"And they're the real thing?" Jamie asked. Something about this did not quite ring true.

"Whatever that is, Jamie. They *think* they're the real thing. That's what matters to us. And I have a hunch that at least one of them knows something that will help."

Allan waved down a cab and they got in and rode toward a destination that he did not reveal. He'd given the driver a set of instructions that ultimately baffled Jamie, and she was afraid she might not be able to find her way back to the train station. She still did not feel altogether safe with him, but better to be with him than alone in this city at night.

As they rode through the maze of streets, Jamie thought about the call she had made earlier that evening to Princeton and worried a little that no one had answered. She imagined that Jorja had taken Devon for ice cream or to a movie to get his mind off his missing mother. She made a mental note to call again as soon as she could.

Allan began to talk to her in a low voice. "I need to just prepare you a little," he said. "You may hear chanting or see some kind of ceremony. These people pray to what they think are the spirits of vampires roaming free in the world. They're trying to lure them to come and select one from among them for possession. That one can then become the Giver to the others."

"Vampires roaming free?" Jamie asked. "They really believe that?"

"Yes. So just act as if it's all normal."

"Does it work?"

"No, not really. They don't know how to use thoughtprints, which is the only real way to bait a creature like that."

Before Jamie could ask him to elaborate, the cab pulled up in front of a three-story brownstone. Allan paid the fare and urged her to get out. She stood looking at the house. Nothing about it seemed all that sinister, except that it appeared to be completely dark inside. Maybe they weren't meeting here. Maybe Allan had gotten some false information, had spent his money for nothing. Or maybe he was setting her up in a rather complicated way. That he'd just spoken about vampires as if they were real spooked her. Jamie steeled herself against the possibility that Allan had something in mind for her as she followed him up a half dozen concrete steps.

"These people have money," said Allan. "It's a lot bigger inside than it looks."

He knocked on the door. Jamie thought the double-, then triple-quick taps sounded like some kind of code. She was about to ask Allan to explain his comment about thoughtprints when the door opened to reveal a woman with black, curly hair that fell below her waist. It was so thick and luxurious that Jamie suspected it was a wig.

"Alexandra," Allan said. "This is Ana, the woman I told you about."

Alexandra nodded. "We've been expecting you." Her teeth gleamed white in the darkness and Jamie thought she saw a slightly elongated canine. That disturbed her. It was one thing for these people to don these teeth to dress up for an outing, but another to have them as leisure wear at home. And how could this woman have been "expecting" them? Allan hadn't called ahead. Suddenly Jamie wanted to leave, but Alexandra beckoned for them to come in.

When the door closed behind them, Jamie felt the warm air close in. Allan might be okay with this, but she was most definitely not.

Alexandra led the way inside down a long, candlelit hallway. Their shadows looked like giant aliens undulating along the walls. The strange woman then opened another door. Contrary to Jamie's expectations, they went down rather than up a set of carpeted stairs. She could not even hear Alexandra's tread as she walked before them, her black velvet dress dragging and her long tresses bouncing behind. The encounter seemed ghostly.

They passed through a room that smelled strongly of roses. Several people sat or lay in various positions of contemplation. One young man stared at a candle flame, while another languidly met Jamie's eyes and whispered, "No one will ever know me." A girl wearing a flimsy black robe reached over to caress him. The front of her robe opened, exposing a bare breast. Jamie tried to act as if this were all commonplace. It struck her like some postmodern ad for perfume. She was sure these kids were on some drug and were not really even aware of her, so she turned away from this spooky scene and went down the steps.

The downstairs was very dark. It felt like a large space, but Jamie was unable to see the walls. She reached out and felt heat emanating from something nearby. A long way away, it seemed, she spotted the glimmer of a candle. Allan took her hand and urged her forth. To her right, she felt Alexandra's presence. At least, she hoped it was Alexandra. The place felt like one of those spooky houses of horror set up by a small town Kiwanis Club. Kind of amateurish but still effective.

"Here," whispered Alexandra.

Jamie looked to her right and allowed her eyes to adjust a little more. Some twenty feet ahead, she thought she saw a large, thronelike chair mounted on a three-foot-tall pedestal. It was occupied, but she was unable to make out the figure in the seat. It looked like a rather large pile of dark clothing. Multiple candles off to either side, some burned down to nubs, glinted against something on the arm of the throne, and Jamie guessed it was some kind of ring on the hand of whoever sat there. The swish of material to her side and behind her told her there were others in the room. She had the feeling she'd been lightly caressed.

Then to her left she heard a deep breath being drawn. Allan gripped her arm. She felt herself trembling against him. She wanted to rip away and pronounce this whole thing ludicrous and silly. This was not the way to find Gail. If these people knew something, why couldn't they just tell her?

Then the dark bulk in the chair moved. She heard a deep sigh that sounded both male and threatening. As her eyes adjusted further, she took in the full outline of the person on the throne. Whoever he was, his size was enormous. If he were to stand, Jamie estimated he'd be at least three hundred pounds.

Then Alexandra lit a dark candle with a nine-inch diameter and three wicks. She slipped a long-bladed knife from an embroidered scabbard and held it up. She looked into Jamie's eyes and said, "Give me your arm. We must know the spirit that's in your blood."

For a moment, Jamie was stunned. Then she ripped her arm from Allan's grip, turned, and fled back to the stairs. Without stopping, she took the steps two at a time.

Alexandra shouted something that she did not understand and Allan called her name, but she was past caring. She was not about to stop. She would not be trapped down there with these demented kooks.

She passed through the room where the stoned kids lay on the furniture and somehow found the door to the street. It was locked. Desperate, she ran her hand along the frame until she found a way to release it and open the door. Flinging herself outside, she started to run. She was unsure where to go, so she kept running in her spike-heeled boots until she found a busy intersection on which she could hail a cab. Her entire back felt exposed, and she felt sure that Allan would catch up to her and force her back to that house before she had a chance to get away. Waving her arms urgently, she shouted at two cabs that passed her by.

Near panic, Jamie looked over her shoulder. There was no sign of Allan, not yet, but she didn't want to see him. Whatever this had been about, it certainly had nothing to do with Gail.

Finally the third cab she saw stopped for her. Without a backward glance, she shouted, "Penn Station, please." The cabby pulled away and Jamie sat back in relief as Dr. Ruth's recorded voice urged her to wear her seat belt.

When she was fully on her way, away from any possibility that anyone could stop her, she allowed herself to feel the horror of what she had just seen. Between her shock and the constriction of her suffocating corset, she could barely breathe. It had not been real, none of it. It couldn't have been.

Who *was* that person on the throne . . . or *what?*

She put her hand to her mouth and shook her head. She had to get home to Devon. Allan could not find her now, she hoped. He wouldn't know where to look. Or if he did, she had a head start. She could get to Devon first and make sure they both were safe. Then she'd take him away to a hotel. Whatever else she had to do to find Gail, she'd do it alone, but first she'd get her son out of the way of any potential harm. Silently urging the cabby to hurry, she thought only of getting back to Princeton.

Five

Christian

Dantalyon had departed from the train in Princeton, where he'd left his maroon Mercedes. It reminded me what he'd done there with Jamie's boy, and depressed me a little. I rode the extra ten minutes to Trenton, walked to the protected structure where I had parked my black Jaguar XJ6, and turned it toward New Hope.

I drove up Route 29 to Lambertville so I could cross over the bridge—my favorite way into this riverside artists' colony. There were always ducks and geese on the river, no matter what hour I passed, and the lights of New Hope shimmered on the currents. The river ran fast tonight after the rains of days before. I was happy about that. Whenever I sought a contemplative journey, I stayed on the wooded Pennsylvania side, but tonight my blood was racing. An evening with the consort. I wondered what lay ahead. I half expected Dantalyon to change his mind, and I also anticipated being spun into the Delaware's black eddies by the thing that threatened us. I pressed my ride up to eighty and passed every other car on the road.

During the golden years in the early part of the century, the New Hope area of Bucks County was considered the Genius Belt. Writers and artists of great renown had bought many of the old houses in the greater New

Hope area and formed a community of kindred souls. S. J. Perelman, Dorothy Parker, George S. Kaufman, Pearl S. Buck, and James Michener had all found the idyllic countryside a welcome retreat from Manhattan, and in 1949 Grace Kelly had made her first professional stage appearance at the Bucks County Playhouse. Visual artists like Joseph Pickett and potters, engravers, and sculptors of all kinds had looked for inspiration in the old frame buildings and serene settings.

Even ghosts loved the place, some of them famous. After his duel with Alexander Hamilton, Aaron Burr had sought refuge in a house in New Hope. It was said that when he wasn't walking the halls of the Morris-Jumel Mansion in Manhattan, he was here at the scene of his notorious seduction of the daughter of the man who had granted him sanctuary. ("She should feel lucky," was his legendary retort.) Then there was the TV reporter Jessica Savage, who'd drunk a fatal after-dinner cocktail outside Odette's of brackish canal water when her car took a wrong turn. People claimed to still see her wandering around. In fact, nearly every one of New Hope's inns boasted of at least one spectral resident, from Hans at the Black Bass who was stabbed to death in a fight to Joseph Picket himself, seen painting his pictures along the banks of the creek behind the Wedgewood.

As I drove along, I watched for the phantom hitchhiker, only because he was blond and young and desperate for a ride. He was my type. He pops up everywhere, from Doylestown to Flemington, wearing a brown leather jacket and hauling a knapsack. He stands out to those who've spotted him because even on dark nights, his blue eyes are piercing and vivid. People always remember the eyes. I've never yet heard that he'd accepted a ride, but I could always hope. We vampires had developed a few entertaining games for our local ghosts.

New Hope is a vampire's town, not because it's good for hunting. It's not. The reason we had our dwelling nearby was the affinity we felt for the place. Like us, it embraced the antinomies of soul—the contrary aspects linked inextricably to give the human condition its special friction. Subcultures of all kinds flourished here, from witches of every persuasion to tattoo artists to gays to musicians. Outsiders were insiders here. Marginality ruled.

I parked behind Havana's, the town's rather singular jazz club, and went around to the front. As I entered, I glanced up at the impressively large, preserved marlin that hung over the door beneath painted gray rafters, and then took in the full scope of the room. To simulate a Caribbean atmosphere, there were pictures of pastel dolphins and posters that featured the islands. On the walls were signs handwritten in black felt-tip pen, noting prices and special dates for upcoming events. A *U*-shaped bar dominated the front room, and several people sat around it on long-legged, ladder-back chairs. I smelled beer and wine, and felt at once my unique pleasure at the collective warmth of mortal bodies. This particular pastime worked well in a bar because of the patrons' heightened anticipation of their own sexual prey. I vamped a bit from that.

I noticed at once a girl with hacked-up hair dyed green and yellow. She was alone, as if awaiting Anyone's approach. Against the wall, a man in his early forties, his dark hair going gray, smoked a cigar and scoped out the action in the room, while the band played something that sounded more like folk than jazz. Only one couple was dancing, an Asian man with long hair and an exceedingly thin young girl in a tight red knit dress. She had covered her head with some sort of silver netting, which sparkled with light from different angles.

The bartender was Patrice. She always served drinks in a gum-chewing trance. That night she had pushed her stringy blond hair under a black baseball cap inscribed simply, *Death,* and had tied it behind with a purple satin ribbon. She wore a faded denim jacket and a tie that featured Edvard Munch's image of *The Scream.* She winked at me as I came in and motioned with her head toward the inner room, where I guessed Dantalyon was already in action in some dark corner. Patrice did not know what we were exactly, but she liked it when we came in. We always made her think we'd ordered drinks and left a large tip, and she once told me that our being there gave the club an exotic feel. She had tried hitting on me that night, but it would not work to have a local disappear in my company nor figure out what I was. Better to be discreet. It made her hotter, which translated into my own body as a wave of an undiluted aphrodisiac.

In the other room, the band's lead singer leaned into the buzzing microphone with a lazy stance, singing with a strong voice but affecting indifference. The guitar player, in jeans and a stained white T-shirt that said, *Fear No Evil,* was in his own world, while the frizzy-haired drummer tapped an entrancing rhythmic beat that had the couple on the dance floor in motion.

I squinted through the smoky haze and saw a girl in leopard-skin pants and high heels rise to dance with an older woman with long, gray hair under a cowboy hat who kept her eyes moving all over the room, as if seeking a better prospect. She was a different kind of a vampire, a life-sucker in bad faith.

All around the room were small tables where people talked or watched the band. To my left sat a heavy girl speaking in hushed tones to a dark-haired, one-armed man. She handed him something with such a quick gesture, I knew it was one of the temps' sense-enhancing drugs. I smiled. If only they knew. I took in the odors of urine and semen from down the narrow hallway. Glancing around for Dantalyon, I realized I was being eyed by two women, both of them blondes, from a table across the room. I nodded slightly, then stepped away to the left, behind the tables, to find a place against the wall where I could lean and unobtrusively watch. Several more girls glanced my way, as did a lone male on the prowl, but I gave no sign of invitation. I had something more engaging in mind.

To my delight, Dantalyon was there. He hadn't changed his mind after all. I saw him saunter toward the center of the room in a way that told me he had a plan. His black shirt was open to reveal a smooth, sculpted chest and belly. He did not have to look to know whom he would take. He went by temperature. Somewhere, a girl or boy alone would signal anxiety with a singular type of sweat, or an erratic pulse or pumping heart, and he would know.

I saw him reach out and swing a dark-haired young woman into his arms. She wasn't physically striking, just pretty, but inside her was a blazing fireball of eager trepidation. That was all that mattered to us. She wore maroon lipstick, and a dozen fragile silver wires pierced her ears. Her nose was also pierced with gold. On her fingers were rings, one a silver death's head, the other a green glass eyeball encased in leather. She offered some resistance, but seeing Dantalyon's beauty, immediately yielded and put her arms around him with a smile. To the throbbing beat, they danced together, hips locked into a tempo of hungry friction, hot breath on each other's necks, her breasts rubbing his hard chest. The singer cried out suddenly as if he, too, were part of this ecstatic dance with death.

I didn't know how Dantalyon kept his hunger in check, but his eye was always on the big picture, not immediate gratification. The longer he kept this girl in desperate anticipation, the better the final meal. He was stoking the fire.

He winked over at me as he let this girl grind her need against him. I could smell her readiness all the way across the room, over smoke and beer and everything else. I licked the pulsing heat sensors in my cheeks and felt my venin teeth twitch. I wanted her, too. It would not be long.

I let the suspense wash through me as warm, enveloping waves. I was swelling up, but in a place like this, everyone else was in the same state. I did not really expect Dantalyon to share this with me, not all the way, but for as long as he allowed it, I wanted to ride with him. I loved watching the act. The others teased me about it, but sometimes that was better than doing it myself. Being invited into this venture with the consort was almost as good as being with Naje, in whose presence I felt utterly cowed but ever enticed. None of us, save Dantalyon, had ever seen his method of seduction. In fact, he rarely went out. He was a grand and enticing mystery.

When I sensed Dantalyon's subtle signal, I slipped out. It would not be wise to let anyone see this girl exit with two males. If she went out with one companion, as most women did, it was likely no one would even notice her missing. She did not appear to be with friends, and Dantalyon knew to select tourists over locals, but it was important to camouflage our trail. This was our home territory.

I went out and climbed up to the roof, knowing he would work her a bit more before leading her out. I waited for nearly twenty minutes, still anticipating sudden death, before I saw them emerge. The girl was laughing, happy with her catch for the night. I'm sure she was utterly surprised to have a man of such allure all to herself, but she had been quick to claim her advantage—at least, from her perspective. He let her think whatever she wanted. That was part of the game.

I listened to their footsteps until they faded against the backstreet macadam before I moved. I knew where they were going. Those rare victims that Dantalyon took from this artists' community he liked to bring to a haunted place. A good ghost story stirred the blood. It also gave us a way to manipulate the extra energy in the air.

Vampires have affinity with ghosts, because we have the same ethereal barcode. It comes from our link through the uncanny, perhaps, and we like to exploit it. The idea that the specter of some long-dead human may hover over our clandestine act provides an added charge. It's like being caught looking through a keyhole at someone else. The high voltage chill of a hovering presence coupled with our eagerness for heat makes the seduction electric. Eryx had taught us how to entice them close to profit by their higher vibrations, and while they didn't care for this activity, they generally had insufficient presence of mind to avoid us.

While the bull snake and his little mouse disappeared toward Mechanic Street, I decided to circle around on Ferry to give them extra time. I walked out to the front, where black ironwork lace on the building's facade reminded me of New Orleans's French Quarter. I glanced to my right at the signs for tattoos and "Warrior Body Piercing," and then turned left. Sauntering past store windows that displayed silver jewelry, homemade candy, hand-crafted leather, tarot readings, and original art, I went onto the bridge to listen to the roar of water coursing over the dam. I breathed in the odors from the ducks and geese. On another night, I'd have crossed over to see it better, but I was eager not to miss anything. To the right, the theater's parking lot was nearly empty, with a few stray cars offering protective space for passions that couldn't wait.

Ferry Street was between the old brick Parry House, built in 1784, and the 1727 Logan Inn, haunted by spooks from early colonial days. The yellow inn with the green shutters and the painted Indian sign was a central feature of New Hope. Inside in the bar was a crystal witch's ball that periodically disappeared and reappeared in odd locations. Outside, a worn red carpet hinted at elegance. I'd once drawn a ghost out of the life-size painting at the top of the stairs and vamped its soul before it could steal anything from me. I'd felt a buzz for the rest of the night.

I turned left just before the Dahlgreen smoothbore cannon with its fragrant flower gardens and pile of nine black metal balls—a memorial to George Washington's defense of the town—and went up past the crowd of boutiques. Each occupied the ground floor of a tiny colonial-style town house of frame, brick, stone, or stucco. Proprietors peddled everything from vintage clothing to modern Japanese decor via hand-carved signs.

I crossed the bridge over the canal where, during daylight hours, mule-drawn barges carried tourists north of town. The mules had been out in force that day: the towpath dust still exuded the fragrance of sweat and manure. I took in the brackish reek of the still water below, so unlike the rushing Delaware River two blocks behind me. But there was no time this night to linger. Dantalyon expected me. For only a moment, I watched a mass of fireflies sparkle in the trees overhead, then passed the cramped houses and walked to Stockton Street to cross back to Mechanic.

By the time I arrived at the abandoned frame house where Dantalyon had taken the girl, he was already telling her a spooky tale. His deep voice charged the air. I entered through a broken window and climbed into an unfurnished room. Dantalyon was down the hall. I smelled the girl's ardor and imagined her clinging to her exotic treasure as he whispered phrases spiked for terror. Seeding, it was called. Inserting trigger words into the tale to play havoc with the subconscious. It was our way of gradually constricting the prey like a stealthy python. We called it the hypnotic wrap, and it failed only if the individual realized at the start what was about to take place. That was the only point at which they could still exercise their will. But that moment was fleeting, and it was easy to envenomate it with a disorienting memory. A person has to be fairly wary and somewhat cognizant of what we are to fight it with success.

I didn't have to get too close to them, because I knew Dantalyon would include me psychically in the full sensations, but I preferred the visuals.

Only the moonlight streaming through two small windows illuminated the room where they were engaged. A dusty old couch, a small oak table, and two ladder-back chairs furnished the place. Dantalyon was on the couch with the girl on his lap, facing him, her black shirt hiked up and her legs spread apart around his sides. I listened as he told the story, which I knew to be true, but to have taken place elsewhere. At least he wasn't telling the Abbie Hoffman ghost story. That suicide had been nearby, yes, but she might know it had not been in this house.

". . . and when this handyman, Gerald," Dantalyon was telling her, "had enough of the old man's disdain, he decided just to screw the girl and then kill the whole family, including the maid."

"Wow," said the girl, her voice slurred by liquor, drugs, or passion. Or all three. "He did that?"

"He crept in on the girl one night, right here in this room. She was your age. In fact, she looked a lot like you." His voice took on a breathy, hypnotic cadence. "She was asleep in her bed, over near the window, just lying there, ready. He got himself worked up and then woke her. The moonlight was just as it is tonight, so she could see him. He opened his trousers and showed her what he meant to do. She tried to scream, but he was on her, his hand over her mouth. He cared nothing for her life. He wanted to punish her and her whole family. So he lay on her and drove himself into her. . . ."

The girl put her hand to Dantalyon's crotch and giggled nervously. She rubbed him with the same rhythms that paced his story. He leaned into her ear.

". . . it felt so good he almost forgot his plan. He'd always wanted her and now he had her."

She snuggled closer, settling on his lap, her back arched. She rubbed against him and moaned a little.

"Then he killed her," he said. "He took a knife and sliced her throat, right here in this room. And even as she bled, he continued to shove himself into her."

Dantalyon slid his hand up her silk T-shirt, and I felt her erect nipples against my fingertips as if I were touching her myself. She moved against him with a sweet sigh, then leaned into him and attached her mouth to his.

"Got a rubber?" she murmured, already stoned by her need. He laughed quietly. She had nothing to worry about, but she didn't know that. Not yet.

"Sure," he said, and put into her mind that she would be safe on that score. No matter what he actually did, she would experience it in whatever way made her relax and provide maximum pleasure. Vampires didn't need to work at it. There was an immediate connection between predator and prey that homed each in to the other and gave the predator all the advantages.

"Then wha' happened?" she murmured.

"Then he went around the house and killed everyone else in their beds. In his rage, he stabbed the girl's father over and over in the chest and cut out the man's tongue. From the mother he removed the heart and laughed in delight. By the time he reached the maid's room, he was aroused again from all the blood, so he raped her first and then killed her. He dragged the body to the girl's room and set them together on the bed."

"Eeyoo," said the girl. She let her hair fall loose over her shoulders. "And are they the ghosts?"

Dantalyon held up a finger. "And then Gerald left the house and went upriver, but when the townspeople found the bodies, they were so outraged that they hunted him down and brought him back. They hanged him, and while he was choking to death, some of them climbed up the gallows and skinned him."

"Skinned him?"

"Yes. They stripped the skin from his body. He was strangling and screaming at the same time. By the time he died, he was nearly skinned all over, his meat exposed to the birds. And then the tanner made a wallet and a lampshade from his hide."

"Oh, geez, that's awful!"

"And those things are still in this house, in the basement. They were buried here, deep in the earth."

The dark-haired girl drew a sharp breath. "Really?"

"Yes, really."

I saw Dantalyon push her skirt farther up her leg and knew they were preparing to join. She reached down to unbuckle his belt.

There's a myth that vampires can't have sex, but whether we do or not has more to do with preference than inability. A vampire's body can mimic a mortal's in nearly every way, except to expel fluids—which we don't generate. Once we become vampires, our erogenous zones spread over more of our bodies and our skin gets more acutely attuned to sensory stimulation. Our bodies do respond with all the typical signs of arousal, but some of us like sexual friction as an accompaniment to the long drink, while others dispense with all the fumbling and get right to the vampiric act itself. Still others merely place a sensory image into the mind of the one they seduce in order to raise the temperature. They don't want to get too physically involved, but Dantalyon was a sensualist. He liked to work himself and his victims into the highest pitch. He was a visceral vampire, fully aware of how to exploit his tactile zones, which I suspected was a good balance for Naje's mental approach.

"So Gerald is here in this house," he whispered, "with the others. They're all here, forever entwined." I saw his hips thrust quickly on this last word.

The girl cried out in delight, and I wondered how much of this was her actual experience versus Dantalyon's skillful illusions. Then she started to move rhythmically as he lifted her shirt to expose her breasts. He breathed on her to simulate a breeze, and I was sure his breath was cool.

"Oh, that feels good." She moaned. "Is he . . . is he . . . ?"

"Yes, he's in this room. This is where people see him. I can sense him. I think he's watching us right now."

Dantalyon grinned over at me in the shadows. He wanted me to join them . . . *now.*

I moved swiftly across the room, lifted the girl's hair, and began to kiss her neck, behind the right ear. She seemed only slightly startled, caught up as she was in her own pleasure below. From behind, I cupped her breast, squeezed gently, and for added stimulus I murmured into her ear the measured cadence of my favorite Rilke poem.

" 'My life is not this precipitous hour . . .' "

"Uhmmm . . ." she groaned.

" 'Through which you see me passing at a run . . .' "

With one eye, I watched Dantalyon. He was nearly in a swoon himself, his eyes half-closed, his legs parted, and his nostrils flared, as he measured the moments building toward the full force of this girl's passion. He gripped her thrusting hips and gestured that I should take the first taste. I knew that he was sucking heat from her down below, and for us, that was all that really mattered.

"Oh, God," the girl cried out. "Ahh!"

She was ready. The sweet pain of yet another penetration would only enhance her rising bliss. I kissed her throat again, slowly, lovingly, as she moaned, nearly in tears from the extreme sensations. I was a compassionate nurse, swabbing the target zone with cotton before the prick of the needle.

"Yeah, oh, yeah," she whispered. Dantalyon stroked her leg with his long fingers and grinned.

I went in behind her ear, hard and quick, my fangs coming forward to pierce skin. To get a good grip, I relied on smaller fangs positioned back farther and curved in the opposite way. My venin went in, just enough to enhance her swoon, and then the blood flowed out thick and hot, and I had to restrain myself from ripping through and causing a mad gush. She was not mine, after all. She belonged to him. But I had her, sweetly, for the moment. I indulged.

It was madness, this gripping need to merge into her and take more and more of her elegant esprit. I was pushing her out of her skin to take over her soul. We couldn't both be in this same space; she had to yield, and she did. As Dantalyon thrust, she leaned into me and placed her hand behind my head to have us both. Her breath came fast and her skin was aflame. I sank in deeper and bit to get more flow.

Then Dantalyon tapped my thigh and it was time. I had half a mind to ignore him. He grabbed me, knowing the moment was close. Reluctantly, I pulled out to watch the blood trickle down her neck into her shirt. I licked at it, molding her breast from behind and feeling my hunger rise again like the surf of a hurricane, to a nearly obliterating heat. The girl turned her face toward me, her eyes dilated as she continued to ride her demon lover with fury. She opened her mouth and I kissed her, letting her taste the final moments of her own life. Then I drank again from the place where my teeth had opened her up, pulled away, and leaned toward Dantalyon. His tongue touched mine, taking the first taste of his night's passion directly from me. The thrill of wet urgency between us nearly did me in. I fell to my knees and pressed myself against the moaning girl. I wanted more.

Dantalyon gave me a warning look, ready to strike if I did not back away.

It was time to withdraw. The girl was at a fever pitch. She couldn't go much longer; she was losing heat, and he would want to drink up her fervent summit in full force, without sharing. I backed away, though I continued to watch with fully dilated eyes. I sought to return to the vortex.

She was more vocal now, coming close. Dantalyon ripped her shirt and tasted the blood that had flowed to her breasts.

"Oh, God," she cried again. "Oh, yeah, yeah, keep . . . doing . . ."

In one swift motion, he lifted her and swung her onto her back over his knees to bite into an artery over her breast as she reached the highest pitch. She was screaming now, her legs apart. She fed him her rising fever. He drank deeply, using his skillful fingertips to keep her going a few more seconds. Her knees came up to give him full access.

I fell back against the wall, overcome. I listened in

my own private agony as her wails grew less intense and gradually dimmed to quiet sighs of utter satisfaction. It was no more than a minute before the girl gurgled a dying breath, filled with an enveloping rapture she had never known before. The flow had caught them both, locking them into an eternal rhythm. As fire ran into his veins like a match thrown into a stream of gasoline, Dantalyon moaned the anguish of a man who could bear no more pleasure, and that sound shot through me as if I felt the joy myself. I wanted to get closer inside their embrace.

I couldn't hold back. In an instant I was on my knees beside them, gripping Dantalyon by the hair, demanding more. He laughed and let me kiss his blood-soaked lips as the girl went limp between us. Maybe it was our last moment. Maybe our very last. It seemed so just then. I took every drop of liquid fire off his tongue, seeking it in every fold of his mouth. He pulled me close for a moment, letting me have just a little heat before he pushed me away. He'd had enough.

But then he seemed to change his mind. Without a word he pushed the girl to the floor, all the while watching me with that fierce warrior stare, and then he removed his shirt. I opened my eyes wide in astonishment. I couldn't believe it, but clearly he was inviting me to drink from him—from the very place where Naje had probably done so on many occasions. I could see the bluish puncture marks on his chest, near his heart. I reached to touch them, but he caught my hand. His eyes told me it was all or nothing.

I panted hard and swallowed. There was still an iron taste in my mouth from the girl. I looked at Dantalyon's throat, at the pulsing vein so recently filled with the liquid of life. His pungent scent penetrated my sensors and tightened my skin into an instrument of predatory need.

I wanted to; I wanted it badly. To press my fangs into those holes where ecstasy had merged those two who were like gods to me. But some dim part of my brain warned me that Naje would realize what had been done and would be furious. Maybe deadly. He'd know the instant it happened, because drinking from Dantalyon would deplete him, too. I couldn't risk that. Dantalyon was playing with me, teasing me . . . or else insulting Naje. Either way, it wasn't good. Fighting my desire, I stayed back. I would be a fool to accept the enticement.

Dantalyon's dark eyes shone at me in the dim illumination. He ran a finger over his skin, from his neck to his chest, and narrowed his eyes in a dare. His body radiated from the night's activity and my own begged for more. All of my sensors were inflamed, and a craving began to flood my brain with irrational thoughts. If this was our last night, what did it matter? We'd all be gone anyway, and I'd at least fill the memory fields with this rapturous moment.

Dantalyon held out a hand to me. "Come on, Christian," he whispered. "You want it, don't you?"

I teetered on the precipice. I couldn't do it but I had to. My inner guard collapsed and I began to surrender to the hunger that zinged from my mouth to my loins. I rubbed myself as if that would somehow hold me back.

But then the impasse was over. Just like that. Dantalyon smiled knowingly, as if to say, *You could have had it,* and shook his head. Then he stood, put on his shirt, and zipped his black pants. "Take care of her, would you?" he asked.

I nodded without a word. I couldn't say anything. I was paralyzed. And yet I despised myself for my hesitation, because this encounter would likely never happen again. We'd had our intimate moments, but not like this, never like this.

He turned away and then faced me. I could barely

see his expression but once again felt a disturbance from him. It was like standing in San Francisco and feeling a tremor. Then he said, "He knows something."

With that, he was gone.

Six

Jamie

Jamie knew something was wrong the instant she stepped out of the cab and glanced at the town house. All of the lights were off, which seemed a bit strange. She checked the address again to be sure she hadn't made a mistake, but it was the right place. Her stomach tightened as a wave of anxious nausea passed through her.

Certainly Jorja could have given up on her and just gone to sleep, but why hadn't she at least left on an outside light? Jamie put her key to the door, and when it appeared to be unlocked she felt a bolt of panic. Keeping as quiet as she possibly could, she slowly opened the door. Immediately she smelled something strange.

"Damn," she whispered. "What next?"

Had those people from that awful house somehow followed her, or had they alerted some network of insiders to let her know they didn't care for her reaction? It seemed improbable, but she was dealing with people unlike anyone she'd ever met. She couldn't even imagine why Allan had taken her there. In retrospect, it seemed a hideous prank that had nothing to do with Gail, but she couldn't think of a feasible motive.

As she walked into the front room, Jamie thought back to how she'd managed to get to the train, get on, and disappear into the crowd without Allan following her. Of course, if he truly knew Gail then he knew where she lived, but she could not be concerned with that at the moment.

Stepping into the dark foyer, she stopped to scope out the place by instinct. It was quiet. Too quiet. No rustle of someone turning over in bed upstairs, no footsteps coming to greet her. No one breathing, deep in sleep. It was late, she knew, but Jorja had assured her that she would be up.

"Jorja?" she called, quietly at first, and then louder. "Jorja?"

No answer.

Now she no longer cared if she woke up her son. This was feeling too weird.

"Jorja?" she called again. "I'm here."

Still nothing, not even the quick rustle of someone getting up.

She switched on the hallway light and ascended the steps. The unpleasant smell grew stronger. It was similar to what she'd once smelled in a deteriorating cemetery. Something dank and old. She hadn't recalled that odor when she'd first come to the town house, and it was strong enough to have been noticeable then.

Halfway up, Jamie hesitated. She wondered if she should call someone. Yet she knew no one in town. Should she call the police? And tell them what? It might be nothing. She was not yet used to Gail's place. That smell could be anything.

She took the steps more boldly and practically ran up the last four. Panic gripped her now, panic for her son. She went straight for his room. The door was open, so she reached for the wall switch and flooded the room with light. To her surprise, no one was there. Devon's rumpled bed was empty.

Yet he'd been there. The covers were pulled back

and the sheets slightly wrinkled. The feather pillow lay in a slump on the floor next to the bed, as if someone had come and yanked him out. Even a book he'd probably been reading lay open on the floor across the room.

"Devon!" she cried. She screamed his name over and over as she went back into the hall, glanced in the bathroom, and then went to Gail's bedroom.

Maybe he'd just gotten lonely. Maybe he had crawled into her bed, but her mind raced to the fact that Allan had persuaded her to stay longer, to join him that night. Had he set something up here? Had he kidnapped her son, or was Jorja somehow in league with him?

Then she saw the girl.

Jorja lay on her back in Gail's carved antique French bed. The flowered sheets were pulled back and she was nude. A trickle of blood had darkened against the skin of her small left breast. There were no wounds that Jamie could see, but she knew instinctively that this girl was dead. A pile of clothing lay on the floor. Jorja stared with empty eyes up at the ceiling, but seemed not to have been frightened of her attacker, as if she had known him and perhaps had him there as her lover. Her pretty face was still and serene.

Backing out of the room, Jamie made her way down the steps. She had to call someone, get help. This girl had been murdered and her son was missing. She had to get to the phone.

Trembling, she dialed 911 and found herself unable to remember the address, give directions, or do anything helpful. Forcing herself to concentrate, she finally managed to make herself clear to the patient male dispatcher. She could barely use the word *murder,* but there it was. A young woman that she had brought into Gail's home had been murdered, and Devon was gone without a trace.

By the time the police arrived, Jamie was shaking and sobbing. She could barely tell them what she knew. She was frantic. Where could Devon be? How could she have brought him here? Who would do this?

Several uniformed men came in and out as one of the officers, Leonard Goleman, interviewed her. At first he looked at her askance, obviously making a quick judgment about her clothing. Then she remembered how she was dressed and realized how it all looked: she'd gone into Manhattan to party—a rather wild one from the looks of it—and had left her son with a sitter who was probably as irresponsible as she was.

Quickly she explained that she'd been looking for her sister and was relieved that Goleman was familiar with the case. She assured him that she had no connection with the Goth underground. She'd just been trying to move among them and ask questions.

He relaxed a little but said, "That was a pretty risky thing to do."

"I know, but Gail took risks and she seemed to know these people, so I thought it would be okay."

Goleman remained unconvinced.

A mustached officer with dark brown hair came in and said they had seen no sign of the boy outside, nor any tracks in the grass, and there were no notes to indicate abduction for gain, but Jamie begged him to keep looking.

The next hour seemed a blur of dark blue uniforms, white jackets, men asking questions, talking to one another, shaking their heads, looking over at her. People were stepping around with little feather brushes and powder containers, lifting prints and taking measurements. They even took her prints, placing her fingers in ink and then against a stiff card. Someone made a drawing of the scene, placing yellow markers here and there, and a lean man with longish blond hair was taking photographs of everything. Then he switched to a videocamera. A red-haired woman in a white shirt and jeans, a detective, Jamie thought, asked her if she knew whether there was anything missing or some object present that she hadn't seen before. They were looking for anything out of place.

Jamie's complete inexperience with the apartment made her feel helpless. She shrugged at most of the questions. She just didn't know. If something were missing, she wouldn't have a clue, and Jorja could have brought things or moved things around. She couldn't really tell them anything.

Had Jorja mentioned inviting anyone over? Jamie shook her head. She wouldn't have allowed it, but she didn't know the girl that well. She hadn't seemed irresponsible.

"There's pretty good evidence that someone else was here," the female officer said, "but unless we know who comes in and out, we can't pick up elimination prints."

Then there were more questions. Did Jamie know anything about the people with whom her sister associated? Might they be involved in her son's disappearance? She could only shrug once again in response and shake her head. Princeton hardly seemed the place for a vampire cult like she'd seen in New York. It made no sense to mention the house where she'd just been. None of those people had ever met her before, and she didn't have an address, so she just stuck to details about the club.

Someone suggested she check into a hotel for the night and let them know where she'd be. She nodded, numb. She could not move. She was barely aware that they were taking Jorja's body out of the house, covered with a sheet and strapped onto a gurney. Blood had leaked through in one spot, and the crimson blotch stood out boldly against the stiff white material. She overheard a man say that there'd been no obvious wounds, but her body appeared to be oddly devoid of blood. That room was now a crime scene, she was told, and no one would be allowed to enter it. In fact, the house itself was a crime scene and Jamie needed to leave as soon as possible, but remain within easy contact of the police. They would be talking with her again the next day.

Just at that moment, Allan entered the room. Jamie was speechless. What was he doing here? How did he know? Then she realized that he'd probably been there before.

He walked through the room, talking with one of the officers as if he owned the place. Her surprise turned to fury. She nearly told the detective at her side that this man knew something about her son's abduction. But she really didn't know if that was true. If she said something like that she'd sound like a total fool, and if he *had* set her up, she would be stupid to cross him. She had no evidence for her suspicions and he'd have the advantage. She quickly made a decision to play this out as if she still trusted him, despite what had happened in New York. She had to smarten up fast.

Allan walked over to her and reached for her hand. Jamie allowed him to take it.

"I'm truly sorry," he said. "I had no idea you'd left a child here. I'd have warned you not to do it."

Goleman was suddenly alert. "Do you know something about this?" he asked.

"This is where Gail lived," Allan said. "I'm sure you're no stranger to the fact that she's missing, too. If someone abducted her, they might be watching this place. We don't know anything about where she is or why she's gone. I would expect this place to be potentially dangerous."

Goleman continued to question him about his association with Gail, but Jamie thought about what he'd just said. It made no sense to her. Allan hadn't said anything about the condo being dangerous when she'd let him know she was staying there. Why would he say that to the police? However, she let it go. He obviously had his own reasons for giving that impression to investigators. There was something in his manner that warned her to go along with him. She figured that she could always call the police later if she had to, but she intended to get some answers herself when she could. She firmly believed he wasn't telling the truth, or at least not the full truth.

"I'll take Jamie to a hotel," he said to Goleman. "I'll make sure she gets to a safe place."

Goleman looked at her for confirmation and she nodded. She wasn't sure she really wanted to be alone with Allan, but she did want to find out what he was hiding.

After assigning one officer to watch the house and cordoning the perimeter with wide yellow tape, the police finally left. With some trepidation, Jamie got into Allan's car. She was a little shocked that she'd caused this by coming here, but her overwhelming feelings were for her missing son. She was certain that Devon, wherever he was, was terrified by now and wondering where she was. She hoped to God he hadn't been hurt.

Allan looked at her and said, "I think I may know where to look for your son."

She stared at him with a mixture of astonishment and anger. "You know? How? Why didn't you tell the police? Where is he? And how do you know?"

"I don't know for sure. And I can't tell the police. It would be too dangerous for us both, but especially for your son. This isn't a matter for the police."

"How can that be?"

"Just believe me, it isn't."

Jamie trembled. She pressed her lips together and sat back in the seat. "If you think he's in danger," she whispered, "then you think he's alive?"

"I'm sure of it. I think I know who might have done this. They were people Gail knew. I think we should go there and see."

Jamie shook her head. None of this was making any sense. "No, no," she said. "I'm not just going someplace with you again, not after what you just put me through. First, you tell me something. You tell me what all that was about back there . . . in that place. What was that . . . that thing in the chair? What did you mean to do with me? Why did you want me to go there?" She was beginning to think it had all been some theatrical distraction to keep her in the city while someone kidnapped Devon. She doubted that Allan would own up to that, but she wasn't about to let him slide through this without some explanation.

Allan shook his head. "It was nothing. Just role-playing. They gave me a false tip at the club. It was stupid. I expected something different, but that's the problem with the vampire scene these days. It's like bad drugs that look like the real thing. You can't tell the ones who claim to be vampires from the ones who're only pretending. After you ran out of there, they took off their costumes and laughed. It was just some idiots having a joke. They'd been alerted by their friends at the club to give us a good show. I guess they thought they were getting into the *New York Times*."

Jamie relaxed, but only slightly. She did not entirely trust this man, but that explanation wasn't entirely unfeasible. He was her only lead at the moment, the only one who might know where Devon was, although even that could be another lie. She just didn't know where to turn.

"Are you ready to go where I think he might be?" Allan asked.

"What about the police? I'm not supposed to leave."

"I've got an idea about how to get around that. But you need to trust me and not go running off when things look weird. This underground is a strange place, Jamie, but it's what Gail was involved in. You've got to be more tolerant of how people look and act, especially if you're going to pass yourself off as her. Now we've got a whole segment of these people closed off to us because they know you're a fraud, and where we go from here may be even stranger. Do you think you're really up to this?"

Jamie nodded, feeling numb. "I can do it. I have to do it for Devon. I have to find him. They're just role-players. I can do it. Let's go."

Allan looked at her as if he didn't believe her, but finally he said, "Okay, then. The place I have in mind is half an hour from here."

Jamie looked at him. "It's three-thirty in the morning. Do you really think we can just go there now?"

"We're going to New Hope. That town is full of night people. But first I'll run you by one of the hotels so it looks like that's what we're doing, just in case we're being watched, and then we'll just go."

Allan reached into the inner pocket in his coat and pulled out a small handgun. Jamie was startled.

"It's Gail's," he explained. "I grabbed it just now when no one was looking. I know where she'd hidden it. I was the one who showed her how to use it. I thought she ought to have it, in light of the type of people she was hanging out with."

"And you think we'll need it?"

"You never know."

He started the car and pulled out to the street. Allan drove Jamie to the Hyatt on Route 1 and instructed her to walk through the lobby and come out another door. He'd make it look as if he were leaving, but he'd be waiting at the other side.

She did as she was told. She strode casually through the lobby as if she had a room there and was just coming in for the night. A young man in a suit looked up at her from the registration desk. She smiled and nodded, and continued into the spacious and empty lobby. Before walking out the door to which Allan had directed her, she considered going to the concierge and just renting a car herself. But then she realized she had no idea what to do once in New Hope, so she went outside. Allan was waiting.

They drove mostly in silence, aside from Allan's brief description of the directions to New Hope. He seemed oddly uncommunicative and would not give a straight answer to any of Jamie's questions, so she finally stopped asking. Instead, she fell into thinking about Devon and wondered if he was hurt or scared. She tried to establish some psychic link, but had never put much stock in that. Besides, wherever he was, he might be drugged or simply asleep. She tried to keep her anger at Gail in check, but she had no doubt that this was all linked to her wayward sister's dark ventures.

They took Route 1 south to the first exit for I-95. After a few minutes on the road, Jamie noticed that Allan kept looking into the rearview mirror, so she finally turned around to see who was following them. There was nothing back there. He looked at her, so she asked, "What's wrong? Do you think the cops are tailing us?"

He shook his head. "No."

"Well, there's no one back there."

"No one we can see."

"What do you mean by that?"

He took a deep breath and said, "Jamie, there are things about all of this that you just won't understand."

"Try me."

He was silent a moment. Then he said, "Just because you can't see them doesn't mean they're not there. They have ways of befuddling the senses so that you see things that aren't there and don't see things that are."

Jamie was utterly confused. "They? Who's they?"

"Look, let's just wait for all of this till we get to New Hope. I have things there I can show you that will explain it all."

Frustrated, Jamie sat back on her seat. However, now she was spooked. She didn't like the idea that Allan sensed things following them that she couldn't see. As they turned off onto a smaller road and drove along the Delaware River on the New Jersey side, Jamie began to realize again how isolated and vulnerable she was with this man. She'd heard of New Hope but had no idea why they would go there. She wasn't even sure it was their actual destination. The whole thing bothered her, but she did not dare to let go of her one slim thread of hope. Devon was surely afraid, wherever he was, and she needed to find him as soon as possible. She thought again about how he'd looked at her with big, sad eyes when she'd left the morning before, and how his tears had nearly made her cry. She even felt guilty that she'd been thrilled at the freedom to wander on her own around a city like Manhattan. She should have been with him. To just pick him up from his home in Arizona, take him to a completely foreign place, and leave him with a stranger now seemed reprehensible to her.

Then she remembered the thing she'd tried to ask Allan in New York. They'd been interrupted before she'd had the chance, and his comment had been strange and disturbing.

"When we were in the cab, what was it you said about

thoughts or something?" Jamie asked. "You mentioned that—"

"Thoughtprints," he corrected her.

"Right. Thoughtprints. What is that exactly?"

"That," he said, "is everything."

Seven

Christian

I had no idea what Dantalyon had meant, none at all, and I squatted near the girl's corpse in utter confusion. *He knows something.* Did he mean Naje? But surely, then, he too knew what it was. Their two minds were like one. Did it have something to do with the approaching danger? I couldn't guess, and as I sat there alone, it made me afraid.

Yet I had a job to do. I couldn't just follow him back to our comforting nest. I looked down at the wretched girl, squatted toward her, and touched her face. To end the poem I'd begun for her lethal encounter and perhaps to steady myself, I whispered, " 'And the song continues sweet.' "

She was already decomposing. Our venin contains a protein that accelerates the process. She would go through the stages of algor, livor, and rigor mortis in record time, and then turn to bones within two or three days. I sensed that her body temperature had already dropped two degrees.

In that tender moment, I wondered where she had come from. Would anyone miss her? What might she have become? The others called me maudlin for the way I lingered over victims, but I had a passion to know them deeply, so much more thoroughly than even this heightened union offered. I loved them in their stages of death. She wasn't strictly mine, since Dantalyon had taken her, but I was alone with her now, and that gave me some feeling of ownership.

Had I been the one picking her up this night, I wouldn't have just danced with her. I'd have spent hours asking her about herself, playing little games of entice-ment, and anticipating how her life might have un-folded. To my mind, the person's full subjective presence gave the blood a special aura. I understood Dantalyon's urgent passion, as well as his need to return to Naje, but I preferred to linger. That he had used a ghost story to work her up was probably rare for him. And now *she* was the ghost who would haunt this house.

Even so, he had honored me tonight. I had never been in his presence in such a way. The images of that encounter—and dreams of what might have been—still excited me. I couldn't help but spin my imagination over the possibility of drinking from his body, even at the risk of termination. Naje would not have been sat-isfied to cast me out; he'd have destroyed me. That meant to me that the experience would have been ex-quisite beyond all words . . . forbidden knowledge.

And perhaps, in light of what was coming, I should have just leaped over the cliff.

With some lingering regret, I carried the girl through secret shadows to my car. The moon loomed large over the buildings, which made this more difficult, and I re-called that tomorrow night would be an eclipse. I felt a surge of dread that this lunar event might energize our nemesis. Perhaps it was just waiting for the blackest night to make its move.

For just a moment, I caught a quick flash of a pres-ence nearby. I weened its nature but felt no threat. Yet there were other vampires afoot in New Hope tonight. That was no surprise, since one of our own had a shop there, and others would come in this way from the city. Whatever they were doing, I didn't want to know. I shut them out. If this was my last night, I had other plans.

I belted the girl into the front seat, got in, and drove downriver to Washington's Crossing State Park. I could have taken her to our morgue, I knew. We had a stack of corpses there, and fresh ones were always welcome for experiments. However, I wanted to go down to the park, to the place where my mortal life had been dramatically altered forever. Somehow it seemed poetic that if my vampire life was going to end, I ought to spend some time where it had first begun. The great General Washington may have crossed the Delaware there on that frigid 1770s Christmas Day, but I'm sure he had no idea how his strategy to save the country would one day inspire a much darker act.

I parked close to the river's edge and saw that the place was deserted. Even if people were there, I could always perform a mass entrancement and walk right into their midst with the body without anyone seeing me. I got out and carried my sad encumbrance down the slope to where the air was cooler. I knew the night spiders would be sedulous, as they always were nearest the rushing water, spinning their delicate dew-catchers of morning's first light. I had little time.

The girl was weightless in my arms. That made things easier. I laid her down, pulled the crease from her skirt, fastened a button that had slipped loose, and smoothed her torn silk shirt over her breasts. She had obviously dressed herself with some thought toward seduction that night. She couldn't have known that her beautiful lover was death itself. I caressed her hair, giving her one last moment of male appreciation. Already her stomach was turning greenish and her jaw and arms were growing stiff. If I gave it another hour, I'd be able to watch her eyes and tongue protrude and the bacteria inside busily devour her. But I didn't care for the putrefying gases. I actually preferred the latter stages of decomposition, after the bloating receded. It was always interesting to watch the skin slough off and the bones begin to protrude. But not tonight. There was no time.

I stood, grabbed her ankles, and swung her in an arc around me. When I had momentum, I cast her out into the water.

She went in flat, with a shimmery splatter, far enough into the deep part of the urgent current to be carried between the white concrete bridge pilings not far away. I watched her bob for a moment as she joined the summer debris of Coke bottles and crumpled hot-dog wrappers that swept by. Across the river, I spotted a large black inner tube floating by, a refugee from some riverfront business. No one was in it, though some kids were mad enough each summer to answer the river's seductive call for human flesh.

The girl was almost to the high metal bridge that spanned the water. No one driving on it would even see her. She might make it all the way to Philadelphia before anyone noticed. I wondered if she had ever seen the Liberty Bell.

I watched in the moonlight for half an hour. Nearby I smelled an animal, a coon or rabbit, inspecting me as I stared into the illuminated ripples. I imagined the girl twisting and rolling in the cold swells, caught in an embrace that she had never anticipated when she'd walked out the door with that beautiful dark stranger. Then, only then, I let myself remember.

This place reminded me so fiercely of Graham. We had grown up nearby and had come here together many times on balmy summer nights like this. Never would I have dreamed what he had in mind on that last nocturnal venture. It was years ago now, a dim impression, a dying ember.

* * *

We were both seventeen and it was the 1960s. We'd been friends since boyhood, and had done everything together, had even bled ourselves into each other's veins. We'd lost our virginity with the same girl. At the same time.

Graham was a dreamer. He was always spinning some fantastic vision for what we would do together one day. First, it was that we would be poets, drunk with talent and cheap wine in some tiny pension in Italy. Then we were going to run off to an exotic African country to squat in the brush and observe the rituals of animals we'd never seen. On another day, he had us in the hot Caribbean. He always had a plan that would keep us together and assure us of some wild quest. I was special, he claimed. He wanted to stay close to me. Even if one of us got married, he insisted that we vow to remain best friends. No woman should keep us apart.

That night he told me he wanted to do something special, something for me. I had to use my best skills to slip away that late, but the moonlight drew me as much as Graham's insistent pleading. The water snakes would be out and I loved to watch them wriggling near the river's edge with the dim illumination glinting off their scaly skin. There'd been times I'd wished I were one of them.

Graham arrived before me and was waiting in the shadows of the old blacksmith shop. I joined him and he led me toward the river.

A chill went up my back but I thought it was merely the effect of the deepening night. Graham looked back with his Labrador grin and reached for my arm. His grip was warm and damp.

"I want to be with you forever," he whispered. "I've been reading, and I've learned how to achieve it."

"What are you talking about?" My trembling voice charged the air with a resonance that startled me. The evening was just too still.

"You'll see," was all he would say.

We neared the river's edge and he asked me to press my back against a thick tree. I shrugged and leaned against the jagged bark. It poked into my skin, and as I was adjusting myself to find a comfortable spot, Graham brought a strap from behind the tree to tie my hands behind me.

"What are you doing?" I demanded to know.

He pulled the rope around my body, took it around the tree, and wrapped me again.

"Graham, what are you doing?"

"You'll see," he said with a grin. "Don't worry; it's not that tight. You can slip out, but not quickly. Not until after I'm done."

"Done with what?"

"Just watch."

He walked away into the shadows. I tried the knots around my wrists, but the leather dug into my skin. I took a breath to yell for him, but he was back. He had a bag in his hand, which he dropped at his feet. I heard the chink of metal against the compact ground.

"What's this about?" I asked. I pulled at my cords and again felt the pinch. "Come on, Graham. Let me go."

He just shook his head. I watched as he unbuttoned the top button of his shirt. He smiled at me. I shook my shoulders to show him I wanted to be turned loose. Now.

He undid the next button on his shirt.

"Graham . . ."

"Don't worry," he said. "You'll be so happy."

In a moment, his shirt was off and his narrow white chest gleamed in the moonlight. He dropped his shirt next to the bag. Then he unfastened his pants and removed everything else that he wore. In a moment, he stood completely naked before me. He was obviously excited by what he was doing.

"You think that's what I want?" I said, trying to push a scornful timbre into my voice. I wanted him to stop this craziness. I felt in that moment that I did not really know him at all. I thought possibly he'd become demented and meant to kill me.

He just smiled again as if he were in complete control and knew there was nothing I could do about it.

Leaning into me, he kissed me on the right cheek. I jerked away.

Then he knelt in front of me and rummaged through the bag. He pulled out a long silver knife. It flashed once as he angled it toward the moon.

"Graham, don't," I said. I could not believe he might hurt me. He had never done anything bad to me, not intentionally. I pulled with all my strength against the rope, but it failed to yield.

He approached me with the knife. I struggled frantically. I couldn't imagine why he'd changed. I wondered if he was on LSD or mescaline. We'd taken them together a few times but he'd never been this psychotic.

"Don't be afraid," Graham whispered. "Just watch. I'm going to be with you now forever. This is a sacred place. This is where Washington led his troops across the river to win the Battle of Trenton. He created an Immortal Moment. Everyone comes here to honor it. No one will ever forget. That's why this will work. There's magic here. I can make it work. And then we'll never be apart through the rest of time."

"No!" I screamed. "I don't want to die."

He stepped closer to place the sharp edge of the knife against my throat. Paralyzed, my whole body went still, except for my panicked breaths. I wanted to shout and get someone's attention, but I couldn't find my voice.

"We should both go together," he whispered. "I thought you'd want to."

"I don't," I said. My voice was a hoarse whisper. "And I don't want you to go, either. Why can't we just leave things as they are? Come on, Graham. . . ."

"Because they won't stay that way. Something will change and you'll be gone. I want to stay with you. Forever. I'm going to join you now. Take me."

With that, he stepped away from me and went down to the rushing water, raised the knife to his throat, and made a swift cut. I saw the blood spurt forth.

"Graham!" I screamed. "Graham!"

He turned and grinned for a brief second. Blood gushed from his neck wound down his chest. "I'll see you soon," he said, and then partly jumped, partly stumbled into the river's current.

I screamed again. I couldn't stop. All I heard was the sound of my voice for what seemed like hours. I didn't care if I died there. Graham was gone! He'd done this awful thing and he was gone. I screamed and pushed against the ropes until they burned and bruised my skin.

I think finally someone heard me. I remember only that hours later I woke in the hospital in terrible pain and hoped fervently that it had all been some awful dream. But it hadn't. They told me as they dressed my raw abrasions that Graham's swollen body had been found downriver, snagged on a fallen willow tree.

I wept for days. Everyone looked at me as if they feared I had gone crazy. I would not go to the funeral. I could not go near the river. I was afraid he'd come, afraid he'd be waiting for me in some spooky form.

Then he did come back. I started to see him. Usually at night, but sometimes during the day. He'd appear in my room, sitting on my bed, staring at me with his crazy grin. Sometimes he spoke.

"I told you I'd come back," he said several times. I never responded. I sensed he wanted me to join him and the thought repulsed me.

I began to fear everything afterward that even hinted of death. I walked a long way to avoid a cemetery and refused even to carry a dead mouse from the kitchen out to the yard. I stopped my ears whenever someone spoke of a neighbor passing away or a fatally sick child, and I feared that Graham would somehow cause a fatal accident. My mother thought I was being silly, but I could not abide anything that would bring back the sight of my other self loosing the torrents of life from his body in that manner and leaving me so abruptly. I hated him for that. I still hate him.

So when a transient vampire one day offered me eternal life, I took it. I took it to spite Graham. He had died and I would live, though it brought me closer to death than I had ever been. Though I would compulsively seek the blood of life to fill the infinitely empty chambers of my heart. I would never join Graham, never. I punished him with an unbridgeable chasm that stretched between us from heaven to hell. Wherever he was, he was not—would never be—with me. Vampires can see dead people, but we can also shut them out.

Still, the river always made me think of him. This many years later I have some perspective. I can understand the romance that had driven him and I can grieve for his unrequited craving. He is a brand on my soul, but not in the way he'd hoped. It was I who had made the Immortal Moment mine.

The girl was gone and the sun would soon peek over the Bucks County hills. There was no more reason to remain in this place. I returned to my Jag, got in, and drove upriver to Dark Hollow Road, where the others in my *kamera* were moving toward their daytime trance. I wanted to indulge in a contemplative space, but there were more pressing concerns now. I—we—had survived this night, but I suspected that the next twenty-four hours would prove eventful, and I wanted to be with my group. For all we knew, the thing could take us by day, in our sleep. Yet if it didn't then we were going to have to pull ourselves together and use our best skills to thwart whatever this thing was.

I thought again about Dantalyon's enigmatic words: *He knows something.* His mood on the train, his little game with me, that declaration—it all seemed incongruous to what our group had become. That meant that something was truly amiss at just the wrong time. I needed to get back and see what the others thought—now, before they dropped off to sleep. I pressed on the gas and shot along the river, racing to beat the sun.

Eight

Jamie

"They're everything?" Jamie asked. "What does that mean? I don't even know what a thoughtprint is."

Allan shrugged and continued to watch the road. "They're like mental fingerprints."

Jamie waited, but when he said nothing more, she pressed him. "And what do they have to do with any of this?"

"They're extremely important to what we're doing. In fact, they're our best protection. It's a way to get into the minds of others and decode them. They don't know that you're doing it so they're not guarded. You can use them for both offensive and defensive strategies. All you need is something they've written or said, but really good communication analysts can do it telepathically."

"I don't understand." Jamie wasn't sure which was better: silence or to have this kind of bizarre conversation.

"People have a lot of subconscious agendas," Allan continued, "and those bleed through in the patterns of their words or the types of things they say. Even in what they don't say. You can match an unknown author to a piece of writing, or you can use various things they've written and said to piece together a character profile. You can figure out their motives for doing something and even predict their behavior. More important, you can find out things about them you may need to know before you deal with them. You prepare yourself in ways they can't begin to comprehend, and you know their weaknesses better than they do."

Jamie felt even more confused. "But what does it have to do with Gail? Was she involved with that?"

Allan was silent for a moment, as if considering carefully what he ought to say. Now Jamie was certain he was hiding something. Her impression was that he'd offer her just enough to keep her involved but not enough for her to figure out what he was up to.

"It's just a way of seeing beyond the obvious," he responded. "Gail understood the method although she didn't learn how to do it very well."

"Is it like handwriting analysis?" Jamie asked.

Allan shook his head. "It's much more sophisticated and refined. It's based on the work of a maverick psychologist who said that we have more intelligence in our perceptions and communications than we realize."

"Intelligence? Like some little man living in our heads directing everything?"

Allan looked at her as if assessing whether she was serious. "The subconscious contains our actual level of intelligence, but we blind it and hamper it with our everyday fears and cultural biases. Nevertheless, it works to pick up on more details of the underlying reality of the world than we're aware of and gives us the guidance we need. If we pay attention, that is. Everything we do has some underlying motive. Sometimes we know what it is and sometimes we only think we know but we're wrong. There's a subtext of communication that very few people can read, but to those who can it says a lot. Our conscious mind is limited but our subconscious is vast. It's also truthful. It won't let us get away with much. Sometimes you can get at it through hypnosis, but it's generally clearer in certain behaviors. You just have to read between the lines."

"So tell me again, what's a thoughtprint?"

"It's a symbolic communication of the deeper intelligence. It tells the truth about us no matter how hard we try to deceive someone. It's like when someone tells you he's being faithful but all of his behavioral clues tell you he isn't. He thinks he's convinced you, but if you're astute, you've read what's really going on. A thoughtprint is like that kind of behavior. The truth of your own subliminal intelligence picks up on the reality no matter what the spoken message may be. You might get at that truth through the symbolism of a dream, but if you're really good at reading the communication, you'll spot it right away."

"Like women's intuition."

"Something like that, yes, I guess. But it's more than just an impression or a feeling." Allan guided the car around a sharp curve and Jamie felt her stomach jump at his speed. She wanted to ask him to slow down but sensed it would be futile.

"So it's a skill," she said.

"It becomes a skill. It's an ability, and you can sharpen it into a skill, as we have done."

"We?"

"The people with whom I'm associated. We've discovered that the human mind has extraordinary capabilities, and we're working to tap them."

Jamie suddenly grew alarmed. "I thought you were a reporter."

Allan nodded. "That's my day job. And because of it I discovered this group. They intrigued me so I joined, and it's changed my life. I understand a lot more about what people are communicating than I used to, and it actually makes me better at my job."

"But you said something about baiting something . . . how did you put it? Baiting these Goths?"

Allan shook his head. He maneuvered the car onto the side street of a small town, which he told Jamie was Lambertville. Then he responded to her. "That was not what I said exactly, but we don't have time now to go into it. Just rest assured that I have certain things figured out based on what's been revealed in some pretty dark thoughtprints. I'll explain it later. We're almost there."

Jamie looked out her window. She couldn't recall Allan's exact words back in New York but now it seemed important. It was about vampires. Baiting vampires, but surely he must have meant those people at the house. She felt frustrated at the mystery. Her son's life was at stake, Gail was missing and possibly dead, and Allan was spouting some obscure philosophy about mind cults and telepathy.

The streets of the small town of Lambertville seemed deserted as they drove by the Victorian buildings. Jamie noticed signs for antiques, art supplies, food, and books. Then they passed the Lambertville Station on her left, a nice-looking restaurant, and spotted a flock of geese in the parking lot that sat one level down near the Delaware River. Through her open window, she could smell the river water on the breeze and feel the humidity clinging to her skin. She wished now she had thought to change her clothes. The leather corset she wore felt ridiculously hot and bulky. Back in Princeton she'd barely noticed it with everything that was going on, but she'd had time in the car to feel its construction bind her and rub against her skin.

There was only an hour—maybe less—until sunup. Would any of these "night people" still be awake?

"This is the most haunted town in Pennsylvania," Allan said as they drove across the steel-girded bridge. He slowed down to maneuver in the narrow lane.

"Haunted?" Jamie asked.

"Yeah, and that's why I know that it's the key. There are ghosts in every B-and-B, nearly every shop. The Logan has several. And they're proud of it, too."

"The key?"

Allan nodded but didn't explain. Given the circumstances, it seemed an odd subject to raise out of the blue, but Jamie let it go. She didn't want to antagonize this man just as they were nearing their destination. He'd said he would explain—would even show her things to prove his point—so for now, he had all the leverage.

As they left the long metal bridge behind and entered the quiet town, Allan turned left onto the main street and then right onto a dark street that went up a hill. He then found a place to pull over and park the car.

"We'll walk from here," he said. "My place is on the canal."

"You know," Jamie said, "I think you need to tell me something now, before we go anywhere. What did you mean about baiting vampires? Is that what we're about to go do?"

Allan's face suddenly went hard. He turned to her and she saw a fierce look in his eyes. "Jamie, listen to me. As strange as this sounds, there *are* vampires in this world. Real ones. Gail knew that. It was Gail who showed me the proof. She was with them."

Jamie opened her mouth in astonishment. "You are—" Then she realized what he was saying. "You think . . . *vampires* took my son?"

"I'm sorry, yes, I do think so."

"You're crazy, Allan; you're just nuts. I thought you had a real plan." Jamie opened the door to get out, but he grabbed her arm.

"Just come with me," he insisted. "I'll prove it to

you, and then we can come up with a plan. I know how to get to them, but I need your help."

Jamie hardly knew what to say. Then she recalled what the medical examiner had said about Jorja. No obvious wounds but drained of blood. *Vampires.* She closed her eyes. This was not happening. It couldn't be.

Allan squeezed her arm. "Trust me for five more minutes. I have an apartment here with some stuff that will convince you. Stuff that Gail gave me."

Then he opened the door and got out. Jamie thought she saw movement to her right in the ebony shadows of a narrow alley, but she could not be sure. She got out of the car on her side, and suddenly felt as if she were going to lose her balance. Her stomach lurched and her thoughts blurred. Allan failed to notice; he gestured for her to follow him as he started toward an alley.

Jamie sensed something desperately wrong and stopped. She did not want to follow him. In fact, she suddenly panicked at the thought. Her memory of those people in New York was still vivid, and she was not about to go into such a situation again. Allan had called them role-players, but they'd seemed to her more sinister than that. Even worse, she suddenly believed that Allan wanted to trap her. In fact, she knew it.

Another flash in the shadows.

Now she was sure she had seen someone else. She felt the sensation of that person, whoever it was, watching her. It wasn't just observing. It was waiting for her. At first she was scared, but then she was flooded with sweet feelings from childhood, when her mother had waited for her at the door each day. It was warm and inviting, and she wanted to get closer.

Allan turned to say something, but stopped. She saw his mouth drop open in apparent surprise just as she felt a strong grip on her left arm from behind. Jamie whirled around, ready to fight, but when she saw the face of the one who accosted her, she was too stunned to resist. He was a freak of some sort, an animal. His entire face looked reptilian, although the features were human.

Jamie pulled away as hard as she could but he had her in a strong grip. Before she could cry out, he swept her off her feet, slung her across his shoulder as easily as if she were a light summer blanket, and carried her away so fast she had no time to catch her breath. Her stomach felt as if she'd just been punched very hard.

The thing opened the door of a black van and tried to shove her in. She grabbed the metal frame to prevent it, and then twisted around. When she saw his eyes, she was once again shocked into compliance. There was something old and commanding deep inside the slitted pupils. She pulled her hand back to fend him off, and he moved fast to push her inside onto a seat. There was no time to try again. The door slammed closed and she was trapped.

Unwilling to give in, Jamie tried to open it, but just as she found it locked, she was grabbed from inside the van by someone sitting next to her. A small female was in the front seat, ready to drive, and the engine was already running. Jamie turned to look at her captor but saw only the silhouette of a man with short hair before a hand went over her mouth. Then the strange one got into the front passenger's seat. With three of them in the car, Jamie knew there was no hope of escape.

They shot away from the curb. As she gasped for oxygen, Jamie recalled Allan's astonishment and realized that this hadn't been his idea. Yet somehow they'd known she was coming. They'd been ready for her. Reminded of Allan's paranoia over being followed, she realized now what he'd meant. Somehow they'd tracked his car and crept up on it. Jamie struggled, but the cold hand over her mouth blocked her air, so she finally quit. The hand loosened only enough to let her breathe. There was nothing else to do but surrender and wait for an opportunity to escape. Obviously they had some intention for her. They had not grabbed her randomly, and she thought that they might even be the same people who had taken Devon. Maybe she was about to see him, and even find Gail. Whatever was going on, she felt certain it was all connected. The best thing to do was keep her wits about her.

Glancing into the side-view mirror on the passenger side of the car, Jamie met the front seat passenger's quick look back. She felt that she was looking straight into the eyes of a human lizard. There were no whites as in normal eyes, just a dark horizontal line through greenish brown. She stiffened and fell back against the seat.

Then she remembered something about what she'd read in the library on that vampire access answering machine: contact lenses. That was what it must be. Special-effects contacts. These people were just role-players; they had to be. No one could really look like that.

The car picked up speed so fast she thought they were flying, and they soon left the town far behind. Jamie saw the last of the buildings and then there were only trees and darkness. They were heading out into the country.

Then a heavy feeling seemed to come over her that started from somewhere within her mind. She fought it, trying to remain alert, but it was no use. Her head went loose on her neck and she lost all sense of time or place. She felt the pinch of something at her throat and the close embrace of the man next to her, but she couldn't fight it. Before she could ask him what he wanted and why he was so cold, she was flooded with a honeyed sense of enveloping darkness.

Nine

Christian

The large three-story house at the end of a quarter-mile-long dirt drive, with its long wings stretching out to either side, was mostly dark as I approached. That meant nothing, since most of the activity took place underground in the layers of chambers that we'd built over the years. They were heavily sealed against intrusion, both physically and mentally, and guarded by the most aggressive venomous snakes, so even if some shadow wandered through the house above, there was no way he'd find the passageways to our beds . . . or at least no way he'd survive his discovery.

It was an hour before dawn, and each vampire there was preparing for it in his or her own unique way. Naje had a heated bed of soft Hawaiian sand, into which he sometimes invited the other elders of our family. Eryx, like a monk, kept a solitary cell, as did Lethe. Stiletto and Phelan would likely be together, although Stiletto also had a secret place in New Hope. Viper stayed in the lab, and Bel was probably in the cage. I parked my car and went in the front.

To my surprise, Phelan was in the library, reading. His albino boa was spiraled in several layers around his waist and slung up over one shoulder. Its head was somewhere behind him. I knew that meant he was getting ready for bed. We'll often commune with a serpent before retiring for the day, partly because it deepens the resonance but also because it's so sensual. I watched as the snake shifted its thick body across Phelan's bare chest and around his middle, its tail slung between his legs. I could almost feel the muscles beneath its scales gripping for leverage. We all had a "pet" like this—my favorite was the deadly black mamba for its speed—and on any given day there might be several of us entranced together in the well-stocked, room-size snake cage downstairs. That was my own destination that morning.

Phelan looked up as I passed and smiled. I laughed to myself at the black-framed glasses he wore. He didn't need them but he liked the appearance he affected with them on. He didn't look like a scholar to me with those enlarged hazel eyes and that head of curly blond hair, but he liked to believe he did, so I said nothing. Technically I was the "baby" of the family, but Phelan drew out the protective instinct in us all.

His special gift was an ability to read our hearts. He weened our need, our sadness, our joy, and even our lies. In his presence, we got away with nothing. He throve on honesty.

I sensed that he had not gone out that night and was in need. He liked to starve himself at times because he knew one of us would always feed him, and that to him was preferable to taking someone himself. It wasn't an ethical issue. It was the penetrating intimacy he derived from ingesting the juice from another vampire whom he loved—and he loved us all without reserve. Apparently no one else had offered him a drink.

I leaned on the door frame to tease him a little with the possibility that he might yet get something from me. I knew he'd feel my warmth right away.

"Have we learned anything yet?" I asked.

He shook his head. "Not really. Ana's still missing.

Tomorrow night we should know something. Her sister's here, but she's entranced. She doesn't know yet where she is. Her son is also entranced."

"Anyone not come home?"

He shrugged. "Lachesis, but she may be with her lover in Manhattan. You're the last one in."

I nodded. "I guess I'll go bed down with the snakes," I commented absently. "Bel's calling me."

He shifted his eyes downward. I saw a shudder go through his boa as it closed around him. I waited a moment to see if he would ask. Surely he sensed that I'd been with Dantalyon. He must be dying of desire, yet he kept his eyes on the backs of his hands. I saw him swallow. Finally I was the one who yielded.

"How do you want it tonight?" I whispered. "It's really quite special this time. Wait till you taste."

Phelan met my eyes with a smile of relief and I went in to him.

When I woke up that evening, I was alone. I was still alive and grateful to be so, but I knew the others were already in the momentum of preparation. It was the night of the eclipse, which meant the spiritual energy was dense and might assist us in what we were doing. I turned over and bumped into a full-grown, thick-bodied boa, which moved slowly away. When you sleep with snakes, you never know what you'll find upon awaking.

I took a moment to recall my dreams, since Naje had taught us how to use this medium to communicate with one another. We could even learn a new language or develop our gifts. The whole secret to immortality was gaining the ability to move through layers of energy formation, and our special kind of dreams helped with that. Naje had also taught us how to use shared dreaming for maximum physical pleasure and deeper resonance—a form of vampire sex that superceded anything humans could do together. By sorting through the images, I learned that Eryx, Lethe, and Viper had grabbed Jamie in New Hope, and that she'd been there with the reporter. I also weened from several recurring symbols that I felt disturbingly unsafe.

I knew where to find Eryx, since the tabloids were always his first order of business and he liked to read them alone in his office one floor up. If he wasn't scanning the papers, he was watching some schlocky vampire movie. Eryx—whose name was Latin for boa—was a lean, muscular creature, albeit only about five-foot-nine, with ivory skin and dark brown hair that he wore short and neatly styled. He surrounded himself with the latest computer gadgetry to the point where one could barely enter the room. I remained at the door. He looked up from his paper, which bore the headline, *Senator Sells Sex Secrets to Venusians,* to tell me that Jamie had come into our care not a moment too soon.

"We took blood from her to compare with Ana's," he said. Then he told me that Viper and Naje were already at work on an analysis down in the lab.

"Where's the girl?" I asked.

"I'm not sure. In one of the rooms upstairs, I think."

I left him to go to the steps, but saw Lethe was in the library. She was our energy translator, and that's a rare talent. She knew a myriad of languages and could ween the shifting currents of the various quantum fields like a meteorologist reads environmental nuances and tells us the "weather." We'd often depended on her to alert us to Naje's moods. She was mostly standoffish to the group, but she adored Naje because he taught her how to refine her abilities. I stepped into the room and was about to speak when she said, "She's upstairs."

I squinted at her. She was looking gaunt and cold, even a bit pale, despite the golden color of her Asian skin. As a mortal, Lethe must have been one of the tiniest women ever created. She was less than five feet tall and surely weighed around eighty pounds. Yet she was slender and perfectly made, like some fragile little black-haired doll. She was quite stunning to look at.

"Are you all right?" I asked.

She nodded, brushing me off. Ordinarily I'd have left her alone, but none of us knew whether this thing that was coming for us would leak in through an infected insider or hit with full fury like a devastating tsunami. Cacilian had been alone when he succumbed, and we had no map to this thing's behavior.

"Have you been out at all?"

"I'm fine, Christian. The girl is upstairs. Go talk to her."

I stood there for a moment, torn between respecting her wish and protecting the group. She gave me a piercing look that revealed how much life she had in her should I care to take her on.

Rather than argue, I left. Telling Lethe to go revive herself was like persuading an anorexic to eat. The one thing we value above all is our privacy, and that's respected as long as it doesn't negatively affect the *kamera*. She had shut the door on my concern, and unless she showed some obvious symptom, that was the end of the discussion. I went in search of Jamie Farrelly.

I knew that she had probably slept most of the day, bound and entranced and locked into a third-floor room, with only the most rudimentary way to care for herself. Not very considerate. It was hot in her room, which I enjoyed, but I figured she had not. Yet there wasn't really any other place to put her—it wasn't like we kept a guest room—and none of us could have attended to her during the daylight hours. Only Naje had that ability, but he generally remained in the underground caverns below the house. In all the time I'd been there, which was more than a decade, I'd never known him to leave. Perhaps he did so secretly, but I suspected that Dantalyon brought him whatever he needed.

I went into Jamie's room and saw her in bed. I felt like the Prince coming to awaken Sleeping Beauty. Was I the first one she would see after her abduction? That could give me some advantage.

I wondered if anyone had given her something else to wear, but soon saw that she was still dressed as a vampire wanna-be. Then I looked more closely. The scarf and corset sat discarded on a forest–green velvet chair. I wondered who had done that. Viper? I didn't think so. Although he'd spent a lot of time with Ana, the only thing that really got his attention was his snakes. Maybe Lethe.

I went without noise to the edge of the bed and looked down at the sleeping woman. I saw right away where they'd taken blood from her arm. Someone had placed a small bandage over the artery, and a spot of blood had leaked through and dried. Jamie seemed at peace, despite the circumstances, so I assumed that whoever had entranced her the morning before had given her something to dream that would replace her more stressful concerns. That was more to keep her calm, I knew, than an act of compassion. I focused my ability to pierce through the thought fields to alert her to my presence. Rather than break the trance by touching her, I thought it was better to lead her out gradually with gentle and enticing images.

Then I realized that someone had already been there before me. She'd been awakened and prepared, and then entranced again. That meant that things were already in motion. I was probably interfering, but I was curious about her. I'd taken great delight in Ana, who shared my impish ways, and wanted to know how closely these two resonated in spirit.

In a few moments, Jamie opened her eyes. She blinked at the ceiling as if not fully aware yet and then saw me. She sat up, hugging the sheet close to her breasts. Then her eyes blazed with the same piquancy that I'd weened when I followed her through the Village streets. Still, I could tell she was also deeply afraid. I smelled it under her black nylon as she sat there on the bed, her wrists loosely bound to a thick oaken bedpost.

I detected in her a combination of attraction and confusion, which made sense. I knew what she saw: a tall, slender young man with dark blond hair that fell into waves just below his ears. I was dressed casually in loose unbelted jeans, bare feet, and a T-shirt the color of dark cabernet. Undoubtedly I looked less threatening than any of the elders—especially Viper. When I smiled, as I was doing at that moment, the corners of my mouth turned slightly down, which made my wide grin seem flirty. I was considered the one always ready to laugh, and it showed on my guileless face. I believe she saw in me a potential savior, someone who appeared kind, intelligent, and open, with only the merest hint of life experience. I appealed to her, I could tell, although it was her anger that won out.

"Who are you?" she demanded to know. "What do you people want with me? Where's my son?"

I told her my name and saw a quick flicker of interest again. She thought I was beautiful, I saw from the way her pupils dilated. I wondered how much time I'd have with her before she was taken to those who would fill her body with such need and desire that she'd forget everyone else. I figured that either Dantalyon or Eryx would be asked to manipulate her memory fields, since they were the males among us who were most adept at this.

Jamie said nothing in response but kept her fierce eyes steady on me. I wanted to smile because there was nothing she could ever do to harm me or get past me, much as she obviously wanted to. The struggles of a weaker one always amuse me. It's like a bug kept in a box running from one side to another, certain in its tiny brain that it will eventually find a way out. But I did feel some compassion for her, too. If Bel were here now, she'd be rolling her eyes.

I came close to Jamie and stood, legs apart, looking down at her. She tried to rise, but her shackles stopped her halfway up.

"What do you want with me?" she repeated. How like Ana she was in that moment. So much fire! I reached to caress her hair, to warm my hands around her intensity, but she jerked away from my touch.

"We didn't mean to be so rough," I told her. "But others nearly had you. And they'd have been far worse. Viper—"

"Viper! That . . . that thing! That snake! What *is* he? What are you?"

I smiled. "I can assure you, none of us are like him. Yes, he's a snake. He thrives on snakes. In fact, his blood is made entirely of venom."

Jamie looked utterly confounded but she seemed to be losing some of her fear. "No one can live like that."

"He can and does, fortunately for us. We need his special abilities now. And we need you." I didn't think it mattered that I revealed things to her. She'd already seen enough to know that something unusual was happening.

Jamie shook her head. "What are you talking about? Is this some game? That's what you're doing, aren't you? He's wearing contact lenses and you're pretending to be some kind of . . . of . . ."

I laughed. She truly delighted me. "If only the role-players could even come close," I said. I extended my hand, palm up, and said, "Feel that."

She looked at me and then at my hand. She didn't want to touch me, perhaps afraid it was a trap. Then hesitant, but urged on by her need to know, she placed her fingertips into the palm of my hand, just barely making contact. The cords that bound her tightened, but she was able to fully reach me. Feeling nothing at first, she pressed harder and then looked up at me.

"You're so cold."

"For now, yes. I warm up fast but I can't generate it on my own. Are you getting the picture?"

She shook her head. "You just put your hand inside a refrigerator or grabbed a cold bottle of water."

I smiled again. I liked her spirit. "Okay, let's do this again." I held out my hand and urged her to touch it in the same spot. She did so.

"Now leave it there for a minute."

I used the point of contact to start taking heat from her. She didn't feel it at first but in under a minute, Jamie sensed her own hand going numb. Still, she left her fingertips against my palm as if not quite believing. I sucked in more of her heat and my fangs began to twitch in anticipation, but she finally drew away. Astonished, she looked at her own hand. Then she looked into my eyes. I knew what she was feeling. Her hand, probably up to the elbow, was as cold as that of a corpse.

"How did you do that?" she asked.

Then she seemed to see something in my eyes that revealed all. "You're not . . ." she said.

"Not alive in the way you know it," I finished for her.

She reacted. "You're hypnotizing me. You want me to—"

She glanced over my clothes, apparently confused by the fact that I didn't dress the part. She'd been told a story about us and she'd believed it. Now the narrative was falling apart. I could feel her heart rhythm speed up. She was scared. She was beginning to believe me. Her chest rose and fell, keeping pace with her fear. In fact, I felt the temperature rise on her skin, which drew a visceral response from me. I wanted to lean into her and get closer. I longed to penetrate her with my fangs and absorb her warmth.

"You know Gail," she whispered. "She told me she'd met some people. . . ." Her voice trailed off.

I nodded. "We know her, but we don't know where she is."

"You think she's alive."

I wasn't sure how to answer this. In fact, we did believe she was alive, but to explain how we knew was complicated.

Then Jamie got fierce again. "Do you have my son? Did you take him?"

"I didn't—"

"Your son is safe."

I turned around at the sound of that powerful voice. I heard it so infrequently that I hardly believed it was him. I felt at once both shamefully caught in the act and aware that I was in the presence of a greater force. I had an inclination to bow but didn't. Instead I backed quickly away from the bed, only glancing surreptitiously to my right.

Naje stood framed in the doorway. I was astonished. I hadn't expected him to just show himself to a temp so easily or so soon. Then I remembered what Dantalyon had said early that morning. Naje was aware of something that we weren't.

Whatever it was, it must mean we had little time. Even to me and the others he rarely showed himself. Around his chambers was a forbidding aura, like a parents' locked bedroom door. That energy shifted only when he wanted one of us to come in. Even then, though we craved contact like starving addicts, we dared not touch him.

I kept my eyes on the floor as he entered the room. I didn't have to look to know that Jamie was transfixed. It was like Zeus or Odin coming toward her out of a bank of textured clouds. In mortal life, Naje had been extraordinary. As a vampire, he was superb.

Thick silver-white hair flowed away from his face to his hips, but it wasn't the dry, brittle hair of old age. It was as shiny as that of a Lippizaner stallion that had been thoroughly groomed for best in show, cut through with a few darker strips to indicate it once had been black. His eyes under incongruously dark brows were deep ebony, as if the pupils had usurped the irises, and a deep crease on either side of his face ran from his high cheekbones to his firm jaw. Dressed in black tonight, with a fine thread of gold sparkling at his throat, he seemed shamanic. He was six-foot-five in stature, with a massive chest and muscled thighs. Both he and Dantalyon had known long in advance that they would become vampires, and both had worked themselves into peak physical condition for their eternal form.

I looked at his graceful hands, which never failed to arouse me, and saw that his long fingers were full of exotic silver and gold from different eras. These were the rings of the magicians he had known, given as gifts and tokens of honor. Whether Hawaiian *kupuna,* British warlock, or African *Imanujela,* he had learned from them all, and according to Dantalyon, each had embraced him with profound intimacy. He made no sound as he walked into the room, and I saw that his feet, like mine, were bare. Gold rings with rubies encircled two of his manicured toes. I wanted to fall to the floor and kiss them, he seemed that majestic.

Behind him, Dantalyon hovered. His eyes were swollen from the trance and he looked concerned. He gave me but a swift, darting glance as he watched his mentor approach Jamie. He knew I shouldn't have been there, but something more profound seemed to concern him now. Otherwise he'd have made me leave at once.

As yet, Jamie had said nothing. She just stared as Naje stopped in front of her. He held out a hand to her, and as if against her will, she placed her small hand in his. I was sure he was even more disturbingly cold than I had been, but now she was prepared for that. Or he didn't allow her to feel it. His eyes never left her. I doubt that he even blinked. He was sending something into her without her awareness, but it would accomplish its purpose. There was no way she could guard herself against it, or even guess what was happening.

I was so thrilled to be there. I'm the most voyeuristic of our group. I thrive on the finest details of activity and motion. It doesn't have to be sex or even a vampire's embrace. With almost equal delight, I can watch a mortal eat an extended meal or engage in a heated debate. I often imagined what it would be like to be in Naje's presence for several hours, although none save Dantalyon ever got that much exposure to him. Viper and Lachesis sometimes slept in his bed, but that wasn't the same as being with him in full awareness. I hoped now that he'd be so concerned with Jamie that he wouldn't notice me.

Wishful thinking.

Just as I thought it, Naje looked over his shoulder at me. It was as if he'd placed his hand under my chin and lifted me off my feet. I knew that he wished me to go, but I didn't want to. More than anything, I desired to witness his effect on a mortal, but it was not my place to question his unspoken mandate. I slipped past Dantalyon, who barely moved to give me room, so intent was he on the scene before him. I felt his heat from three feet away, the residual digestion from his carnal meal that morning.

As I went through the door, I came near enough to feel the conflict in his heart. Something was amiss with all of this, but I couldn't ween what it might be. That meant it was likely an emanation from their heightened state—the level of soul they had reached that was beyond the likes of me. He shut me off and mentally pushed me away. I wasn't allowed in. Whatever we had shared the night before was at best a vague memory for him now. It meant nothing.

Down the hall, I saw Eryx. He watched me with caution. Then he quickly withdrew. That told me he knew something as well and didn't want me to get it from him. He was afraid. I narrowed my eyes, trying to ween his particular strain of fear. I sensed at once that he wasn't scared of this demon that was coming for us. He was scared of Naje.

I wandered all the way to the cellar. We had five lower levels down here, hewn over a long period of time out of the rocky land, and we tended to seek one another here in the cold air. It was more home to us than the house above, which was merely presented as a façade to the mortal world. In one room full of plush sofas I found a vampire named Destiny talking with Bel, while Phelan listened nearby. He gave me a little wave of greeting. He was wearing his glasses, so I knew he'd been reading. I wondered where Stiletto was. Generally he stayed pretty close to Phelan.

"Have you seen the girl?" Destiny asked. She didn't live with us but she often stayed here to deepen her resonance. She was certain that she was some kind of fallen angel, and we didn't contradict her. For all we knew, she might have been. Her black hair shone almost red at times, and her build was so willowy we thought she could easily have flown away. If not a dark angel, she was a shape-shifted raven, but her manner was always gracious, warm, and nurturing. Except when she worried about her teeth, which were her obsession.

Even now, in the midst of our crisis, she asked me to check them out. Pulling back her lips, she asked if she needed to get some work done. "I think maybe my front teeth are interfering with how my fangs come out," she said. "What do you think?'

It never really mattered what I or anyone else thought. She didn't listen.

"They look fine," I said. "Stop worrying. If you can inject venin and suck blood, that's all that matters, right?"

"But maybe I can do that more effectively if I file them down a little."

Bel gave me a look of annoyance. She didn't care for Destiny's vanity.

For Destiny, being a vampire among the most refined of our species was the ultimate spiritual experience. In fact, she'd already advanced to the third level, though she'd been around us only a decade. I expected her to become one of us fairly soon, but I wasn't keen about losing my status as the baby of the family.

"So have you seen her?" Destiny asked again. "Bel says you tracked her."

"I did," I admitted, "but I didn't take it very far. I don't think this was the best way to bring her in. She's resistant and afraid."

Destiny and Bel exchanged glances. They'd obviously already discussed the situation and come to their own conclusions. Phelan looked uncomfortable.

"What's wrong?" I asked. "Did something happen?"

"What's he going to do with her?" Phelan asked. "Will he make her one of us?"

The idea was so absurd I nearly laughed, but Phelan was clearly disturbed. I sat down next to him and patted his hand. His unrelenting vulnerability was so poignant. Though he was fully grown, he seemed more a very young boy, and his curly hair only supported that illusion. In fact, in that moment he seemed to be near tears.

"Naje can't make her one of us," I assured him. "You know that."

"He can. There's nothing to stop him if he decides to do it."

"He'd have one of us do it, not him."

"It's different," Phelan insisted. "It's not just a matter of transforming her. It has to be done through him."

I shook my head. "I don't believe that."

Bel and Destiny watched me closely, as if I had some secret knowledge that would put their fears to rest. I began to realize what it was that disturbed Dantalyon. As the consort, he'd be destroyed if Naje made another vampire. Yet the scenario was absurd to me. Jamie was pretty, even beautiful. She was also spirited, but a replacement for Dantalyon? Never. I shook my head. "There's just no way that would happen," I said.

"If Naje thinks the only way to save us is to make the sacrifice," Bel pointed out, "he will. He's lived much longer than any of us and has seen members of this *kamera* come and go. This is a desperate situation, Christian, and no one seems to know what he's going to do."

"What makes you think that making her one of us would save us?"

"Eryx has it figured out," Phelan interjected. "He's worked it all up on the computer. He said that the logic of the procedure that Naje was going to attempt with Ana entails the possibility of turning her. And he's the only one who can make her as powerful as she needs to be to protect our center."

Suddenly I was lost. I had no idea what he was saying, and I couldn't even imagine the possibility that our fate might mean Dantalyon's destruction. Could Naje really go through with it?

"He'll find some other way," I said, but it sounded empty. Only Naje seemed to know what had to be done, and it had to do with the esoteric marriage of metaphysics and biology. There was something about Ana, and now Jamie, that offered us a way, but I didn't understand how it worked. But maybe Dantalyon did. Maybe that was why he was worried. Naje's sudden abduction of this woman had surprised us, and it seemed now that it was going to have some negative repercussions.

I suddenly realized that the existence we'd all enjoyed for so many years was about to be drastically transformed. I couldn't even imagine losing Dantalyon. None of us got to be near him very often, but just to look at him inspired the most exquisite sensations. Beauty was what we loved, and perfection of form. He was a magnification of the most sublime Michelangelo sculpture.

"He'll talk to us first," I said, and I believed that. "He's not going to do anything without talking to us."

Bel shook her head and looked away. She despised my optimism. Naje was usually inscrutable, and there was no reason to believe he'd take us into consideration on an issue like this. In fact, there was probably no time. Whatever he had in mind, he'd already set it in motion. He made our *kamera* possible and he defined its essence. We didn't depend on him for our existence, but from him flowed our means of elevation. If he destroyed the center, we'd flounder and possibly wander into oblivion.

"Do any of you feel . . . ?" Destiny began, but didn't finish.

"What?" Phelan asked.

"Nothing."

"Feel what?" Bel pressed her.

She shrugged and leaned her head into her left hand. "Just this sort of . . . I don't know."

I looked at Bel.

"Anyway," Destiny said, "it's probably nothing. Just the stress of this thing, and we do have a more pressing problem. No one's heard from Lachesis. Eryx told me that she didn't come back from New York last night."

No one said a word. We all knew how important it was right now to check in. Lachesis was an early riser. Even if she'd stayed in the city, she'd have let us know.

"What is this thing?" Phelan asked. "What's going to happen to us?"

"It's an emotional leprosy," Bel spoke up.

We all looked at her. I read from her face that she wished she'd said nothing, but she went ahead and explained: "It just makes us stop feeling. We're spiritually asphyxiated. Then we deteriorate. We just sit there and rot."

I noticed Destiny watching her with horrified fascination.

"How do you know that?" Phelan asked, wide-eyed.

"That's what happened to Cacilian. He's down in the morgue. Go look at him."

The image of that wasn't particularly intriguing to any of us. I hadn't realized he'd been brought here, but of course it made sense.

"But how do you know that's related to this thing that's after us?" Phelan asked.

"Because he wasn't the first, and all of the victims are part of our network. They had some alliance with us."

Leave it to Bel to have done her research, although I wished she'd deliver it with more sensitivity. For her, to know was to have options, and to have options was to have power.

"So tell us," I said, with a pointed glance at Phelan, "who else? What happened to them?"

"It's not what happened but what's happening," she responded. She'd read me, but she didn't believe in sugarcoating. Phelan sat forward to listen, like a kid with a wild imagination hearing a horror story that could keep him awake for weeks.

"There's another *kamera,* mostly in Asia," Bel explained. "Naje founded it long ago and then left it behind, or at least that's what Dantalyon said. They could only develop so far, so he removed himself, although they were clearly based in his essence the way we are. And they were hit first. They're all gone. It's like whatever this nemesis is, it picks a resonant thread, sucks it dry, and then moves on to another."

Phelan looked concerned. "So it's like a vampire. Like us, but it's against us. Like a snake eating its own tail."

She nodded. "We've already lost a few, some of them close by. It's closing in quickly. Naje knows he has to move fast."

Then I realized something. "Maybe it's here," I said. "Lethe hasn't gone out for several nights. She's been keeping to herself. Maybe whatever it is, it comes in through someone and then infects the rest."

No one looked at me. No one wanted to deal with that. It meant the possibility of casting her out. It also meant that any of us might be infected from contact with her. Better to think of it as some random whim than a contagion.

Before we could say much else, Dantalyon came in and interrupted us. His dark eyes were intense and his jaw was set in anger. Something had happened.

He looked at me and said, "You need to go to Manhattan. Stiletto's going with you. Lachesis is up there and she wants help."

"She's okay then?" I asked.

Dantalyon ignored my question. He also blocked my attempt to probe his state of mind. "Just go," he commanded. "Don't take the train; drive, because we need you back here tonight." He told me where to meet Lachesis and then he was gone.

I looked at Bel. *Something's wrong,* she communicated to me, though she said nothing. I understood what she meant. Dantalyon's obvious agitation was unrelated to anything Lachesis had said. It must have something to do with what had gone on in that room where Jamie was kept. He was definitely worried.

"Where is he?" I asked Phelan. He and Stiletto were in continuous contact, if only mental.

"In New Hope," Phelan told me. "He was going there to get something."

"Well, let him know I'm on my way and he should be ready."

With no time to waste, I grabbed some shoes and went to my car. The feeling of dread from my daydreams lay heavy in my stomach, and the concerns I'd just heard made my head race. Whatever Lachesis had discovered, it had better be good. When we were attacked, I wanted to be with the others.

Ten

Jamie

As scared as she was, Jamie was filled with curiosity about this man, this being who approached her. The slender blond who'd come in first had seemed harmless, even sympathetic, and she'd thought she could persuade him to help her escape, but all thoughts of that now disappeared. To her surprise, looking at this one almost made her believe what Gail had been telling her. His eyelashes were thick and long, framing large black eyes that were like deep holes into which she could fall and then float downward for a very long way. He seemed as calm as stone, with a wisdom rooted in the origins of humankind, or beyond. Yet more compelling was his facial beauty. She wanted just to gaze on him without speaking for as long as he would allow. In that moment, she believed she knew what an artist felt when gripped by the muse—an absolute obsession to possess and express the feeling of submersion into boundlessness.

More than with the one who had called himself Christian, she now believed she was among beings that were not human. This one, at least, was vastly more.

"Do you want to see your son?" he asked. To Jamie, his voice and manner were layered with the complexities of darkness and light. There was something bad here, and something good, as well as things that defied a label. She was certain that he never once blinked as he shocked her system with the fiercest look of compassion she'd ever seen.

"Of course, yes," she whispered. She hadn't meant to whisper. She'd meant to sound firm and determined, and not about to be intimidated. But it was as if her will were no longer her own. He commanded the room, as a darker creature hovered nearby, and he also commanded her inner world. What she would feel, she sensed, now would be under his control.

And yet the thought of that didn't bother her. She wanted to deliver herself to him totally. As he stood before her, she felt the urge to sit closer, grip him, and press her face against his belly, his crotch, his thighs. She craved to have his fingers touch her hair and bring her closer.

Without even a visible gesture, he seemed to tell his companion to unfasten her bindings. Jamie heard and saw nothing in his manner, but she sensed that there had been a communication between them and it was something that the dark one did not want to do. He looked unhappy, even angry. And he seemed sufficiently strong to refuse, yet he didn't.

He came near and knelt before her, his black hair falling over his shoulder. As he looked into her eyes, she saw a vicious guarded expression that told her he viewed her as a threat, an enemy. But she had no weapons, nothing whatsoever that she might use to strike out. She was completely at their command, yet this one with the dark brown eyes full of fire wanted her dead.

With deft fingers, he removed the thick bondage cords from around her wrists. His touch was like a feather and she felt chills at the contact. To her shock, Jamie imagined herself locked with him in erotic combat, loving and hating and trying desperately to join.

She quickly banned the images from her mind but they returned. Was he doing this to her?

His hands moved to her feet. Again, the soft whisper of a caress, his fingertips touching under her arch as if surreptitiously he were seducing her.

Yet could anything be hidden from the powerful white-haired man who waited just a few feet away? She felt like Guinevere and Lancelot in King Arthur's presence, except that their intimacy was delicately threaded with antipathy and treachery.

When "Lancelot" was finished, he stepped back but still kept his eyes on her like some cornered viper. That was when she discovered his name.

"Dantalyon, leave us now," said the white-haired one.

She could tell it was with a great effort of will that he did so. It seemed that he felt danger here but had no choice in what was to be done. Jamie also instinctively felt when he closed the door behind him that he'd been given another task. There was urgency in the air. Whatever plan these things had in mind, it was moving with some rapidity.

But now she could see Devon. That was what mattered. She knew he was here, she believed that he was safe, and she expected to be reunited at once. She stood up, rubbing her wrists and waiting expectantly for their next move. She hoped her enigmatic liberator might say something by way of explanation or tell her his name, but he merely gestured for her to come with him.

There were a thousand things she wanted to ask as he ushered her toward the door, and yet she couldn't voice any of them. They walked abreast in silence down a long corridor that seemed to be the interior of an old house, but below ground. Stone walls were visible on both sides. She saw no windows, only doors, and dim bulbs in rusting iron sockets spaced far apart cast the merest light. The cold floor, too, felt hard like stone and was dusty with cement powder.

Jamie had the feeling this creature, whatever he was, could see perfectly well in the dark. His presence just a step behind her seemed at once ominous and courtly. He was both a threat and a protector. She suddenly feared that he was not taking her to see Devon but to go elsewhere, to a place that would be even worse than the room where she'd been bound. And yet she wanted to go. She didn't know why, but she felt propelled by some inner urge to stay as close to this man as possible.

Just ahead about ten yards, she spotted the shadowy, stooped figure of a man who stood staring at them. He appeared to be frightened, and Jamie expected him to yell out at any moment, but he remained silent. Then he moved suddenly to his left and was gone. When they arrived at that spot, she looked for a doorway but all she saw was a stone wall. How could the man just disappear like that?

Feeling a shock of cold air, she glanced at her escort, but he seemed oblivious to what she'd just witnessed. Rather than ask him, she remained silent, but just ahead she saw what appeared to be a very young woman, possibly sixteen, and wearing a light-colored dress that came to midcalf, dart across the hall. Jamie thought she could see right through this figure, but it was too dark to be sure. In fact, she didn't trust her eyes in that hallway at all. She wanted this massive man by her side to say something reassuring or at least to acknowledge that they weren't alone in the building, but he seemed to have no sensitivity to her confusion. Or else he just didn't care.

Near her feet she heard a distinct hiss and the quick scrape of something rough on the floor. She jumped back, bumping the creature, but couldn't see where the noise had come from. It had sounded like a snake. Her captor steadied her, made a gesture with his hand into the darkness, and kept walking.

"Here," he said with such quiet grace Jamie almost didn't hear him. She turned to see him opening one of the doors to their left. A boy sat with his back to them inside a small room.

"Devon?" she cried out. It was him; she was sure of it. Ready to sweep her son into a relieved embrace, she stepped toward him, but just inside the threshold she ran into a glass wall.

"What's this?" she asked. "How do I get through?"

"You can't go to him," the creature said. "I only want you to see that he's alive and unharmed. We'll feed him and keep him safe."

Indeed, as her eyes adjusted, she was able to see Devon at a table on which a dim light sat, playing a game with some exotic woman with mahogany hair. She didn't look up, though she faced them, as if unaware of their presence. It was like something out of science fiction.

"I want to speak to him," Jamie insisted. "He may not be physically harmed, but I'm sure he's afraid."

"He's not. Children are the easiest. He's malleable and perfectly happy. At the moment, he doesn't even have memories of you."

Jamie looked up at the man, ready to burst forth in anger, but suddenly everything looked different. She felt her inner world unraveling, her memories sliding like clay immersed in water. She barely even knew she'd been brought to this place. All at once, she believed she was home, yet it was not the home she had known over the past ten years. She was "home" in another way, another world. She nearly believed that she'd been living here for a decade.

Suddenly afraid, Jamie struggled to find reference points, but instead went further into a quicksand of shifting images that included a different name, a different homeland, and even the feeling that she was only five years old.

Through all of this, the creature watched her. She felt his eyes on her, working her like a puppet master. She stepped toward him and laid a hand on his powerful chest.

"What are you?" she whispered. "What are you doing to me?"

A dark eyebrow went up. "You asked me to take you here," he said.

She shook her head. "No, I . . . Why?" Looking back toward the glass she saw a woman and a boy with his back to her, but didn't recall their names. Maybe she'd never known them. Puzzled, she looked back at the man who waited at her side.

"I'm sorry, I don't . . ."

He smiled. "You feel well now, don't you?"

Jamie took a deep breath. "Yes," she acknowledged. "But what are we doing?"

Then it came back, as if a veil had been lifted. That boy was her son, Devon. She wanted to see him. And yet she'd just now believed that she didn't know him. Astonished, she was about to ask how this could happen, when the creature lifted a finger that bade her to be silent.

"You see," he said. "He doesn't know anything but what he's doing in the moment. He's not afraid. All reality exists for him in the moment."

Jamie felt completely disoriented. These demons, whatever they were, could manipulate at will. No matter how she might resist, they could melt that down before she even had time to think of a plan. Never had she felt so helpless. It was an ungodly prison.

"Now come with me," said the creature. "We have

work to do. Devon won't be hurt as long as you cooperate."

He gripped her arm with hypothermic fingers and guided her down the hallway to another door, which opened without his touching it. Just inside, she saw another one of these beings, surrounded by computers, speakers, monitors, and other electronic contraptions. He looked human but Jamie knew he wasn't. This experience was nothing like that of the role-players in Manhattan. It was almost like being among moving mannequins. Yet these things were real, and they obviously had some dark intent.

This room felt even colder than the hallway, and Jamie was hesitant to step inside, but she clearly had no choice. The new creature, a young man with dark hair and a thick body who dressed in a blazer and slacks as if he were going to a casual business meeting, placed his hand on her back and guided her past all the equipment to a chair.

"Have a seat," he said. Jamie sat down and then looked around. Different brands of computers were stacked one on top of another, with several laptops and organizers tossed haphazardly on different chairs. Then, when she noticed that the white-haired one had disappeared, she felt as if someone had removed her wool coat on a winter day. Where had he gone?

"I'm Eryx," said the creature. "You're in a house not far from New Hope. We brought you here last night and we don't want to hurt you, but we need your help."

"You've already hurt me. You've taken my son from me."

He shrugged. "He's in no danger."

"What could you possibly want from me?" Jamie asked. Her voice sounded weak.

"Well, frankly, you wouldn't have even caught our eye under other circumstances, but you're Ana's twin and that makes you extremely valuable. Are you her identical twin?"

"Ana? You mean Gail. You know Gail?"

"She's Ana to us. Which of you was born first?"

"Is she alive? Is she here?"

"Please. Identical or not?"

"Yes. I was born first. Why? Is she here?"

He shook his head. "She's not here. If she were, you wouldn't be. And I think she's alive, but we're about to find out for sure."

Jamie flinched away. "What do you mean? What do you want with me? What are you going to do?"

He smiled. "Don't worry. I'm not that powerful. That's why Naje asked me to do it."

"Naje?" Jamie figured he meant the one who'd taken her to see Devon and who'd left her here. He seemed to be the leader. "Asked you to do what?"

"The others could overwhelm you if they tried this, and he especially could kill you with his mental abilities without necessarily meaning to. But I can't. Or I don't think I can."

He moved away from her for a moment, and she felt as if he were going to place a metal cap on her head and zap her with electricity. How could they possibly use her to find out something about Gail?

"Can't you please tell me what you're going to do?" she begged. Her immediate thought was to rush to the door and just run. There were so many doors out there. Surely she could find a place to hide, maybe even a way out. She could hit him with one of these computers and go.

Yet even as she thought it, Eryx turned back to her and said, "I'm going to help you relax now. This won't take long."

Eleven

Christian

We arrived in the Village in record time, partly because Stiletto could ween a cop a mile away and was able to shift his perceptions just long enough to prevent the officer from realizing we were passing at such a speed. I loved this, and I could almost feel the heat in the air from the many temps cursing us as we did what they dared not do. Stiletto took his name from a venomous African serpent, also known among the natives there as "shroud bearer" and "bite dead." These stealthy assassins stare for a moment at their prey and then strike with a backward movement. Unless you know this, they have all the advantage.

I'd picked Stiletto up at his metalwork shop on a side street in the artsiest part of New Hope. None of us could fathom why he applied his energy to mortal commercial pursuits, but he loved the feel of the different kinds of copper, steel, and iron, and he could spend hours in a Zen-like trance imagining how to transform heaps of junk into art. The odd thing was, he looked as though his only concern might be to hang out in bars and bash in people's heads. He was like a prizefighter, and he even shaved his head. But his work sold. People came from foreign countries to admire the black man's art and take it home with them.

"I don't like this," he said as he got into the car. I knew he was thinking of Phelan. Stiletto was Phelan's special watcher. They were nearly as inseparable as me and Bel.

And speaking of Bel, she'd been unhappy with Naje's order.

She'd wanted to come with us but was told to stay. Naje needed her there. Personally, I'd have gladly ,raded places with her just to stay near the two most advanced souls of our *kamera,* but Naje knew whose talents would best match the jobs he needed done, and given our precarious situation, this was no time to question his judgment.

"I don't think any of us like this," I told Stiletto, "but none of us really knows what to do. We can't just sit around and wait for this thing to come and get us. They're working on the girl now, so we at least have some direction."

"So what does Lachesis have?"

"I don't know, but it's obviously important."

Stiletto said nothing more. He was a loner. While he respected Naje, had been with him since forever, and had a place in our house, he kept to himself. Even Phelan barely knew him. He was the third one to come into the *kamera,* following Lachesis and Viper. At that time, they'd lived somewhere in Europe, and Naje had wanted someone of Stiletto's strength and stability. People who choose to become vampires, which all of us had, tend to be a fairly strange bunch. Stiletto was grounded. He understood and supported Naje's vision but processed every piece of information before he acted. Like the snake of Norse mythology that holds the earth together, he encircled us with a mindful perspective.

Dantalyon told us once that Naje had started the *kamera* four different times, and had failed the previous three times to achieve an operational manifestation of his spiritual ideas. After each failure, he'd gone out alone to learn more, and this time he'd been more astute in his selections. Not every vampire invited had made the cut. It took decades just to get the first three, and once they came together to the States, that was when Naje had spotted Dantalyon.

As we drove along, I thought about all of this and wondered how Naje evaluated us now. Did he care that we stayed together, or were we as dispensable as the others? You can never tell with vampires. We care about one another but we're attached more firmly by need. Naje created our center, and I doubt that any of us knew how he really felt about anything. I figured we'd find out before the end of the night.

We finally crossed into New York, befuddled the toll collectors, and shot into the city. Lachesis met us at the old hanging tree in the northeast corner of Washington Square Park, the graveyard for tens of thousands of plague victims. She was dressed in tight black clothing, as usual, and I weened that she'd been with the male temp who'd beguiled her over the past month. She went through periodic infatuations that took her away from us, and always came out of them having terminated the guy and declaring that she'd never get so caught up again. I'd seen her go through at least three. Climbing into the backseat, she said, "I know where Ana is."

I looked at her in the rearview mirror, about to ask where to drive, when Stiletto said, "So? We only need one of them."

"She has something," Lachesis continued. "She was looking for one of us to tell us. She's got something hidden away somewhere that's meant only for us, and it might be here in New York. Even if we can't get her out, we might get close enough to read her memories and then go find it."

"What does she have?" I asked.

"I don't know, but Naje managed to get that much before Cacilian was totally lost. He thinks she was abducted by someone or some group who might be turning this thing on us."

"How? And for what reason?"

"We have enemies, Christian, and if she has something that could be used against us, there are those who'll take advantage of that."

"So this is bad," I commented.

"Maybe," was her reply. "Even if they intend us harm, they might unwittingly give us what we need. We just have to be artful about it. That's why Naje sent you two. We may need your agility, Christian, and Stiletto, you're always good with a plan."

Stiletto shook his head. "This isn't a time for us to be dividing our forces. We need to stick together."

"Naje agreed that we should check this out. Otherwise you wouldn't be here."

There wasn't any good reason to argue. Naje called the shots, so we followed Lachesis's directions until we arrived at a house in SoHo that looked dark and uninhabited. It was obviously not the abode of vampires of any breed, or we'd have weened that right away. Secretly I was relieved. I didn't want to tangle with predators of a different resonance.

"What makes you think she's in there?" I asked.

"I got a tip," was all Lachesis would say. She stepped out of the car and we followed her inside. Since we could see in the dark well enough, we left the lights off. I saw at once that the rooms were nearly empty. Here and there was a piece of broken or moldy furniture, and the air was thick with the smell of dope and cigarettes, and even the hint of blood from some needle, but clearly no one lived here.

Stiletto stood in the middle of one empty room,

hands on his hips. He was peeved. I had to admit, I was skeptical, too.

Lachesis ignored him and went to a door. She tried it but it was stuck. I came up behind her to help. Between the two of us we managed to pry it open and saw a short flight of steps. They weren't tall enough to go all the way to another floor, which meant there was probably some sort of hidden chamber—probably once a storage area.

Lachesis proceeded and we followed until we were standing in a cramped, windowless space. Given how warm the night was, I could hardly breathe. Lachesis didn't seem to notice. She held up both hands, using her palms to take in the nuances of the atmosphere. Stiletto and I waited while she read the currents.

"She was here," she finally said in disappointment. "We missed her. Ana was here, and not that long ago."

"Lachesis, what's this about?" Stiletto demanded. "I don't see the point."

She breathed out in exasperation. "We're in a crisis, Stiletto."

"I know that, but—"

"No, you don't know what I'm saying. This other woman we've brought in, she's the threat."

"How do you mean?" I asked.

"I've been talking to Dantalyon. He thinks she's a plant."

I snorted. "A plant? How? She didn't come to us. We grabbed her. She's totally naive."

"That's what it seemed like, yes," Lachesis continued. "But you know who she was with."

I shrugged. "Allan Coyne. So?"

"Coyne's been tracking us."

"We all know that," Stiletto broke in. "He's impotent. He can't touch us."

"He just did. He put this woman in our midst. Think

about it. We discovered that Ana's blood was the perfect genetic gateway for our transformation and escape. She disappears. This twin of hers shows up. Of course we'd grab her."

I nodded. I was following this now. "She meets up with Coyne and he tells her that Ana's in trouble. That's how he gets her to agree to be grabbed so that she can transmit to him where we are."

"Right," Lachesis said.

"But what does he want with us? Does he fancy himself some kind of modern-day vampire hunter?"

"In a way." Lachesis hesitated a moment, and then revealed what she knew. "Ana told Viper that Coyne wants the venin. But not just any venin. He wants it from Naje."

I was floored. "How does he even know about Naje?"

Lachesis shrugged and said, "He knows. I can only guess that Ana told him or he got it from her some other way. He apparently discovered the source of a rather potent drug that's marketed as high-caliber Ecstasy—a vampire, as you know—and he expects to create something even more alluring and addictive by trapping a vampire as old and skilled as Naje. He tried to force Ana to show him how to penetrate our retreat."

"But she didn't do it," I pointed out. "She wouldn't, either. She won't betray Viper." Much as I loved heat, I longed to step out of this tiny room and get some air, but Lachesis was intense. She wanted us to see her point.

"It's not a matter of what she wants to do," she insisted. "If Coyne finds her first, he may get her cooperation in some other way, or else he's trying to get to us through her sister. At any rate, he clearly knows things, and that's not good for us."

Stiletto threw up his hands. "I still don't see the danger. So we scramble the mental fields. Any of us can do that. This twin won't even remember him, let alone be able to help him. And even if he finds us, what leverage does he have? He'd be trapped. We'd just kill him."

"It's not just about him," Lachesis continued. "It's about her."

I was about to ask what she meant when Stiletto stiffened. He was listening. I quickly focused and heard it, too. Someone had come in. I made out a light tread, and then another.

"We're trapped," Stiletto whispered. He looked accusingly at Lachesis. She looked quickly around and saw no obvious opening.

I motioned to both of them to be quiet. I couldn't quite tell what we faced, but I didn't sense vampires. Still, if we stayed there, we were blind. We needed to know precisely what we faced. On impulse, I went out and down the steps. Lachesis shot a warning for me not to go, but I ignored her. Someone had to do something or we'd all three be caught. We'd be pretty intimidating if our adversaries were just temps, unless there were enough of them to overpower us. I, for one, did not have the ability to telepathically scramble the thoughts of more than two or three people at a time, but at least I could distract whomever had come in while Lachesis and Stiletto looked for holes. Even a small opening would allow escape. Then they could rescue me from a position of strength.

I weened the intruders before I was on the first step down and knew they were waiting. The psychic field informed me that they'd watched us enter. They'd been there before us and they knew what we were. Whether they had actually known we were coming and what their intent was I couldn't tell.

I came into the dark room and made out three silhouettes. All were male and all were looking at me. I tried to flow into the shadows so they couldn't clearly see my form, only that I was there.

For a few moments nothing was said as we sized one another up. I could see that they were young and without many skills but knew more than most of the vampire kids who dominated the clubs. It was clear that they wanted something quite specific, although I couldn't read what it was—and that alarmed me. They definitely weren't vampires, though they dressed in black, so that was in my favor. What they actually knew of our *kamera* and its specific abilities, I couldn't say.

I threw out a mental block and found it ineffective. That had never happened to me before. These shadows had some metaphysical force on their side and they knew how to use it. I had to think of something else, fast.

Most other creatures underestimate the snake, and that's because some snakes have only one means of defense, such as making themselves look larger or blending into the foliage. That was not too impressive, but since those in our *kamera* who've absorbed the lessons can call on the entire range of serpentine weapons, I had more going for me than these would-be captors realized. Even so, I was outnumbered and had to do this with some finesse.

I sent a coded communication—*black mamba*—to Stiletto and Lachesis to be ready to streak through to get out. They, too, had weened the extra power these temps had and warned me to be careful. Then I prepared to take on the trio who barred my way.

I tried again to ween from them what their purpose was, although I sensed they were just following the orders of someone else. Then one lurched forward to grab me and I leaped easily beyond his reach. I quickly assumed a defensive posture, ready to strike, but going for one would make me vulnerable to the other two. I had to be careful.

Of the three, one was short, only about five-foot-eight, and he seemed the least comfortable with his role that night. That meant that he was possibly the weakest link. Yet I couldn't just push past him and escape, because I needed to create a diversion for my companions. We all had to get out of this. I tried to read his thoughts so I could penetrate them and spook him.

I was about to let my cohorts know that the three of us could take them on, but then two more came through the door. Both of these were tall and strong, and they looked like real predators. They carried a net and something else that I couldn't see. Then I sensed others outside, but how many I couldn't tell. Now my only recourse was to keep their attention on me. They had a vampire nearly in their grasp. I used whatever I could find in the memory fields surrounding us to make them believe I was a real prize.

Then I worked to condense my internal juices. I had to be ready for more than one.

The two who had mostly recently entered came right at me and grabbed me from either side. Finding myself held tight, I let loose a hot streak of stinging poison that hit one dead center in the eye. This was the trick of the spitting cobra and it worked. My enemy let go with a cry, and I turned toward the other, but he shielded himself from the spray.

And that was it. I had no more. The others rushed in to grab me. I slipped away and found a slight grip on the wall where most people would think there was nothing. Clinging to it, I moved upward toward the ceiling, but then found no more toeholds. I pushed away, leaping over the heads of the three who had tried to subdue me, and landed in a crouch. Then I flipped around to see that two of my assailants were out of sight. I turned again to find them and suddenly felt leather go around my neck.

A snake catcher. They'd been prepared.

I reached for it to try to slip out, but they pulled it tight and two of them held it from behind me. I gripped it to rip it off and found it to be too thick. Then a nylon net came down over me and one of the temps—a large one—used his full weight to shove me off my feet. Once down, I was vulnerable. There was no way to get loose from the net.

They draped another net over me, from my feet to my head, securing me past all hope of escape. I could barely move.

Yet I'd accomplished my goal. With all of the activity they failed to see Lachesis and Stiletto streak through the shadows and out the back door. I was relieved about that, certain they wouldn't abandon me.

The five men bound me and dragged me across the floor, out the door, down the steps, and across the small yard. The hard ground hurt my back. I tried rolling, but one of them kicked me down. Then they lifted me and shoved me into a windowless van. It reeked of male perspiration, alcohol, and stale cigarette butts. My only consolation was the benefit of body heat from the males who sat in the van near me. Their recent exertion paid off for me, and I worked at taking what I could to build up my strength.

Lachesis communicated to me that she and Stiletto were free. They would follow the van in my Jag if they could. She also let me know that whoever this group was, they were also the ones who had taken Ana.

Twelve

Jamie

Jamie grew slowly aware of the room again and she realized that Eryx was talking to the white-haired man who had so enthralled her, the one he'd called Naje. They both looked grim. She listened harder to try to hear what they were discussing.

"I'm sorry," Eryx said. "I can't make it work with her. It's not hard to get a trance, a deep one, but I can't get the connection from Ana. I worked it from every angle I could think of. Maybe there is none. I can't tell, but it could just be that I'm not skillful enough. Maybe Dantalyon can do better."

"No," said Naje. His response was definitive and Jamie sensed in it something troubled. "It's time to try something else. Wake her and take her over to the serpentarium."

With that he left the room.

Jamie stiffened. A "serpentarium." What in the world was that? Just the word itself hit her with a vivid image of the room from an adventure movie she'd seen in which the floor was so thick with every variety of snake that the explorers couldn't walk without stepping on one. The snakes had dropped on them from the ceilings and circled around their feet.

Eryx returned to her. When he saw that she was awake, his frown deepened.

"What was that about?" she asked. "Were you talking about that thing that grabbed me last night? That . . . that . . ."

"Viper? He's not a thing. He's our scientist."

"Scientist?"

"Yes. He works with the snakes. But he handles them well. He breeds them and studies them. Their bite can't kill him, so he's been able to record all the nuances of their venom." Eryx helped her to sit up as he continued: "He's actually discovered that some venom has a substance that keeps blood from clotting, some relaxes the muscles, some paralyzes them, and some dissolves tissue. More interesting, some actually inhibits the growth of tumors. He's actually published articles about it in medical journals."

Jamie couldn't imagine how this creature before her just chattered on as if this were all commonplace, as if they were buddies or something. And she was definitely not going to get near this Viper thing again, or his snake laboratory.

"What does this have to do with me?" she asked.

"You're about to find out."

"What do you mean? I hate snakes. I don't want to get near any. Please don't take me there. What is it you want from me?"

Eryx shrugged. "I don't have any choice. What I tried here didn't work, so I have to take you."

He came closer to bind her and she kicked at him with all her strength. "No! I'm not going!"

He stood there looking bemused. "You'll go willingly or you'll go in a trance. It doesn't matter to me."

Jamie stared at him. "In a trance?"

"Yes. So you won't know where you're going and

you'll just find yourself already there. Maybe that'll be easier for you."

He lifted his right hand to move toward her and she sat back and shook her head. She didn't want to lose control or awareness. She wanted to know as much as she could about this place in case there was any chance of escape. And she didn't want to be so vulnerable to these things.

"Okay," she said. "I'll go. But please don't let the snakes get close to me."

Eryx laughed. "I can't imagine what you're afraid of. Most snakes aren't even venomous, and they rarely attack unless they're really provoked."

"Just . . . just promise me. . . ."

"Okay, come on then. It's not far. And don't try to bolt, because if you're afraid of snakes, you could really get yourself into a mess."

Jamie thought he must be saying that to keep her under control. She couldn't believe they would just let snakes roam around in the halls. Then she discovered what this place was really like.

Eryx made her walk a few paces in the lead, although the hallway was dark ahead. He told her to just keep going straight, that he'd stay close. Jamie stepped lightly, keeping close watch on her feet and recalling the hissing sound she'd heard earlier, but overhead on a shelflike ledge to her right she saw movement. Then she saw a large, dark body undulate and knew it was some kind of exotic constrictor. She sensed it was watching her. At any second it could fling itself off the shelf straight at her. Looking left, she spotted several black holes in the wall. Although she saw no movement she was sure that slick, creepy things lived inside those holes.

From behind her, Eryx flashed a light against the wall to show Jamie a detailed painting. "That's an ana-

conda," he said. "The longest snake in the world." Its
body was thick and its length disappeared well beyond
the light into the darkness. "It kills by suffocation."

Jamie remembered that this was the snake with which
her sister identified—as Ana. She wanted to close her
eyes. She couldn't believe she was in the midst of all
this, and she cursed Gail for running off as she had.
Even an alcoholic husband was better than this.

"Here," said Eryx. He opened a dark door and light
slipped into the hallway. Jamie had no time to adjust
her eyes before Eryx urged her within. He touched her
arm and she was acutely reminded that he wasn't alive.
She reacted to his cold grip, and then looked inside the
room. She gasped in horror. On every side were cages,
both wire and glass, filled with snakes. She heard a hiss
and several angry rattles, and saw a cobra rise up and
swell its neck into a flat oval. In a large glass cage several
thin black reptiles writhed together.

"Oh, my God!" she cried. "I'm not going in there!"

Despite what Eryx had warned her about, she turned
to leave and ran straight into Naje, who was following
her into the room.

"I can't do this; I can't do this," she cried. "Whatever
it is you want, I can't be here with all these snakes!
Please let me out."

He gripped her arms and turned her around. "Go
straight across the room and through that door," he
said, pointing. "It's better in there."

Jamie turned and looked again at all the serpents on
every side. She felt sure that if she took a step deep into
their lair they would all come slithering out of their
cages and attack her. She could imagine them writhing
at her feet, encircling her legs, hissing at her and stab-
bing her with their sharp little fangs. She felt faint.
Nothing could make her walk across the room. She fell
back against Naje's solid body. Eryx looked over her

head at Naje and shrugged. Then he went toward the door on the other side. He opened it and waited.

Just then Jamie felt her fear displaced by a sense of calm. Instead of a room full of snakes she saw a garden. On the other side was a feeling of warmth and light. Urged from behind, she breathed deeply and went where she was directed. She only vaguely remembered being afraid but didn't know what she'd been afraid of.

She was walking barefoot now and the soft grass felt delightful. Purple, blue, and golden flowers surrounded her with a pleasing fragrance. She felt good here, as though she belonged. She even began to think that maybe this was *her* garden. In fact, it looked very much like one she'd often walked through as a child. But where was she going?

Then all of a sudden she saw the thing, the snake creature, the one that had grabbed her in New Hope. He was standing a few yards away, apparently waiting for her.

Jamie stopped and backed up hard, slamming once again against the man behind her. He held her fast. The viper-thing watched her in amusement. Then he looked at her captor.

"Is she ready?" he asked.

"It doesn't matter," said Naje. "There's no more time. Just take her blood again and tell me what you see."

"No!" Jamie cried. "Don't let him touch me."

Jamie woke up and found herself strapped to a wooden armchair in the middle of what appeared to be a sophisticated science lab. She had no idea how she'd gotten there or what had happened. Three large computerized screens were active, and there was a low buzz from a generator of some type nearby. She recognized a bulky gas chromatograph–mass spectrometer on one side from work she'd once done in a serology lab, and the various comparison and compound microscopes sitting on counters were clearly expensive. She thought she recognized a scanning electron microscope. The viper-creature that had frightened her was leaning over one of the comparison scopes and there were others in the room: Eryx was busy at a computer while an Asian female—the one whom Jamie had seen with Devon—stared at the ceiling. Around her neck was a thick black eel-like snake. Fear at the thought that Devon was alone nearly made Jamie vomit, but she convinced herself that the boy was asleep. She tugged at her restraints in a futile attempt to get up and away. The woman with the snake looked at her but said nothing. Near her was a young blond man wearing dark glasses, and standing behind Eryx, gripping his chair and looking over his shoulder at the computer monitor, was the ancient Naje.

The blond noticed her watching them and he brightened like a kid on Christmas morning. Leaning toward the female, he whispered something. She looked again at Jamie and nodded, and that seemed to be the sign that he could approach. He got up and walked over. Behind his glasses his hazel eyes were wide, even awestruck. He pulled up a stool next to her and pressed her hand, bound as it was to the arm of the chair she was in. His touch was warmer than the others' had been, and she didn't want to think about what that might mean. She didn't believe it was possible that he was human and living here with these demons—although that was what Gail seemed to have done.

Naje looked over at them and then returned his attention to the computer.

"How are you?" the blond one whispered. "Do you want something? Water, maybe?"

Jamie was struck by his childlike eagerness to please her. She glanced at the others, who were busy, and then back at her sudden companion. Under her breath, she said, "I want to leave here. I want to see my son."

He squinted at her as if disappointed by her answer. Apparently he'd hoped she'd ask for something that he could accomplish. "I can't let you go," he said. "We need you. But I'll get you something to drink."

Jamie shook her head. She almost felt as if she were talking to Devon, yet the boyish man beside her was clearly in his twenties.

"What are you?" she asked.

"I'm Phelan." Then it seemed to occur to him what she'd meant. "Oh, are you asking what are we, all of us?"

"Yes. What are all these snakes and why am I here? How long before you let me go?"

Just at that moment the door opened and the one she'd seen earlier with Naje entered the room. He looked at her with that same fierce expression and then went over to Naje. Although they appeared to communicate, no words passed between them. She sensed from his taut body and set jaw that the dark-haired one was agitated about something. He glanced over at Viper, who nodded almost imperceptibly.

"That's Dantalyon," said Phelan, apparently in awe. Jamie glanced at him and realized that he was completely infatuated. His eyes followed Dantalyon like those of a puppy hoping for a crumb from its master's dinner. Then Phelan turned his attention back to Jamie. Quite simply, he said, "We're vampires. You know what that is, don't you?"

Jamie didn't quite know how to respond. Any number of people whom she'd met over the past two days could have said the same thing. All of them wanted her—or anyone—to believe that. Yet there was some-

thing about Phelan's expression, and about the composition of this group, that made her think that she'd
come among creatures that really did thrive on blood
and cleave to the night. They'd left her alone all day,
so maybe they slept in coffins somewhere inside this
underground crypt.

Carefully, she said, "I've met a few vampires in the
clubs. Is that what you mean?"

Phelan drew his eyebrows together as if puzzled by
her response. "You think I'm like them?"

Jamie suddenly thought she'd hurt his feelings. Her
intent had been to see how he'd react. She'd not expected such simplicity.

"No, I . . . you're not like them."

Phelan tilted his head as if trying to read her mind.
"Are you really afraid of snakes?"

Jamie was so struck at the absurdity of this question
that she nearly laughed. It was the query of a boy she
might encounter in a field who had one in his pocket.

"We've learned so much from them," Phelan continued. He pointed at Viper. "He harvests venom and
sells it to researchers, but he tells us what snakes can
do. He also makes antivenom, so if you get bitten, it'll
be okay."

Jamie's mouth dropped open. She couldn't believe
what he'd just said, but he continued: "Most people
don't understand snakes, but they can be helpful. The
devil was a snake, and some religions think they're evil,
but Moses used one to heal people, and Jesus even referred to that to explain who he was—that if they looked
on him as they looked on the snake of Moses, they'd
have eternal life. Did you know that? That's just like
us!"

Jamie looked around. She could not imagine why
they were having this conversation. Finally she said,
"No, I didn't know that."

"And the Egyptian goddesses held snakes to prove their power over life. In ancient Egypt, there's a story about how a snake tried to keep the sun god from bringing daylight to the world—so that's like us, too—but the priests chanted over a wax snake and cast it into a fire. That way they ensured that the sun would rise, and they made the snake into a symbol of resurrection. Then when someone died, they'd write out a text about the way snakes shed skin and get new life, and they put it into the corpse's mouth. That was supposed to help with the afterlife. So do you see why we have them around?"

"Well, that's very interesting," said Jamie, aware now that she had to treat this one as she'd treat Devon, "but it won't make me less afraid. I don't want to get bitten or be around them. I need to get out of here."

Phelan looked over at Naje and then back at Jamie. "Maybe I could take you to another room," he suggested.

Jamie brightened. Suddenly there was hope. She felt sure she could persuade this boyish monster to take her to Devon. At the very least, if she got out into the hallway, she might be able to escape from him. He seemed almost too simple to suspect treachery on her part.

But just as she thought it, he smiled. "No, I can't do that," he said.

Jamie slumped in disappointment. She had to be more careful. These creatures had abilities at which she couldn't even guess.

The door opened again and a young girl rushed in. Her hair was short and almost as white as Naje's, although it had a yellowish sheen. She glanced over at Jamie but went right to the computer. She had a cell phone in her hand, which she handed to the leader.

"It's Stiletto," she said. "They've had some trouble. He says he couldn't get your attention."

Next to Jamie, Phelan perked up. He turned halfway around to listen. Even the tiny Asian woman sat up with a look of concerned interest on her face. The snake adjusted itself on her shoulders for a better perch.

Naje listened for a moment and then said, "If there's a way out, he'll find it. Stay close if you can. I'll locate him."

He turned off the phone and told the others that Christian had been captured.

"Captured," the blond girl said. "By whom?"

"By humans."

"Christian? No way. He'd never let them close."

"He did, and now he's gone."

"Why can't they get through?" the Asian woman asked. "I can't connect to them, either. There's something in the way."

The blond turned. "Lethe, can you get Christian?"

"No. None of them."

Naje didn't respond, but Eryx looked over at the woman called Lethe. Something passed between them that seemed to alarm her. Phelan caught it, too, and he appeared to be worried.

Naje looked at Viper and said, "Let's get her ready." Jamie knew he meant her. Then he left the room.

Thirteen

Christian

I remained alert throughout the ride. Feeling the way the van was managed from one turn to the next, I weened that I'd been taken out of Manhattan into north Jersey. That was good, because when I got away, I'd be closer to home. I hadn't heard a thing from Stiletto or Lachesis for nearly twenty minutes and I thought they must be reporting all of this to Naje. I wasn't sure what he could do, but he wouldn't just sit still. We were all entwined with him; that was the whole point of the *kamera*. Depending on what these people did, my capture could mean nearly as much danger to him as to me.

The knowledge that they had Ana, and that she had something that we needed, gave me a way to plan my reaction once we stopped. If I could get past these temps, I could at least locate where Ana was being kept. I tried working my way out of the net but couldn't get through both layers. I'd seen snake traps before, and it was clear to me that these temps had some idea what they were dealing with. The collar itself was going to be a serious problem. Like any snake caught by the neck, I was rendered helpless to whomever controlled the cord—as long as they kept their distance.

The van was warm inside, which felt good. Still, it made me a bit lethargic and I had to fight to keep focused. Had they turned on the AC, my mind would have been much sharper. Perhaps that was the point. They wanted me weak.

I sensed a communication coming through and wondered if it might be Bel. Surely she knew by now what had happened. From Naje we'd learned how the subconscious can snake out as an *aka* body through an invisible cord and fasten onto another person. That strengthens the concentration and provides an energy conduit. You send instructions along it and the *aka* body finds the information you seek or makes mental communication possible.

I opened my mind to it and was astonished to realize that it wasn't Bel at all. It was Naje. He sent an enveloping reassurance that I was linked to him and that he'd remain aware, through me, of my situation. Just to have this merging with him was worth whatever price I was about to pay for my naive lapse in judgment. I dilated my receptor sites to give him as much room as he needed for weening my surroundings. I loved the feel of him blending his energy with mine. My entire being expanded until I imagined myself huge and invincible, like Gulliver being desperately tethered in vain by the silly Lilliputians.

Then the van slowed down, made a few turns that jostled me away from these spiritual levels, and seemed to pull into a building. The echoes of an engine inside walls and the smell of trapped exhaust alerted me to the fact that we'd arrived. The car lights went out and the engine was cut. In a matter of moments, the double doors slid open and I was dragged out into a dimly lit garage. I tried to pay attention, both with my physical senses and with Naje's awareness, but still could not tell precisely where I was.

"Good work," I heard from somewhere in a darkened room. It was a female's voice, deep and hoarse from years of smoking. She shone a light into my eyes, which hurt me and prevented me from seeing her. "Oh, he's a pretty one," she said with some sarcasm. "Poisonous, too, I'll bet. Bind him up tight. This one can slither out of almost anything. Make sure he doesn't."

That alarmed me. That meant that they not only knew what a *kamera* was and which one I was part of, but more specifically what my own abilities were. How could they know me? Had Ana told them? I'd shown her once on the walls back home that were specially made for me to practice. Or were these temps so adept they'd learned to read memory fields as we did?

Needless to say, I was tied up tight with many types of bindings, from handcuffs (which I could easily slip) to nylon rope to elastic cords. Then I was strapped onto a gurney type of bed, with my head resting against cold steel. The net was thrown over me and tied beneath the bed. They moved me from the garage into a darkened building, and after going down a hallway, they shoved me into a small room that smelled so strongly of turpentine that it clogged my sensors. Two males stayed to guard me while the rest went out and closed the door.

I lay there for some time, trying to ween the atmosphere. I sensed Naje working through me, but there were gaps, too, as if his attention was taken elsewhere. Each time that happened I felt disturbingly alone. From the building itself, I did pick up clear signals that there were a number of people not far away, all of them mortal and all with a shared purpose. It was almost like the cult meetings of the vampyre club's "inner circles," although I didn't hear any chanting. I hoped I wasn't being prepared for some sort of sacrifice. As I lay there in the dark, it certainly seemed that way. Although Naje seemed to be gone, I fed whatever images, sounds, and smells I could get past the thick turpentine vapors through my receptor cells.

Then a light went on in the hallway. I saw it under the door and sensed that someone was about to enter. The doorknob turned and three rather large men came in. They flicked on a bright overhead light, which blinded me, and came over to where I lay bound. But they didn't untie me. Instead two of them wheeled the gurney out the door and down the hall. Since it was futile to struggle, I lay still. I needed my resources for the right moment, and I felt sure that Naje would be with me then. I sensed from him that I was to be quiet and observe everything.

The men took me into a large room, dark except for a few lamps along the walls, where I discerned the presence of at least a dozen people, both male and female. It took all of my powers of awareness to make a fair count. Most of them came across as rather young, but there were elders among them in their forties and fifties. I couldn't see much through the thick netting but I smelled incense, chemicals, and blood. I opened my mouth a little to take in more through my sensors. We have tremendous feeling in our mouths and can distinguish the many temps that we encounter according to their different energy signatures. Generally that's so we can find the best meal, but in this case it helped me get my bearings. If these people were really focused and intense, that would be worse for me than if they had only a vague idea about what they were doing.

It wasn't long before I realized that the room was a mix of many different motives for being there. Some were followers, others leaders; a few had secret doubts, and the leaders had a keen plan. In fact, whatever they were doing, they'd been revising and polishing their idea for some time. I sensed that they believed they needed a vampire for it to work and I was the first one they'd caught. Yet they'd known I was coming. They'd been prepared. I didn't understand how that was possible.

Then I paused. Something familiar came though my receptors. I made my breathing shallow to achieve better focus. There was someone here whom I knew. Someone close by, but not another vampire. Ana? I opened my mouth a little and stuck my tongue through an opening in the net. Naje was with me and he affirmed that, yes, Ana's energy was clear to him. She was somewhere nearby. He urged me to be prepared for anything, and to be careful.

Well, I thought I was doing just that. When four men approached me, I believed they were going to untie me and hold me down or move me to another location. I didn't expect what they ended up doing: one of them cut through the net around my face and another clamped his large hands around my head. Good Lord, I'd seen Viper do this so many times with snakes I don't know why I hadn't anticipated it.

Yet even if I had, I couldn't have fought them any more than a cobra can defy the venom harvesters. They meant to have my venin.

I panicked. I thrashed around to keep them away from my mouth. I sent out distress signals to Naje and Bel, begging for whatever aid they could give from a distance. For that, I received a surprising surge of strength and managed to throw myself off the table, but it didn't work. They had power in numbers. In an instant, men were on every side of me, holding my chest, arms and legs, gripping me so tight it hurt even my toughened vampire skin. Finally I had to give up.

Again, my head was held firmly and some device was thrust into my mouth to force it open. I cried out and retracted my fangs as deeply as they would go into their normal grooves, but these people had thought of that.

They had a pair of fine tweezers that they used to pry my sharpened teeth out. I thought that surely they'd break my left fang, so I had to relax and let them do what they intended. I could replace it, I knew, and had before whenever my fangs got worn down, but it would take time.

Another man held a tube covered with a thin membrane against my right fang and shoved it so hard that the tooth pierced through. I breathed hard to prevent any leakage and tried using my mental control to foil his purpose. He then used his thumb to squeeze against the sac where my juices were stored, awaiting transfer into a victim. Despite my best efforts, I felt it release and the fluid ran through the hollow canal inside my fang. Soon the tinkle of liquid in glass told me they'd gotten their treasure. The man removed the tube and held the amber juice up to the light. The group cried out in triumph.

He then went around to my other side. I tried resisting again, but the others held me fast. The harvester ripped the net further and managed to milk my other fang as well, though there was less venin available. I'd spit the rest out at my captors back at the house where I was captured. As awful as this felt to me, I fought to keep my wits. They'd taken my treasure, but there might still be a way to gain my freedom.

Then I had an idea that I'd learned from the Australian death adder. I relaxed my limbs and feigned unconsciousness to give them the impression that they'd seriously weakened me. I worked to still my breathing, change my skin color, and make it look as if I were near death. Naje, who kept a clear awareness of the entire situation, guided me in this. He slowed my heartbeat and drained some heat. Yet even as I withdrew into my cold body, I knew I had a more complicated task. Now I needed to get away and also get that venin back.

It wasn't that they'd taken something irreplaceable. We regenerate that substance after each encounter with prey, but it wasn't good to have it in human hands. People couldn't handle its effect.

There was one other time that a vampire from our *kamera* had been caught, somewhere on one of the Polynesian islands, but it was a low-level creature with only slightly potent venin. He hadn't even known much about the levels of the soul. We were one of the few strains of vampire, to even produce venin, and it didn't poison. Instead it produced total relaxation and euphoria, which made it easier for us to manipulate the memory fields. In the case of the vampire who'd been caught, the result was a synthetic drug manufactured from its chemical composition, and kids all over the country know it as E or Ecstasy. In fact—and quite ironically—in the vampire clubs, it's the drug of choice. Whoever had patented it had become quite wealthy, and we were aware that if the secret ever got out, others would hunt us down . . . which was exactly what had just happened. Lachesis had warned us about Allan Coyne's ambitions, and now I put it all together. Yet I didn't sense him anywhere nearby.

We didn't much care that it had gotten into the hands of a drug manufacturer, and in fact the Ecstasy product had given them the false idea that vampire juice wasn't really very potent. It's like saying that the devil is a horned creature with a tail and pitchfork. It draws focus away from the real thing. However, now that they had this venin from me, they would find out different. Our juice develops increasing potency with our spiritual accomplishments. That means that anyone with the wherewithal to replicate the chemical formula of the stuff they'd just removed from me would have the world at his feet—literally—as long as they didn't take it themselves. A significant amount of this drug could obliterate the self and dissolve all ambition. Those who experienced it in even the minute amount we inject for the trance drowned in the most undiluted reverie.

What they'd just taken from me was worth its weight in the precious substances, and then some. Yet handled badly it could send a recipient into a potent psychosis and a torturous death.

I had to get it back.

Once the men who'd handled me had what they wanted, they let me go. Suddenly I was no longer their primary focus, and they clearly thought I was out of it for a moment. They walked away to the center of the room and I took that opportunity as I lay on the floor in the deepest shadows to strengthen my link with Naje. What I was about to do would be touch and go, and I'd have to rely on his "eyes" and energy to make it work.

Now, I mentally told him on the *aka* thread. *Give me your spirit.*

As I began to squeeze and collapse my bones to loosen the bonds, I felt the dimming of my own life force. I grew increasingly colder and my heart began to beat with a leaden *thump . . . thump.* I was risking obliteration, but with Naje's help, I could escape and survive.

The cult gathered around the harvesters somewhere apart from me, and several of them shouted. I knew they were preparing for something, and I had little time to make my move. I continued to condense myself to the point of being unable to breathe, and I felt the ropes around my flexible ribs loosen. I wouldn't be able to get out of the leather choker, but I managed to slip my hands from the ropes and cuffs. The hole they'd cut into the net was at my head, so that made things easier. I worked the muscles in my back into a rhythm of pulling and pushing, just like a rattlesnake on roughened rocks, until they worked my body along the floor toward even deeper shadows. I was compact enough now to slide out of my bonds and through the hole in the net. I had to hope that no one would notice, so I kept it as quiet as possible.

I wanted desperately to breathe, but if I did it would expand my chest. I had to trust in Naje's ability to carry my spirit with his own. In a way, I was killing myself by placing my life force on hold to return it into my body when my physical form was safely in position to receive it. I'd been through many close calls, but this one really demanded my greatest skill.

I was now halfway out of the net but I was nearly unconscious. I had to work faster. I felt the urgency from Naje. I didn't know how long he could hold up, especially given the pressures of our situation back home and the impending force of destruction. I wasn't sure if Dantalyon had brought him the sustenance he needed for the night, so I didn't know how much I was taxing his strength with this maneuver. Yet it was my only way out. If they caught me, they'd bind me and cage me much more forcefully, I was sure. There wouldn't be a second chance.

Naje sent me a distress signal. Something was happening there as well. I had to move more quickly. He couldn't keep the connection much longer.

I was nearly out of the net, and most of the ropes were down near my knees. I let my chest expand again but tried not to breathe yet.

"Hey!" A man stood over me and flashed a light on me. "He's getting out!"

He reached for me and caught my leg as I freed it from the net, but he thought he had a solid grip. He didn't. I slid right through, gasped in a deep breath to get my form back, and crouched onto my feet. I was wobbly but had my wits about me. Naje was still with me.

I heard the footsteps of several men, and my venin

sacs were empty, so there was no other defense than to cleave to the shadows and disappear. That was my best trick.

Naje let go, leaving me on my own, and I felt terribly weak but still able to run. Then came another infusion into my brain and I knew that Bel was helping. She couldn't carry me as Naje did, but she could give me a little more strength in my postconstriction stupor. I silently thanked her and shot toward the darkest corner.

The lights went on as the room broke out in pandemonium, but I was already scooting up the wall, finding tiny nicks and abrasions for getting a grip, and into an area yards away from where they expected to see me. I continued to move fast. I was thankful the ceilings were bare of plaster, and I got a grip on one of the wooden rafters. Moving along it over their heads, I made sure they never heard or saw me. I might not find a quick escape hole, but I believed I could hide in the room without detection until they gave up the chase.

I found a dark corner behind some crates on a shelf some ten feet over their heads to rest and gather my strength. They couldn't see me but I could easily watch them from this perch. The combination of losing my juice and having to call on this vampire's trick of near-total bodily collapse had taken its toll. I couldn't really go any farther for the moment. I had to replenish.

Then I received a mandate. I stilled myself to listen. I couldn't believe what he was asking, but then I recalled what Lachesis had said. *Ana has something we need.* That could only mean one thing. For whatever reason, they couldn't use Jamie. Ana was now our only hope.

That meant that I had to recover as quickly as possible and find a place from which to watch for my chance. Ana was here, somewhere close by, and Naje wanted me to find her, rescue her, and bring her back.

Fourteen

Jamie

Dantalyon, too, went out, casting another fierce look at Jamie as if to let her know that she was nothing more than a worm. She sensed that there was some kind of emergency and she hoped that meant a distraction that could work to her advantage. If she could just remember the way back to the room where she'd seen Devon—if he was even still there—she felt sure she could find a place to hide until daylight, and then get out. That is, if they didn't just kill her to keep her from doing anything.

"Take her across the hall," Viper instructed. "I'll get things ready, but I don't want her in here."

The Asian woman, Lethe, came over to unstrap Jamie from the chair and then gestured for her to get up. Phelan watched this from a few feet away, offering an encouraging smile.

"What do you want from me?" Jamie asked again. "Why won't you tell me?"

"Just get up," Lethe instructed. "We're going across the hall."

Then from the other side of the room, Viper looked up from his microscope and said, "Wait."

Jamie caught her breath as he strode toward her. She didn't want him touching her and she prepared to flee, but Lethe's cold grip on her arm told her there was no place she could go. She stood her ground as he approached, but her insides melted.

He grabbed her around the shoulders with both hands and she gasped and tried to back away from him. His reptilian eyes bore into her as if he were taking her measure from the inside out, and up this close she could see that his skin had a rough texture unlike anything human. His mouth opened slightly and she spotted a pair of thin canine teeth that looked like they could pierce metal. For a moment, she thought he was going to pull her close and bite into her.

"Don't," she tried to say as she struggled to keep him away, but no sound came out of her. To her relief, he didn't come any closer.

"Are you Ana's *identical* twin?" he asked. His voice was thick, as if his tongue no longer functioned as a human's. She imagined it was thin and forked, like that of a rattler. He seemed disturbed about something, and impatient.

"Y-yes," she said with a stutter.

She saw Eryx watching her from his seat at the computer and felt that something was amiss with whatever plan they'd had for her. He'd asked her the same thing earlier that evening, and now it was obvious that something was utterly important to them about her kinship with Gail. She hoped her value wasn't diminishing.

The snake let her go but stood staring at her. He seemed to be pondering something. Then he turned away and shook his head. Eryx watched him go back into the heart of the lab and then looked back at her. He nodded to Lethe to continue and told the blond girl, whom he called Bel, to go with them.

"What's wrong?" Lethe asked.

"We just can't get the same calibrations."

Lethe turned Jamie around and guided her toward

the door, which Bel opened. They obviously had something in mind for her, and the idea started to work her into a panic. If Devon had not been there, she would have run, no matter what the cost. She hated that no one was telling her what was in store. It was clear from the group's demeanor that they were looking to her for something and that she had not delivered as they'd hoped.

Lethe took the lead, and Phelan and Bel came behind her. Phelan tried to help her walk through the serpentarium without fear, but his power was not as great as Naje's. Only the knowledge that the hallway on the other side was free of snakes—at least of so many— gave her the courage to get across.

Lethe opened the door to the next room, and Jamie saw at once, although the room was dim, that this was part of the laboratory, too. There was something that looked like a massage table off to one side and several steel gurneys that made the space look like an autopsy suite. Jars of tissues and organs lined the walls, and the room smelled of formaldehyde. Several lamps shed light, but there were clearly a number of powerful lights that could be used for purposes that Jamie did not want to ponder.

Lethe instructed her to lie on the padded table. Jamie did so and felt straps go around her chest, waist, and hips. Then Lethe tied her hands down. She was about to draw a strap over Jamie's neck when Phelan stopped her.

"Don't," he said. "There's no need for that. He doesn't want her tied up."

Lethe looked at Bel, who just shrugged. "It doesn't matter," Bel said. "She's not going anywhere."

"I'll get the snake," Lethe said.

Jamie's heart started to pound. What snake? What was this "preparation" that Naje had mentioned?

Lethe left the room, giving Jamie a few torturous minutes to imagine what was about to happen. Phelan touched her hand and smiled slightly. She couldn't figure out if he was truly compassionate or a deceptive little imp who wanted to keep her off her guard to feed some sadistic pleasure.

The door opened across the room and Jamie felt the change in atmosphere that she had come to associate with Naje. Despite the sinister nature of his altered existence, she felt better when he was there. She looked over and watched him come toward her. For once, he did not have his warrior shadow hanging about, and that made her feel somewhat safer. She could imagine that, had Dantalyon gotten the chance, he'd have plunged a knife straight into her heart.

"I'm cold," she whispered to Naje. In a moment, she felt a strange but pleasurable warmth flow through her body. He had a small pillow in his hand and he placed it under Jamie's head. Then he touched her face, and to her surprise, her body responded with rising excitement. She wanted more. She could not imagine what it would be like to have Naje's daily attention, to make love with him, or even just to sleep next to him. But she desperately wanted to.

Naje looked at Jamie with what seemed compassion, touched her hand, and appeared to finally be prepared to offer some explanation for why they had her here. She waited. A thousand questions demanded to be asked, but she sensed that silence was best. This one clearly did things in his own time and would not be pushed. Even to explain anything to her would serve his purposes, not hers.

"I'm sorry for any discomfort you've suffered," he began, "but we have need of you. There's an infection in our family that's wiping us out, and we're seeking ways to end it."

"Your family?" This statement surprised her. She couldn't imagine what he meant. He merely nodded, and something was conveyed to her that he had feelings similar to hers for Devon.

As he spoke, Jamie felt the vibrations of his deep voice go straight to her loins. She struggled against the effect, but the intense pleasure was such a contrast to everything else she'd experienced that she ultimately gave in. She allowed herself to fall into Naje's mysterious obsidian eyes.

"We experimented with several different . . . subjects," he continued, "and didn't always succeed. Eventually we found a way to accomplish what we need through a specific pattern of human DNA. Do you understand me?"

Jamie shook her head.

"You know biology," he said. "I can read that from you. Before I tell you what we're going to do, let me assure you that you'll experience no pain."

Jamie breathed deeply, feeling herself become more fully immersed in that soft and confident voice, as if she were sitting in a tub with the level of warm, gurgling water rising around her. She felt Naje's hand on her waist, oddly warm now, and she wanted him to touch her more intimately. It didn't matter that the others were watching. All that mattered was this overwhelming sensation of fluidity.

"We make a substance with our bodies that acts like the injection of a drug," Naje said. "It fits the brain's M-4 nerve cell receptors, which control pain. You really won't feel a thing."

"What are you going to do?" Jamie whispered.

He didn't answer. He just continued to look at her and she felt him penetrate her as if he were on top of her in bed. She gasped and tried to raise her legs, but the straps held her down. His lips never moved, but she

heard him say, "You like that, don't you?" All she could
do was nod.

"We need to readjust our energy patterns," Naje said,
"so we can transform ourselves."

Jamie tried hard to have a conversation with him, but
all she could manage was a brief question: "How?"

He smiled and she felt the love of a father for his
favorite child. "You'll help us."

She said nothing. She only wished he'd continue to
look at her, caress her, and talk to her. Nothing else was
real to her in that delicate moment. She smelled something good, something male and exotic, that had the
fragrance of freshly ground hazelnuts. Her skin began
to tingle, and something slightly sweet spread across her
tongue. She licked her lips and nodded, as if to say, of
course she'd help. She'd do anything he asked, just
keep touching her.

"We have one among us who's managed to change
his chemical structure," Naje explained. "So we have a
model. He did it with snakes, but we need to do it
through a mortal. The one pattern we were able to work
with was Ana's. Gail's. She was willing to help and was
just about to do that when she disappeared."

"Gail?" Jamie hardly even knew what she was saying.

"We know that you share the same DNA with her but
not her same desires. More important, you're a mother,
so you may have reason to resist."

Jamie was astonished at the implication. "Ana wanted
to die?"

Naje shook his head, and a long strand of silvery hair
came over his shoulder. "Not die, although she would
have risked that. She wanted something else. With her,
we'd have changed our own biological map and she'd
have changed hers as well. She'd have gained a more
magnified existence and a way to climb into another
level of her soul. It's what she wanted."

"Why would she?"

"Her reasons were . . . complex."

"She'd be one of you, a vampire?"

Naje didn't answer. Despite her erotic immersion, Jamie began to understand that what they wanted from her would alter her life forever. "What are you going to do?" she asked again.

"We'll put you into a chamber that will cool your blood until it calibrates to the right temperature for me to merge with it. Then I can make it work for my family. It's something like a transfusion, but its more generative than that."

"How does it work?"

"Jamie, we have little time left. I can't ask you if you'd be willing. We just need to go forward."

"You did this with Ana?"

Naje shook his head. "No. We did it theoretically, and initially it was for a different purpose. This procedure is a little different, but we've looked at all the variables and we think it will work. Everything is ready."

Jamie understood. They didn't know the real risks; they were just guessing. Her stomach lurched and she could see that Naje was aware of her fear, and sympathetic. "What about Devon?" she asked.

"He's fine. He'll remain fine as long as you cooperate."

Jamie blinked through her confusion. This creature was telling her that her son might get hurt, even killed, if she resisted, and at the same time he was seducing her. The net effect, oddly, was to diminish her concern. She loved her son, but she was also growing obsessed with this man. She wanted to give him whatever he needed in the hope that he'd feed this craving in her belly. She needed him to take her away, be alone with her, and fill her up. Looking into his eyes, Jamie knew he was fully aware of what she was feeling. It was like a physician watching a patient succumb to the effects of anesthesia. Soon there would be—*could* be—no resistance.

"I can't die," she whispered. "I need to be with my son." Then she gathered her energy and cried out, "Please don't kill me!"

"I want to teach you to breathe," he said. "You'll need to know how. It'll help you. It brings your three minds together so the subconscious can use the energy. That was the *mana,* the sustenance." As he spoke, his voice was deep and even. It massaged her with gentle pressure in the most sensitive places. "If you learn to breathe properly, you'll increase the amount that's available. You take a breath as deeply as you possibly can and hold it. The energy permeates your body and goes to where you need the most healing. You don't think, because that depletes the energy. You just pull it in and surrender to the *manaloa.*"

He was right; it did feel good. As she followed his instruction, it felt like helium filling her up and making her light. Then she felt herself sink into the warm undulation of a dream state. The vampire was with her. Everything was good. She had exactly what she wanted. Everything was ready. She was ready. Whatever he wanted.

It was the sound of an opening door that woke her. The woman named Lethe came in and in her arms was a large brown snake. Jamie stared at it and wished fervently that she'd tried to flee when she was between rooms. She did not want that thing anywhere near her. Lethe placed the reptile on a shelf not far from Jamie and then said, "As long as you lie still, he won't do anything. He'll just lie there. But try to move and he'll strike." Then she smiled. "Just keep breathing," she said, and walked out, leaving Jamie alone.

She was groggy, but surprised that no one was in the room guarding her. It occurred to her that she'd dreamed the entire scenario with Naje, and she tried to recall the details. Something about DNA and transformation. Some impression of the way he'd touched her. She had no idea how much time had passed.

Jamie watched the snake adjust itself to its uncomfortable bed. Its small eyes stayed on her as if waiting for some signal—any signal—to strike. She couldn't believe they had left a snake so close to her, and she wondered if it might really hurt her. She knew nothing about these legless lizards, so anything she tried might backfire. Yet she couldn't just lie here and do nothing.

Thinking hard, Jamie pushed a little against the straps that bound her and wondered what was happening across the hall. She wanted to know what they were doing with Devon. Having time alone at last, she felt the urge to just let go and cry. The situation seemed utterly hopeless. Her only source of consolation was the idea that Allan had not abandoned her. He'd seen with his own eyes that she'd been abducted and he had every reason to find her. After all, he'd led her into this thing. It was his fault. But could he find the place where she'd been taken? They'd gone in a car at high speed out into the country. What chance did he really have?

She lay there for some time, processing the same thoughts and fears and finding no answers. For a few moments she indulged in a fantasy about Naje, but then felt guilty. It was her duty as a mother to figure a way out. She'd already been here a full day and several hours into this night. She'd been put under so often she had no idea what time it could possibly be. Maybe when the sun came up, maybe then she'd have a chance. But they'd put her out the morning before;

they'd probably just do the same thing again. Whatever plan she made, she'd have to do so while she was still conscious here in this room.

The door opened and the snake rose slowly up. Jamie held her breath, keeping as still as possible so as not to provoke her dubious guardian to attack her. She saw a silhouette, followed by another, and then a dim light came on overhead.

Viper had a syringe in his hand. He came over to her, oblivious to the snake's hissing. He reached over and used his thumb to rub its throat. Eryx moved her sleeve and tied a stretchy rubber tube over the crook of her arm. He avoided looking at her eyes. Viper turned back to her, tapped the swollen vein, and stuck a needled syringe into it. She jumped at the sharp pinch and the snake jerked its head back. Viper looked at her as if annoyed. Red liquid flowed into the syringe.

"There's something different about you," he explained. "You're not exactly like your sister, and we need to find out how that will affect what we're doing."

Jamie tried to breathe evenly, searching his eyes for some flicker of compassion. "Can't you take this snake away?" she begged.

Viper smiled. "Just lie still," he said. "Snakes don't attack unless provoked. We'll be back soon."

Then he and Eryx left, and the "guard" settled back onto its perch.

It seemed like only moments had passed when the door opened once again. Jamie's stomach jumped. She wasn't ready for this, whatever it was. Yet to her surprise, this time there was no response from the snake. She looked at the form of the man who came in and knew it wasn't one of the vampires.

He placed a finger against his lips to urge her to be quiet. She peered at him more closely in the dim light and realized it was Allan. Her mouth opened in aston-

ishment, but she remained quiet. How he'd managed
to just come in through a door that was right across the
hall from where the vampires were at work—from
where they could emerge at any moment—mystified
her, but she was utterly relieved to see him. He lifted a
short pole from which dangled something that looked
like a leather loop. Jamie had no idea what it was, but
he aimed it at the snake.

She couldn't imagine what he thought he was doing.
It was too dark to try to catch the thing, let alone slip
a rope over it, but he continued to hang it over the
snake's head. It held still for several moments, making
no sound, but its large body registered its watchful pose.
Then without warning it struck at the leather and Allan
moved just as fast to grab it by the tail.

The snake's head swung around, just grazing Jamie's
arm, and she jumped at the feel of its scaly skin. She
thought it would surely bite her. Yet Allan snapped the
tail and forced its head away from the bed. The snake
went after him, but he danced out of harm's way. Clearly
he'd handled snakes before. While it hissed and struck,
he got leverage with the pole and slipped the leather
loop around the snake's head. Its entire body writhed
in reaction, but he had it fast. This thing was not going
to escape, not unless he lost his grip on the pole.

Jamie watched him lower the snake until its body
touched the floor. It undulated again, and he placed
the head down onto the floor, held it with the pole,
and reached into his back pocket. What he had wasn't
clear, but he bent toward the floor and made a quick
motion with his arm. The sound of something slicing
through a solid and wet substance told Jamie that Allan
had a knife and he was using it to cut off the serpent's
head. She waited until he was finished, as grateful to
have the thing dead as to be rescued.

Allan held up the decapitated body and flung it into

a corner. Then he came to cut through Jamie's bindings. She smelled the sweat on him and realized that he'd been more nervous about what he'd just done than he'd seemed.

"Thank you," she breathed out. "Thank you so much."

"Sshh," he whispered. "We're not out of here yet."

He helped her to sit, removed the straps from her legs, and urged her to stand. "Come on," he said. "I know the way out." He made his way toward the door, but Jamie grabbed him to stop him.

"Not that way!" she insisted. "They're out there. They'll see us."

"They're busy," he said. "Besides, I have protection, but only for so long. We have to move quickly. Just stay close to me. I know how to get out without their seeing us."

Jamie stepped gingerly around the mess on the floor where the snake's head still lay and joined Allan. He opened the door and they slipped together into the hall.

Fifteen

Christian

I remained still in a dark corner and watched them search for me. I'd left behind a secretion from my skin—a scent plume—that would throw them off my trail and send them in the wrong direction. It was so distinct they wouldn't miss it, although they wouldn't realize that a scent was drawing them. Then I climbed fast to a dark place up about fourteen feet, from which I had a good vantage point to see, listen, and absorb the chemical array of impressions that guided me more surely than sight. I found a way to blend in with the walls so they couldn't see me and then opened my mouth slightly to allow the air currents to inform me. While kinesthetic clues are best, I was too far from the scene for these to be much value. I had to take what I could get.

I counted thirteen people, and from that I thought they must be adhering to some superstition. Significantly, there were no vampires among them, nor had any been in this building, but I weened that these temps clearly knew that Real Ones existed. Since most of them were dressed in dark clothing, I figured they'd formed some sort of religious cult. I wondered if these were the "others" that Naje had thwarted when he'd had us grab Jamie. I hadn't really heard those details. If he knew about them and even tracked their movements, that meant they were more than a silly band of humans with big ideas, but were actually a threat.

What they would now do with my vampire juice I had no idea, but if I could I meant to get it back. To me, that was just as important as finding Ana. She was our *kamera*'s salvation, I knew, yet retrieving the substance from which a potent—even toxic—mind-altering drug could be manufactured had larger issues for us all, including temps. They really had no idea what they'd stolen, even if they had an inkling of how it could be used.

After observing them for a few minutes, I pinpointed a leader among them, a woman. She was tall, around five-foot-nine, with small breasts, a thin waist, and narrow hips. Her black hair was braided in multiple layers of thin plaits, and she wore a silver lace headpiece encrusted with deep red garnets that looked like a skullcap. She also wore several layers of necklaces and a number of rings. I could see that she'd spent a long time on her facial paint, especially the intricate Egyptian swirls around her eyes that ran to her ears and down her jaw, and her figure-hugging dress was a cotton-knit weave of black, silver, and royal purple. Around her throat above the necklaces was a beaded black choker an inch wide, with a silver symbol on the front that, try as I might, I couldn't make out. It appeared to be in the shape of some animal. It was this woman who directed the search for me, sending her people with harsh commands over to this corner and then that one, and she grew increasingly frustrated when no one could find me. She smacked one guy hard with a flat leather paddle. Although he was much larger than she was, he cowered. From that I guessed that he thought she had fearsome powers.

"He can't have gotten far," she thundered in a voice

that reverberated with a depth that spoke of the fourth decade of life. "It's just some trick. Keep looking!"

Her lackeys scoured the room, nowhere near where I'd found an effective hiding place. I counted three females and nine males, all in their early to late twenties. Although they wore loose black garments, I estimated that they were in good athletic shape. Several were bald, but the others wore their hair in some ornamental fashion, either braided or tied with silver chains. The females seemed fairly ordinary in contrast to the males, who struck me as the type of guys who become models or Broadway dancers. Those who weren't bald had died their hair red or black.

They did catch the deflection scent that I'd left but couldn't track me. I watched in amusement as they discovered places in which they felt sure I'd hidden myself, and after about twenty minutes they had to report to their mistress that they'd failed. I drank in the heat of their anger from the air currents, using it to restore some of my energy. I heard one of them call the woman Sabbatina, and I almost laughed out loud. Had she really adopted a name like that? How kitschy, in a Goth sort of way. She was furious with this little wart, and issued further heated instructions. Losing the vampire was unacceptable, obviously, but another matter also seemed to needle her.

In exasperation, Sabbatina finally said, "It doesn't matter. Once the Dahaka is here, he'll show us where this creature is. Nothing can hide from him."

I inched forward and strained to hear. The Dahaka? What was that? And how could it penetrate my defense?

Again I probed for some connection with Naje but couldn't grasp him. I hoped he hadn't just withdrawn and left me here. I had a feeling I was going to need everything he could give me. I tried probing for anyone else, especially Bel, but couldn't get them. That meant something serious was happening that I couldn't ween. I didn't want to think about what that might mean.

I still felt an ache throughout my chest from constricting myself to such an extent, and my heart was pounding wildly as it worked to restore my processes to their normal functions. It would be better if I could just go crawl away for a while to recover, but there was no time. I sensed that I needed to finish my business here as fast as possible.

Then I saw Sabbatina pick up the vial of amber liquid that they'd taken from me and set it up in a test tube rack on a clean steel table. She switched on an overhead light that directed its narrow beam straight down. I was tempted to leap out of my dark cubbyhole, grab the vial, and run, but Naje had insisted that Ana was my priority. I had to bide my time until I saw her. In the meantime they might withdraw just the slightest amount of liquid to preserve. That meant that even if I managed to get the vial, they'd have what they needed to re-create the product. Anyone with access to a polymerase chain-reaction device could replicate the DNA molecules many thousands of times. I guessed they understood what an opportunity they had here, but I didn't yet realize that their ambitions went far beyond material gain. For this group, something much larger was at stake.

As I crouched on my perch, I saw them wheel in an unconscious girl strapped onto a padded steel gurney, and despite the black hair, I weened at once that it was Ana. She wasn't drugged with some chemical but entranced in the superficial stupor that some humans can produce with hypnosis. It wouldn't last long, but apparently they didn't care. They merely wanted her under control.

I watched as they placed her in a specific spot under the intense beam of light and tied her more securely in place. She moaned a little as if regaining awareness but then dropped back into her dopey state.

The tall woman picked up the vial of my substance and poured it into a small beaker. Then she stuck a syringe into the liquid and pulled back the stopper. I could almost feel the hot juice flowing up the needle's throat, and I felt angry again that she'd violated me.

Gradually I began to form an impression of what they were doing. While we experimented with Jamie for our own purposes, her twin was about to undergo something similar but possibly far worse. This substance that we manufacture is a threshold for ecstatic experience, but it must be doled out in measured portions. Our fangs are equipped for that; we know what our quarry can endure and just how much will produce euphoria. Even a measure more will erupt in the most ungodly psychosis. I felt sure this woman had no clue how much was too much.

The reason it's so powerful is because it works with the brain's serotonin neurotransmitter, which derives its very name from the Latin words for *blood* and *constriction*. To be more precise, there are sites on the brain's nerve cells that receive this chemical, process it, and act on it, and those same sites are fooled by our vampire molecules. The same receptor site that seeks the brain's natural sedative will suck up our mimicking chemical because it effectively blocks serotonin, starving the brain. Our juice affects sexual responses, aggression, sleep, and general well-being. In fact, it's similar to the way LSD works by producing sensory and emotional responses unlike anything the mundane senses offer. By altering the brain itself, we can alter consciousness and give someone multiple layers of internal awareness.

To put it in scientific terms, our "stuff" is entheogenetic, mysticomimetic, phanerothymetic, and psychodysleptic. It produces quite visceral feelings of the mystical and divine, but it also seriously disturbs the mind. In other words, it's a psychotoxin. Even as it heightens and enhances perception and sensation, and magnifies suggestibility, it can bleed into a horrifying psychosis. Energy transforms quickly into anxiety and then terror. Generally we take our prey during the celebratory mood before the substance gets that bad, so to them it seems only a wonderful psychedelic.

Now I was beginning to guess what these people were up to, and I looked for some way to stop them. I didn't want this to happen to Ana. I didn't know her that well, but she'd been fun, and her quick affinity with Viper had endeared her to us all. I knew that Naje had taken a special interest in her, and even Dantalyon had relaxed his jealous guard over Naje's door to allow her to spend a few moments in there. We'd never before let a temp so deeply into our center, but Naje had seen something in her that served his purpose, so she'd gained a few privileges. And she'd been good about it. She'd never attempted to become one of us, to divide us, or do anything but accept what she was offered. She'd even found one of our snakes injured outside during the day and had nursed it herself until Viper woke. That was why I felt protective of her now. She wasn't a vampire but she had a connection.

Yet I could plainly see that even if I were to swing down from my hiding place like some martial-arts hero and take out a few of them before they could react, I couldn't have grabbed Ana from their clutches. She was firmly strapped to that heavy table. I had no choice but to sit and watch so that I could report back to Naje. I also had to hope that, in the event she was overdosed—a strong possibility—she wouldn't survive. If she did, she'd never recover and would exist in the worst kind of evolving nightmare imaginable.

Then I had an idea. I couldn't believe I hadn't thought of it before, since I'd watched Bel do it countless times. Despite my weakened mental powers, I searched the air for spirits. They were always around, and although they didn't actually obey us, it was possible to penetrate the energy field and manipulate them a little, as Dantalyon had done when he was with his short-lived New Hope inamorata. I needed to create a disturbance down below.

To my disappointment, the room was mostly clear. I tried hard to connect with the dead but failed to draw anything close. Yet I knew that spirits travel, often at high speeds, and I had only to wait to get access to one. As they prepared Ana for her ordeal below, I opened up my sensors as wide as they would go and beckoned some mindless entity forth. I wished Naje would merge with me and help me, but I seemed to be on my own. My job was to do the best I could with what I had, so I concentrated on my own ethereal skills.

There are many different types of ghosts, and the ones that get the most play in spooky tales are those that wander without sight or hearing, who terrorize with their unblinking, mindless demeanor. People fear them because no one wants to believe that brain death is also mind death. To have no aim and nothing better to do than go through repetitive motions for years, even centuries, is hardly the way temps view the ultimate state of their souls. They can't bear to see these spooks as afterlife extensions.

Another type of ghost comes from the disincarnate senses, which means an odor like perfume or tobacco that was once associated with an intense incident. It might also be a spooky voice, a footfall, or the cold touch of an invisible hand. Those didn't interest me, either. They're like place memories, which are just the result of the magnetic fields in a certain area trapping the residual image of an emotional event. A murder, for example, might be reenacted over and over, though only one person died in that particular spot. The other person also appears in the transparent scenario because the emotional energy got attached to the place. They're not really ghosts.

I was seeking the aware spirit, a rare type of entity. That's the one that's defied the web of the memory fields, has gone over to where spirits gather, and for some reason has come back into our realm. It might be to watch a loved one, it might be out of curiosity, or it might simply be that the soul has an addiction to something that in life it couldn't release. What we vampires have learned from the spirits is that the psychology of life is continuous with the psychology of death. Who we are and how we direct our lives—or not—influences what traps our spirits or frees them to evolve. I sometimes think that was what motivated some of us to become vampires—just to avoid this fate altogether. There was certainly truth in that for me.

Anyway, these aware spirits rove around, observing us, bumping things around, moving objects, and creating cold spots. Sometimes they try to communicate as well. You might hear them as a voice, record them on tape, or even get a disturbing phone call from them. I heard that one being actually managed to send a fax. Often they can speak only briefly because it takes so much energy to shift onto the plane at which communication with living beings is possible. Many try and fail, and even those who succeed may get only a few phrases across, like "Help" or "He hit me with a chain."

There are temps who know about them and who spend hours attempting to record their messages. The results range from fuzzy to clear. These people aren't mediums who can hear and converse with the dead.

They just have sensitive taping devices and plenty of patience.

The problem with these spooks, of which I was acutely aware in that situation, is that in order to bridge from their world to ours, they need a certain type of energy, and they can pick that up only from someone with a good abundance of it. Hence, a group of people engaged in a séance may contact a spirit more easily than a person alone. There's just more ectoplasmic substance available, even if it's visible only to the spirit who needs it. Once the ghost attaches to it, it can become partially or fully visible or move objects, make noise, and produce odors. It may even transport objects through the air as "apports" from some unseen place to the middle of the table.

These spooks don't much care for vampires, although some of them seek attention from wherever they can get it. If they can't get their mortal friends and relatives to acknowledge them, and they get lonely, they can generally count on us. The thing is, though, we *are* vampires, and we'll exploit them and suck energy right out of them. That was what I was hoping to do at that very moment, but I had to be clever about it. Too many spooks were wising up to us, so I had to bide my time until I sensed a naive one in need.

We like the continuity of the spirit world. It all meshes in the memory fields, which can make the mundane seem extraordinary and the extraordinary supernatural. For example, a human with the talent to read the memory fields may be viewed as a medium in connection with the dead. He can say that your grandmother is nearby and even name her and say what she died of. He'll be able to tell you about the medallion you forgot to bring to the session, pinpoint the start of a depression, or explain a family secret that has haunted you your entire life. It will seem as if he could know these things only by communicating with the dead, yet all he's really done is tap into the energy field in which memory is stored.

We, too, can use this electromagnetic energy to entrance prey and scramble what they think they know. But we're aware of the difference between a memory and a soul that's passed through the threshold of death. The difference is so striking that one can never be mistaken for the other. The dead who remain aware can actually communicate what it's like over there, albeit briefly. Their knowledge is transcendent. That's how we as vampires learned about the levels of the soul and turned that knowledge into a way to enhance our own existence. And that's why our venin is now so potent.

That's why I worried about Ana.

Most of the ghosts resent us, of course, believing that we abuse the immortal treasure toward an evil end, but some of them actually help us. They teach us because they're so stuck in their own narcissism that they'd rather suck up the attention than protect the other world's secrets.

I remained on the lookout for one of these, and it wasn't long before I hooked one. It was easy to read the memory fields around her, since she was one of those defined by guilt. This was a young woman who'd died while causing a thirteen-car pileup. She'd been riding with her husband when she suddenly saw people flying up into the air and believed that the Rapture was at hand. She thought Christ was calling forth all the righteous souls, so she demanded that her husband stop the car. Then she saw Jesus walking along the road, so she jumped up from her seat and went through the sunroof. She expected Jesus to grab her, but instead she flew out of the car and into the road. It turned out that the "people" she'd seen were helium-filled blow-up dolls that had flown out of a truck transporting them to a party—the same party for which "Jesus" had dressed up. It wasn't the Rapture after all.

Though her spirit was of flimsy substance, I could still see the pretty girl with long auburn hair she once had been. As she grew attuned to my ability to see her, she rolled herself into a ball of light and zipped over to get closer. The air grew measurably colder around me, but I felt the quick burst of energy blips.

The people below couldn't see this, of course, although it can be caught on infrared film. Ghosts are quick but not totally elusive. Once she drew near me, she unfurled from her round shape into a filmy ectoplasm and began to fill in around her shoulders and arms. I felt her tugging at my energy to feed her form and I opposed her. I had little enough for myself without giving any over to her. She persisted and I resisted. I knew that she wouldn't give up but would tug even harder at the field that surrounded me. What I hoped to do was use it as a sort of rubber-band effect. The more I held back, the more she pulled. Her spirit was fairly strong, so I knew I couldn't endure this much longer. Yet I had to work it just right. If I failed, she'd escape with the energy I needed and I'd have no leverage to invite another spirit close.

I felt her gather for a more concerted effort. Just as she was about to exert her greatest force, I released and she lost her "grip." As I'd hoped, she zipped across the room over the heads of the mortals below, leaving a sudden cold breeze in her wake. A few of them looked up, startled. In moments, she was gone through the far wall, but the energy that attached to her was sufficient to create a stir in the material world and she managed to topple a glass jar that sat directly in line with me but across the room.

It had the expected effect. The group thought that

I was over there, and at least half of them rushed over to grab me.

In the meantime I looked for a way to swoop down and pick up the jar that contained my elixir. I prepared to jump, contracting my muscles to give me the greatest distance, but then I froze in place.

Sabbatina had guessed that I was up to something and had grabbed the jar herself, keeping it close to her body. Damn, she was informed. She commanded three of her followers to surround and shield her.

I slid back into the shadows. The moment had passed. There would be no getting that stuff away from her. She obviously knew its value. But she still did not know where I was, which was my single advantage just then.

Ana moaned again and the woman snapped her fingers at her crew, who were still snuffling about in some far corner. "Forget that," she instructed. "We have something more important here. The moment is approaching. We need everyone in place."

I wasn't sure what she meant by that and tried to read the fields for more information, but I was too weak. My tug-of-war with the ghost had depleted me of anything more than the basic physical energy to keep breathing. I might be able to run if I had to, but I couldn't do anything of spiritual merit. I sent out a mental pulse to Naje once more but got nothing back.

Then I watched as two of the men untied some cords that were attached to the high ceiling and used them to open a four-by-four-foot panel overhead. Moonlight streamed in and I recalled that we were heading into a full moon eclipse that night. Then I knew: that was what they'd meant by "the moment." They were going to tap the shifting electromagnetic energy of the eclipse, just as we meant to do with Jamie, but to perform some ceremony with Ana. That meant that they knew that certain energy forms would be most intense during those few moments, and for some reason they were going to exploit that. Now I was really getting nervous. These people were more sophisticated than I'd realized.

Suddenly I missed Bel. She'd understand this better than I because she reads voraciously and pays special attention to the effects of astronomical dynamics on the spiritual plane. It was Bel who had taught us how to use the energy of planetary movements to increase our mental powers. I remembered how she'd won Naje's admiration for this feat, and she'd basked in that for over a week. If only I'd paid more attention. In fact, I ran through several scenarios where one of our *kamera* had taken time to teach me something, and I'd neglected to follow through. I was sure that things would be different for me now if I had. No doubt Elizabeth or Viper could have taken care of this situation without much effort. Even Bel.

Yet I couldn't even communicate with her now. She might be sending me one pulse after another of information and support but I couldn't receive it. I'd used up my energy keeping the connection with her and Naje earlier. Until my powers regenerated, I was on my own.

I sensed the room dimming and saw that the eclipse was moving toward its dark peak. That told me it was nearing midnight. I wondered how things were going with Jamie and how Naje was exploiting the energy of this lunar event.

Lights were dimmed and black candles on stands were lit below, all around the table where Ana was tied. There must have been three dozen. I leaned closer to see. I hated that I was so helpless, but there was little I could do about it.

I still had one potential weapon but it meant the possibility of recapture, and I would use that only in the event that I could not find another way to prevent them from injecting Ana. If I didn't see my chance, I'd stay right where I was, because there was no sense losing her and me together. This was going to be tricky.

Several more spirits came through the walls and traveled toward me. I scanned them to see if I could use one. In my experience, ghosts often travel in groups, and one of these had discovered from the female I'd just cast across the room that a creature—me—was near that could acknowledge them. They were always and forever looking for someone to whom to tell their pathetically repetitive stories. I didn't care but I didn't want their nearness to clog up the receptor fields. If one came, others could shoot in quickly, and that could be troublesome.

I tried to think of a way to be rid of it. As the woman below gave orders to each of her people as to what their role would be in her ceremony, I mentally beckoned this hovering spirit closer. It was leery of me, I could tell, because it offered nothing of its origin, death, or gender. Sometimes we confuse ghosts with demons, and that was the last thing I needed to mess with that night. I sent out a signal to assure this entity that I was interested in its woeful tale.

It wasn't long before I received an impression that this one had never quite reached the other side but had been trapped since death in a spiritual malaise. It was seeking a rescuer because it had just enough awareness to know there was something better but not enough to realize that it could never get there. Whatever it had been in life, it had blown its chances on the other side. Probably this one was a murderer or a corrupt politician. It needed to convey its distress. There's nothing worse than a whiny ghost, but I had to reach for something.

Again, I urged it to come closer. What I had in mind

would work only if I could get it to attach to my energy, what little I had. If it sensed there wasn't much there on which it could feed and strengthen, it might wander away in search of better company. I used my resources and all that Naje had taught me to transmit a false reality of great strength. Most ghosts at this one's level weren't well versed in the spiritual universe. Otherwise it would know better than to trust any images I thrust at it.

Fortunately for me, this one was even more naive than the last one. It moved a shade closer.

I looked below to gauge how much time I had and realized that the room was darkening and the ceremony was under way. Apparently they intended to inject Ana at the height of the eclipse's shadow. Sabbatina was chanting something. I sensed that I had only moments, and I wasn't even sure that I could pull this off. I turned my full attention back to the ghost.

It had taken a step closer.

Then I "heard" a quick flurry of words that acted as feelers for my interest and awareness. I maintained my focus, which encouraged it closer. It began to feed on the outer circle of my energy field, but that wasn't quite close enough. I needed it to come all the way inside, as the other spirit had freely done.

Naje had taught us this trick. It works through the channels of the right temporal lobe, in the same way that we access the memory fields. It meant first cleansing our perception of the limited cultural ideas about physical boundaries and brain functions. We had to understand how fluid were the mind and body before we could hope to manipulate their connection. This ability opened up doors of all kinds, both for what we could take and what we could create. And that comprehension was only the second of seven levels of spiritual maturity.

I saw movement below and realized that the woman was preparing for the injection. She lifted the syringe. Exhausted as I was, I had to work faster. I sent a pulse to Naje but got nothing back. Desperate, I turned back to the ghost. It hovered but came no closer.

Sixteen

Jamie

Jamie followed Allan through a labyrinth of dark hallways. He held a tiny light in front of him, and all she could manage to see was his silhouette. It soon became clear that while he'd come for her, he didn't seem to realize that Devon was somewhere in the house as well. Jamie wasn't going anywhere without her son.

She grabbed the back of Allan's shirt and tried to get him to stop. He reached for her, shushed her, and urged her forward.

"Devon is here," she whispered.

Allan looked at her, his face shadowed and uncomprehending, and then he said, "We'll have to come back for him."

"No, we can't leave him. They may get angry and kill him."

"They won't," Allan assured her. "They'll need him to lure you—"

He stopped talking to listen. Under his breath, he said, "Shit! We've gotta get out of here."

Opening a door, he dragged Jamie inside a dark and clammy room. The odor of decay overwhelmed her, and vomit came up in her throat so fast it gagged her. Allan slapped his hand over her mouth and whispered to her to find a place to hide. He held the light up to the ceiling to spread its power, and Jamie realized they were in some kind of morgue. She saw the forms of human bodies stacked on shelves that went up every wall. Some were clothed but most were naked.

Catching her breath, she backed away, but Allan pushed her farther into the room and urged her to keep quiet. He turned out the light, and that made things even worse. She stepped on something that felt thick and solid and tried to back away, but he was behind her, sending her forward. Jamie almost stumbled, but she forced herself to breathe through her mouth, as she'd once learned to do in a forensic lab, and entered the dark chamber. She could only imagine what might happen if she fell. She figured that this had to be one of the experimental parts of the lab that Naje had mentioned, though she hadn't expected something this gruesome. Had they done this genetic procedure on these people, killing them and stacking them in here for further study?

No, Naje's comforting presence belied that. He'd intended her no harm. He'd been so gentle with her. Surely he'd protect her. In fact, she wasn't so sure now that she ought to follow Allan. She didn't want Naje to be upset with her.

Allan pushed her against a wall and she felt herself crowd up against a cold corpse that exuded a sudden foul odor. She kept her hand over her nose and mouth. Her dress felt wet in back, and she tried not to imagine what kinds of bodily juices might be leaking out of the thing next to her. She experienced something slip, believed it to be skin, and knew this thing had to be several weeks old. Again she fought the urge to vomit.

Outside the door, they heard running footsteps. Quickly, they crouched down against the wall. One of the creatures passed by but then stopped. Jamie held her breath as the door opened. She saw rather than heard it, and she had the creepy feeling that these things could see her there in the dark, though she could not see them. She wondered which one had come inside. Then the door closed again and Allan breathed out, but Jamie wasn't so sure that the vampire had left. Her senses were on alert, and she believed they were not alone.

The corpse next to her suddenly moved. She nearly shouted as she felt it shift, and realized that she'd pressed too close to it. Panicking, she thought it might fall and give them away, but it rocked only slightly and then went still.

"We need to find a different way out than I came in," Allan whispered. "There's a tunnel out of this room. That's how they bring these bodies in here. It goes some ways but comes out into the yard."

Jamie was suddenly suspicious. She wondered how he could possibly have this piece of information. He had to have been in here before. Or else he'd been told by someone who had. In either case, it felt all wrong to her. It seemed to her that she'd left one bad situation only to jump straight into another, and the fact that Allan seemed to have little regard for her concern for Devon gave her further reason to question his motives. He'd gotten her into this mess by pretending to care about finding her son. She'd informed him of Devon's whereabouts, but he'd failed to respond as she'd expected. Something about this situation was terribly, terribly wrong.

"I can't go without Devon," Jamie said.

Allan gripped her arm and came close to her ear to whisper, "We've got only a slim chance of getting out of here at all, right now, in the next few minutes. Once out, we can come up with a plan, but if we stay here, they'll get us and you still won't have Devon. This is your only hope. You don't even want to know what they'll do to you if they catch you trying to escape. We have to get out!"

Jamie had to admit to his logic. She knew almost nothing about these creatures, and she feared that they'd certainly retaliate. Keeping contact with Allan, she felt him rise to his feet, and then got up herself and followed him through the darkness as he felt his way around a pile of at least three decomposing corpses. One lay on its stomach across the other two, and they all seemed fairly fresh. She couldn't imagine that this many people were missing from the area without raising an alarm. These vampires obviously got them from elsewhere. Grave robbing?

And besides the biological hazard, there was another concern. At any moment, Jamie expected that she'd encounter a snake, or that her thoughts would suddenly get scrambled in some manner to make her forget what she was doing. Naje had done that so effectively earlier, and it seemed strange that the vampires hadn't yet resorted to this. It was clear that they'd discovered her disappearance and the dead guardian reptile. She wondered if Allan, with his expertise in mental graphology, was somehow immune to this hypnotic trick, and could even extend that protection to her. He obviously was more than he seemed.

"There's a door here," he whispered. Reaching for her hand, he led her through it into what she sensed was a rough-hewn tunnel. She didn't want to touch the sides for fear she'd contact some kind of insect or spider. Surely if this tunnel was that close to a room full of dead bodies, it would be teeming with cadaverous things like maggots and mausoleum flies. She maintained her focus on Allan.

Within moments he came up against a wall. Only then did he venture to turn on his tiny pocket light. He shone it over the resistant stone, searching for an opening. Jamie saw the pointed tail of something disappear into the shadows along the floor and she froze. There were things in here with them, probably quite close. She looked overhead but saw only darkness. Was there something up there just waiting to drop down on them? Instinctively she used her hand to cover her head.

Allan turned to his right and found another wall there. Then he ran the small beam of light over the wall to his left. He found a three-foot-tall narrow hole, but going into it meant they'd have to crawl on their knees.

"No way," said Jamie. "I have a dress on. I can't go through there."

"You'd rather stay here with the vampires?"

"I can't do this, Allan. There has to be another way."

"Jamie, do you know what they're planning to do with you?"

She was struck by his question. How could he possibly know what they had told her? Or did he know something else, something they hadn't told her? She couldn't imagine why Naje had offered such an elaborate explanation if it hadn't been true, but she also realized that if they truly meant to hurt or kill her they'd hardly admit that to her.

"What do you mean?" she asked. "What are they going to do?"

He came close to her until his face was only inches away. She could feel the heat of his anxiety. "Listen to me," he said. "Your sister told me everything before she disappeared. She said they were going to use her as some sort of incubator. They wanted to give her an infusion of their blood so they could transform themselves into something else. She believed that she'd change, too, but from what she told me, I think they'd have killed her and used her as a gateway. She was so desperate to have this incredible experience that she was blind to the dangers." Allan's eyes blazed with the intensity of what he was saying. "I tried to tell her but she wouldn't listen. Surely you can see what I mean, can't you? They're vampires. Don't you know what that means? A vampire thrives off the resources of others. It takes what it needs and it doesn't give anything back. All you do is lose. They don't care about you, but they can make you think they do. That's how they draw you in and manipulate you. They can make you feel so utterly desirable, but you can't gain anything because they can't give anything."

Jamie hated to hear this. Her feeling from Naje had been real, not an illusion.

"I'd risk my life for Devon's," she insisted.

"You'd risk it for nothing, then," Allan said. She heard the frustration in his voice. "They'd kill him, too. In fact, his best chance is for you to get away."

"How?"

"If they have him, they'll believe they can lure you back. They don't have much time. They won't lose their leverage. He'll be fine as long as we get away. But once they have you and they do to you what they were planning with Gail, Devon becomes extraneous. He's meaningless to them. Think about it."

"What do you mean, they don't have much time?"

"Their enemy is coming. In fact, it's already here."

"Their enemy?"

"The one they're trying to thwart. It's the whole reason they grabbed you."

"What is it?"

"Jamie, we can talk later. I have things I can show you to prove all this, but we need to get out of here now. If it destroys them, then we can go back in and get Devon. Until then, he'll be fine."

Jamie looked again at the hole and shook her head. "I can't go through there."

Allan was clearly exasperated. "Look, I'll check it out. You stay here. Maybe this part only goes a short way. I don't think it's wise to try to go back in there and look for some other way to escape. We have to go this way. You stay here and I'll see what's ahead."

Allan crouched down and used his light to peer into the tunnel. He seemed satisfied that there were no imminent dangers, so he got on his hands and knees, placed the penlight between his teeth, and went forward. Jamie was suddenly enveloped in darkness.

She heard a rustling behind her and turned to try to see what she could, but it was hopeless. Whatever was back there had a clear advantage. It could probably smell her, and if her vague recollection about snakes was correct, she knew they sensed things through some kind of infrared images or heat receptors.

Something was watching her, she was sure of that, and Allan's shuffling into the tunnel had diminished sufficiently to tell her that he wouldn't get back fast if she suddenly needed him. She moved closer to the opening where he'd disappeared and kept her ears attuned to the slightest noise. She hoped it was just a mouse or rat. Anything was preferable to a snake.

Then she went still. Something was definitely in here with her, and she felt sure it had intelligence. It wasn't a snake or a rat. It was aware of her.

She edged over to the hole into which Allan had disappeared.

"Allan," she whispered. She tried to make her voice loud enough for him to hear, but he didn't respond. She thought she heard some scraping pretty far into the tunnel. Pressing against the wall, Jamie tried to see in the dark, but it was impossible. There was only one thing to do, she finally decided. She crouched down and forced herself to follow where Allan had gone. Expecting at any second to be grabbed from behind, she rushed forward. The rough stone floor pressed sharp edges against the palms of her hands and her knees, but no matter how far she had to crawl, she was determined now to escape.

Seventeen

Christian

I had learned that this ghost was male and that its mortal body had died in prison, the victim of another inmate's shank attack. This incident had happened several decades earlier, and for all that time he'd been caught in this particular spiritual fold, only growing gradually aware that he was stuck. He'd found several mediums to play with who'd initially been pleased by his presence, but then they'd realized he was a psychopath and had had a devil of a time shooing him away. To him, I was just one more in a long line of people he could dupe, and I allowed him to continue to believe that. He was too dim to sense that I wasn't human at all. That's the trouble with narcissists: they believe what they want to believe, and it's not hard to use their own delusions to trip them up.

Using my mental muscles the way a snake pulls its body along a hard surface, I drew him closer. To bait him I had to give up some of my limited energy, but he proved difficult to hook. He'd come close and then move away, retaining the compact roundness with which he could instantaneously shoot across the room and through the wall if he had a mind to do so. I needed him to shift into a form that I could hook into, and his current one would not do.

I saw Sabbatina raise the syringe over Ana. Fortunately, she seemed to need some sort of ritual to accompany it, because she continued to urge her followers to behave in a certain manner, so that bought me some time. The temps around her formed a circle and chanted something in a foreign and ancient language, using the word *Dahaka,* and I sensed that they believed that their collective force was opening some kind of invisible door. I sent an emergency pulse to Naje.

Then I felt a tug at my heart that took my breath away and knew the ghost was hooked. He was trying to form himself off my substance so that he could better show himself and communicate. That was what I'd been waiting for.

Before he could react, I sucked him toward me and rolled him into a tight ball. He struggled, surprised, but I had him. I rose, risking exposure, and aimed straight at the raised arm of the priestess. While this entity had no material substance to affect her, the condensed ectoplasm could have some force. I was counting on that.

But I'd never practiced this particular skill. Eryx and Bel were much better at throwing ghosts than I was. Like the gunslingers of the Old West, they could knock bottles off shelves with this balled energy. It didn't hurt the ghosts, actually, although it startled them to find themselves trapped in a form that generally served them. That was probably another reason they didn't much like us.

At any rate, I rolled this one in, let it pass through me to pick up speed, and then flung it straight at the arm of the woman who intended to put Ana into a psychotic trance. I watched like a pro bowler to see if I'd get a strike. The white orb went shooting straight toward the intended target. I knew I'd thrown true. I could feel it.

Then, to my shock, the spirit ball shifted slightly, like a bowling ball that had hit a slight warp in the floor. It was off track. I could see that it was going to smack one of the true believers in the side of the head, which would have no effect at all, aside from the feeling of a refrigerated egg cracking against a wall.

The woman moved the syringe toward Ana's arm.

Then the ghost shifted again, as if trying to right itself, and it was back on track again. And then . . .

It missed.

Instead of knocking the woman's arm, it flew straight at the jar of fluid, knocking it to the floor. It shattered and the liquid smeared across the cement.

Disappointed, I slipped back into the shadows.

The only effect I'd had on the ceremony was to alert the priestess to my shenanigans. She looked up in my general vicinity, although I knew she couldn't actually see me. Yet the damage had been done. Just as the moon went dark, she quickly injected Ana with the vampire hallucinogen.

My mission had failed. Now Ana was on her journey, and it was one from which she might not return a whole person. Even worse, I'd failed Naje.

The group waited for the serum to take effect, and as I watched from the shadows, I went mentally through the stages of what she would experience, wondering if there were some way to stop it even now.

Sometimes we vampires did this to one another just for a kick, like an LSD party at college. One of us would inject a recipient by biting down on some area where the nerves were close to the skin and allowing the potent juice to flow. This produced a wave through the other's body and caused certain parts of the brain to vibrate to frequencies that merged the giver and the taker. It was like giving a temp an intravenous psychedelic, yet more powerful, because our bodies could more efficiently process it and magnify its effect. We were going for a psychic "flashpoint," or the point at which the temperature in a smoke-filled room reaches a degree that it will burst into such an intense flame that everything is consumed. Vampires at lower levels can't achieve this—they're annihilated rather quickly—but if the right mental discipline is used, the effect is spectacular. The closest that temps come to this experience is through the flood of hormones at birth, during sex or deep meditation, and at the point of death, but even then it's the merest whisper to a shout.

Ana was about to feel the first tingles of hallucinatory experience. That, at least, would be pleasurable. But that would soon flow into something else. I saw her open her eyes and knew she was flashing on the trails of eidetic imagery that precede a colorful visual fantasy, which were something like the last legs of bursting fireworks as they burned themselves out. Soon she would feel a touch of nausea and a slight trembling as her body awareness expanded and made her feel that she was growing out of her skin. Her blood pressure would elevate and her heart begin to pound, but all of this would feel euphoric. She wouldn't mind. She'd enjoy it.

Only when the scenes began to flash by in quick alternating motions would she panic. If she was used to this loss of control, she might ride with it, and knowing Ana, I guessed that she'd had a few psychedelic experiences. The faces of the people around her would appear as masks, and when the moon began to show its edges once again, that would become a luminescent glow in her visual field. She'd also see a lot of geometric patterns, and the various objects around her would appear to melt into one another. Then she'd hear singing, faint at first, but eventually it would become loud and clanging. The odor of flowers or fragrant nuts would flood into her nostrils, and her skin would become so charged that she'd crave to be touched. These experiences could last for about an hour or so, before they shifted over into the meltdown of the self that preceded the sense of an encounter with the divine and finally a fragmenting and painful psychosis. Flashpoint for her could be a complete and unsurvivable shock to the system.

I had no doubt that Viper had given her a taste of this experience, but only as a recreational high. He'd never have harmed her and made her afraid. I could only hope that her fun with him might help her now with a little homeopathic immunity.

On this night, Ana had been given more of this drug than we generally injected into our prey. The fact that she'd received it in the dark indicated that those who administered it realized that it had a more potent effect under diminished light. Certain bodily processes shut down in order to enhance others that would resonate well with the molecular structure of our venin. Ana would suffer for that, but I couldn't be sure that she would die. I still needed to grab her if I could and get her out of there. I had to watch for an opening.

Then I sensed Naje coming through. It was weak at first, and I could tell he was distressed about something. That was unusual. I'd never heard of anything shaking his practiced equilibrium. Now I was certain that something had happened back at home. I tried to ask, but he pushed me back and communicated a single question: *Do you see a book?*

I glanced down at the ceremony. Under the eclipse, it was pretty dark down there and farther away than my night vision generally stretched. Yet clearly he needed this information, so I called on other senses beyond vision to help me "see." I looked over the tables and beyond but saw nothing that resembled a book or a manuscript, just a few pieces of paper. I thought perhaps that Sabbatina had memorized the ritual. At any rate, I hadn't seen her consult any book or manuscript, and I communicated this back.

Down below, Ana moaned and writhed on the metal bed, and then arched her back and opened her legs. That posture called to me and I wanted badly to go to her with the only response she craved. I felt my entire body respond and then realized that I was receiving an infusion of energy, but didn't know from where. It was different from what I'd felt from Naje or even from Bel. It wasn't localized but was filling the room from some central force. I looked below, and as the emerging moonlight brightened the room a little, I saw that the temps were feeling it, too. Something was definitely happening here. I tried to form some sense of this for Naje but felt him quickly withdraw. Once again, I was utterly alone.

Ana started to say something but at first it was incoherent. The group gathered close, but the priestess gestured for them to keep to their places.

"It's blue," Ana shouted. "They're all blue."

I knew that for her whatever colors she saw were vivid, intense, and multidimensional, more so than anything in the natural world.

"There's three of them," she mumbled. "They're touching my face." She gasped and then said, "It's yanking me away. It wants to take me somewhere. It says, 'Let's go!' and it's flying. I can't fly with it."

"Try," said the priestess. "Try to go with it."

Ana writhed on her bed, as if resisting the order. "It itches," she cried out. "But I can't feel my body. My arms are gone. It's cut them off. I'm going into a maze."

"Tell us."

"It's cool in here, and green. My neck hurts; it bit me. There are little things all around me. They have bells on. They're pointing to something they want me to see, but I can't see because it's dark. It's a dark purple out there. Something's coming."

She lay quiet for a moment, breathing fast, and the priestess urged her to say something more. I waited, wondering how long it would be before Ana would submerge into a fragmented reality that would make it difficult for her to function or talk. She was already mixing up her thoughts and getting close to speaking in the word salad of the unmedicated schizophrenic. I knew her tongue would thicken soon.

Ana's hard breathing told me that her blood pressure had shot up, but eventually over the next few hours it would drop to a level that would not support her. Not unless she was taken into our world.

"There's something large over there." She pointed with her hand, although nothing was visible in that area. She was seeing something that no one else saw. "I see the eyes. He's looking for someone. He's so large. . . . They . . . It's too many. My neck is burning. I can't taste my throat. Someone is taking me away in a cart. I'm feeling . . . I'm feeling . . ."

Her voice trailed off. I'd already felt the energy growing more intense around me and it was getting heavy and corrupted. It wasn't the pure force that I'd felt from Naje but a dark, dense cloud of chaotic forms and images. The group was responding to it, too. This was no psychedelic trip of hallucinatory images. Ana had tapped into something and it was using her to come through. In fact, I could see a thin stream of black smoke trailing out of her mouth, as if she were internally combusting.

My instincts told me to stop it at all cost. It was the thing, the nemesis, that vampiric force that was infecting us. Searching the fields for Naje but failing to connect, I decided to suck up all the energy I could, even if some of it was bad, and then work it into something that might protect me. That seemed to be the only defense I had, though I knew it might just as easily destroy me.

I concentrated on the channeling function in my right temporal lobe to bring it closer to me, and felt at once the smothering contamination. This was putrid and foul. Whatever this energy source was, I didn't want it in me. I had to purify the waves, if possible, to strengthen myself for what I was about to do. I was no genius at this and knew I risked everything, but I couldn't let it flow forth without a fight.

Unsure whether I could actually pull this off, I moved noiselessly off my perch and down across the shadowed wall. No one seemed to notice, so intent were they on Ana's struggles to grapple with the emerging entity. It was like she was giving birth psychically, and they were a rapt audience in the birthing chamber. I had to act fast.

I made it to the floor without a sound and stayed there for a moment to rest. I'd regained my equilibrium but was nowhere near full power. And I'd never had to scramble the thoughts of this many people all at the same time to produce a mass hallucination. There were those in my *kamera* who could do it: Naje, of course, and Dantalyon. Lachesis was a skilled mind-bender, and even Bel was good at it because she practiced. Naje had obviously chosen the wrong one for this night's work, but I had to make the most of those powers that I had.

Ana began to cry out and then to scream. No one administered to her distress. Instead they watched with an air of anticipation, as if she were merely the disposable channel for something that they would welcome into their midst, regardless of how mentally rending the experience might be for her. Regardless if it destroyed her.

I was only a few feet away, crouching in the darkness, when I saw something in the room just beyond the smoke. It was a dark, dense humanlike form attempting to merge with her aura. It was outside her attempting to get in rather than coming into the room through her. I weened that Sabbatina was trying to use her physical form to control it, like running a river through a conduit. Ana screamed again and I knew it was now or never. I had to act before the thing fully attached to her.

I leaped into the midst of the group and used every bit of skill I had to create a group hallucination. Like a cobra that flares its neck to appear larger, I stood up tall on the bed, straddling Ana and seeding the collective imagination with the image that I was this entity they were calling forth. It had taken form.

Oddly, it worked better than I'd anticipated. They'd been so determined to see this Dahaka thing that they believed I was it. I saw the awe on their faces, although the priestess looked vaguely doubtful. I then worked the image into a tornadic whirl to hold them back, and while they were in that confusion, I tried pulling Ana free of her constraints.

But she was held firmly in place.

Then something knocked me off the bed with the force of a giant balled-up fist. I flew straight at the priestess and knocked her over. She cried out and grabbed for me, but I was already on my feet. Ana was shrieking now, her eyes wide in terror and her mouth sloppy with drool. I saw burns on her face and neck.

I jumped at the bed and gave it a push, knocking back four of the group, even as two of them tried to grab me from behind. One ripped off my shirt, but that made things easier for me because in an instant I could make my skin slick and difficult to grip.

Yet my burst of energy was draining out. I didn't have much time.

Then, miraculously, Naje was there within me full force. I felt the quick infusion of power and rose up tall, knowing that he'd make them see whatever they needed to see to be utterly afraid of me. All I had to do was let him perform through me. In a moment, I sensed them drawing back.

But the priestess was tougher. She didn't accept her fears. Rather than withdraw, she moved into them to disperse them. She watched me with eyes glazed with a brilliance that revealed that she was high on something, and then took a step toward me, her hand out as if to grab me. I tried to think of a way to free Ana while also duping these temps, but it's difficult to do something physical while making such a concerted mental effort.

The priestess picked up a large hook attached to a short rope, and I realized that her intent was to fix it to the leather collar I still wore. That meant that what she saw was me rather than the vision that Naje was spinning. Somehow she'd managed to fend that off, which told me she had powers beyond what I had guessed. How she'd acquired them I couldn't imagine.

Suddenly I was grabbed from behind. I lost the sense of Naje's force and realized I was on my own again. This wasn't good, and whoever had me was clearly stronger than me, yet no mortal had that kind of power. I struggled but found myself held tight.

Then I saw a dark shape leap in behind the priestess and grab her by the hair. She dropped the hook to turn and fight, and that was when I saw her nemesis.

Lachesis!

Before Sabbatina could turn around, Lachesis had her locked around the neck in a constricted hold that would soon suffocate her. It was the strangler's hold, the one that body snatchers used to do when they ran out of fresh corpses to sell. Then Lachesis put her fangs against the woman's neck and in less than an instant had paralyzed her.

"Don't kill her!" I tried to shout, but my own breath was shallow in the grip of this other around my chest. I was dragged away from the group and shoved against a wall.

"Stay there," said Stiletto. "I'll take care of this."

I was too stunned to do anything but obey.

Already the temps were on their feet, the spell broken, and their concern for their ceremony was driving them toward certain death. Two went for Stiletto and he flung them against a set of wall shelves as if they were flies that he'd swatted away. The whole thing came crashing down and I weened that one of the temps was badly injured. The other just didn't want to move. Stiletto pushed another hard into two females who were trying to run for the door and they fell together to the floor. Then he ripped the straps off Ana as if they were duct tape. She'd gone silent and still, so he picked her up off the bed, flung her over his shoulder, and beckoned to me to follow him. He stopped for a quick look around, and I wondered if he, too, was seeking the book that Naje had wanted to know about. I didn't see anything like that.

I looked back at Lachesis, who was finishing off the priestess to her own satisfaction, and moved quickly in Stiletto's wake.

Then I stopped. I had to be certain that the venin had been destroyed. I went to where the rolling orb had smashed the jar and saw that whatever liquid it had contained had soaked into the cement floor. I picked up the test tube that had originally contained my fluid and saw that it was empty, but I smashed it against the floor as well. Then I grabbed a nearby temp, slashed his throat with a broken piece of glass, and directed the flow of blood over the venin. I could only hope that would contaminate it sufficiently to prevent anyone from scraping up a pure sample. I rubbed it in with my shoe, and for good measure I took a quick drink from the hapless temp. I was starving. Once I stuck my fangs in—only one of which worked properly—the most difficult thing in that moment was to remember what was happening around me and to let go.

But there was one more thing. I dropped him into a heap at my feet and looked for the syringe. Even one precious drop still in it would be sufficient for some dark and clever chemist to duplicate its composition.

I picked it up just as Lachesis grabbed me by the arm and insisted I leave at once. Her skin was hot and my instincts were aroused, but her eyes snapped at me to *move*. Naje was waiting.

With one last glance around, I realized I couldn't get closure. Part of me might still be in this room and I couldn't do anything about it. I broke the needle off and pocketed the syringe body before I turned and followed Lachesis out the door. At least I could ensure that no one would get *that*.

The moon was shining bright now, almost fully emerged from its shadow, as we slipped into the car. Stiletto stepped on the gas and we were out of there. I worked at the leather collar and finally peeled it off. I didn't have to ask how they'd found me. I was certain that Naje had pinpointed my location and directed them there. I fell against the backseat, feeling temporarily safe and protected.

Ana lay unconscious beside me, so I pulled her close to place her head on my lap. She moaned a little as if I'd hurt her, and I saw that there were further burns on her that had singed her dress. Whatever that thing was, it had fried her to some extent. Saliva trickled from one corner of her mouth and I wiped it away. I knew that she was already deep in some nightmare that defied human reaction. It was beyond screaming, crying, or begging. I believed there was no hope for her. While I hadn't done anything to her and no one would ever blame me, I felt responsible. She was suffering from my stuff.

"We should help her die," I said. "She's in a bad way."

"No," Lachesis snapped back. "Naje wants her."

"Does he know how damaged she is?"

She looked at me. "We bring her back alive."

Stiletto looked at me in the rearview mirror. "The other one escaped," he said.

It took me a moment to realize that he meant Jamie, and I was shocked. "Escaped? How?"

He shrugged. "Somehow that reporter found his way in."

"Reporter?" Then I remembered that she'd been with Allan Coyne. He'd been a mild threat to us, since he knew we were real, and what Lachesis had said about him earlier that evening had made him a little more imposing, but no one had considered that he might actually locate and enter our home. That made him deadly, and I felt as if someone had exposed our crypt to the sun. "How could he come in without Naje knowing?"

"We're not sure. That's why we have to get back and put our heads together. I think someone betrayed us."

My head was reeling with each new bit of news. First this nemesis, then Ana, now Jamie and a traitor among us. But who in our *kamera* would put us in such danger? We'd all been carefully selected, and for all of us survival depended on this experiment with Jamie working. If it didn't, there would be no more *kamera*. We'd be wiped out. Even beyond that, the foundation of our group was trust in the larger force that empowered us beyond anything the lone vampire could experience. We'd all been tested on that long ago. How could any of us have done this?

I couldn't ask, and I knew they wouldn't express their private thoughts on the matter, not before we were all together. Lachesis had been the first one to join Naje, so she probably had the most accurate sense of the situation. She'd also be wise about it.

"It wasn't Destiny, maybe?" I pressed hopefully. "Or Cacilian?"

They said nothing.

"Can we still use Ana, then?" I asked.

Stiletto shook his head. "Viper will tell us that."

The thought of bringing her to Viper sent a steel blade through my stomach. I could already feel those snake eyes silently questioning me about what I'd just done. In some ways, that was worse than being accused. I hadn't really done it, but that was how it would seem to him. My venin had poisoned his friend.

Lachesis was strangely silent. I thought it might be from the aftereffect of her hasty meal. It must have been interesting to take the blood of a woman so steeped in awareness and power. I wanted her to tell us but knew that she'd speak in her own time, if at all. It was unlikely that she'd even apologize for getting us into that situation. She'd done what she had thought was right and the consequences were another matter.

"Why did you kill that woman?" I finally asked her.

Lachesis breathed out in exasperation, as if it should be obvious. "She knows about us. She knew how to lure and grab one of us."

"Lachesis, she knows other things, too. For one thing, she knows how to bring something forth from another place. I saw it. I don't know if it managed to get through, but it was there, and I think it had something to do with this thing that we're all afraid of."

"We saw it, too," said Stiletto.

"Well, that woman knew what it was and how to do it. We should have kept her and made her talk."

Lachesis half turned toward me. "Christian, you're so young!" This was her ultimate insult. She had little patience for immature vampires. "She wasn't the leader of that group."

"Yes, she was. She was running things."

"That means nothing. She was a puppet. There's someone else behind all of this. She had powers, yes, but she hardly knew what she was doing. She was quite stunned that her incantations even worked, but the fact is, whatever came forth had nothing to do with what she was doing or saying. Otherwise she wouldn't have tried to come at us the way she did."

"Why not?"

"She would have known she didn't need to. But she didn't know that."

"Well, she must have known something. I mean, she managed to trap us and catch one of us."

"Only because you weren't thinking," Stiletto cut in. "You shouldn't have just walked off like that in that house. I tried to stop you but you zipped out too fast. We don't divide forces in a crisis. That's why Naje sent three of us to go do this thing. But you just took off on your own and put us all at risk."

I was astonished. "I did that to divert them so you two could get out."

"As usual, Christian, you're thinking like a sole operator," Lachesis scolded. "That's not what it means to be part of a *kamera*. We don't just live in the same house like a group of fraternity brothers; we're connected. Had you waited, we could have formed a plan collectively and all gotten out just fine. They were only temps. They were helpless against the three of us, no matter how many there were. When you made your own plan and blocked us, you weakened us. You can't be one of us, Christian, if you're going to be a loner."

I was stung, more so because I realized it was true than because I felt their ingratitude. In fact, hearing this now from Lachesis made me aware that I'd wasted precious time that night and nearly had my venin come into human hands. Not to mention that Ana wouldn't be in her current state had they not had it to inject into her. From this perspective, I'd nearly brought about a real disaster. I was deeply embarrassed.

And the fact that Naje had assisted me, despite my mistakes, made me even more ashamed. He'd already warned me several times about my independent streak, which was all well and good as long as it didn't harm the group. Autonomy within the collective was part of spiritual maturity, but that was not what I'd done. I wasn't sure how I'd even face Bel. In fact, I wasn't sure I'd be accepted back into the family. The thought of that possibility injected my heart with negative adrenaline that made it shrink and pound at the same time.

I fell silent for the rest of the trip as Stiletto sped down back roads, and kept my hand on Ana. Just then, the last thing I wanted to do was arrive back home, and yet that was all I wanted. And I desperately hoped it still was my home. It's not easy getting into a *kamera*, particularly one like ours, where most of the members are highly skilled in some manner. The way it's done is that you come to the attention of one of the other members and they propose that you be watched for a while to measure your worth. You have no idea you're under surveillance, but then one day you're approached. You understand immediately that you're being offered a great privilege, and it's one that can be withdrawn instantly. It's also one that comes with certain sacrifices and risks.

In my case, it had been Bel and Phelan who had liked

the look of me. They'd been out on a rare jaunt together one night in Manhattan and had spotted me from afar. For a few weeks they trailed me, and then Lachesis had taken over. She's generally the gatekeeper. Had she vetoed their idea, I'd have been rejected without ever even knowing what had taken place. But she didn't. She made her decision, told Dantalyon, and he had gone to Naje to get the final word. It was also Dantalyon who'd eventually approached me.

At the time, several decades ago, I'd been a loner like most other vampires. I knew vaguely that there were vampire collectives here and there, but I had no idea what being part of one could really do for me. I'd just thought they were vampires who wanted to hang out together. For myself, I'd avoided other predators.

One night I was in Brooklyn, walking through the Green-Wood Cemetery. (Vampires love cemeteries, and our *kamera* especially indulged in the artistry of the nineteenth-century garden cemeteries around New York and Philadelphia.) Suddenly I was boxed in by other predators who seemed to intend me harm. It felt like a scene out of *West Side Story*, as if I'd crossed into their forbidden turf and had to pay. I was usually alert to these boundaries, but on this night I'd been so caught up with the moonlight shimmering on the intricate marble statuary of angels and saints that I hadn't paid proper attention. They were close, too.

I'd tried to shift my path, hoping that might work, but they'd followed me, so I threaded my way though the stones and looked for anything that would provide some cover. They could see me in the dark, so shadows wouldn't work, and at the time I didn't know anything about the various predatory resonances, so I didn't realize what their strengths and limitations were. I only knew that I had to find a way to "disappear."

I wasn't far from the Charlotte Canda monument,

a huge edifice erected to commemorate the death of the girl in 1845 on her seventeenth birthday. She had in fact designed it herself, intending it as a symbol of hope for her deceased aunt, but it was she who ended up inside. The gothic white marble arches, Grecian urns, and angelic statues made for a rather eclectic mess, but it was busy enough to provide a means to break up the energy pulses that gave me away.

As I wove my way through it, I sensed a cold patch of something to my right. It was the foggy substance of ectoplasm, and though I'd experienced ghosts running through me, I'd never tested the experience in reverse. Yet I knew that a merging of diverse energy patterns would surely be confusing to anyone tracking me, so I shifted direction and jumped right in.

The chilling mist enveloped me like a Venus's flytrap closing itself around an insect's meat. It had more substance than I'd expected, which meant that at the moment I'd interrupted it, it had been close to apparitional form, and it had felt the opportunity to fill itself up with my own life source. My heart began to pound hard to keep my substance fed, and I had to fight an urge to stop right there and yield. I wasn't experienced enough to know how to manipulate the fields to my advantage and thought briefly that I might drown inside this soul-sucking specter. But I also had sufficient speed that I managed to pass through and out, though it tried to keep a grip on me, and by the time I recovered myself outside the cemetery, I felt utterly drained. Yet I was temporarily free of the predators.

I found a perch from which I could ween the approach of my enemies should they pick up the scent, while I drew my resources together. If they came now, I'd be lost. I couldn't even think ahead to another defensive strategy.

Yet they seemed to have fallen back or lost me. Much

as it had cost me, my trick appeared to have worked. I sensed no life-forms around me at all and was preparing to relax my guard when I was startled to find a tow-headed vampire with large hazel eyes sitting right there behind me. The possibility that he'd crept up on me without my knowing so stunned me that I couldn't even move, although I'd always felt confident of my speed in camouflage and escape. Yet he seemed harmless, and the energy pulse from him was surprisingly sweet and friendly. It could have been a trick, but I didn't think it was.

Then I saw the other one. He stood on a shadowed wall, and even in poor lighting I could see that he was both intimidating and magnificent. He sent a quick greeting to assure me I was in no danger. Still, I remained alert and kept an eye on the one behind me.

Then somehow I realized without anyone saying anything that they'd driven back the gang that was after me. I wasn't sure why.

Dantalyon had such presence that I allowed him to come close and talk with me. As he approached from out of the shadows my mouth dropped open. I'd never seen such splendor. He wore tight brown leggings that I sensed were made from animal hide, but tanned to such supple flexibility that they were like his own skin. His lustrous black hair framed a remarkably chiseled face with intense eyes that took in my measure in a glance, and before he even said a word, he'd spun a vision of his group that enveloped me in a veritable haven. I'd never communicated like this before with anyone, and the influx of images and feelings overwhelmed me. I looked at the blond one and he was grinning like the Cheshire cat.

"Come and see for yourself," he said. "Come now, tonight."

I looked back at the dark one and knew I had no

choice. I'd been invited in a way that said there was now no turning back. So I went with them to New Hope.

In retrospect I realize that they'd revealed very little that night, only the feeling of belonging and growth that Dantalyon had weened would most appeal to me. Only as I became acquainted one at a time with the various members did I realize how powerful they all really were. Bel especially caught my fancy because she was so sophisticated in her awareness and knowledge about our association with the paranormal world, and because we had fun together. She freely taught me, and it was through her that I advanced. Even so, I grew increasingly aware of how little I actually knew and how much more I needed to learn, in terms of both knowledge and skill. In a manner of speaking, I had to rebalance my entire perspective. I once asked Naje why I'd been picked and he'd told me, "It wasn't for what you can do right now, but for what we believe you eventually can do." In fact, I learned, they rejected most candidates at some point along the way because they couldn't break through in a way that enhanced the *kamera*. That was always Naje's decision, and no one ever questioned it.

And it had been a long time before I even knew about him. He'd shown himself only after I'd been fully accepted by the others and had evolved onto a spiritual level sufficiently refined that he could have some connection with me. I'll never forget how overwhelmed I was by him. Initially I had thought Dantalyon the group's dominant focus, and they'd allowed me to believe that as a way to protect Naje. I'd gone off with him on several occasions to learn his special tracking skills. "If you stay on your own," he told me one day, "you're no greater than the sum of your personal power. That may seem like a lot to you in comparison to what you once were as a shadow, but it's a drop of spit to an ocean compared to what you can be with us."

Then we returned and I learned about the multiple levels of the underground chambers. Phelan and Viper showed me the ways of the snake, which thrilled me to the bone. As a mortal, I'd once encountered a small black snake on a weedy path. It tried to slither by me unseen, but I'd stepped in front of it. Then it tried a different route and I blocked it again. This time it went straight under my shoe, obviously finding some impossibly small opening. I watched, waiting to catch it, but it didn't emerge on the other side or behind me, so I lifted my foot, expecting to see it curled into a ball. To my astonishment, the snake was simply gone. I checked in the grass and looked all over the immediate vicinity, but it had disappeared. I was utterly stumped but impressed, and now these vampires were telling me that I could learn to do this, too, just like the snake. And not only did I learn, I eventually surpassed most of my cohorts in this particular ability.

Then Bel instructed me in the initiation process that would allow me to be in Naje's presence. The whole thing was so mystical and arduous as they carried it out one night that I'd thought they were just playing with me. I had to prove myself in certain ways and pass mental tests that I didn't understand before Dantalyon finally gave the signal. Then Bel took me by the hand and led me to the entrance to Naje's private underground rooms. She told me to enter on my own but didn't prepare me in any way for what I would encounter. I wasn't too keen on just going in unaccompanied, but I had already learned not to question the ways of advancement. It wasn't about thinking my way through; it was about allowing the process to unfold within me.

At first I believed I was alone. I was aware only that I was in a cavernous chamber where a variety of dangerous snakes enjoyed complete freedom. The reptiles lay curled on a floor and along walls roughened specifically for their convenience, or they basked in lamplight softly illuminating small gardens or sandy rock beds. Someone had carefully studied what each species preferred and had developed an enormously varied terrarium, from desert sand to a thick foliage of trees and flowers like night-blooming jasmine. Even the air temperature and the types of fragrances seemed to shift and change as I walked through the place. A few of the serpents watched me, and one black-and-gold-banded cobra raised itself up defensively and spread its neck, but the room's atmosphere was so placid that my entrance was but a minor disturbance. I reached into a bush for a light green snake known from its jutting hood as the eyelash pit viper and let it sink its tiny fangs into my skin. I'd already learned from Viper that receiving the venom is like humans taking a hit of speed, although the effects don't last as long for them. The serpent pulled out and I let it go.

Then I realized that another vampire was there with me, but one with abilities that surpassed even those of Dantalyon. He'd been there all along but was able to make the room feel empty as he surveyed me. So skilled was he at camouflage that I looked right at him and failed to see him. Only when he was satisfied in his silent assessment of me did he appear, and it seemed that he had suddenly emerged as figure to background in a pastoral painting. Like one of those camouflaged images that you look at for the longest time, and once you see it you can't believe you didn't spot it at once.

To be in his presence was like coming out from a dark, damp hole to bask in the desert sand after the sun has penetrated it all day. This feeling came not from his long white hair and the bright red Polynesian attire that he wore, or even the regal furnishing of his inner chamber, but from the way he radiated a depth of secret knowledge and a vast store of mental cunning that awed me to silence. I wasn't generally one to pay much respect to anyone's position, but this vampire's ability to feel his way subtly into my most primal needs got my attention. He was different. He seemed a boundless source for something I didn't yet comprehend.

Then he stepped forward. He was taller than me and more muscular. He was also centuries older, and I was allowed to know that he had made a point of gaining a multitude of experiences around the world, residing in many different places from islands to mountains, before settling into this vast underground chamber. I had the impression he hadn't left here for decades. He seemed nearly a deity, like Neptune in his ocean, yet he didn't make me feel as if he expected reverence. Even so, I gave it freely.

He was so pleased to have me among them, he assured me, and he predicted that I'd eventually be an important member. He was aware of my skills at concealment, my quick wit, and my ability to escape the tightest confrontation. He told me that being part of the *kamera* that honored the snake would enhance those skills considerably. More important to me, when he touched me I felt so enveloped by his expanded aura that I realized how much my vampiric existence enlarged reality and spiced my every move. I understood that there was much that I could aspire to. I never wanted to lose that, although I'd often slipped in discipline and failed to develop as quickly as Naje hoped I would.

Now, as we drove along, I remembered those rarified moments with him and contemplated the possibility that I was now going to be released. That meant not being shoved out as an ex-communicant but essentially destroyed. That's part of the pact: if you get far enough inside and agree to membership, you in essence agree to a total restructuring of your identity. You have to lose something to gain something. If I were considered an outcast, my memory fields would be permanently scrambled, my abilities corrupted, and my deep bonds severed. I might as well be torn limb from limb. All I would have would be some vague sense that I'd been cast from heaven and cursed to wander the earth without purpose or connection.

In a way, I hoped the incident with Jamie would take the heat off me. And after all, my heedless escapade had helped us locate Ana. She might still be of use, and that had to count for something. I pulled her a little closer to make her comfortable, although she was clearly unaware of where she was. I feared that she was lost somewhere deep and dark that was crushing her ability to cope. At least she was still alive.

I watched the road, and it was only as we approached New Hope that I realized something had shifted. Stiletto and Lachesis looked at each other. They'd obviously gotten a communication to which I'd not been privy. Now I was really worried.

Eighteen

Jamie

As Jamie crawled slowly into the tunnel, forcing herself not to think about creatures that lived within, she silently cursed Allan for bringing her into this mess and then leaving her. Yet just as she thought it, she saw his tiny light. He was coming back for her. She forgave him instantly.

"It's not that far," he said. "You can make it."

"There was something back there," Jamie insisted. "Something that was aware of me. What if it catches us as we come out?"

"Don't worry," Allan assured her. "I told you, I've got special protection."

"How?"

"Don't ask, because it might not last long. I'll explain when we're out of here. We've got to get moving *now.*"

With difficulty, he turned himself around in the small space and crawled forward. Jamie followed. Something sharp cut into her knee, and she was sure she'd scraped the skin raw, but she kept going. It seemed forever before Allan finally whispered to her that they were near the opening. He gestured that she should remain perfectly quiet. Then he said, "When we come out, we'll have to make a run for it to my car. It's parked about a quarter of a mile away. Can you do that?"

Jamie thought about the ridiculous heels on the boots she'd bought for her vampire outing in New York. That wasn't going to make things easy. "I'll try," she whispered back.

Within minutes, she felt the fresh air currents that told her there was an opening. She breathed it in and felt refreshed. Then Allan grabbed her and pulled her through the opening. Rather than being thrust out into the open yard, they found themselves protected by dense bushes and trees, as well as a thick blanket of darkness, yet Allan was still wary. He turned off his penlight, looked around, and then looked up. Jamie followed his gaze and noted that the round shadow over the moon blocked most of its light but was slowly moving.

"Come on," Allan said, and started running. Jamie followed as best she could, but was unable to keep up. He slowed down to grab her and then pulled her along. If not for the rocky ground, she'd have removed her boots, but having her feet cut up wouldn't do her any good, either. She just kept moving.

They reached Allan's car, and rather than unlock it automatically, which would have been noisy, he shoved the key into the driver-side door. Jamie opened the passenger door and jumped in, relieved to be off her feet and away from that house, but fully aware of how dirty and soiled she felt. The image of those corpses flew through her mind, and she thought of Devon still trapped inside. It felt awful to be leaving him.

"I can't go," she said. "I can't leave my son here alone."

"I'm telling you, Jamie, either they've already killed him or they won't touch him. Your leaving isn't going to change anything."

"Already killed him?"

Allan started the car and backed out of the spot

where he'd parked. "How can I make you understand?" he said. "They are not human. They do not care about you." His tone was condescending. "They kept your son alive only to manipulate you, not because they have any feeling for children. So if they think they need him to force you to do something, they'll keep him around. But the truth is, they may only make you believe they have him in a room someplace. They can put his image in your mind and you'd never know the difference."

Jamie was only half listening. She could attend only to the last glimpse she'd had of Devon in the room with that woman. She needed to touch him and to know that he was okay. Then something else flowed in that she'd expected, thanks to Allan, but was wholly unprepared for.

Naje.

He knew she was gone and he wanted her back. He needed her. Though the car was in motion, she sat up and reached for the door handle, but Allan was ready. To Jamie's surprise, he stepped on the brakes and reached around her, binding her arms to her sides with a tight elastic bungee cord.

"What are you doing?" she demanded to know.

He didn't answer. Instead, he used another cord to bind her hands together and tie them onto her lap by winding the rope around her thighs.

"What are you doing?" she practically screamed. "You're hurting me!"

"Sorry," he mumbled, and then stepped on the gas pedal. He roared out of there down a long, dark drive and then turned onto a main road. Then he looked at her and said, "I don't like this any more than you do, but he's going to try to get you and he won't stop till he does. You're vulnerable. You might jump right out of the car if he gets into your mind. That's what he's trying to do; I can tell."

"What are you talking about?"

"What he does. He makes you feel like you need him, like you can't exist without him. He did that to Ana—I mean Gail—and she bought it. She knew better and she still bought it."

Jamie suddenly felt defensive. "Well, maybe she knew something that you don't."

Allan looked at her and then gunned his car up to a speed so fast it slammed Jamie against the car door when he took a sharp turn on the road. Once they'd straightened out again, Allan said, "Let me tell you about your sister. She went into this place and she listened to them explain what they wanted. She played along because she wanted to get as much information as she could. But they worked her. She thought she was outwitting them, and they let her think it because that made her vulnerable. She never had a chance, and it wasn't long before she fell for one of them. She believed he loved her and that he'd give her what he had." Allan snorted. "But he didn't love her. He's a vampire. He can't love. He saw her value for himself and used her. Then he handed her over to a group of people who were going to use her tonight to channel some foul creature into existence."

"Oh, God!" Jamie responded. "This is all so absurd. How can you possibly think I'd believe any of it?"

"I'll show you," Allan said. "I've got it all on tape in my apartment in New Hope. I have a teleconference device that's scanning the place where this group is doing their ceremony. They're doing it right now."

"I'll see Gail?"

"I think you will. I left to go get you before they started, and I don't know how long it was going to take, but I recorded the whole thing, so we'll see together. Then you'll believe me."

Jamie moved uncomfortably in her seat. "Can't you untie me?" she pleaded.

"Sorry, no. They'll come for you and you'll be tormented into returning to them."

Jamie sat back. There was clearly no sense in arguing. Allan had his own ideas about what to do, and she had to go along with it. At least he'd come for her and taken her out of that house. She had to give him some credit for that, because it had been dangerous. But what his motive had been still troubled her.

He drove around another curve, and there in the middle of the road stood Naje.

Jamie screamed, certain of impact, and Allan hit the brakes, but then seemed to become a demon. He drove straight at the white-haired figure, and then right through him.

But there was no impact. Jamie was stunned. She looked behind them but saw nothing.

"What's wrong with you?" Allan asked. "You almost made me lose control."

"You hit him. You didn't see him?"

"Who?"

"The . . ." Jamie couldn't tell him. What she'd seen had been meant for her. It was just an image, some projection. No one had gotten hurt. "Nothing," she said. "I just thought I saw something on the road." She fell back against the seat to let her racing heart slow down.

Allan was silent for a minute. "It was him, wasn't it?"

"Who?"

"The vampire."

"Obviously it wasn't anyone. You didn't see anyone or hit anyone. I'm just tired. I'm seeing things."

"He's coming for you. He knows you're gone and he's coming. We've got to get to my place before he tries anything."

"What's going on?" Jamie wanted to know. "How do you know what he is and what he'll do?"

"I just know." Then as if rethinking his words, he said, "I have a book. I've learned everything I need to know about them. Now, that's all I'm going to say until we get to my place. We have very little time."

Jamie watched the road. She didn't want to see Naje again, not like that, but she wondered what he was up to. There was no doubt he knew where she was and that he wouldn't let her get away easily.

She didn't know what to believe anymore. Had Naje lied to her about Gail, or had Allan just done so? She couldn't understand any of this, but if Allan did indeed know where Gail was and could prove that, then he'd regain his credibility. It wouldn't be long before at least that question would be answered. They were nearing New Hope's town limits, and Jamie was grateful to see streetlights. Yet she was afraid of what Naje might do next.

Nineteen

Christian

When we arrived, we drove into the underground garage so we could carry Ana into the house undetected. If Coyne had penetrated our fortress, there was no telling what else he was up to, or how many others he might have recruited to help. Ordinarily, we'd have just left that place in search of another, but we had other pressing matters that night. It was now nearing two A.M. There was little time left.

I carried Ana inside myself, partly to attach myself to her as the one who'd found her. The closer I got to Naje, the more nervous I became. I couldn't even imagine looking into his eyes and seeing him shut off from me. I'd know in an instant, I was sure, and I wanted to delay that moment for as long as I could.

Eryx met us. He looked at me and shook his head. Obviously everyone there was aware of my blunder, which made me feel doubly ashamed. Then he took Ana from me and left me defenseless. He was taking her to Viper, he said. I let her go.

Stiletto and Lachesis had already walked away, so I went into the reading room in search of Bel. I had to know that someone here forgave me, and I counted most of all on her. If she turned away, I didn't know what I would do.

She was there, sitting on a plush velour couch, deep in conversation with Lethe. They both looked up together, and for an instant I truly believed I was outcast. Neither of them moved. I hardly breathed.

But then Bel came running. She threw herself at me and let me feel the wash of hot relief that flooded from her. She'd been out feeding and she felt wonderfully warm against my body. Only then did I realize how hungry I was, and how cold.

"I'm so glad you're back," she cried. It was a rare moment of emotion from her. "I thought you were gone for good. I tried to contact you but I—"

"I was just weak," I said, and then hugged her hard against me. "We'll get a few more trips to the city together." I didn't want to say what we both knew: things were closing in. None of us knew how this night was going to turn out. And if she knew what was in store for me there, she didn't give it away. She just hugged me again.

"Is Naje angry?" I asked. But she was looking past me to the door. I turned and there he was. My stomach churned in anxious waves, but I couldn't take my eyes off him. I prepared myself, fearing that he might order me to leave the house at once. Maybe he even thought that I was the traitor who had given Allan Coyne our secrets. After all, I was the one who'd been close to him. I was the one who'd alerted them.

I don't often feel fear, but I did in that awful moment. Naje's dark eyes nailed me to the spot. I felt Bel back away, and behind me Lethe got up and went out another door. I was certain Bel had followed her, but I felt so weakened I couldn't focus. Even Dantalyon was absent, which meant that the *dominie* had insisted on seeing me alone. I wanted to defend myself and beg for another chance. I tried to think of anything that could make a difference, but I knew that whatever my fate was to be, Naje had already decided. Nothing would change his mind.

He raised an eyebrow to let me know I'd used poor judgment. I wanted to slither away. I knew better, and it wasn't the first time he'd chastised me about this, but it certainly was the most inconvenient episode.

But then he astonished me. He held out his arms. Both of them. I hesitated only a second and then went toward him and into an embrace that welcomed and forgave me. He pulled me against his body and merged his aura with mine so that I would feel how much a part of him I was. Having no shirt, I felt the hardness of his chest and the vigor that emanated from deep within him. I was profoundly grateful for this and exotically warmed. I wanted to keep pushing into him but could go only so far against his solid form. He received my need and silently assured me. I sensed that he was satisfied that I had learned something that would now advance me, painful as it had been for the group. Yet I also believed that I'd done some damage for which I couldn't forgive myself.

"I thought you were gone from me," I whispered. "I couldn't connect with you."

"I was never gone." His statement was brief and quiet but overwhelming in its fullness.

Then he let me know that it was time to step back. I did so, but kept my head bowed in humility.

"All of us are here now," he said. His voice was deep and hushed but clearly concerned. "We need to discuss together what to do, but first let's see what we can do for Ana. If we can restore her, we can possibly get Jamie back."

I looked up and could barely keep looking into his black eyes. "Why do we need Jamie if we have Ana?"

"Because Ana's been corrupted."

I was stunned. "Corrupted? How? By me?"

But he was already on his way out the door. I weened the signal for all of us to gather in the lab, so I figured the others had received it, too, or were already there. All but Bel. Her small hand was there in mine. She handed me my favorite red cotton shirt, and I looked down at her in gratitude. Then we went to the lab together.

The others were already standing or sitting in various places around the large underground room. Naje and Viper were next to Ana, who lay at the threshold of no return on Viper's steel autopsy table. I noticed that he'd put down some padding for her. I watched him putter around and realized that this was difficult for him. He and Ana had developed a special rapport. He'd taught her all about his snakes and had even given her the idea to change her name. I think she'd fallen in love with him, and for him, she'd been an engaging respite from his usual isolation. With all that snake venom pumping through his heart, I had no idea what feelings he was even capable of, but we all sensed that he cared in some way about her.

I glanced to my left and saw Dantalyon sitting up on a shoulder-high ledge against an enormous sleeping python. He wore form-hugging suede pants decorated with rattler skin that Viper had made pliable in a special solution. He seemed lost in his own private thoughts.

Eryx was reading a tabloid newspaper to Lachesis and Lethe, and Stiletto sat in a chair nearby. The headlines said, *Three-legged Woman Opens Dance Studio*, and *Frog Spits up Shrunken Head*. Bel beckoned for me to join them. I looked around and saw Phelan with his finger in the cage of a tiny red racer that watched him suspiciously. Everyone was clearly waiting but not very willing to start this dark meeting.

"Where's Destiny?" I asked. Eryx looked up from his

reading. I felt everyone's eyes on me and I knew that whatever had happened, I was the last to know.

"Naje didn't tell you?" Lachesis asked.

"No."

"She's gone," Eryx said. "Just like Cacilian."

My mouth fell open. "What? How? She was here in the—" I couldn't say it.

"We don't know. We put her in the snake cage an hour ago, but she hasn't come around. She just sits there, staring."

"Was she in the house when it got her?"

Bel nodded. "She was upstairs."

"This thing, whatever it is, knows us," said Lachesis. "It knows how to get to us by picking us off one by one. It can't attack us as a group, but it seems to come in through our weakest members."

They looked at me and I held up my hands. "Okay, okay. I've learned my lesson. So I guess I'm next, then."

The others weren't about to indulge me in this; I was looking for reassurance but no one offered it. In fact, if anyone was next, it would be Phelan, and none of us could face that thought. He'd been in the *kamera* longer than I had, but his vulnerability was almost an art form.

I felt someone at my side and turned to see Viper standing there with a syringe. Much as I liked him, it was always disconcerting to look at him face-to-face. He'd long ago lost the ability to blink, and his eyelids just didn't work the way I expected. Even worse, whenever I got this close, I could see how truly inhuman his expression was. Maybe it was just the way his pupils had elongated into slits, but it seemed to me that he'd taken on a snake's persona entirely.

"Open your mouth," he commanded.

"Why?"

"I need some of your venin."

"Viper, I haven't regenerated it. They squeezed it out of me, both sides."

"Okay, then give me your arm. There's some in your blood, Christian. Enough that I can get the chemical composition for an antivenin."

I felt cornered. I'd already been violated once tonight. I didn't need this. "I hate needles," I said. "Just . . . can't we do it another way? I hardly have any blood in me."

"You won't even feel it." His frosty stare told me to stop whining and pull up my sleeve. I did it. Then he gripped me and his fingers were so cold I pulled away.

"Christian!"

I looked away and let him do what he had to do. I saw Bel's look of amusement, which further annoyed me. The needle went in and I flinched. He poked me three times before he found a vein that offered up the treasure. It didn't hurt, but I hated having anything taken from me. It went against the grain. Vampires take; they don't tend to give, and they certainly don't let others take from them if they can help it. I saw Eryx squirming the way someone does when watching a friend get a broken arm reset. At least *he* felt some empathy.

Viper quickly withdrew the needle, left me to plug up the pinprick hole with my finger, and walked away. He didn't even thank me, which I didn't expect. Vampire etiquette is organic to vampire nature. I rolled my sleeve down and joined Bel. She rubbed her fingers along my back and gave me a little smile.

"Listen to this," said Eryx. Phelan left the snake and came to join us. He rubbed my arm where the needle had been as Eryx picked up his tabloid and started to read. The article was about some group of temps who claimed they were channeling a powerful vampire. I listened closely.

" 'We're using the power of the darkened moon,'

one person was quoted as saying. 'We believe that to-night is the night that the world's energy will shift and open the door to the most potent form of evil ever seen on this planet.' "

Eryx looked at me. "Does that sound like what you saw tonight?"

I shrugged. "I saw a cult using the eclipse to conjure up something, but I didn't see what it was, and I didn't get the feeling that it was quite that cataclysmic." I thought for a moment and then added, "But there was something definitely sinister about it." I asked if there were any names mentioned, and he read off a few. I thought I'd heard one or two of them but couldn't be certain. Sabbatina wasn't mentioned. "It seems a bit too coincidental, don't you think, that the very same group that caught me is the one quoted in—" I stopped. There was a link—an obvious one.

Ana cried out and then began to scream. We all looked over. Viper appeared to have given her some-thing to try to counteract the effects of the overdose of my venin while he worked on the antivenin. I flushed in shame. Even if she survived, she wouldn't be okay. She'd already seen things in the tangled nether areas of her mind that would significantly damage her as a human being. It's the very same experience that had influenced our own transformations, but even to bring her over to be one of us now risked an incurable aber-rance that couldn't be tolerated among us.

Eryx looked back at me, and I was grateful that he wasn't accusatory. In fact, it was his unrelenting objec-tivity that often kept us balanced. "What were you going to say?" he asked.

Naje came toward us and I hesitated. I saw him glance up at Dantalyon, who remained completely still. I looked at Bel and she raised an expectant eyebrow. The moment was at hand.

"Well?" Lachesis pressed me. "Is there something you haven't told us?"

I shook my head. "I don't know. I may be wrong, but I'd say the link is this Allan Coyne. He's a reporter, so he could have gotten access to this group I saw and made sure this piece got into the paper. And he knew Ana."

"But why would he?" asked Bel. "What's the point?"

"Tabloid journalism," Eryx said with a shrug.

"It's more profound than that," said Naje. "He's not just a reporter. He coded that piece. It's a message."

We all looked at him. Even Dantalyon sat forward as if surprised. His python companion stretched a little.

"Coded?" Eryx asked. "For us?"

"Quite specifically for us."

"Why?" Stiletto looked supremely curious, as if trying to solve some puzzle. "He planted that piece and he lured us in. I don't see it. The timing seems off."

"It's not about coordination," Naje explained. "This is simply a message, a warning, regardless of anything else. He's letting us know that he's got all the leverage now and intends to use it. As long as he didn't know where we were, only those of us who ventured out alone were vulnerable." Naje turned to me. "I thought you might be next, but it was Destiny, and that means that he figured out how to target us. Now that he can get to us, we're all in serious danger."

"He knows about this nemesis?" Bel asked. "He's part of it?"

"He knows something. He knows enough."

"How?"

Naje didn't answer, but clearly this event troubled him. It wasn't like him to talk with any of us this much. He was pulling us together for defense, something we'd all known could happen one day. It was partly why we'd each honed a particular ability, so that we could complement one another, but there was more. On short notice, such as now, we had to become cohesive and unified—a single coordinated mind.

"Who betrayed us?" Lachesis demanded. "I want to know."

I looked at the group, scanning their faces one at a time, and then came back to Naje. "It couldn't have been me, could it?" I asked. "I didn't get close to him, but—"

"He reads thoughtprints."

"What?" Bel asked. "He can read our minds?" I knew that she was thinking about how she had warned me not to go down to the club.

Naje shook his head. "He's not a mind reader. To read a thoughtprint he has to hear the patterns of how you speak or else read something you've written." I saw Eryx squirm. He was the writer among us. I'm sure he was feeling some panic, but Naje continued: "He didn't get in here through thoughtprints, but that's how he can now do his damage. All he needed was a way in, and for him to learn where we keep our beds and find his way down to this floor, he had to have been told directly."

Naje looked at Phelan and we all knew right then that this traitor could be discovered . . . and soon would be. No one escaped Phelan's ability to distinguish honesty from deception.

"Maybe it was Ana," I said. "He knew her. Maybe he forced her to talk. Maybe he told her that we had her sister, so she sent him to get her. She knew the way in."

Naje said nothing, and I sensed that he already knew who had done it, and it wasn't Ana. However this all turned out, whether or not we survived, I felt that something about us would dramatically change in the next few moments.

It was Stiletto who spoke next, although he didn't

communicate in words. In a silent challenge, he asked Naje not to force Phelan to be the spiritual decoder. Stiletto wouldn't beg, but he'd certainly use the force of his displeasure to advance his request. Naje stood his ground and turned his regal gaze to Phelan, who stood trembling in our midst. I could feel him pleading with Naje as well.

Yet I knew that he'd do whatever he was asked, even if he was broken in the process. That was what Stiletto feared. To save the group, he would have to expose a member, and that was not his way. Even so, the point of our participation as a whole involved our individual gifts. They were to be used as needed, whether we liked the situation or not. That meant that in shifting contexts, they could be riches or curses. Phelan now bore the curse.

He reached into his shirt pocket and pulled out his glasses. Quite deliberately, he opened them and put them on. His shoulders drooping, he shuffled past Naje and went over to Viper. I nearly laughed at his decision to begin with the least obvious one. Viper was the beating heart of our *kamera*. He lived endlessly in these dungeons experimenting with snakes and corpses so we could learn. To have let in an intruder was to deprive himself of his own home.

Phelan approached and stood in front of him, silently begging him to understand. Without hesitation, he took Phelan's right hand and placed it over his own heart. His slitted eyes gazed without fear into Phelan's as he said, "I did not invite the intruder in here," and we could see that the youngster was visibly relieved.

But the idea that Phelan would have to do this with each one of us was excruciating. I didn't move and neither did anyone else. I don't think anyone even breathed. In a way, I really didn't want to know who had done it. What did it matter now?

Phelan came back among us. He looked like he needed some guidance, and Bel and I exchanged weary glances. I gestured for him to go next with me. I knew my heart was clean, but possibly my subconscious knew something that I did not. If I was some inadvertent traitor, I'd put an end to this suspense for all our sakes, no matter what it cost me. I'd already been bad that night; I might as well take the heat.

Phelan came and stood in front of me, his babyish eyes behind those absurd glasses magnified with suffering. I'm sure he was thinking about all my kindnesses to him and fervently wishing he had any other gift but this. Like Viper, I boldly took his hand and looked directly at him.

"If it's me," I instructed him, "you say so. I'm ready." I knew that to be thus revealed could mean being torn apart by my closest friends . . . even Bel. I tried not to imagine that. I'm sure she was feeling the same way. And yet to be outcast from this group would be so awful that I'd rather be destroyed than sent away to the eternal torment of knowing what I could no longer have. Naje watched, his expression hard, and I knew before Phelan even touched me that I was not the one.

Then Lachesis stepped forward and insisted on a reading. "I was out there," she said. "I led us into that trap. And I got the lead from someone who'd spoken to that reporter. I must be the one."

But Phelan was frozen into place. I saw the look on his face. He already knew who it was. I glanced around and realized that everyone else was aware of this development. Eryx actually paled—which is pretty white for him—and Lachesis gasped.

I thought Phelan was going to fall over, so overcome was he. He looked at the floor, possibly to keep himself from looking at the person whom he'd have to turn over to Naje. Removing his glasses, he started to cry in dry, heaving sobs.

Naje said nothing. He merely waited. It was an immensely cruel moment, I thought, but I wasn't as wise as he.

I was sure I'd burst from anger over this pressure on Phelan. I couldn't bear to have it continue, and I was not alone. Stiletto had already risen to defend his companion, but Phelan stopped us all. He fell to his knees in front of Naje and cried out, "It was me. I did it. I'm sorry." He continued to cry, and still Naje said not a word. His expression was unreadable.

It was in that instant that I realized. Phelan loved us all, but there was one whom he'd be utterly unable to cross in any manner. I looked at the dark Apache and saw him locked in mental confrontation with Naje. Their fierce eyes performed a complex battle that spoke of an anger that only those who love deeply can feel.

Bel rushed to Phelan's side, hugging him with a surprising burst of compassion. "It wasn't him; it was me," she confessed. "Destroy me."

Naje didn't even look at her.

Viper, who'd stayed in his lab close to Ana, came over to watch in curiosity.

Then Eryx joined in. "I was the one," he said. "I told him how to get through the tunnels. I showed him the spot."

Phelan continued to sob but more softly now. "Don't," he whispered. "Don't."

Naje then held his hand to Phelan and gestured for him to stand. He put two fingers under his chin to force him to look up.

"This is enough," he said.

Then Dantalyon shoved himself off his ledge and came forward. The air was so thick with passion that we all began to imbibe the heat. It was an automatic reflex, awful but intoxicating. Dantalyon was clearly enraged.

"I did it," he said. "I told him to come in here and get that girl out. I gave him access and I shielded him from your awareness. You know I'm the only one who could have done that. There's no reason to put everyone through this. You've known all along it was me!"

Naje appeared unmoved, and I began to understand that we'd just endured an important spiritual crisis. He *had* known, but he'd had a purpose in this exercise. We'd all protected the integrity of our collective bond over our personal survival. We'd passed a test—an excruciating one. I sensed that the reason Naje had put us through this had to do with something far larger than punishing a traitor. He actually seemed to approve of what had just taken place among us, or was at least pleased with the result. And yet some infected blister had been opened and now the pus was pouring out. None of us could stop it.

I recalled Dantalyon's words to me the evening before: *He knows something.* Had Dantalyon done this because he'd resented being locked out of a mind he'd shared intimately for more than one hundred years? Or had it simply been to save himself? I recalled what Lachesis had said in New York: Jamie had been a plant, and she was a threat to the consort.

The room went silent, but it was pulsing with emotional fervor and suspicion. I couldn't bear that these two were in such conflict. It could mean that Dantalyon had to go, even possibly to be destroyed, and that was something our family would never tolerate. Yet it was Naje's decision. Dantalyon belonged to him, body and soul.

"You don't know what you've done," Naje told him quietly. "You think he's just some idiot mortal who's trying to find the real vampires, but he's far more dangerous than that. He's both more than you know and less than he himself knows, and that makes him lethal."

In a rare burst of anger, Naje grabbed the tabloid newspaper that Eryx had been reading to us and said, "He planted this article to provoke me. He made sure that Lachesis knew where to find Ana and he set the trap. He brought Jamie right to us and now he thinks he can use her to lure us out again." He hit his chest. "To lure *me* out."

"Well, he can't succeed," said Eryx.

Naje looked at each of us and then at his protégé before he said, "Yes, he can. He has. I have to go."

Before Dantalyon could respond, Naje stepped toward Phelan, who was still trembling, and kissed him on the cheek. It was both an apology and a way to bestow his approval. Then he looked at Dantalyon and said, "Your fate has been decided." With that, he left us.

Even Dantalyon looked shocked. Then he faced us. Clearly he was stricken. Phelan kept his eyes on the floor. Dantalyon made a move as if to leave, but Lachesis stopped him.

"You can't just go," she said. "You put us in this spot. We deserve to know why."

Dantalyon turned around and faced her. It was almost amusing to see this powerful brave confronting a tiny wood nymph who stood her ground. Lachesis had been with Naje long before Dantalyon came along, and she had enough of her own shadowed layers to give her leverage.

Dantalyon stood there for a moment. He looked at Phelan, who could barely return his gaze, and then at me.

"None of you even realize that he's using you," he said. "You were all pawns. That reporter didn't set you up tonight; he did."

I raised an eyebrow, not quite believing. I wondered

if Dantalyon was saying this to deflect us from what he'd done.

"How could he have set us up?" Stiletto asked. The skepticism evident in his voice perfectly echoed my own sentiments. "He sent us all together. We could have taken that gang if Christian hadn't gone off on his own."

Dantalyon's laugh was brief and harsh. "You think he didn't know exactly what Christian would do? He could have sent Eryx. He could have sent Bel. He didn't need them here. Instead he sent the one most likely to separate and get caught, which gave *him* a way inside. That was what he wanted. He knew what he was doing."

"He wanted me to get caught?" I asked.

"Yes. Even if it risked you, he needed eyes and ears inside that place. They would have known if there were vampires around, so we couldn't just go in. We had to give you up to them."

"Why?" Bel asked. "Why would he risk any of us?"

Dantalyon looked at her and then faced Lachesis again. "Why don't you tell them? You know what this is about. In fact, why don't you enlighten Christian as to why you didn't just grab him yourself when you had the chance?"

Fire blazed in Lachesis's eyes, but before she could respond, Dantalyon stalked out.

I looked at her and realized that she did indeed know something. She could have rescued me tonight had she so chosen. Dantalyon was right: I'd been thrown to the wolves. On Naje's order, Lachesis had lured us to New York and to that house. She'd known what was going to happen. Bel realized this, too, and I saw her body tense up with anger and confusion. It was as though these older ones were playing chess, but with rules that we younger ones could not comprehend. But were they playing for survival for all of us or just for themselves?

"Well, are you going to tell us?" Eryx asked. "Is there some reason why we nearly lost both Christian and Dantalyon tonight?"

I looked at Stiletto, standing with his arms crossed, and wondered how much he knew. If he was surprised, he wasn't showing it.

Lachesis nodded, but her mind was clearly far away from this room. Her eyes were unfocused, as if she were picturing some other time or place. "The Dahaka is his . . ." she began, and Viper looked up from across the room with a warning expression. Now it was clear that he was in on this, too.

"We have to work together," she told him. "We don't have much time."

"It's not for you to say."

"What is it?" Bel asked. "What's the Dahaka?"

"Yes," I agreed. "That was the word I heard from that group."

"It has something to do with Naje's *kumu,* his guide."

Viper let out a quick, exasperated breath and shook his head. "Don't say any more!"

"We're all at risk here, Viper, even you. We stumbled tonight. We've got to get our footing back, and that will happen only if we're all together. That was what Naje just did for us; he forced us to act together, because he has to know what he's got here with us before he faces this thing. They should be told."

"Naje's guide?" Phelan asked. It was the first time he'd spoken up since Dantalyon had gone. "He had a teacher?"

Lachesis nodded.

"Was he a vampire?"

"I—"

"Lachesis!" Viper warned.

"So?" Bel pressed. "We know he's had teachers all

over the world. What does it have to do with any of this?"

But I was beginning to see, and I wasn't the only one. Allan Coyne, too, must have discovered something if he'd coached that sorry group of shadows to ritualize the power of the eclipse for raising the specter of Naje's mysterious guide. He'd kept his distance but had orchestrated it from outside. That way he was safe from whatever happened, but I felt sure he was monitoring it from somewhere. Possibly even feeding it. How could he know more than we did? It must have something to do with the thoughtprints that Naje had mentioned. Then I recalled the book he'd wanted me to find. The temps didn't have it, but possibly Coyne did.

"It's . . ." Phelan began.

"What?" I pressed. "What is it?"

"It's revenge."

I wanted him to say what he meant, but Ana suddenly screamed from her bed. Viper went to her and then beckoned Lachesis to come close.

"Read her," he commanded. "You're the most skilled. You've got to get into her thoughts and find out what she knows before she's lost to us."

The rest of us came closer to watch.

"Link with me," Lachesis said. "We'll read her together. She's more likely to respond to you, but I can get you more deeply inside her."

Viper nodded. I wondered what he was feeling. Clearly this moment gripped him in some inarticulate way.

As I watched, I felt Bel's small hand come into mine. I looked at her and knew she wanted to feel close, just in case. This night had been difficult for her, she seemed to be saying, and these revelations had shown her how fragile everything was. There was so much we didn't know. I put my arm around her shoulders just as Stiletto made the same protective gesture to Phelan. I thought I saw tears in Phelan's eyes, and I wondered if it was because of Dantalyon's curt response to his generous devotion. Something important was cohering for us, but something was falling apart, too. Our center was gone and we had to find it again, or create a new one.

I watched Lachesis concentrate on Ana. I knew something about the way advanced vampires ride mental waves to read the mood and content of thoughts, but I'd yet to master this myself. It came with hours of practice over a period of decades, and I just didn't have the patience. But when I saw it in action, I castigated myself for taking shortcuts. This was truly a unique and significant skill.

Viper, too, was trying to focus, but I could tell from the strained expressions on both of their faces that we weren't making much headway. Eryx stood off to the side, his arms folded over his chest, with an expectant look.

"There's something," Lachesis murmured. "She wants to tell someone something but I can't hear what it is."

Viper nodded.

"She has something or had something . . ."

"She's here," he said. "She's trying to connect. I can see her soul."

Lachesis put her hand on Viper's shoulder as if physical touch magnified their mental power. I wondered what they were experiencing. I felt a shift in energy, and it was evident from the way my body went on the alert that they were generating heat. I guessed they must be taking it from Ana.

She moved as if in pain. Viper narrowed his reptilian eyes. She started to move her mouth as if speaking, but nothing came out. We waited several agonizing moments before Lachesis pulled away and shook her head.

Then Viper looked over at me and indicated that I should come closer. Curious and a little wary, I let go of Bel and went to the gurney.

"Drink from her," he said. "It'll diminish some of the strength of your venin."

"You think?" I asked. "Won't it be more dangerous?"

"Christian, I don't have time to develop an antivenin specific to your stuff. I have to attach the molecules to tiny gold beads and inject them into mice to get the best reactant. That will take days. You're the only one among us, besides Naje, who can tolerate it without overwhelming side effects. So you do this, and do it carefully. I've got a pint of blood from her sister that I can use to replace what you take, and I'll monitor her heart to make sure you don't damage her."

"What about an inhibitor?"

"Don't you think I've tried that? They put too much in her. You have to get it out."

"This is like leeching someone," I said.

"Something like that," Lachesis snapped. "Get to it."

I took a deep breath, glanced at Bel, whose eyes betrayed her concern, and then bent toward Ana. Doing this in Viper's presence was like making love to another man's wife. It felt all wrong. However, time was running out, and I was sure that he'd figured out all the angles. If he was asking me to do this, then it must seem to him the only possible route.

He rolled back the light blue sheet that covered Ana and used scissors to cut away her black dress. It was apparent from small stains and numerous wrinkles that she'd been wearing it for quite a while, possibly since the day she'd disappeared. Underneath was a crimson bra made to lift and plump her breasts. Viper moved the left strap so that I could get close to a major artery near her heart.

I didn't like this plan. I could already feel the warmth

of her body working on my brain to release the drug that drove us to indulge without limits. It was like testosterone fueling the male libido, but much stronger. Once the act was begun, it was difficult if not impossible to stop. And yet Viper expected a measured approach. Easy for him—he wouldn't be the one in the throes of physical craving, and aside from one hasty drink I'd been starving all night. I felt Bel's hand on my back and was grateful for her awareness of what I would need in order to keep from killing this mortal girl.

I bent closer and smelled Ana's skin. It was stale, with the merest trace of soap and old perfume. Her heart was beating and I felt the warmth. I closed my eyes and let the effect pervade my body. Then I licked an area just over her left breast. I felt Viper's eyes on me. Despite this, I began to feel the rush of breath and the tingling in my belly and crotch and down my legs that starts the dance. My fangs came forward to prepare for plunging into Ana's soft skin. My lips drew back and I ran my left hand up her body to hold her in position as I readied myself for the assault. I had no idea what it would be like to draw my own powerful juice back into myself, but there was no turning back now. The worst thing was that Naje wouldn't be there if I needed his help. We were experimenting here like children without supervision, and I could get into real trouble.

I bent over Ana and gripped her ribs. Then I stopped. Surprised, I pulled away and my fangs retracted. My fingers had brushed against something just beneath her left breast, something hard that didn't belong there. I drew away and straightened up.

"What's wrong?" Viper asked. I heard the possessiveness in his voice that told me he wasn't too keen about this procedure.

"There's something here."

I moved Ana's bra, exposing her breast, and then

lifted the soft, supple flesh to see what I'd encountered. I saw a badly bruised area and a small stitched cut that appeared to be fresh. In fact, a line of yellow-white pus had crusted around the edges of the skin. A lump beneath begged to be explored.

Viper instructed me to stand back. He grabbed a lamp for better light. Everyone crowded in to see what I'd discovered.

"Let's cut it," Lachesis said. "She won't feel it."

Viper grabbed a scalpel and snicked it through the thin layer of skin. Whatever had been sewn there was right at the surface, so he didn't have to dig into muscle. In moments he had a piece of bloody metal in his hand.

"It's a key!" Bel said. "Why would she sew that under her skin?"

"Obviously she wanted to keep someone from getting it," Lachesis said. She looked at Viper and he nodded.

"That was what she was telling us. This key opens something important. Something for us."

"Or Allan Coyne," I reminded them.

Viper flashed a dangerous look at me.

I shrugged. "There's something going on that none of us grasps. At least, I don't. But I think Coyne does, and it's very likely he told what he knows to Ana. Now he's got Jamie. And he appears to have something that Naje needs."

"Well, we still have the boy," said a voice from the doorway. We looked over to the shadows and saw Dantalyon leaning against the frame.

"We need to get this key to Naje," Eryx said. "He might know what it's to."

Dantalyon shrugged. The look on his face made it clear that something was wrong. "He took my car," he said. "He's gone."

"Where?" Stiletto asked.

We gathered around Dantalyon, not quite believing what he'd just said. Since I'd joined the group, Naje had never been outside. I was surprised he even knew how to drive, although I was aware that he'd somehow traveled all over the world. Still, the fact that he'd gone out seemed incongruous.

"I don't know," Dantalyon said. "He said we were to stay here so he could draw this thing away."

We all looked at him, and I felt the strained energy of our mutual horror. Naje could be destroyed somewhere away from us, where there was nothing we could do.

Then Viper broke the spell. "We've got to get to work," he said. "Christian, get on with this."

Now there was no hesitation. Naje was out there, exposed, and we had to see if we could possibly purify Ana. I quickly prepared my fangs and plunged right into the area over her left breast. Fear drove me, and then hunger and desire took over. I felt the powerful smack of my own psychotoxin coming into my body and nearly lost my grip on her, but I continued. The flow of hot blood trickled at first and then surged into me and tightened all my cells. I grew increasingly more ravenous, and was only vaguely aware that Bel and then Viper were trying to separate me from my prey. Someone pulled my hair to jerk my head back but failed. My fangs were deep in Ana's soft flesh and I wasn't letting go. Her heart beat loudly in my ears and this was all I wanted, all I cared about.

Then Naje was there. He was inside her mind, commanding me to move away. Surprised, I pulled out and stood up straight, then nearly fell over. Someone caught me from behind, and then another came up on my other side. I didn't even know who was touching me. They set me down in a chair, and I felt someone wipe at my mouth with a warm, damp cloth. But I was in the full grip of a hallucination.

"Naje . . ." I whispered. "He's going to . . ."

I felt a large hand on my chest and then Dantalyon was close. "Stay with it, Christian," he said. "Use the *mana.* Just tell us what you see."

"He's found her. . . . He's found Jamie."

Twenty

Jamie

It wasn't easy getting up to Allan's second-floor apartment while tied, but with his hand under her right elbow, Jamie managed. He'd untied her legs and led her along the canal until they'd reached some wooden steps, and then they went up, with Jamie going first. Allan looked carefully around, clearly nervous, and then unlocked a door and shoved her in.

Once they were in his cluttered studio, she asked to be untied, but he would only remove the bindings from around her arms and chest. He left her hands tied.

"I can't risk it," he said. "You don't know what they're like."

"What's the risk? I wanted to get out of there."

"For now. He'll call to you again, and you'll want to go back. I saw it happen with Gail until there was no reaching her at all."

Exasperated, Jamie found a place to sit near one of several computers that were all showing different screensaver patterns. "So where's this proof?" she asked. "And when can we go get Devon? I want to just get him and leave this place." Once again her son's frightened face came unbidden into her mind, the way he'd looked the morning she'd left on her ungodly odyssey.

Allan gestured for her to calm down. "Everything in time," he said. "Let me get this set up." He moved toward a desk where Jamie could see a twenty-inch monitor.

She had never seen a teleconference device. It looked like an ordinary computer but it had the capability of showing in real time what was happening in some other place, even as far away as overseas. It used some sort of satellite connection to digitize the images from one place and re-create them on a screen someplace else.

"I got this from a friend who does teleforensics," Allan explained. "He can access a crime scene even though he's in some other country. They can show him fingerprints, blood spatter patterns, the position of a body, and whatever else he needs to offer an assessment. Sometimes the first officers at the scene just don't have the experience to know what to do."

He hit a button, and a small blip on the screen opened up to show an empty room that seemed in obvious disarray. He appeared perplexed. "It can't be over already," he said. Looking at his watch, he then tried to focus the picture.

"What?" Jamie asked.

Instead of answering her, he pressed another button and she heard a tape rewinding. He fiddled with the equipment for a few minutes and then brought up an image on the screen that had obviously been recorded in that same room. This time, however, there were people in it—a lot of them.

Allan backed away to watch and Jamie sat forward. As she did so, she hit her arm against the chair, and a sharp burst of pain reminded her that the vampires had taken her blood. She thought about Naje and his request.

In the video, she saw at least a dozen people, maybe more, and most of them were young men. As she watched, she was reminded of things she'd read out in Arizona about satanic rituals performed in the desert areas. Everyone was dressed in black, and some wore exotic hairstyles.

"What is this?" she asked. "More of these role-players?"

Allan assured her that it was something far more powerful, but his attention was focused on the screen. He seemed disturbed. Then Jamie looked more closely and realized that she knew the person lying on a table in the center of it all. Her hair was black, but there was no mistaking who it was.

"That's Gail," she said. "Where is she? What are they doing to her?"

"I told you," Allan said. "Those vampires gave her up to this group. They're experimenting with her, and they were about to do the same thing with you."

Jamie watched in horror as Gail was given some kind of injection. At least she was alive, but what was happening to her looked dreadful. After a few moments, she started to speak, but then the images on the screen scrambled and blurred.

"Damn vampires!" Allan said. "They're interfering." He wouldn't say anything more, although he mumbled something that sounded like, "They must have found it."

Then he flipped open his cell phone and was soon talking with someone who appeared to know about this ceremony. He sounded upset. "How could you let it get out?" he demanded to know. Then he gave some instructions, pushed a button on the phone, and came over to sit near Jamie.

"What's this about?" she asked. "Is Gail all right? Where is she?"

He took a deep breath and said, "No, she's not all

right. I'm sorry to be the one to say it, but the vampires grabbed her and they're going to kill her."

Jamie pulled away in shock. "Kill her?"

"Yes. That's been their plan all along. They lied to her, lured her in, and she believed that they wanted her to become one of them. She was foolish and now she's as good as dead."

"How do you know that?" Jamie asked. "Did that person on the phone tell you?"

Allan nodded. "She said they came in, broke the place up, and took her."

"But we didn't see that."

"They wouldn't let it record. That's the kind of power they have."

"But why would they give her to that group like you said and then come and take her? That doesn't make sense."

"I don't know. Their plan must have changed." Allan was visibly disturbed, and it seemed to Jamie that he just wasn't getting his story straight.

"They gave her to this group," Jamie said in a measured tone, "and intended to do the same with me. They then go get her by force . . . so . . . what does it mean now that I'm gone?"

"It might mean that she was taken by a completely different group. I really don't know."

"Different group?"

"There are more out there than just those that you saw. And they don't get along very well."

"Where would they take her?"

Allan just shrugged.

Jamie began to feel numb with all this information overload—information that failed to even make sense. What he was telling her seemed too unreal. Gail was not going to die. "I don't get it, Allan," she said. "How did this happen? And if you knew where she was, why weren't you *there* instead of with me?"

"I knew where this group was meeting because I'm a reporter. They had talked with me earlier and I printed their story, but they weren't about to let me come in. I planted a device for viewing and that was as close as I could get, but obviously that didn't help much."

"Then why in God's name didn't you send the cops?"

He put his hands on his hips and looked at the floor. "I have reasons," he said, "but I'm not sure you'll believe me."

"Well, Allan, you have to tell me something. Otherwise I'm going to get out of here somehow and drive back, and I'll find Gail and Devon myself."

He snorted. "You'll never be able to do that. You don't have a clue what these creatures can do. That's exactly what they want. They'll be waiting. You'd walk right into a trap. Then none of you would get out."

"I won't leave my son with them. I intend to get him back. And if they have Gail or know where she is, I'm going to find her."

Allan watched her for a long moment before he asked, "Did you see him? Did you see the lead vampire?"

Jamie was astonished. Why was he shifting the subject like this? Didn't he understand her primary concern?

"Did you see him?" he repeated. "Did he show himself to you?"

Jamie stuttered out a response. "I . . . I don't know."

"You'd know. Gail said he's magnificent. Looking into his eyes is like finding the most amazing depths of peace and safety. When he was mortal, he was a powerful *kupua*."

"A what?"

"A Polynesian wizard. He was one of the wayfinders,

the intuitive men who directed the course of the travelers who set out in canoes a thousand years ago to cross the ocean to the Pacific islands. They were exceptionally skilled, and even among them he had special perception. He knew how to merge the forces of nature with the subconscious to get what he wanted. Most of us are aware of only two selves. He's in touch with four."

"I don't have a clue what you're talking about."

"That was because you haven't studied this stuff, but I have. He can move in and out of the different realities without any real effort because he's connected to the most basic force of the self, which is pure will. He can change his experience entirely from the inside out, and he can make his group follow and protect him by harmonizing their energy. That gives an added dimension to anything he focuses on, which means if he wants to destroy or seduce someone, he can use their collective strength to enhance his own. He's nearly invincible."

Jamie watched him and realized he was obsessed with this creature. It was like looking at the title of a book that spoke of infinite details within once someone opened to the pages. Allan knew a lot more than he was saying.

"So why are you taking him on then?" Jamie asked.

"Because I control the only power that can do it. I have what will bring down Achilles. I understand his vulnerability, and through that chink in the armor I can direct his enemy against him. Once he's crippled, I'll have my chance at him, and then he'll be damaged beyond hope. I won't have a thing to worry about, and thanks to him I'll become the most powerful man on the planet."

Jamie watched Allan's demeanor change. He was hungry for information, even fixated on it. Something was going on that she didn't comprehend, something beneath appearances.

"So you would know if you saw him," he continued. "He has white hair, long hair, and he's very tall."

Jamie shook her head. For some reason she didn't want to reveal her experiences there. Something intimate had passed between her and this creature that had the aura of a shared secret. Despite her shock at the idea that vampires existed, her horror over what she'd seen at that house, and the things she'd just heard about Gail, part of her wanted to return and know him. He had something for her.

"Well?" Allan prodded her. "What kinds of things did you see?"

"Nothing really. They wouldn't let me see much. They kept me in a room." Jamie thought about the pretty young man who'd first revealed what they were, and the puppyish blond who'd been so eager to explain all about snakes. She didn't understand how such things could exist, and still half believed they were highly experienced role-players, but that older one, Naje, did truly have powers. A wayfinder.

"You were in the underground when I found you," Allan said. "You had to have seen something." He got up and paced the room.

"Snakes," said Jamie. "I saw lots and lots of snakes."

Allan shook his head and looked at her askance. He didn't believe her, she sensed, but neither could he get her to talk.

"What can we do to get Gail?" she asked.

"Nothing. I told you, they intend to kill her."

"They can't. They need—"

Allan raised an eyebrow. "So you do know something."

"They told me they needed her. They didn't tell me why."

"Jamie, if you want Devon back, you need to be straight with me. I have the tools to get inside that nest of vipers, and I have a way to destroy them, but I need you on my side. I have to be able to trust you, and that means you can't hide what you know."

She shrugged. He was persuasive, but something held her back. "I really don't know anything. They grabbed me, tied me up in a room, took me downstairs, and told me that they knew Gail . . . or Ana . . . or whatever you all call her."

"And you didn't see the leader?"

Jamie shrugged again. She couldn't bring herself to lie outright.

Allan returned to the computer screen and tried to get some images but it was still scrambled. He fidgeted with more buttons, as if looking for a new channel, but it appeared that his efforts were in vain. He pounded the desk with his fist.

Then he went still, as if listening. He cocked his head to the left. Jamie was about to say something, but he gestured for silence. Then he went over and lifted the heavy curtain away from the window. "Shit!" he exclaimed. "One of them's out there."

Jamie jumped up, nearly losing her balance from her hands being tied, and went to see for herself. She wanted it to be Naje. She wanted to believe that he'd come for her, even if there was nothing she could do about it. He hadn't been real when she saw him on the road, but if Allan sensed this, then maybe he was actually out there. Peering into the darkness, she strained to see what Allan had sensed or spotted, but he pulled her away.

"Don't let them see you," he insisted.

"Why?"

"I don't want them to know where you are."

Jamie wanted to laugh. "From what I've seen, they won't have any trouble tracking me. I don't think we got out of that house because we're clever. They let us leave."

Allan looked at her. "What makes you say that?"

"Because they know things. There's a lot of them in there. You don't just walk in and walk out."

"You don't have a clue of the power I have. I'm protected. I told you already that I can destroy him, and without him, they all go down. And that's going to happen soon, very soon. I have his thoughtprints."

Now Jamie was interested. They were back on the subject that he'd claimed was "everything." This time Jamie wanted the details. "What do you mean?" she asked. "How can you have something like that?"

"Things get written down; they get passed around. A long time ago—centuries—he wrote a manuscript. Gail got it for me. She went into their house and stole it."

Jamie was stunned. "She wouldn't have."

"She did."

"Where is it? I want to see it."

Allan hesitated and then said, "It's locked away. But I've studied it thoroughly. I almost know it by heart, and I figured out his story by reading between the lines. He thinks he's put his past behind him, but he hasn't. He'll kill his own lovers without hesitation, and has. He's killed his children. Don't even begin to think that he cares that you're protecting him. You won't get any points for that."

"You talk like they're all a bunch of psychopaths. They were human once, from what I could tell. I saw evidence of feelings. They were taking care of Devon."

Allan snorted. "You're a fool, like your sister. Their only traffic with you is what they can take and use. You're meaningless to them. But that Naje, he's worse. He's an annihilator. He'd destroy that whole group if he thought it would save him. He can always re-create it with others. They mean nothing to him except fuel for the power he gets from the collective mind. He put them together and he works them into a unit, but it's all for him. Don't kid yourself."

"How do you know all this?"

"It's all there in his manuscript. It was just a short thing, only about thirty pages long, but if you know how to read subconscious patterns, it's easy to figure out."

"Figure out what?" By this time Jamie was losing patience. She wanted to know who was out there. Yet something about this document intrigued her. If Naje had truly written it, she wanted access to it herself. That her own sister had stolen it made her feel that she had some kind of family obligation to Naje. Especially if it contained the formula, as Allan implied, for his destruction.

"Who was out there?" Jamie asked. "Which one?"

Allan peeked again through the curtain. "I don't know," he admitted. "I just caught a glimpse. They like to play cat and mouse. They're— Shit!" He took a sharp breath, which sent Jamie back to the window. She didn't care if they saw her. She wanted to know.

To her astonishment, standing there in the shadows across the canal was Naje. He was holding something close to him but looking up and right at her. Jamie expected to hear some kind of voice in her head, but there was only silence. Then he stepped out into the moonlight, which was brighter now, and she saw what he was holding. It was Devon. The boy had his arms around Naje's neck and he appeared to be sleeping against his chest. Naje supported him with one strong arm.

"My son!" Jamie cried. "He's got Devon!" She turned to rush from the room but Allan caught her.

"You can't go to him! It's a trap!"

"It's not. He's brought my son. I'm going down there."

"Don't, Jamie. If you stay here I'll tell you everything. If you go, you'll be bound so firmly this time that you'll never escape, and neither will Devon. He's just using your kid as bait."

Jamie struggled to free herself and managed to get rid of the bindings around her wrists. She hit Allan hard and made it as far as the door before he caught her again. He used his whole weight to throw her against the wall.

"You can't leave here!" he shouted. "I won't allow it."

Jamie turned and hit at him again. "You can't keep me here!"

He grabbed her wrists, forcing her back into the room, and she cried out from the sharp stab in her arm. Allan shoved her against the couch and pinned her there with his knee.

"You're not going anywhere," he said.

Afraid now, Jamie stopped struggling. Allan decreased the pressure on her. Then she heard the call. Naje was out there beckoning to her with the full force of his presence. Jamie could almost feel him caressing her, using a rhythmic connection that went deep into her and caused her to crave his touch. She made a move to leave, but Allan held her fast.

"Allan, I need to go," she pleaded. "Please."

"No. I need you here. Don't you see? He can't come in to get you or he would. There's a reason for that. He knows he can't get near me."

She pushed again but he held her fast. Then she screamed out, "Devon!" Looking to the window, she hoped he could at least hear her, but that was her mistake. Allan slapped her hard and then pulled her off the couch and over to a chair. Before she realized what he was doing, he'd bound her hands together again and then tied them to the chair.

"No!" she cried. "Don't."

"I'm sorry," he said. "I can't let you go." He took off his leather belt and forced it into her mouth before wrapping it around the back of her head. Jamie had no idea how he'd fastened it, but it held her tongue so far back in her mouth that she could barely make any noise. He rummaged in a drawer and found a cord that he used to tie her feet to the chair. Then he strung it behind her and wrapped it around her neck. She made as much noise as possible to try to dissuade him.

"He's a siren," Allen said. "If I don't tie you, he'll lure you out." Then he pulled another chair close and looked at her. "He doesn't care about you, Jamie. How many times do I have to say it before you'll believe me?"

Jamie just stared at him. She tried to move her tongue to shift the belt, because it hurt the corners of her mouth.

"He'll be gone soon and then you'll have Devon back," Allan assured her. "I know the way. You'll be thanking me."

Jamie's eyes widened in distress.

"Yeah, I can see that he's worked on you. So you've seen him, after all. That's why you won't talk about him. But you won't gain anything by it. Now just listen. When Ana was with them, she found this manuscript that this Naje wrote, only he didn't use that name. It was written hundreds of years ago, but there were translations of it in several different languages. She showed it to me and I studied it for the thoughtprints. I figured out pretty quickly that he'd been associated with a powerful being that he'd somehow trapped and stolen the powers from, sort of like Prometheus stealing fire from the gods. The manuscript is meant for shamanic practitioners, to teach them how to do it, but it was clear that he'd learned the stuff from his own experiences. I studied the document and figured out how to find this other creature, who needed a human channel for coming back through. He was trapped in an energy field that prevented him from returning for revenge, and that was accomplished with Naje's magic." Allan was panting as he related all of this. "So to make a long story short, I contacted him through a medium and made a deal: I get him through to destroy the one who trapped him and stole from him, and he gives me the most seductive substance the world has ever seen. Look at Ecstasy or heroin and imagine something even more powerful and addictive."

Jamie looked away. She didn't want to hear any of this. But what he said began to sink in. Naje was a vampire. What would he possibly want with her, other than something he needed for himself?

But this deal troubled her. Had Naje actually been treacherous when he trapped the other one, or protective? And if the other one had nursed a grudge for so many centuries, what would it be like unleashed? In moments she began to realize something frightening: Allan was so caught up in a large-scale, self-enriching vision that he was blind to the obvious: what he himself had said was that vampires take but don't give. What would stop this other creature from just destroying his enemy and then killing Allan and her, too? Once it was free, why should it give anything up?

In that instant Jamie knew how she fit into this scheme. He didn't need her there to talk to her but for something else, and it was probably related to what Naje had told her about her genetic map. Those other people were using Gail for that very purpose, and now Allan wanted to do the same thing with her. *It needs a human channel,* he had said.

Now what she'd just seen on the computer screen made sense. Allan wasn't just some reporter; he was directing that group in the procedure for bringing the other creature through. From the tone of his voice on the phone earlier, she guessed that something had gone wrong. Then she recalled his words: *How could you let it get out?* Whatever *it* was, the thing was no longer under his control. That meant it was going to the vampires, and they had Devon.

She had to get away.

Allan was on the phone again, completely ignoring her, so she challenged her bonds to see if there was any weakness. To her despair, he'd been thorough. And yet Naje was out there. . . .

She held still and listened. He had said something to her about breathing deeply to increase her perceptions, so she held her breath. All she could hear was Allan's voice and the unrelenting chirping of crickets. Trying again, she pulled the air in more deeply still and held it. It was only when she thought she'd burst from lack of oxygen that she felt him near. He was with her, inside her.

Be still, he whispered. *Wait.*

Jamie let out her breath and took it in again as she tried to adopt a meditative pose to help Naje communicate. She fervently hoped he'd somehow help her contact Devon. Surely he knew what she most needed right then.

Suddenly Jamie realized it wasn't Naje or Devon with whom she was connecting; it was with Gail, her sister, as they'd done as kids when they didn't want anyone to know what they were thinking. They'd learned to be aware of each other's thoughts and feelings as only twins can achieve, and here it was again, the same feeling.

Gail, where are you? Jamie silently asked. She filled her lungs more deeply.

Gail seemed dazed and unable to speak coherently, but gradually her voice emerged through a haze.

Get . . . get it . . . the manuscript.

Gail, please tell me where you are. I'll come and get you. Don't let him . . .

Jamie let out her breath and the connection was lost. Allan glanced at her, but he was still talking to the person on the other end of the line.

Surreptitiously, she breathed in again and Gail was still there. *Jamie, get the key. Get it . . .*

Then she was gone again.

Long moments dragged by, and Jamie felt sure that Naje was no longer there to connect her with her sister. She feared the worst. Gail had seemed terribly weak, even in pain.

Then her voice drifted in again. *Jamie, I took it. I wanted to know. Allan got it. He has it. I tried to get it; I couldn't. I took the key. Get the key. Get it.*

Then to Jamie's great surprise, as she held the air in her lungs nearly to the point of blacking out, she saw her sister. Gail emerged from a swirling grayish haze and came toward her. In spirit form, they embraced. Then Gail whispered into her ear, and when Jamie pulled back in shock at the communication, the spell was broken. Gail was gone and Allan stood over her with a fierce expression on his face.

Twenty-one

Christian

I felt a hand on my belly and a mouth closing over mine to force air into my lungs. Vaguely I knew what to do from years of practice every morning before the trance shut me down. I took in the breath, knowing if I inhaled deeply enough and held it in, it would begin to counteract the force of the venin I'd just swallowed. I could still sense Naje's presence, and there was something he needed, but I couldn't speak beyond the announcement I'd just made. My tongue seemed paralyzed. Then I felt other fingers touching me, and it seemed as if the entire *kamera* surrounded me to lay hands on me. We'd been trained to multiply our energy with total focus, so they were aiming this at me, and gradually the mist cleared and I regained some awareness but felt utterly weakened.

I opened my eyes to see Bel watching me. "Christian," she said. "We think Naje's trying to communicate. You've got to concentrate."

I shook my head. "Can't," I said through what felt like thickened syrup.

Then Dantalyon took my face in both of his hands and forced me to look him in the eyes. "We're running out of time," he said. "Use the *aka* thread." Then like a medic giving CPR to a wounded soldier, he came close and pushed breath into me. The warm contact with his moist tongue woke me up further, along with the realization that if he was saying and doing this to me, Naje had cut him off. I closed my eyes again and tried to see inwardly. I knew what he meant about the *aka* thread. I had to connect with Naje to form a psychic conduit. To facilitate this, I imagined a golden cord shooting out from my belly to him, braided into a strong rope by the joint mental efforts of my companions. Then I truly did feel their energy run through me. It was a rush, sexual and mystical and potent.

A message pulsed at me, but it ran through me like water into a hose. I couldn't catch it, though I sensed it was from Naje. I started to fall away. I had connected, but for some reason it had been difficult and bumpy, like talking on a cell phone from within a tunnel. I shook my head. The others counted on me but I couldn't do it.

Then I smelled cold flesh and felt a wrist push against my mouth. I wanted just to sleep, but my fangs twitched forward and soon I was penetrating skin; I didn't even know whose. I reached for the arm and knew from the feel and foreign taste of it that it was Viper. The liquid that flowed forth was bitter and I jerked back, but he held my head still and forced me to imbibe the snake's essence.

"It should heal you," he said.

I took it in, nasty as it was, and soon began to feel better. When he pulled away, I had no more urge to sleep, but I still felt weightless.

Bel knelt beside me, facing me, with her arm over my leg, and said, "Christian, what did he tell you?"

I blinked and tried to mentally reach for the message, but only one word came through. "It's just . . . apport."

Bel looked puzzled, as did the others. An apport is a physical object that mysteriously appears at a séance or some other physical location, as if it were moved through some spiritual dimension. Mediums call them gifts from the spirits, and they could be anything from a dish of candy to a block of ice to a human skull. It's just suddenly there where it hadn't been before, and it's physical and solid.

"He's sending something?" Lachesis asked. "I don't understand why we're blocked. Any of us should be able to understand this."

I shrugged. I didn't know.

"It's this thing," Stiletto said. "It's between us and him."

"Christian hears him because of Ana," Phelan said, "because he penetrated her."

"Oh!" Lethe exclaimed. "An apport! The . . ." She clapped a hand over her mouth.

We all looked at her.

"I shouldn't say it," she said. She looked around, hoping one of us would connect.

Bel leaped to her feet. "I know!" She went over to where Ana lay and picked up the key that Viper had removed from her skin. Viper looked perplexed, and Dantalyon, too, seemed confused, but I was beginning to see what she had in mind. Now it was Bel's special gift that claimed the moment.

With a finger to her lips, she beckoned to Eryx to come close. "I think we need to practice our little sport," she said. His eyebrows came together in question, but then he smiled and nodded. I didn't think this plan could possibly work, but Bel knew a lot more about the capabilities of ghosts than I did. It wasn't an apport that we intended to bring forth, but an asport that we wanted to send. That was the word: *asport*. Naje was making his energy available to the spirits, something he disliked doing, to provide the right channel to get this key to him. The main problem with this little trick is not getting it to work; it's keeping the spirits from stealing the object and transporting it elsewhere—especially if they want to get back at us.

Bel closed her eyes to better read the room, and I got a kick out of watching this little white-haired pixie use her awesome sense of paranormal discernment. She could process the room with the speed of light and catch a ghost like a frog snaps up a fly. There were ghosts of every variety in this place, so it didn't take her long to lure one close—one that was sufficiently solid for even me to read his energy signature. It was the revenant of an older man who'd died from some illness in this house over a century ago and who seemed rather mindless. I wasn't sure if that trait was better or worse for what she had in mind, but as we watched, she pulled him toward her and quickly rolled and packed his apparitional form into a ball. I felt his protest. He wanted to talk, but Bel was not one for ectoplasmic chitchat. Especially not now.

Once the ball began to form, Eryx placed his hands around it to hold it steady. I could barely see the glow between his fingers, but Lethe nodded as if to say that the concentration was nearly right. Bel held the key over Eryx's hands and waited a moment.

"Okay," he said, and she dropped it.

It went right through and clattered on the floor. We groaned together in disappointment.

"I can't hold him," Eryx announced, and the orb shot away from him and went through a wall across the room. His shoulders sagged. "Sorry," he said.

Bel looked at me and I gave her an encouraging thumbs-up. I felt sure that Naje knew this could work. It was just a matter of trying again with some other spook, but we had to do it quickly. He might not hold the channel open for long.

I glanced at Phelan and saw him watching Dantalyon

with some concern. The Apache's face was grim and his expression distant, the way he looked when he was tracking invisible forces. He caught my eye and looked down.

"It's close," he said. "It's coming."

"Where's Naje?"

He just shook his head. He wouldn't show us his distress, though I knew he must be feeling a deep loss over this disconnection. It probably helped that the others were cut off as well. Yet at the same time, he and Lachesis were the two we looked to now. He couldn't just indulge himself. He had to come up with a plan for our protection in the event that Naje failed to return before the annihilator arrived.

Bel had caught another ghost. This one was female, the kind of person who in life had devoted herself to helping others. She had died a long time ago, when New Hope had been a stopover along the canal for mule barge crews. I weened that some drunken lout had stabbed her to death. Unlike the elder spirit, she seemed willing to be manipulated; she even appeared to like it. Bel smiled slightly as she formed this unearthly illuminated snowball. Phelan watched with great curiosity, while Stiletto crossed his arms in a waiting pose. Lachesis couldn't look. I saw her catch Viper's eye and believed they both felt somewhat hopeless.

Eryx cupped his hands and Bel placed the whitish orb into them. This one glowed with an opaque brightness, which told us this spirit had more energy than the previous one, and more density.

"Tell her what you want," Dantalyon suggested. "Then throw the key into the air."

Bel nodded. It made sense that this procedure might require energy in motion rather than the passive mass we'd used in our first failed attempt. She talked to the orb as if it were her friend, asking permission to use its energy and instructing the spirit to take the key to the open door. It was something like a medium urging a spirit to "go to the light." If this was going to work, the ghost had to connect with Naje's *aka* thread and travel along it. That is, if he was still pushing it toward us. A lot depended on all of the elements coordinating just right.

"She's ready," Eryx said. "Toss the key and I'll launch her."

Bel fingered the small metal key and then flipped it into the air about six feet over her head. Just as she did so, Eryx pitched the orb. We watched, breathless, as the key hit the apex of its arch and began to descend. Then it disappeared. It was just gone. Bel looked at me and grinned, but her triumph was short-lived. In seconds we heard a clang against the wall to our left and then a tinkle of metal on the cement floor. Viper was closest, so he reached down and picked it up. It was the key. He looked over at us with his unblinking eyes.

Lachesis shook her head. "She can't get it out," she said.

Stiletto breathed out. Then he said, "Let's take it outside."

"No," said Dantalyon. "We're too vulnerable out there."

"I'll go. Bel and Eryx and I. They can do this and I'll keep watch."

"No!" Dantalyon was adamant. "We can't separate."

It wasn't good for us to be without our center, but it was clear that only one of us should call the shots. Stiletto backed down, though I saw something in his face that told me he would not be subordinate for long. Lethe went over to stand near Ana. She put her hand on the unconscious girl on several spots as if looking for something.

"Calm down, everyone," said Eryx. "Let's just try it

again. Apports aren't stopped by walls. However they work, it's not about being carried on this plane." He looked around. "Can anyone sense Naje? Is he still ready to receive this?"

"I can," Lethe piped up. "I don't know why, but I read him a few minutes ago. He's there. He's put Jamie and Ana together. He's—"

"Oh!" Bel cried. "That's how!" She went over to Ana, who'd been utterly silent all this time but was still breathing. I saw that she was hooked up to an IV with a small pack of crimson blood dripping through a tube stuck into her right arm. Yet even if she were given a complete transfusion, I believed it was too late for her. Bel laid her hands on the girl and then said, "This is where the channel is. We have to direct the ghost here."

Eryx looked up. "She's back. That same one is back. She wants to help."

He was right. A thin ectoplasmic cloud formed overhead that we all could see. It floated near the ceiling as if waiting for the next command. In an instant, I knew, it could roll up and shoot away. We had to hurry.

Bel took the key from Viper. She held it up to make it clearly visible and went to lay it on Ana, but just as she was about to let go, the key disappeared from her hand. The ectoplasm was gone as well.

"He's got it," Lethe said with a smile. "She connected and he sucked her through."

I collapsed back into my chair in relief, but Dantalyon was not about to let us relax.

"We have to keep vigil," he said. "I'm going to draw it to us."

"What?" Lethe asked. "Why?"

"To keep it away from Naje. I can mimic his energy and make it come here."

"No," said Lachesis. "You can't bring it here." She glanced pointedly at Phelan and continued: "It's too risky for the younger ones. It won't go after you until you're the last one standing."

"It wants Naje."

"If that was all it wanted, it would have had him already. It came like some murderous Passover angel and took Destiny. No, it's not going to just attack the one it wants. It's going to hurt him in every way first, and that means us."

"Besides," said Stiletto, "you betrayed us. You collapsed the center and you let Phelan suffer for it. We're weak now because of you."

Dantalyon didn't even flinch. He stared steadily at Stiletto and said, "We're not separating and we're not leaving Naje to face this thing on his own." His chin came up in defiance and his eyes flashed hot.

Stiletto met his challenge with protective anger. "I won't let you put Phelan at risk. Or Christian."

"What difference does it make?" I interrupted. "If that thing goes after Naje and takes him first, we're all done for anyway. I'm not going to survive without him or all of you. I don't want to. It might as well come here first."

Then Phelan stepped forward. He didn't look at Dantalyon, but instead kept his eyes on the floor. With intense bravery, he said, "I'd die for Naje. If that was what it means, I'm ready."

Dantalyon watched him in silence for a moment and then said to Stiletto, "We should all be ready. This is what Naje prepared us for. You think we're weak, but we're much stronger than we were before this night began. Naje uses everything, even our mistakes. What's real is the moment—*manawa*—and everything that's made it what it is. We have to move into it together and stop thinking like separate souls. That's our only hope. He may not be here with us physically, but if we harmonize our resources he's here spiritually. That's been the whole point of the *kamera*. A single energy source. What good is it to learn the bow if you never shoot the deer?"

None of us could argue with that; we'd all heard this from Naje. The question was, who would lead us?

"What are you going to do?" Lachesis asked. "How can you get this thing here?"

Dantalyon didn't respond, and all eyes turned to him in expectation. He remained silent.

"Look," I said, "I don't know a lot, but I know this: whatever's going on with that manuscript and Jamie, Naje could walk in there, kill the reporter, and get whatever he wants. For some reason he's not doing that. Something else is going on that he understands better than we do. None of us could even be in this room without having a deep sense of trust in him, and I for one don't want Dantalyon to violate whatever binds them. If he can't tell us, I accept that."

"I agree," said Eryx. He took a step toward Dantalyon. "Just tell us what you want us to do."

Dantalyon waited on Stiletto, who stubbornly stood his ground. He obviously needed all of us, and this deadlock was consuming precious moments. Phelan touched Stiletto's arm to get him to relent, but he continued to stare at Dantalyon. "What you did was self-serving," he accused. "That corrupts the nucleus. I can't trust you, and I think Naje left because he couldn't, either."

I knew Dantalyon wouldn't defend himself, although I understood Stiletto's resistance. I looked to Lachesis to dissolve the impasse, but she, too, was watching Dantalyon. Bel came over to me and leaned against me. When she gripped my shoulder, I sensed some fear in her.

Then Viper came forward. "Tell them," he said to Dantalyon. "We won't cohere without the truth." Dantalyon flashed a look at him as if to silence him, but he continued: "You tell them or I will."

"Tell us what?" Lachesis said.

Viper looked from one to another of us and said, "Dantalyon didn't betray us. It was my idea to get that girl out of here. I knew there was something wrong. Genetically she's identical to Ana, but there was something more: she's pregnant. That was an element I didn't calculate and that meant we had an unknown factor that posed some real risk, not just to her but to Naje. And we knew that with time running short, he'd go through with it anyway."

This surprising bit of news silenced everyone, and it was Stiletto who first found his voice. "So you let that reporter in here?" he asked Viper. "Why not just take her and drop her off in New Hope or Princeton?"

"It would have been obvious, and Naje would have stopped us."

"But how did you fool me?" Phelan asked.

"I didn't." Viper turned toward him. "You were asking for honesty, not truth. You sought the one who showed the reporter in. I told you I didn't do it, and I didn't. All I did was keep Naje busy while Dantalyon let him in."

"I still don't see—" Lachesis began.

"Giving Coyne access," Dantalyon said, "made him think he was getting some special privilege, so he was willing to give something for it. I was getting rid of the girl anyway, so I used it as leverage."

"What did he give you?" Lachesis asked. "What was worth making ourselves that vulnerable?"

"Did you get the book?" I asked. "This manuscript that Naje wants?"

"No. But I know that Coyne has it and he's read one of the translations. When you told me he was at the club with Jamie, I suspected he had it. He lied to me about its contents, but as he talked I was able to track its energy."

"And . . . ?" Stiletto pressed him.

"I now know what this thing is."

Just then, Lethe looked up in horror and said, "Something's here."

Twenty-two

Jamie

Jamie continued to focus on staying open to Naje's voice, although she was bound so tightly there was no chance that she could get to him. Allan had seen to that. Clearly he'd been afraid that she had found some way to communicate with the vampire. And he'd been annoyed, so he had added an extra strap to prevent Jamie from escaping to Naje. Yet just having Naje this near brought back all the powerful feelings she'd experienced in his presence. She completely forgot the things Allan had warned her about.

Then he was there. *Open your hands,* he communicated.

She couldn't imagine why, but she struggled to shift her wrists in such a way that she could make a small cupping space with her palms up. Naje instructed her to keep them level. That was a trick. Every few seconds, Allan glanced over at her as he punched in numbers and talked on his cell phone. It sounded like he was giving urgent instructions to someone, but he kept his eye on her. She bent her head forward to look as if she were giving up and he turned away. At that moment, Jamie felt something cold and hard in the palm of her right hand. Carefully she looked at it and saw that she had a small metal key. She couldn't imagine how it got there and had no idea what it was to, but it seemed that this was what Naje had wanted—that she receive it. She couldn't begin to fathom the ways of these creatures. How could a key just appear from thin air? And what did he want her to do now?

Just as she looked up, Allan was in front of her. He saw what she had and darted his hand to grab it. Jamie clamped her fist shut.

"How did you get that?" he demanded to know. "Where did you find it?"

Jamie stuttered that she didn't know.

"Was it on the floor?"

"I . . . no . . . yes, yes, it was on the floor, down by my feet." It was the only thing she could think of to say. He surely would not believe that it had just materialized in her hand from out of nowhere.

"I thought *she* had it," he murmured to himself. "He gave it to you, didn't he? He wanted you to get that manuscript from me. Isn't that right?"

"I don't know what you mean," Jamie said.

Allan held out his hand. "Give it to me."

She didn't know what to do. Obviously Naje had sent it to her and would not be pleased to have it come into the hands of his enemy. Yet her resistance made no sense. If she'd just picked it up from the floor as she'd claimed, why not give it over? Weakly, with a stinging awareness that she'd failed Naje, she opened her hand and allowed Allan to take it.

He immediately went over to a small, reinforced case under the desk where his computer sat that looked like the type of fireproof box in which people kept important papers. Inserting the key, he opened the beige container and exclaimed in triumph, "It's still here." Then he put his hand deep inside and Jamie could not see what was there. She suspected it had to be the document he'd just mentioned, the one from which he'd read the thoughtprints. Gail had communicated that she'd taken it from Naje. Now things were beginning to make sense. Gail stole it for herself, Allan took it from her, she grabbed the key, the vampires grabbed her, and they got the key. Naje had given it to her to get the manuscript back. When it all seemed clear, Jamie was unhappy that she'd been so slow. Now Allan had it all.

He slammed the box shut and locked it again. Then he put the key into his pocket.

"Well, my dear," he said. "We have someplace to go. I've got everything I need to destroy that nest of monsters out there who have your son. They can't escape me now. This will be their last night on earth."

"Are you going to untie me?" Jamie asked.

Allan forced a smile. "Yes, of course, although not entirely."

When Jamie protested, he said, "It's for your own good. You'll thank me when this night is over. Believe me, the last place you're going to want to be when I've completed the ritual is with the vampire."

"What do you mean?"

"I mean that I have the means to destroy him, he can't do anything about it, and it's not going to be pretty. He's going to get sucked into a maelstrom of evil souls that will torment him forever."

Panic filled Jamie's throat. "But what about Devon? And Gail?"

Allan began to untie her legs. "They won't be harmed; don't worry. It's not a weapon or a bomb. It's his own worst nightmare."

Jamie looked out the window and wondered if Naje was still out there. When her feet were loose, she moved her legs to restore circulation. Allan freed her arms, too, but kept her hands bound together.

"Allan," she said, holding her hands toward him.

"Please take this off. What do you think I'm going to do?"

"Go to him. That's what he wants. And believe me, Jamie, even if he tries to use you as a hostage, that won't stop me. It just won't. So you're better off letting me handle this as I think best. If he tries to lure you, you won't be able to resist. You won't want to. So despite what you think, I'm protecting you. He wants something that I have and he's not going to get it."

"What is it?"

"It's the secret to his power. I know exactly what evil he performed to get it, and now he'll pay for his mistake. And I'll benefit beyond my . . . beyond *anyone*'s wildest dreams."

"Allan," Jamie said, "what are you going to do?"

"I'm going back to that house," he responded. "And I'm taking you with me. Then I'm going to turn all that energy that this vampire has used to empower himself for centuries directly against him. It's too perfect. I'm beating the devil at his own game. All this time he's been feeding off this force, using it to survive and thrive, and now it's going to circle back on him and exact its revenge."

"You're making no sense whatsoever," Jamie said. From his surge of glee, she sensed that he felt on the edge of triumph and wanted someone to know what he'd accomplished. She was actually beginning to get the picture, and it had something to do with this manuscript, but she thought that if she played dumb she'd get more information.

"I can't explain it all," he said. "But we've got to be there before the sun comes up. The shifting electromagnetism of the geophysical energy right before dawn will make this thing the most powerful it can be. I don't really have to be there. I could do it from here, but I want to see it happen. I want to see the vampire get hit by his own progenitor. He's going to be sorry he ever learned this magic—eternally sorry."

Allan now had her free from the chair and he pulled her to her feet. "We'll have to do this carefully," he said. "Whatever is out there might still be there. And he wants what I have."

"It's him," she said. "It's him with my son."

"No, it's not, Jamie. That was just his trick. He wanted to remind you and bait you, but he wouldn't risk bringing your kid into New Hope. He knows I have people here."

He went back to the box and opened it again. Then he pulled out a sheaf of papers that looked rather ragged and used. He flipped through them until he appeared to find what he was looking for and he placed that sheet on top of the others.

"This is it," he said. "Let's get to my car. You walk in front of me. If he's out there and tries to get you to come, I can stop it." He held up the papers. "I've got this. He doesn't have a prayer . . . so to speak."

Just then the window shattered inward, blasting shards of glass toward them. Some of the papers blew out of Allan's hand and he rushed to pick them up. Jamie protected her face and Allan grabbed her and pulled her toward the far wall. "He's coming," he said. "Let's get out of here."

He opened the door and pushed her through, then kept a firm grip on her arm as they went down a different set of stairs from the one they'd used to come in. "It's the back way," he said. "He'll think we're going straight to my car, but I have a driver waiting for us."

All that mattered to Jamie just then was that they were returning to the house where Devon was. If she could get there, she could find a way to escape Allan and find her son.

They came out into an alley, and Allan urged her

toward a dark-colored van that looked like a vehicle some cleaning company would use. Recalling her earlier abduction, she balked, but he jerked her along behind him. He opened the door to the back and told her, "Get in, quick!" She struggled to do so with her hands still tied together and finally managed it. Then he climbed into the front passenger seat and turned to the driver. Jamie heard a quick intake of breath and "Oh, shit!" so she leaned forward to see.

A young man dressed in black leather in the driver seat was slumped over the wheel, his eyes staring in terror. His head was bent awkwardly in such a way that Jamie suspected his neck was broken. She didn't have to ask to know that there would be marks somewhere on him that would reveal that he'd also lost a lot of blood. The vampire, wherever he was at that moment, was now much stronger.

"Shit!" said Allan again. He handed the papers to Jamie and then got on his knees for leverage. He grabbed the corpse and began to push and shove it until he had it angled between the seats.

"What are you doing?" Jamie asked. She hugged the manuscript against her and had half a mind to pull off a few of the top pages and hide them. They seemed important, and in some small way maybe she could make up to Naje what her sister had done.

"I can't dump him out in the street, and we don't have much time. He'll have to go back there."

"No!"

"Sorry. You'll just have to live with it. I'm sure he'd be happy to trade places with you."

With more shoving, Allan managed to move the victim into the back, and Jamie tried hard not to touch the corpse. At least there was no blood. She couldn't stand to see how his head lay against his shoulder in a way that it shouldn't be able to do. She didn't want to

think about Naje just killing someone in such a wanton
way, though it was obvious that this kid had been among
those who posed a threat to him. This was some kind
of war where enemies killed each other. Closing her
eyes, she just wished they'd get to the house.

Then Allan grabbed the manuscript out of her arms
and placed it on the passenger seat while he got behind
the wheel. He started the car and maneuvered it out of
its spot. Jamie looked at the pile of papers and wondered how hard it would be, with her hands tied, to
toss it all out the window. But if she did that, she knew
Allan would kill her.

As he drove through the quiet streets, he pulled out
his cell phone and made another call. He didn't get an
answer, so he punched a button and called again. It
took a few minutes for someone to finally answer, and
as soon as they did, Allan spit out, "He got Trent. He's—
What?"

Jamie knew at once that something else had happened. Allan drove with one hand as he listened to the
report. "Barefoot. You're kidding! But that was him; it's
got to be." Then he said, "I don't know how he found
us, but I'm on my way to the house right now. Protect
whoever's left in any way you have to. We don't know
how many of them might be out. They'll have to get
back before sunrise, anyway, and I'll be waiting. I'll call
you in an hour." Then he slapped the flip-phone back
together.

"What happened?" Jamie asked.

"I'd say he's fortifying himself. He got three of my
people. Sucked 'em dry."

"Three?"

"Well, including Trent back there, that was four. One
of them he killed with some kind of black venomous
snake. He just walked in with this thing—without shoes
on, if you can imagine—and flung it. One of my guys

was dead in seconds, and this thing just lifted him up and drank him like a soda. He's filling up his tank, I'd say, though little good it will do him." Half turning in his seat, Allan looked back at her. "He's a killer, Jamie. If you didn't think so before, believe it now. There's not going to be any happily-ever-after for you two, no little half-breed brats. He doesn't want you; he was using you. Unless we get him first, he'll kill you and Devon and Gail. Now, are you with me or not?"

She sat back, numbed by this piece of news. She didn't know what to think. Here was this man who kept her a prisoner asking her to side with him against an alluring, exotic creature who seemed to be only defending his territory—yet it was a territory carved from blood. She couldn't side with either of them.

"What do you want me to do?" she asked.

"They have Ana . . . Gail. When we get there, we'll find our way to where she is, and when you see her, you go right to her. When you're in place, then I can start."

"What do you mean?"

"Look," he said as he glanced at her in the rearview mirror. "Let me lay this out. I've told you bits and pieces, but here it is. This Naje is some sort of extradimensional being. He's a vampire but he's much more than that. He empowered this group of vampires around him to protect him from something he did centuries ago. From what I can tell with this document, he tried to increase his powers by outwitting some very bad entities. I don't even know what they are, but they're very mean and destructive. He had a ritual for luring them, but he did it through some shaman who was training him. I wouldn't be surprised if it was the one who made him a vampire. So anyway, he exploited the magic like the sorcerer's apprentice, but he blew it. Things ended up out of control, so he directed all the energy at his mentor and destroyed him. Then he trapped the spirit in some nether region and walked away with the goods."

Jamie was incredulous. "You read all that in this manuscript?"

"No. I said I read between the lines. I read the thoughtprints and listened to what Gail told me about this creature, and I figured out what must have happened. It wasn't hard. He was going to use her to get some more juice, I think."

"Juice?"

"Power. Magic. He was going to tap in and take it without letting the thing out. And he needed a human channel to keep it contained. He could have killed her in the process, and probably still will unless we stop him."

"What if you're wrong about all this?"

Allen glanced back at her. "You've seen him. You tell me. Am I wrong that he's a very powerful being? More so than the others?"

Jamie pondered this. "I don't know," she said. "I don't really know what he is. He's a skilled hypnotist; that's all I know."

"He's more than that, believe me. And he's treacherous."

"So what does all that mean?" Jamie asked. "I still don't get it."

"I've found this entity that he trapped. I've released it and I can use this document to aim it straight at its betrayer."

"You've communicated with it?"

"Yes. Not in language, but in other ways. I conveyed what I wanted in exchange for releasing the thing, and I have assurances that I'll get it. Once this Naje is destroyed, the others will go down with him, and I'll be free to take his precious blood. That's all I want. His blood and his venom. His mentor or whatever it is, can have his soul, if he even still has one."

Jamie just shook her head. She didn't know what to say to this hallucinatory narrative. To her mind, Allan just sounded nuts. Nevertheless, he obviously had a clear goal.

"So," he prompted her, "does any of that make sense to you?"

"I don't see where I fit in."

"You fit in as a conduit. This thing has no boundaries, so it needs a physical form to help it condense and aim its powers. You and Gail can give it that, because this Naje calibrated the process to her genotype, and bringing the two of you together may heal even her. She's been damaged. You saw her. She needs a life force like yours. It'll all work out if you just do what I say. I promise."

Jamie thought about what Gail had reveal to her in the vision: she was pregnant. How Gail could know that when she hadn't been aware herself was disturbing enough, but now this journalist wanted her to put her at risk for his grand plan.

"Okay," she said quietly. "Just tell me what you want me to do." It seemed to her the best way to lull him into believing she'd be obedient. He might even untie her. But channeling some vengeful entity was not in the cards. That he could never make her do. Nor could she imagine being the conduit for Naje's destruction, despite the things she'd just heard.

The rest of the way there, Jamie tried to ignore the hideous corpse in the seat beside her by staring out the front windshield to see if Naje would appear. She just wanted to know where he was, and especially whether or not Allan was right that he hadn't actually brought her son. Could he have killed these people in front of Devon, breaking someone's neck and drinking blood?

Could he have carried a poisonous snake while holding him? She didn't want to even imagine it. Naje had not seemed so cold-blooded to her, but she didn't really know. The little blond back at the house had said they were like snakes.

Allan parked the van in a secluded spot and Jamie looked around to see how close they were to the mansion.

"We're not there," he said. "We can't get too close. We'll have to walk."

"Walk? But I thought you said these things are out killing people. If we go out in the open, what will stop them from just grabbing us?"

Allan reached for the stack of pages. "This," he said. "We've got a guardian angel. They're afraid of it. You should have seen the one who approached me to get you out. Like Geronimo."

Jamie could hardly believe what she was hearing. He had to mean the dark-haired one who wanted her dead, the one they'd called Dantalyon. "One of them approached you?"

"Yeah. He said he'd give you up in exchange for the contents of the manuscript. He wasn't too bright, either. I didn't tell him a goddamn thing, but he thought I did." Allan laughed at his own cleverness. "I tell you something, if I looked like him, I'd probably opt for immortality, too. But he wanted you out and he offered a deal. I could tell that this manuscript bothered the hell out of him, too."

"How?"

"He was just so intent on it. He listened to every word I said. He wanted to see it but I'm too smart for that. I told him I knew he could just kill me and take it. He said he could anyway, and I said, 'Go ahead then.' That's when I knew he couldn't touch it. There's something about it that's like garlic to these vampires. They protect it but they're afraid of it, too."

"So you didn't tell him what it said," Jamie repeated, just to be clear.

"Nope. I gave him a convincing song and dance. I must have, because then he showed me how to get in and he protected us till we got out. What he'll do when he finds himself empty-handed I have no idea."

Allan grabbed a leather pouch from behind his seat and shoved the papers inside. "Okay," he said, "enough talk. Time to go." He got out and came around to help Jamie out. She didn't appreciate being alone in the van with a corpse next to her, but it wasn't long before the door next to her was unlocked and Allan was reaching for her. She practically jumped out. To her relief, he finally untied her hands. She rubbed her wrists to restore circulation.

"We've come around behind the place," he said. "Not where the tunnel came out, but in another spot. It's about forty minutes to sunrise. Let's go. We don't have a lot of time."

Twenty-three

Christian

Lethe cowered a little, but Dantalyon instructed her to translate what she could from the energy she sensed in the room. She shook her head and said, "It's some language I don't understand. It's very old."

"Just tell me what you hear," he insisted, and then to Phelan he said, "You let me know if it's truth or a lie."

Phelan nodded, obviously intimidated. He looked over at me with huge eyes and I could tell he was scared to say the wrong thing. Nevertheless, it was fast becoming clear that whoever was going to lead us in this situation would have to know how to coordinate our gifts. As taciturn as Dantalyon usually was, he was stepping into his role now.

With halting effort, Lethe offered what she could. She strung together a phrase, and then a couple of words. I thought they sounded like a language Naje had spoken a few times, and it seemed to me that Dantalyon comprehended some of it. He didn't say anything to us. He just listened.

Then Lethe broke off. "It's not pure," she said. "There's more than one. And it's hard to hear a single voice."

Phelan nodded. "I sense both truth and lies, and I

can't tell. The true communication is the weakest, but there's more than one coming through."

Dantalyon put his hands to his hips. "It isn't here yet," he said. "This is some forewarning."

"So what is this thing?" Lachesis asked. "You and Viper seem to know something we don't. I think we should be told. Obviously what I thought I knew isn't the truth."

Dantalyon nodded his assent.

"It's something called the Dahaka," Viper said. "But that's just a code name. It's like the *Kana*, a trickster, but it's more than one entity. I don't know how many, maybe dozens, but they all travel together, trapped in some astral current."

"But where does it come from?" Eryx asked. "And how will it attack us?"

"We don't know exactly, but we think that long ago it was once a gang of malicious humans who found a way to blend with certain destructive powers from the supernatural. They brought harm and torment to a lot of people, and there seemed to be no stopping them, so one of the *kapunas* decided to subvert them. First he devised an elaborate ritual of protection and then he ventured out in his astral body to learn what he was up against. From what we could tell, he was tempted to take their powers to enhance his own."

"From what you can tell?" Lethe asked. "If it's what you say, how could you have gotten close enough to this thing to understand it?"

"It was from the manuscript that Ana took," Dantalyon said. "I knew something about it from Naje. What he was doing with Ana was related to it. And I learned more when I talked to that reporter. He thought if he had both Ana and Jamie, he could work the magic."

"I still don't understand why it's coming for us," Lachesis said. "What's our association?"

"The *kapuna* involved was Naje's teacher, his mentor," Viper responded. "He wrote the manuscript. It was meant as a charm against the black magic that he intended to use. It's like those elaborate chairs that some people in Europe carved specially to sit in and send out their astral form. The manuscript's purpose was to protect the one who performed the ritual and said all the right words, but to work it required a human medium, someone apart from him. That was the way it was set up. If he didn't have that, then he'd become the medium. He'd be vulnerable to the Dahaka's attack and would get sucked up into them."

"What exactly did Coyne tell you?" Eryx said. "How could he have understood all this?"

Dantalyon looked at Viper, who shrugged and said, "That was my fault. I told some things to Ana—not much, but enough for her to figure things out once she got the document. Or to think she did. Then Coyne forced her to tell him, and from there, he did some research. He must have found out something, too, because these entities were trapped for hundreds of years and now they're free. They started overseas taking out some of Naje's former *kameras,* the ones he'd left behind. Now they're here. Since he was the one who trapped them, they're coming for him and for us."

"Naje trapped them?" Phelan asked. "Where was his mentor?"

"With them. He's trapped, too."

Phelan's eyes opened wide. "Naje did that?"

No one said a word, but I thought we were all aware of the same possibility: if Naje could do this to an intimate, what did that mean for us? And where was he now?

"There must be something we don't know," said Stiletto. "It doesn't feel right to me." He looked at Dantalyon. "Surely he's told you. The two of you practically share the same mind."

Dantalyon shook his head. "Naje keeps his secrets. He's been close to many teachers, but this one was different, and I think he's trying to communicate. I know the sound of the language, but I don't know what he's saying."

"Maybe he was treacherous," Phelan offered. "Maybe Naje had to trap him and now he wants revenge."

Dantalyon didn't respond to that. "He wanted to touch the Dahaka," he said. "That much I know. He never told me why. He was going to go through Ana to keep a controlled means of escape. When the time was right, we were to protect his spirit while he went among them. But he didn't get that far. The rest . . . was not meant to happen. He didn't free them, but I think he's hoping to trap them again."

"So he needed the key to get the manuscript," Lachesis mused. "He had us send it through so he could unlock the place where it was kept. Ana must have known where it was. That's why she had the key."

I shook my head and said, "I don't think it's that simple."

Dantalyon's eyes were moving as if he was connecting to some invisible power. "Whatever happens, we do what we've been trained to do, all of us. There's no more time to prepare."

Suddenly the whole place went dark. That didn't matter, because we could see fairly well in the dark, but there was something disconcerting about it nevertheless. Someone else had taken control and was sending us this message.

Phelan cried out and I saw around him on the floor a moving ring of black smoke. Everyone looked and it soon began to form a substance that rose quickly to knee level. Stiletto shouted for him to jump out, but he was frozen. Dantalyon went toward him, but Stiletto was closer. He grabbed Phelan and the dark smoke suddenly formed into a long, snakelike rope, slithering up his arm and winding several times around his neck. Dantalyon pulled Phelan away and pushed him toward Eryx, but he stopped short of touching Stiletto, who gasped for breath as the thing choked him. Lachesis came forward, and even I rose from my seat to help, but Dantalyon stayed us both. To get too close risked the same fate. We didn't know what this thing was or how contagious.

Stiletto wheezed and his muscles bulged as he pulled at the thing. I couldn't bear to see this. We don't die like mortals, blacking out when the cells are starved. Instead, we remain fully aware of the torment that our body goes through. To terminate consciousness, we must be completely destroyed.

We watched as Stiletto fell to the floor and turned onto his back, wrestling with the thing that squeezed his throat shut. His eyes bugged and his tongue came out of his mouth. I looked at Dantalyon, who stood over him, his hands rolled into fists. We had to do something.

Yet even as the Apache remained still, I could see that something was at work. He and Lachesis had aimed their full concentration on Stiletto, which meant they were extending to him their energy. I looked at Bel and saw that she, too, had connected in some way, as had Viper. Then Stiletto went still and I didn't know why. Phelan rushed in, but Dantalyon blocked him and pushed him back.

Slowly the black cord unwound itself from Stiletto's neck and one end of it began to snake across the floor. Inside my mind I heard a sharp command to get off the floor and I sprang away. Dantalyon stepped protectively in front of Phelan just as I reached the wall into which we'd chiseled small chinks for practice, and went up.

I was halfway to the ceiling when I looked back and realized that something terribly cold was close to me and was sucking at my body heat. The snake had opened up into a new form, like some Mora that can take any shape it wants. It looked like a small tornado, whipping a freezing torrent at me. Lachesis had been right: it was going first for the weaker ones.

I felt a tug from the others to join my mind to theirs to break this power. We couldn't defeat it if we remained apart, but desperation seized me. I moved across the wall and soon realized that it was close at my back. For the second time that night, but faster than before, I made for a small space, blew out my breath, and collapsed my ribs to squeeze into it. If this thing was fluid, it would follow me, but if it was just seeking easy prey, it might move on.

I squashed myself into a large crack in the wall and found it giving way. Nothing had choked me yet, or grabbed my foot, so I kept pushing. Speed was my greatest advantage. The other side of the wall fell through, and I moved into the hole to come out into the morgue. I fell right on top of a male corpse that had been there a little too long. The stench of decomposition was overpowering. I knelt on the man's chest and felt it collapse under my weight, ribs cracking and liquefied organs bursting out through his mouth. I snapped off an arm to plug the hole I'd left in the wall, and then used a foot to complete the job. Then I took a moment to breathe. Collapsing my ribs like that risked poking a hole into my lung. We do heal, but not quickly.

Nauseous from the organic gases, I ran toward the door and found that it was locked from the outside. I stopped to think. The thing hadn't followed me in, so it was still in the room with the others. I went back to the corpse, shoved it aside, and then removed the spongy foot to have a look.

At first I couldn't see anything and I feared the worst. Then I found a good angle and saw Viper move toward Dantalyon, who'd removed his shirt. Viper handed him a scalpel. Dantalyon took it and sliced into the crook of his arm. I smelled the blood from where I stood and saw it flow forth. I couldn't imagine what he was doing, but then I saw him kneel next to Stiletto, who was prone on the floor. Lachesis and Viper helped Dantalyon to lift the bulky body, and he placed his bleeding wound against Stiletto's mouth.

What had become of the thing that had attacked us, I didn't know. Perhaps they'd managed to shove it out. I tried to communicate with Bel but she was locked into the group, all of whom concentrated their energy on reviving Stiletto. I saw Dantalyon's blood smear against his mouth and cheek, but he didn't move to drink—a response I'd have expected to be automatic. I hoped he hadn't succumbed to whatever had sucked the life force from Cacilian and Destiny.

I wanted to get back through but not the way I'd come. That was too difficult and required more energy than I had. I returned to the door to try it again but knew well enough that it wouldn't budge. We'd made it thick and solid to keep the odors contained. It was the morgue, after all. I went back to see if anything had happened.

Stiletto still lay on the floor, his mouth open, and Dantalyon was now dripping the blood by force of gravity into his throat. He wasn't dead, but he wasn't responding, either. The others remained around him in a tight circle, although Phelan was kneeling and touching the hand of his valiant protector. I felt his misery.

Dantalyon closed Stiletto's mouth and sat back on

his heels. It was clear to me that he didn't quite know what to do next, but he wasn't giving up.

"Maybe I should try," said Viper.

"No. It's not venom that he needs." He looked away and I thought he must be wondering where Naje was. I wanted to return to them.

Then I remembered that we had a tunnel out of this room. I'd seldom used it, but it was a way out. As long as nothing caught me, I could come around and get back in. I searched the wall for an opening. It was only then that I realized just how many bodies we had in here. I pushed against one stack that was piled five high, and there was a slosh of fluid around the bottom. Someone needed to get in here and get this place organized.

Then I saw the open door. That surprised me, but there was no time to think about it. I went through and quickly found the small opening that would get me outside. I sensed at once there'd been temps here recently, so I guessed this was the way that Coyne had taken Jamie out. I followed the scent, crawling along the stone floor and pushing snakes and rats out of my way, until I emerged into a shadowed area of the yard.

Using all my senses, I tried to ween the air to see if something might be waiting for me, but nothing seemed amiss. Then I heard voices close by—human voices. I couldn't imagine who'd be there, given how far off the main road our house sits, but I soon recognized Coyne. He was giving instructions to someone. I figured it must be Jamie. With the silence of a thief, I pulled myself out of the tunnel and stayed flat on the ground until I could ascertain their location. It wasn't close enough for them to see me, and even if they did, I could scramble their perception long enough to camouflage myself. I wanted to get close so I could better hear what their intention was, coming out here like this in the early-morning hours.

It never ceased to amaze me how temps always seem to approach a vampire's lair when the danger to them is most intense.

I didn't think Coyne would make that mistake, so I knew he was up to something else. I crept closer until I could see them. Coyne carried a leather pouch. I weened that it was something extraordinary and figured it contained the manuscript that Ana had stolen. That meant the key had been useless. I smiled. How easy it would be to grab it and run. He'd never catch me. What a gift to give to Naje!

I moved a little closer. As dark as it was, the sky was just beginning to lighten, so I kept to the shadows cast by the many ancient trees around the house. The two couldn't possibly see or hear me.

"I want you to stick close to me when we go in," Coyne was saying. "They'll know we're here the moment we cross their boundaries. They probably already do, so don't relax your guard. They're letting us think we're getting in easily. If they separate us, I can't help you. Just remember what you saw in the van."

Jamie didn't say anything, but I weened that she distrusted her companion and wanted only to find her son. I crouched, ready to spring when they walked past me.

Then I felt a firm hand on my shoulder. Impossible! I had shrouded myself. Caught off guard, I turned.

Behind me, towering over me, was Naje.

He made a motion with the flat of his hand for me to keep still and watch. I felt intense heat coming off him and knew that he'd filled himself like a constrictor devouring a pig. I thought he intended to take the manuscript himself, but to my surprise, he allowed the two mortals to move past us. I looked at him again. His hair shone even in the dark, although I knew they couldn't have seen him even if they were only three feet away.

Without a word, he urged me to go behind and take Jamie. That confused me. If he got the manuscript back, and surely he knew that Coyne had it, then why did we need any of these temps? I looked into his placid eyes and felt assured. Whatever he was up to, he had a plan.

I shot him an image of Stiletto, but he was already gone. There'd been no need to tell him. He knew—had probably felt it when it happened. I had no time to tell him I was running low.

Returning my attention to the temps, I looked for the opportunity to get Jamie away without scaring her too much. No one else would think of this added bit of manners, but that was just me. I'd had only a moment with her before, but I thought she'd liked me. And since Naje had somehow connected her with Ana, she might also know that her sister was inside. That would help.

They were getting close to the opening of the tunnel. It was time to make my move. I tried to imagine what Naje would do, and that gave me an idea.

Twenty-four

Jamie

Jamie tried to stay close to Allan, but she feared he was taking her back to that awful tunnel. No way she was crawling through there again. There had to be a better way in. Sensing something, she looked around and saw movement in the shadows. It had to be the vampires—or one of them, anyway.

Nervous, she stopped and looked more closely. Then her eyes widened. To her astonishment, Devon stood about forty feet away. He looked right at her, smiled, and waved.

"Devon!" Jamie whispered.

Allan looked back at her and then at the spot where her son stood. "There's no one there," he said, but she was already moving away. He would not be able to stop her this time. He grabbed for her, but she slipped away and ran.

Devon laughed and trotted away toward the dark house. Jamie followed. She heard Allan call for her— "Jamie!"—without raising his voice, but she was past caring what he wanted. She was going to find her son, go back to the van, and leave this place.

She spotted him again just turning the corner of the house, and then he was out of sight. Jamie wanted to call him, but she was afraid of alerting the creatures inside.

How had Devon gotten out? she wondered. Had he . . . ?

Then she remembered. *Naje*. He'd had Devon with him. He must be there somewhere, too. She looked around but saw nothing but trees and shrubs.

Jamie heard a door open and close and ran to where the sound had seemed to originate. Once there, she looked back. Allan had not followed her as she'd feared. Yet she sensed someone near.

"Naje?" she asked. There was no response.

Without another thought, Jamie reached for the doorknob and tried it. The door wasn't locked. She pushed it open and found herself standing on the threshold of darkness.

"Devon?" she whispered. She took another step. He couldn't have come in here. He wouldn't have been able to see any more than she could. Yet she'd heard the door open and close. "Devon. It's Mom."

Then she felt the strange sensation she'd begun to know when one of these creatures lulled her. Images formed and she tried to push them away. She stepped farther into the room and the door closed behind her with a sharp *thwack*. Startled, she looked back and then realized she'd been tricked to come inside. Devon hadn't been out there at all. He was still imprisoned somewhere.

From the corner of her eye to the right she saw a quick flame and turned to see a candle held in the hand of an adult male. It wasn't Naje, though, but someone of slighter build. His hands were smooth and young. He brought the flame closer to his face, and from his longish ash-blond hair Jamie realized that this was the one who'd called himself Christian.

She said nothing. Despite his gentle appearance, she

knew he was a killer. He'd caught her through her own need, and he obviously had some purpose for luring her into this room. Allan had warned her about this; they'd separated her from him and now she had no protector.

"Do you want to see Gail?" he asked.

"Gail?"

"She downstairs."

"She's alive?"

He came closer to her and she felt the coldness from his body. "She's alive but hurt," he said. "Your friend Allan turned her into a human straw. He used her to suck something into existence that burned her badly and nearly killed her."

"Allan . . . ? He said it was you. . . ."

"I was there when it happened, Jamie. I saw it. I took Gail away from them and brought her here to protect her."

Jamie felt utterly confused. Any one of these people could be lying to her. This one could be enticing her into the dungeon below to trap her again.

"What do you want with me?" she asked. "I want to see my son."

"Your son is deeply asleep. He won't wake until this is all over."

Jamie looked into the eyes of this being who'd revealed something of himself to her early the previous evening. He'd seemed without guile then, as he did now.

"What's going to happen?" she asked.

"Just come with me."

"The snakes . . ."

"I'll take you another way, not through the serpentarium. I could force you, as you know, but it would be better if you freely chose to come." He watched her without making a move. A small waxen drip formed on the candle and slipped down over his fingers.

"Is your . . . is Naje down there?" she asked.

"I don't really know. But he's aware of you and he wants you to be with Gail."

"He said that?"

"Yes, just moments ago."

Jamie stood her ground, knowing she had no real leverage. Yet this one took no advantage of that. He didn't try to plant illusions or force her. Even so, she knew that time was running out, not just because of Allan's plan, but if these things were truly vampires, then daylight was not long away.

"Okay," she said. "I want to see Gail."

He offered her the candle and gestured for her to walk in front of him. "Just go through the door over there," he said, pointing to his left. "You'll see some stairs. Take them down two flights. I'll open the door for you at the bottom."

"Aren't you coming with me?"

"Yes, I'll be behind you, but there's room for only one at a time on the stairs. Be careful not to slip."

Her heart pounding, Jamie went to the door, which seemed to open on its own. She turned to see the pretty young man close behind her. Then she descended into an even thicker darkness than she'd already been in. It was like submerging into a tube, with rough-hewn steps at her feet. She held the candle aloft to be sure there were no snakes on these stairs. She wondered how this creature behind her could see, and kept going down. The walls felt close and cold, as if carved from rock. Yet claustrophobic as it was, these were palace stairs compared to that tunnel.

Along the way, Jamie wondered what had become of Allan. He'd seen her run off but hadn't followed. Had he gone on alone into the tunnel? He'd been so intent

on his mission that she felt sure he had already penetrated into the building and was preparing for his triumph. Whatever he intended, Jamie could only hope
that she'd reach Gail first. If they were going to die, at
least they'd be together.

Just as Christian had said, by the time she was nearing
the bottom of the second flight of stone stairs, a door
opened. No light came through, as she had expected,
but as she stepped through into a larger hallway, she
noticed that the stairway continued on down into someplace deeper.

"Keep going," said Christian. "Stop at the first door
on your right." He came up beside her and touched
her under the elbow as if to guide her. His fingers were
dreadfully cold.

She stopped at the door, and Christian opened it like
some courtly mortal. It was a nightmare, this bizarre
normalcy with these preternatural creatures. Gently he
pressed against her back and urged her inward. For a
moment she hesitated, afraid again that she was walking
into a trap. Then, across the candlelit room, she saw
her sister on a table that looked like something from a
surgery.

"Gail!" she cried, and rushed toward her. She was
vaguely aware that the room was full of these creatures,
some of whom watched her in surprise. She ignored
them and arrived at Gail's side.

But Gail was unconscious. She lay under a blue sheet,
her eyes closed and her hair incongruously dark from
some cheap black dye. Jamie touched her and then saw
the snake-thing approach. She backed away.

"She's alive," he said. "But she's not well."

Jamie swallowed hard. She had no idea what to say
to this thing. Looking around, she saw Christian go to
the one called Dantalyon, who stood shirtless in the
middle of the room. His chiseled body nearly took her

breath away, but around his arm was a blood-soaked bandage. She glanced around for Naje but failed to see him.

Then she saw someone on the floor, leaning against a wall as if dead. He was large and dark-skinned, and his head was slumped onto one shoulder. Blood had smeared the side of his mouth and dripped onto his shirt. Was he one of their victims? Some person who'd mistakenly wandered the grounds? The blond who had been so eager to help her earlier knelt next to him, patting his chest, rocking slightly, and weeping.

"What happened?" Jamie heard Christian ask. "Where's Naje?"

"He's not here," Dantalyon answered. He looked at Jamie and then said to Christian, "Where did you go?"

"You warned me to get out."

"No, I didn't. I tried to keep you here but you were already through the wall."

Christian looked confused and then he glanced at Jamie, too, and something seemed to dawn on him. "It must have been Naje," he said. "He was outside."

He went over to the corpse and knelt down to offer comfort to the blond. Jamie recalled that his name was Phelan. He seemed utterly grief-stricken.

"He's gone," said the slight woman called Lethe. "We just can't do anything."

Just then the lights came on. Jamie moved closer to Gail and touched her face. It was cool but not cold, and then she noticed the horrible burned patch under her chin. Exactly as Christian had said. She looked at the snake-thing, who despite his strange eyes actually seemed concerned, and forced herself to ask, "Can I do anything for her?"

"You could give her blood," he said. "She needs it."

"Hook me up, then."

He glanced over at Dantalyon, who nodded. Viper

moved to get the apparatus he needed. Jamie spotted a wooden chair nearby, so she dragged it close, sat down, and rolled up the sleeve of her ridiculous black dress. It seemed so long ago that she'd bought it and put it on. Another lifetime. She suffered the rough touch of the half-human lizard as he prepared to strap rubber tubing around her, and kept herself from looking into his eyes.

Yet before he could tie it, the door opened and Allan burst in like some Old West bank robber. "Everyone just stay where you are," he commanded.

Dantalyon made a move toward him and then stopped. The others froze, too, as if they'd all heard the same inaudible instruction. Still, Jamie saw the hint of a fang protruding over Dantalyon's lower lip, and Lethe had drawn back her upper lip in a posture of aggression. Allan seemed oblivious. He held up the black leather pouch and said, "I've got the manuscript. No one touch me or I'll release this thing on you."

Jamie saw Christian look uncertainly at Dantalyon, and the slender blond girl moved closer to him. No one said a word as Allan scooted across the lab and toward the table where Gail lay supine. He saw Viper and stopped in surprise. Apparently he hadn't expected this one. Then he looked at Jamie.

"Just you and Gail," he said. "I want you two right there and everyone else away from the table."

Viper looked at Dantalyon, and Jamie thought they'd communicated something. She knew that Allan had no idea what he was getting himself into. There were eight vampires in this room who all could jump him at the same time, and who all had mental powers beyond what he seemed to comprehend. Yet it did appear that they had a healthy respect for the thing Allan held, since none had tried to take it from him. Viper moved away to stand closer to Dantalyon, and Allan backed up to-

ward Jamie, holding the manuscript in front of him.
Jamie got up from the chair.

"It's coming," Allan said. "Can you feel it? There's
no escape now for any of you." He pointed at the dark
one on the floor. "In just a few minutes you're all gonna
end up like that. Where's your leader?"

No one answered him.

"In the house somewhere?"

Again, not a word was offered.

"Well, he can't hide. No matter where he is, this thing
will get him. You can't protect him."

Jamie saw something above them, near the ceiling.
A dark gray cloud seemed to be forming, as if someone
had boiled black ink into steam. An odor filled the room
that reminded Jamie of the morgue she'd been in that
night. The vampires seemed intent on Allan, and only
one of them looked up, the one who had taken her to
the serpentarium on Naje's orders. He looked afraid.

"Eryx!" Dantalyon spit out. He wasn't looking at anyone, but Jamie recalled the name. These vampires had
a plan, she sensed, and they were converging their powers, perhaps as a shield, perhaps as a sword. Eryx re-
focused his attention.

Dantalyon stood his ground, and Jamie thought he
must have been magnificent among his people when
he was human. He looked unbelievably intimidating,
yet he didn't make a move. Allan must have been right
that he feared the document. Otherwise why wouldn't
he just smack Allan to the ground? He looked strong
enough to do it all by himself.

The ceiling became an undulating mass of shapeless
forms, and for the first time Gail moved. She made an
"ungh" sound and bent one leg up slightly as if in pain.
Jamie wanted to go to her, but Allan grabbed Jamie's
wrist. "Stay close," he said. "I need you." Then before
she could move, he pulled a pair of steel handcuffs from

his back pocket and with one hand snapped one cuff on her. He placed the manuscript under his arm, and though she struggled, he managed to get the other cuff on himself.

Suddenly she realized what he was doing. Christian had told her that he'd used her sister like a straw to channel this thing. Now Allan wanted her for the same purpose. She remembered the burns. Shocked, Jamie looked at Christian. They'd had the perfect opportunity to overpower Allan while he was struggling with her and had done nothing. Now she was certain they couldn't touch him. She was trapped.

Then she sensed that Christian was trying to communicate. An image of Naje came into her head, but before she could attend to it, the cloud on the ceiling shifted and changed, and multiple voices began to chatter as if from a distance. Some began to scream, male and female alike. Jamie then saw a montage of hideous leering gray faces poking out through the clouds. Where their eyes had been were dark holes, and their mouths were open wide. They appeared and disappeared like human flotsam from some shipwreck floating in an angry ocean. The cloud seemed to grow dense and to come closer, and the voices grew increasingly loud. Jamie had the impression that this was hell: it was some floating gaseous debris that sucked up souls as it passed by. Long black tendrils seemed to snap here and there into the air. One came down near Christian, who flinched slightly, and near the head of another woman Jamie had never seen before. Neither of them looked up.

To Jamie's surprise, the vampires remained as they were around the room, as if they'd been turned into pillars of salt. Only their eyes betrayed the vigorous energy present. Something was happening, but Jamie couldn't tell what it was. Somehow they were shielding themselves. Christian held the hand of the young girl at his side.

"It's time," said Allan. "It's over now." He held up the leather pouch. Jamie tried to crouch down toward the floor, but Allan jerked her back up. When he looked at her, his eyes had changed. He was no longer the same person.

The place darkened again, and even the candles began to flicker. Several went out altogether. Allan began to speak some words that Jamie failed to understand. The massive cloud undulated and thickened. More faces appeared. More shouts and jabbering came through. Jamie wanted to stop up her ears. She thought she saw one face open its mouth and devour another, which sent a bolt of fear through her stomach. She wanted Allan to stop. Whatever he was saying was making this sadistic vapor gather its forces. There was no telling what it was going to do.

Then a more powerful voice filled the room. It seemed to be everywhere at once, drowning out the cacophony and reverberating off the walls. Jamie looked at Allan. To her shock, the voice issued out of him, though it wasn't his. He was mouthing the words and yet it seemed as if he was struggling not to. He grasped the manuscript close to his chest as if to ward off whatever had possessed him. Jamie wanted desperately to get away from him. She could feel heat coming from him and it began to burn her hand.

The thick gray cloud formed itself into a tight roll that showed many random faces, hands, and legs as it swirled around and around. It was becoming like a giant's spear, ready to aim itself at some target. The omnipresent voice continued and seemed to be joined by a second male voice, not as loud, that came from within the monstrous collage. It wasn't a dialogue but a rhythmic chant by two people who both knew it well.

Then the ghastly legion stopped rolling, though its internal components continued to shift and cry out. It hung overhead for a moment, and the tendrils came out like the oars of a Viking ship. In a flash it shot directly at Allan. Jamie cried out and tried to jump as far away as the handcuffs allowed. She squeezed her hand as small as she could get it but couldn't slip out. Allan dropped the manuscript to shield his face. The entire rush of voices, heads, and figures came at him, and in that blazing moment, a solid figure shoved itself between Jamie and Allan, snapped the chain as if it were cotton string, and pushed her into the wall. She knocked her shoulder hard and fell to one knee, then turned to see what was happening.

Allan screamed, "No!" as the cloud of entities disappeared into him through the top of his head. Behind him, holding him around the chest, was Naje. His fangs were sunk deep into Allan's neck, and Allan let out another piercing scream that seemed to come from the darkest pocket of his soul. He wailed long and hard, and Jamie was horrified at the expression of sheer terror on his face. Naje was killing him.

Through the gloom, Jamie could just make out that the others seemed astonished. Christian put his hand to his mouth as if he could not believe what he was seeing.

The reporter flopped about like a windup doll out of control, obviously filled to the brim with the energy of that hellish shaft of tortured souls, and within moments he went still. His arms slumped down at his sides. Naje dropped him and then stepped back as if in a swoon, sitting down hard on the chair that Jamie had vacated moments before. Whatever he'd imbibed from Allan's life force, he was badly affected. He leaned on the gurney on which her sister lay, laid his head against his left arm, and seemed to pass out.

Twenty-five

Christian

We'd been commanded to remain still, to keep away from the manuscript, and stay fully joined to the center, which was now Dantalyon. Having seen Naje outside, I'd felt that he was somewhere close, but I didn't spot him until he rushed in and grabbed Coyne. When the Dahaka flowed into the reporter's body, I figured that was it, the end, but Naje surprised me. I hadn't expected him to penetrate the body while it was filling with all those tormented souls. I could tell that Dantalyon was surprised as well, and alarmed. I felt his heart pumping from four feet away. Then Naje dropped Coyne and fell back.

"Naje!" I cried, and moved toward him, but Dantalyon blocked me so hard with his arm I thought he broke a rib. How could he stop me, let alone not rush himself to Naje's aid? Lachesis gripped my arm and held me back.

"Don't," she said. "He needs space."

He? Who? Dantalyon? Naje? I didn't get this. I looked at Bel, who was watching Naje as well, with concern but without fear. Lethe came up on my other side and put her finger to her mouth to keep me quiet. I saw Phelan get to his feet, leaving the still form of Stiletto on the floor. Eryx remained perfectly still as if listening. And that was what I was supposed to be doing. I realized that only the keenest focus would join me to the group mind. Despite my panic and concern, my job was to do exactly what Naje had invited me into the *kamera* to do: listen, blend with the energy, and be ready to support the whole with my gifts.

And then I realized: Naje had sent his astral body out with that mess of things that had come to attack us. It had gone into Coyne and right through him, and Naje had hitched a ride on his soul. But why? It seemed to me he was risking everything.

Though it was only minutes, it felt like forever that Naje lay against the table. I feared that he'd fall to the floor. But I also felt strength in the room from the power radiating from Dantalyon. I had to trust that the many intimate hours he had spent with the *dominie* had honed his knowledge of what to do. Whatever it was, it had to be fast. I felt the dawn not more than twenty minutes away.

Then the lights came back on. From her bed Ana shrieked, and I saw Jamie watching her, apparently uncertain what to do. It was then that I saw Naje's hand gripped firmly around Ana's wrist, though he otherwise seemed dead. Ana's legs came up and she cried out, "ungh, ungh!" Viper went to her side, but I could tell he didn't dare touch her. I wondered if Naje was coming back through.

Then behind us, Stiletto moaned. Phelan knelt beside him and gasped. He touched Stiletto's chest. "He's coming back!" he said. Phelan was right. Eryx, Bel, and I watched as Stiletto slowly emerged back into awareness and life came into his eyes. He blinked but stayed where he was, as if too exhausted to move. I watched Dantalyon, who nodded but kept his eyes on Naje.

"We have to bring him back," he said.

"He can't come through Ana," Viper said. "She won't bear it a second time."

"We have to try. We can't just guide him back. He has to be cleansed. He's been among those rotting souls."

Jamie stepped forward. "Use me," she said. "I'm stronger than she is. Whatever it is, I can do this. Don't risk her."

"But you risk a mis—" Viper started to say.

"I know. But maybe it will help. It's life energy, it's pure. Gail . . . Ana . . . told me. Just . . . just tell me what to do."

Viper looked at her and then at Ana. There was no time for calculating the ramifications. He nodded. "Okay," he said. "We'll need to prepare you. Lie down here next to her." To make room, he pushed Ana to one side, careful not to disturb Naje.

She walked toward him and I could see that she was trying to calm her fears. Getting close to Viper had to be disconcerting.

Jamie climbed onto the table and lay down next to Gail, and Viper beckoned Dantalyon over. They whispered together and then Dantalyon leaned over Jamie. "I'm going to help you to be more receptive," he said. "It won't hurt and it will help show him the way back."

Her fear was palpable to all of us, but she bravely nodded. "Okay," she whispered.

I looked at Bel. She raised her eyebrow as if to signal her doubts that this would work. Behind me, Phelan was helping Stiletto to his feet, and Eryx lent a hand. Lachesis and Lethe went over to Naje to support his body for the moment of reconnection.

Dantalyon moved the edge of Jamie's dress from near her neck and bent close. She took a deep breath as if preparing for the doctor's needle, and he pierced her skin with his fangs. She gasped as if penetrated by a lover. He put his hand on her breast to enhance the pleasure.

He was giving her venin, not taking her blood. She moaned at the rush, and I knew the euphoria she felt. Viper walked around them and reached into a glass cage for one of the sleeping cobras. This he wrapped over Naje's shoulders. That was wise, I thought: Naje's special resonance. Lethe held its head to keep it from striking Jamie.

As Dantalyon injected his juice, we all felt the connection. I could tell as I looked around at the others. Jamie relaxed into the flow of the moment, moaning her rapture as her physical boundaries melted away. I imagined she was in some fantasy with the creature who had so beguiled her, though at the moment I wasn't sure whether that was Naje or Dantalyon. No longer feeling her physical shape, she could connect with a floating spirit and let it merge. Naje had already prepared the calibrations for himself through Ana, although that had been for an entirely different purpose. It was but a slight shift to return through Jamie, as long as he saw the way—and as long as her pregnant condition worked for him rather than against him.

Then he moved. His eyes still closed, he mumbled something I didn't understand. Dantalyon pulled away from Jamie and went quickly to Naje's side. Lethe stepped away to give him access.

"Naje," he said. His hand went to Naje's chest to massage him back to awareness. On the table, Jamie cried out, "Oh, aagh," and Viper went to attend to her, to be sure she didn't roll off.

Yet Naje was not yet back. His chest wasn't moving.

"Give him the breath," Lachesis said. She looked around. "Everyone concentrate."

As he'd done with me earlier, Dantalyon opened Naje's mouth and exhaled into him. I saw his chest fill up and I focused all my effort into the *mana* that would move through Dantalyon into him. There was no response, so Dantalyon tried again.

Jamie drew a sharp intake of breath. She arched her back and Viper grabbed her shoulder.

Then Naje drew a breath on his own, and another deep into his lungs. He opened his eyes, and then closed them again and shook his head. I thought he looked different, as if he'd been changed somehow by what he'd seen in that chaotic morass.

Jamie opened her eyes, saw Viper, and seemed unafraid. "Did it work?" she whispered. He nodded. Then he helped her to sit up.

Naje, too, had straightened up. He looked worn out, but he embraced Dantalyon like a lover returning from the sea, and then received kisses from the women. Bel and I went forward to touch him as well, and Phelan ran up behind us.

"Did you see your teacher?" he asked in a rush. Only Phelan would have dared such a question.

Naje nodded but his eyes seemed shadowed.

Then Stiletto pushed his way through and knelt before Naje as if coming before a king. Naje pushed the snake off his shoulders into Lethe's hands and moved to get up. I reached to help him, and when he was on his feet, he drew Stiletto up to full height and they embraced in what could only be described as great relief. Phelan began to cry again, and he joined this hug. Next to me, Bel squeezed my hand. I looked at her and realized that no matter how much we all wanted to stay there together, the sun was rising.

Naje looked to Eryx and he turned quickly and left the room. Then he said something to Dantalyon, who looked at Jamie and deferred. She walked shakily toward Naje and he reached for her and held her against him. "You'll have your son now," he said. Then he stepped back and broke off the handcuff.

Jamie's hand went to her mouth and tears sprang into her eyes. "Thank you," she said. She hugged him again and tried not to look where Allan's body lay in a heap. The door opened and Eryx came in with the sleeping boy in his arms. Naje took him and held him for Jamie to kiss. Then he told her it was time for her to go, and asked Lachesis to help her up the steps. He would carry Devon, and the rest of us were to go bed down.

When they were gone, I turned to see Dantalyon embrace Stiletto, and both were grinning—a sight I never thought I'd see. I wanted to get to the warm sand of the snake cage, but I also wanted to know what had happened.

"How did he bring you back?" I asked Stiletto.

He shrugged. "A gift, I think, from his *kumu.*"

"I thought his teacher was trying to destroy us," said Bel.

"No, no, he was an illuminated soul, caught in a maelstrom. He kept me close to him. Naje reached us on the *aka* thread; I could see it." He looked around. "It was your power, all of you. Had it broken, we'd all have been lost. Naje sent me along it first, and I didn't know until I was here that he'd come back, too." He gazed again at Dantalyon and said, "He did well picking you."

Twenty-six

Jamie

Carrying Devon, Naje accompanied Jamie outside. The female had left them at the door. Jamie noticed that he walked barefoot across the gravel driveway without a hint of pain until they came to a maroon Mercedes parked in the turnaround area. The light of dawn was threatening to peek over a distant hill, but Naje seemed unaffected. He gave the sleeping child over to her and opened the passenger side door. "Take this car," he said. "The keys are in it. Park it outside at Ana's and close the keys into the trunk. We'll come for it tomorrow night."

"No, I couldn't—"

"You can't take the van you came in and you need to leave now. We'll get rid of the van and we'll wipe down Coyne's apartment. You'll have no connection with what happened here. He'll disappear and no one will ever know how or why."

"I won't forget," she said. "I'll never forget."

He smiled and touched her hair. "You go back to Princeton. Put your son to bed and let the police know that he's safe, because when you both wake up, neither of you will remember. You'll believe that Ana is safe and that she's where she wants to be, and you'll return to your life."

A little disappointed, Jamie said, "You don't want me to know—"

"It's better that you don't."

"But Gail needs blood. I should come back."

"We'll take care of her."

Jamie looked down and then back into his eyes. "If you're going to mess up my memories, can't you at least replace them with the memory that I'm brave and bold and can choose the life that I want?"

Naje smiled. "I don't think I need to. You've been changed. You know what matters. And your daughter will be quite unique."

Jamie raised an eyebrow, wanting to ask what he meant, but knew there was no more time. She placed Devon gently on the front seat. He didn't stir. Then she straightened up and looked at Naje. "Just for the drive back, so I can stop wondering, did my sister really take something from you?"

"Yes, and that was my mistake. She had potential for something we were trying, but she wanted more. She didn't mean to put us at risk, but she failed to see through Coyne. Once he knew what she had, there was no stopping it."

"So she started this, then. It was her fault." Naje said nothing, so Jamie continued. "That's why she let you use her. She owed you."

"It's not clear who owes the debt. It started with the promise of something great, and it ended badly, at least for Coyne. We'll see what happens for the rest of us."

"He didn't really know how to use the manuscript, did he?"

"He knew well enough how to unleash the monster, but he didn't know that whoever does that—if he doesn't do it right—has only one destiny, and that's to be trapped with them. He needed a human channel to guide the thing, so he grabbed Ana and you, but he forgot that his body, too, was a medium. Once he opened up to it by using those words, and as long as he had the manuscript, he was the greater magnet. And his was a greedy soul; he'd have attracted them, anyway."

"He told me about your teacher. Is that what happened to him?"

Naje's response was whispery and sounded full of pain. "My teacher, yes."

"But why did you give me the key? Why did you want the manuscript back? Wasn't that like"—she nearly said, "like holding a poisonous snake" but changed it to—"like lighting a match over gasoline?"

"I didn't want it back. I wanted Coyne to believe that I did so he'd keep it with him. But he needed the key, because it was locked away and Ana had taken the key to give to us. By giving it to you, he assumed you got it from us to steal it back, which to his mind increased its value. All that was important was that he have it in his possession when he performed the ritual. That made him a clear target. And they were guided in part by my *kumu,* my teacher. He was trapped with them, but he protected us however he could."

"That was the other voice."

"Yes."

Jamie nodded. "So it's done then. Will I ever see Gail . . . Ana . . . again?"

Naje waited a moment before he replied, "If she recovers, it will take a long time, and even then, she knows what it means to be with us. She won't contact you. It's better that you just think of her as . . . gone."

Jamie looked away, tears choking her. The thought of Gail with that snake-creature was appalling, but she had always wanted something different. Beauty and the Beast. She probably couldn't do better. "You won't punish her?"

Naje shook his head, and Jamie saw sadness in the gesture. "She did only what I myself had once done. When I first saw it, I took it, too. It has that effect."

"Then why didn't—"

"It belonged to my teacher." Naje hesitated and then said, "He was more than my teacher; he was my father."

"Your father?"

"I was human once. I had a father. He worked magic and I was curious. So I freed the demons and the only way he could save me was to sacrifice himself. He conferred his powers to me and made himself vulnerable. What happened was my blunder. So I kept the document because I thought one day I'd find a way to release him. That's what Ana was trying to help me do, and it's done. He's free."

Jamie started to ask what he meant, but he said, "You leave now. It's time."

Naje moved toward her and kissed her on the forehead. His lips were surprisingly soft and warm. Whatever last moments she had to remember him, she would savor as long as she could. Difficult as it was to leave him, she had Devon to think about. She went to the driver side of the Mercedes, and when she turned to wave good-bye, Naje was gone. Over the hill, the first rim of light promised a very warm day.

Twenty-seven

Christian

I was nearly asleep when I heard the glass door to the snake cage open. Though my body was heavy with the weariness that floods in when tension ceases, I opened my eyes and saw Naje enter. Dantalyon stayed at the door while he went from one of us to another, as if to assure himself we were all still with him. Stiletto was dead to the world when Naje touched his shoulder, but Phelan opened his eyes and smiled. Naje whispered something to him and his grin broadened. Of all of us, Phelan, our eternal child, was likely to recover the quickest, especially after Dantalyon's gesture of protection.

Eryx reached up to put his hand in Naje's. For once, he was here with us instead of alone, and I weened that he wanted connection.

I was next. Lethe was in her own private chamber, and I suspected that Lachesis and Viper were invited into Naje's. This had been a hard night, and he would surely extend certain privileges. Or Viper might be with Ana.

I shook Bel gently. She opened her eyes just as Naje came near us. He crouched next to me and ran two fingers through my hair as he smiled. He seemed illuminated from somewhere within. I wanted to say something, but the intimacy of silence felt right just then. We'd all survived something together and protected our center. I sensed he was proud of us, and grateful. He felt my cheek as if taking my temperature. I realized he was trying to determine if I'd been injured when the venin was forced from me.

"I'll take care of this tomorrow," he said. "But you're so cold. Are you hungry?"

It was too much to believe what he was offering. I couldn't respond, but when he held out his wrist to me, my fangs came forward and I drank. His blood was thick and warm, and seemed imbued with a special magic. I freely indulged. It seemed only a minute before he removed his arm, but I felt as if I'd absorbed the full heat of a sun-baked rock. I floated in the warmth of his awareness.

Then he kissed a finger and reached over me to touch it to Bel's cheek. She received this gesture without a word, but when he stood to leave, she rolled close to me and put her head on my shoulder. We nestled ourselves more deeply into the sand, but I forced my eyes to stay open so I could watch Naje leave.

Dantalyon stood back as he walked out and then fastened the snake door behind him. They went together to descend to their private rooms. Satisfied and toasty, I prepared myself for rest.

Feel the Seduction of
Pinnacle Horror

When Darkness Falls
Grab One of These
Pinnacle Horrors

Scare Up One of These Pinnacle Horrors

__Haunted
  by Tamara Thorne   0-7860-1090-8 $5.99US/$7.99CAN

__Thirst
  by Michael Cecilione 0-7860-1091-6 $5.99US/$7.99CAN

__The Haunting
  by Ruby Jean Jensen 0-7860-1095-9 $5.99US/$7.99CAN

__The Summoning
  by Bentley Little   0-7860-1480-6 $6.99US/$8.99CAN

Call toll free **1-888-345-BOOK** to order by phone or use this coupon to order by mail.

Name_____

Address_____

City_____ State_____ Zip_____

Please send me the books that I checked above.

I am enclosing	$_____
Plus postage and handling*	$_____
Sales tax (in NY, TN, and DC)	$_____
Total amount enclosed	$_____

*Add $2.50 for the first book and $.50 for each additional book.

Send check or money order (no cash or CODs) to: **Kensington Publishing Corp., Dept. C.O., 850 Third Avenue, 16th Floor, New York, NY 10022**

Prices and numbers subject to change without notice.

All orders subject to availability.

Visit our website at **www.kensingtonbooks.com**.